Manifestations of a Phantom's Soul

A Phantom of the Opera Story Collection

Michelle Rodriguez

DEDICATION

This book is dedicated to my fellow Phantom phans. Thank you for making me who I am as an author. You have changed my life.

ACKNOWLEDGMENTS

A special thanks to Sara Schwabe for her beautiful cover artwork.

And to the people who always continue to push me when confidence wants to waver, especially Katie, Mary, Diane, Noelle, and El. You have always believed in my stories and my talent, and I am forever grateful.

And thank you to all of my readers and reviewers on fanfiction.net and The Phantom of the Opera forum. You guys are amazing!

Manifestations of a Phantom's Soul

Introduction

I have been a little bit in love with Erik since I was 14 years old. As a naïve girl believing wholeheartedly in fairytales, I was truly convinced that he existed and that one day he would appear in my life. Yes, I favored being on the dramatic side of things, but at the time, discovering my voice and love for performance, I held a certain affinity with the Phantom of the Opera story that made it take root in my heart. I wanted to *be* Christine, insisting that *I* could give her the guts she didn't have and love Erik for who he was. I wanted to rewrite their story, find the magical ending Erik deserved and make up for all the loneliness and agony he had suffered. A man of passion and music, told again and again by a cruel world that he didn't belong because he didn't look the same as everyone else. Of course, at 14, I didn't explore the darker facets to Erik's character and his Opera Ghost antics, but that was the hopeless romantic in me. I preferred the love story.

Fast forward almost a decade. I decided to try and give Erik that denied love story my own way, to tell his tale from different angles and with different variations. One story became a dozen and onward to over 60, but I was writing solely for my own enjoyment. I truly didn't believe anyone would be able to love my stories the way I did or fully grasp how anyone could write over 60 stories about a disfigured Opera Ghost and still have more ideas to tell. Obsessive? Yes, I freely admit to it! Two years ago, I took a chance and posted one of my stories, "Blessed Are The Forgotten", on a couple of fanfiction websites. I was a nervous wreck until the first reviews came in, terrified that my portrayal of these so-loved characters would be called erroneous and torn apart. But...the first review I got was so amazing that it made me cry and to this day holds a special place in my heart. I learned with that very first posted story that there were many people equally as in love with Erik as

I was, eager and willing to read my stories and become lost in my dreams of romance.

Over the past 2 years, I've posted more than 30 of my stories, and that is just so far. I am constantly and continuously humbled by the support I have gotten from the Phantom community and the fans always anxious for my next post. I have gotten to know people all around the world who have been touched by my words, which is something that amazes me to no end. It astounds me to think that I almost didn't go through with that initial post and let fear be my guide, especially considering that wish at 14 to *be* Christine and be brave enough to love Erik. I feel like through sharing my stories, I have fulfilled that wish and given him the love story I thought he should have had dozens of times over.

So now I invite you into my world of the Opera Ghost. I yearn to inspire, to show the transcendental power of love and hope, to give fairytales a reality. And above all else, to change perspectives. A face does not define the heart of a man or the love it can hold. Erik taught me that. He has been my greatest inspiration in life, and writing him has been my greatest joy.

Contents

"Blessed Are The Forgotten"
After the unmasking, Christine escapes and seeks answers to her destroyed illusions, only to find herself once again at the mercy of Erik's wrath.

It took every ounce of remaining strength Christine possessed to fight wind and snow and pull open the thick, wooden door. She was only too relieved to escape such brutal conditions and steal into the stone walls of the warmly lit building, its glow like an unspoken welcome and promise of peace. And wasn't that just what she was looking for tonight? Peace and the sense of safety that was connected to it. ...And forgiveness. Dear Lord, she needed forgiveness.

Lingering in the back of the small church, she purposely avoided thought to survey the details of her surroundings, desperate to find something that could matter. Dozens of sconces encased flickering flames around an upraised altar and down the short, wide aisle that led to it. Their glow glinted off images trapped and portrayed in stained glass panels on the walls, portraits of faith, and hanging above the altar was the cornerstone of Catholicism: a large, carved crucifix.

Immediately, she made the sign of the cross and bowed her head to behold it. Reverence for such religious icons had been engrained in her from birth by a father who had only been able to face the death of her mother with prayers and God at his side. When he had realized that he, too, would be abandoning his only child to live alone in the world, he had reminded Christine again and again that her faith would be her salvation. And she had believed him so completely that it was no wonder she had chosen the path she was now walking. Faith was a blind commitment. One wasn't supposed to question or doubt; one was just to believe. ...She had believed, and how foolishly disillusioned she now was for it!

Tears were choking the back of her throat again; their earlier counterparts had blended with the melted treks of incessant snowflakes leaving her pale cheeks tinged pink from a frozen burn. Their demise meant nothing when too many more were ready and eager to take their place. When was the last time she had been their victim? ...It must have been months ago, after her father's death. She would have cried more often for his loss, all the time even, but faith and hope had materialized into reality and tears had become forgotten in the background. What was their use if she was no longer alone? ...She had had an angel...

A breath suddenly fled her lips caught in an agonized sob. *Angel...* How naïve she had been! In her head thrived vivid pictures of golden halos and shimmering wings, visions of heaven. ...Did heaven even exist? Perhaps it was as childish a belief as angels. Perhaps *everyone* in the world was alone, ...and yet wasn't alone better than cursed by the devil himself? Haunted by the devil; it was a bitter reality to face, but it was indeed hers.

Crying soft and incessant, Christine forced her legs to carry her down the aisle to the front pew and reverently knelt before the warm glow of a faith that was suddenly cold and foreign to her. One moment of one day had changed everything; one hasty act had shaken her very foundation to its core like a violent earthquake, and nothing could possibly be the same. She couldn't help but feel she was being punished. ...But punished for what?

In the farthest recesses of the shadows, Erik watched her, crying his own silent tears. He had followed her, stealthy and unnoticed as always, from the opera house, unsurprised by her chosen destination. The good Catholic girl, seeking answers in her faith. His eyes trailed over the back of her bowed head, her dark curls glistening with strawberry red in the candlelight, and a fleeting memory of their silken texture tingled his fingertips. *One touch.* He had had one touch, and was that to be enough to last him to eternity? Because he knew it never could be.

Had it really been only last night that his dream had been realized, and he had held her in his arms? It felt as if ages had passed since, and miles of distance had been ripped like an endless chasm between their hearts. He knew the dull, empty ache as acutely as any physical pain he had ever endured, and he was desperate to remedy it.

Oh, Christine... He thought her name, terrified to breathe it aloud, trembling with the very idea of alerting her to his observing presence. She was the love of his life, the only woman he had ever wanted, and at the same time, she was his condemner, his tormentor, single-handedly shattering his dreams with her small, white fists. Why couldn't she have let well enough be and not pushed for more? Why couldn't she have remained the innocent child, willing and eager to believe and grasp onto anything he could give her with greedy hands? But no, she had fallen victim to the lure of curiosity and allowed it to pull her into its devious arms. ...Foolish girl. She had expected a glorious angel. Was it a surprise then that she had cowered in disgust and terror when faced with the visage of a demon instead? Time and time again he had endured such reactions from a superficial world, and yet never had they broken him until today, until it was the beautiful features of his Christine screaming revulsion at him. In that one moment and one response, hope had been shredded along with his dignity. He had lost everything; she was to blame. He found himself hating her as much as he loved her.

Continuing to watch from the darkness, he spied her slowly lifting her eyes to the cross. He himself had no taste for religion; funny then that he had so eagerly accepted the role of angel...

Gazing into the image of salvation, Christine began to speak, her voice ragged from tears and yet echoing through the small space to her unknown audience, "Why am I being punished...?" It was the agonizing question of her soul, and Erik cringed to hear it. "You took my father from me and left me alone and now... I thought I was blessed. I thought that I hadn't been forgotten... An angel. He was supposed to be an angel..." Her voice broke off in a sob with the true reality, and it took a calming breath for her to continue in hushed tones. "Whatever wrong I have committed, I beg Your forgiveness. Perhaps it was my readiness to believe without question and follow the devil's plans; I didn't know. I didn't realize what... *who* he was. I was a gullible child. ...Perhaps I deserve this."

Erik's heart felt constricted in his chest, and he stifled the full extent of a sob, catching it between lips that he could only consider were misshapen, ...*unworthy*. But pain was laced so deeply with resentment that he suddenly found himself retorting, "And I, Christine? If you are so deserving of this unjust punishment from your ignorant God, am I equally as deserving? Was I as deserving as an infant to be born with the face of the devil?"

Christine went rigid at that voice, frozen with her back to him a long, held breath before she could find the ability to rise and turn guilt-ridden eyes to the shadows. At first, he was only a gleaming mask with one radiating green eye in its casing and one the same caliber shine but brilliantly blue exposed, both gazing at her with contempt before he reluctantly stepped forward into the far reaches of the light, as if he had been delivered to her from out of the dark itself.

A man... She had to remind herself that he was only a man, even when her soul cried out that such an explanation was a blasphemy and he *must be* an angel yet. A trick of the devil, trying to corrupt her soul against her. And how weak she was to desperately yearn to believe it all over again!

Erik strode with the elegance and grace of a true heavenly being into the aisle, approaching even as he took note how she shrank into her pew, her hand clutching the wooden back as if he meant to pry her away when he had yet to lay a single finger on her.

He would have laughed at her ridiculous fear if it didn't sting him so deeply. As he neared, his eyes casually roamed the church, catching the silhouetted bursts of snow against the stained glass windows and the echoes of howling winds outside. No one else was here, and no one would come; they were alone. He wondered if she realized, and yet she seemed too preoccupied regarding his approach at the moment, her wide, blue eyes locked on him.

"God, Christine?" Erik dared to taunt with a mocking gesture to the cross she had so reverently praised. "You called yourself a gullible child for believing so readily in an angel, and yet here you are bowing before a pathetic faith, equally as gullible and foolish."

She made no reply, words evading her when in the vicinity of his powerful aura. It was still so new to her: to hear that once-beloved voice and see it attached to a being, and beyond that, to feel the sheer essence of this man as it exuded past a seemingly inconsequential body to touch her. It made her knees shake beneath the dark blue wool of her skirt and her heartbeat hold and mutter erratically in both a warning and a failure to stay strong. She wondered if the power he possessed was a reflection of his soul and, nervous with the idea, if it was tied to the dark and evil, the very legend of his existence: ...phantom, Opera Ghost, murderer.

"Now I don't believe in a god," Erik went on as he halted mere feet from her, desperately seeking anything beyond fear in her eyes. "I find it a pointless endeavor to live one's life under the fear of pleasing some potential higher being that will determine our fate in the afterworld. It is futile and a manmade attempt to control the race of human beings as a whole, to establish order. What better threat to keep the peace than an invisible, omnipotent creator? The first of this species were wise enough to see the charms and advantages to such a story."

"I...I don't believe you," she softly protested,

and he could tell she was fighting with better judgment to form words. Was it really only the day before that she was so unguarded of her tongue in his unseen presence, eager to speak freely, teaching him what it was to be ordinary even if she did not know it?

"You," Erik replied, "have been manipulated to follow your faith your entire life. I wouldn't expect you to believe otherwise."

His implication ignited a wave of argumentation and a need to prove him wrong. "What about the soul?" she demanded, a bit less timid. "If you don't believe that God exists, do you believe in a soul? Or is all we are *nothing* to you?"

Months ago, he would have instantly referred to every living being as precisely that *nothing*, but she and her very existence had proven his views wrong. Whereas the rest of the world was a faceless blob of cruelty and pain, she shone like a beacon of salvation and had taught him so much more. ...But he couldn't tell her that, not after the day's traumas.

"Soul," he instead spat back. "Souls are another of your fairytale stories meant to ease the fear of death. Consider how truly ridiculous such a notion is, Christine, and how utterly narcissistic to believe in a piece of yourself that will go on forever. According to your stories, mine would be black, tarnished, and shriveled up beyond recognition. And that would be all that I am. Ignoring and contradicting your very belief as a Catholic in forgiveness and redemption for all, I am supposedly meant for hell by your teachings, already condemned and set on the path to burn. If your merciful God exists, how is that fair?"

"You are a murderer." The accusation tumbled out even though she did not will it. Part of her grew immediately terrified what his response would be with a fleeting memory of his fiery, enraged outburst and how sure she had been at the time that he would kill her and add her name to his list of victims. But to her surprise, his casually debating demeanor did not alter.

"Perhaps, but your God is supposed to forgive

all and rule with mercy and love. Isn't that correct?"

She gave the smallest nod and insisted, "He forgives the penitent... Are you sorry for your sins?" A bold question, and she found herself admiring her own courage to ask it.

A scowl creased what bits of his features the mask allowed her to see, and he abruptly snapped, "I need not answer to you or to your God. You know *nothing* of my life save the lies I placed before you, and yet you are as willing as your God to pass judgment over my supposed soul. What you are neglecting to consider is the simple fact that if there is a God, why does He punish the undeserving? It was your very own question but minutes ago, and yet you have bypassed its validity to defend your faith to me so adamantly. But what is your answer, Christine? Why does God punish the undeserving?"

No response came even as she contemplated or rather, no response she knew he would accept. It seemed that he was seeking the answer as urgently as she was, that he wanted and needed to know for himself. If she could find the right reply and convince him of it, would it really matter so much? Was it that important? ...Would it save his soul?

When she said nothing, he snapped his fingers before her and pointedly said, "Another contradiction then! The Lord God is fair, but not to all. To some, He closes His eyes and forgets they exist, allowing cruel humanity to destroy them and their supposed souls, and for no reason other than He didn't care enough to save them."

"No," she immediately protested. "That isn't true."

"It isn't?" he taunted back. "You yourself were just His willing casualty, manipulated by lies, very nearly the next victim of the Opera Ghost. And was it His divine intervention that saved you? Did His influence keep me from snapping your pretty, little neck earlier today?"

His temper was flaring at both her and himself,

and his eyes landed a beat on her clenched fists gripping the pew, stretched white with her viselike hold. He was almost pleased to know he was frightening her, and daring to push further, he leaned close until he was breathing her heavenly scent into his lungs, intoxicating himself on it like a heady wine before he sharply bid, "And yet if it is solely due to His saving grace that you are still alive, why did He deliver you right back into my clutches? Why did He bring us together in His very house, alone as it seems? Will He save you again when the danger comes for you, or will He turn His back this time?"

Tears rimmed her blue eyes, but her legs were frozen in their place, keeping her captive to the intensity of that stare and the contrasting gentleness of his every ragged breath as each breezed across her features. A man, this was a man, not an angel, and this man had bloodstains on his soul. An angel might have loved and protected her, but this man would not hesitate to kill her. With a fire in his eyes that consumed, he stared at her, long and hard, taunting her to argue, to beg maybe, but words were reserved for a terrified mind and would not come forward.

With an impatient growl, Erik suddenly caught her upper arms between his hands, yanking her without thought to benevolence into the wide aisle, finding it surprisingly easy to sever her grasp on the pew. She did not scream or sob; all he received was the smallest whimper like a distraught child as the tears held still and shimmering in her eyes, cutting him to his core.

"Where is your God now, Christine?" Every bit of his self-hatred was served into his hiss and the fire of his rage. His hands dug into the wool of her coated arms, likely bruising white skin beneath. No, he wouldn't care! He wanted to hate her as he hated himself! He wanted to blame her for the pain eating a hole within him! Shaking her in his grasp, he demanded, "Will God save you? Will He smote the wicked phantom and preserve your innocent body from harm? Or will He allow you, as pure and undeserving of such cruelty as you are, to fall to my sins? Will He turn a blind eye on you? Let's see, shall we? Go on, Christine. Cry and beg. Pray for God's salvation! Pray that He comes for you! *Pray*, damn you!"

She could only cry silently, and every tear glimmering like a diamond in the reconciling candle-glow tore at him with even more bitterness, reminding him so vividly what a monster he was. To hurt this beautiful woman he so loved... What could be a more heinous sin?

Practically roaring his disdain, his hands abruptly caught the collar of her coat and ripped it wide open as buttons darted everywhere, bouncing off pews and getting lost along the carpet. A cry fell from her at the viciousness, and she fought to suck a breath into terrified, constricted lungs.

"Pray, Christine," Erik commanded again, not permitting a single flicker of compassion to enter his stare as it concentrated on her fear. "Pray! Say, 'Dear God, save me from this deformed madman'. Say, 'Preserve my innocent body'."

As he spoke, his fingers curled in the neckline of her blue, wool gown, lacking any gentleness. This wasn't *her*; that was what his mind kept insisting. No, not his Christine because he would never be so heartless to his Christine. No, this was only the chit who had robbed him of his every dream, the one who had ripped away his mask and his self-respect with it. Yes, that was what he saw, not the small, sobbing woman before him. It wasn't Christine's gown in his fisted hands; it wasn't Christine's gown that he tore open, creating a deep gash down the center to her waist. *No!* And it couldn't be the creamy flesh and white silk undergarments of his Christine meeting his horror-stricken stare.

"Pray!" he shouted at her. "Damn you! *Pray*! God must save you before I put my hands on your body! God must strike me down and destroy me! He can't think that you deserve to have my sin-laden hands upon your pure flesh! You don't deserve that!"

Christine stared at him as she sobbed, her entire frame quivering in his grasp. Chilled air passed over exposed skin, making her shake harder inside and out as gasped breaths entered her trembling lips. To her surprise, as those fiery eyes trailed over her, taking in the flimsy barrier of her chemise and the fitted outline of her corset before they raised to her accusing gaze, she saw realization peek through and then in its wake, guilt.

"Christine," he moaned as tears rapidly clouded his vision of her. It was the beauty of her, that flawless perfection that insisted everything he would rather have denied. His body spasmed with the power of his sobs, his hands daring to remain on her arms, palms open and flat; she could have pulled free, but she didn't, staring with her blame as blatantly on display as the violent tear in her gown.

"No," he whined miserably. "No... It isn't supposed to be this way, ...not with you. This isn't what I wanted..." As he sobbed, his hands slowly made a path over her shoulders and neck until they cupped her face between them, his sense refusing to consider how she shuddered to bear his touch on her skin. Not even gentleness would wipe away her disgust or suspicion, and cringing with self-revulsion, he curved his fingertips into his palms, nails digging into skin, yet kept only the slightest pressure on her cheeks. No... He wouldn't hurt her again.

"You don't deserve this," he softly told her. "You deserved an angel, a real angel, but you were given a demon... And yet was my sin so great? I lied to you, yes, but I gave you something to believe in. I gave you the answer to your prayers that your God never could. And you weren't alone anymore. ...And neither was I."

His words broke with a sob, his head ducking as if its weight was too great to hold up any longer, and unworthy, shaking hands lowered to grasp her concealed shoulders again. No, no, ...he didn't deserve the pleasure of touching warm, silken skin. Without daring to meet her eye for fear what he would see, he admitted, "For one moment, I did believe in God. My entire pathetic lifetime, I had been sure that if He did exist, He was a cruel, unfeeling bastard, that He had cursed me for no reason but being born. It's easier to deny His existence than accept His unqualified hatred. ...But then I saw you, and you were so beautiful, so pure... You needed me as much as I needed you. I was certain that you were my salvation and...my proof that I wasn't forgotten."

Christine listened intently as he spoke. *Forgotten...* Had she not thought the very same thing? That his presence proved the same for her? Her heart twisted within her chest in a sudden bout of regret. What had she done? She had destroyed the illusion he had almost lovingly created for her and them both with it.

Still, he would not meet her constant gaze, staring at a spot of smooth skin just below her collarbone, part of him desperate to forget that his own actions had exposed it. "I should have remained the angel, should have confined myself to being the voice in the darkness and nothing more by whatever means necessary. I should have never come to you as I did. But angels can't be touched... And how I longed to touch you!"

It was odd that his words did not upset her; perhaps had anyone else said such an intimate thing or had he not spoken with that exact longing in his golden tone, brimming over with it, then she would have remembered to be timid and at least a little afraid. But he spoke as if the voice itself came from the sharp-edged recesses of a broken heart, and she was shaken for a second time that day off her foundation. Before she could rationalize and fathom the meaning it brought, he grew suddenly bitter with a distant sneer.

"But then," he muttered half to himself, "you

betrayed me."

Her frame went rigid, and though his grip on her arms tightened to keep her from fleeing, he still did not grant her a glance.

"I never considered that the mask would hold such a lure for you. Anyone else, maybe. But in my mind, you were above such mundane things. I was expecting questions; you do possess quite the inquisitive streak. ...I did not place it within your character simply to act."

"I...I'm sorry," she stammered softly, hoping to thwart the festering embers of temper beneath the surface. Everything felt unstable, even the solid ground beneath her feet, as if at any moment, the earth would part and swallow her whole with one wave of his ferocious rage.

Abruptly, his eyes shifted to her, searching deeply into her own, penetrating to her soul to seek his answer for him as he demanded, "Are you, Christine? But what are you sorry for? Are you sorry for betraying my trust in you and acting like a frivolous child? Or are you sorry that it was not the ethereal visage of an angel you found? ...Perhaps you are only sorry with the hope of saving yourself. I would never have taken you for such ruses before, but...I also would never have expected to be stripped of my rights as a human being by you and your curiosity either."

Shaking her head slowly, she insisted, "I *did* act like a child. I *did* betray you."

"And you are sorry for it?"

"Yes!" she vehemently replied, catching his immediate flicker of doubt. "You know me, *ange*, better than anyone I'd say. You'd know if I was lying to you."

Erik was searching her unceasingly. His gut believed, but his heart had to question, terrified more that she spoke true. To believe her meant to be vulnerable. *Vulnerable...* Keeping her eye captive in his, he lifted one hand from her arm and brought it, trembling in mid-air to the corner of his mask.

"My face," he said as his suddenly clumsy fingers worked the lacing they usually knew so well, "is disfigured and ugly. I have spent my lifetime hiding it away behind my mask, hiding *myself* away from every cruel person in this self-centered world. But you...you could learn to see beyond it; I know you could. Christine, I've seen the heart of you, the *soul*, as you would call it. You're strong and as passionate a creature as I am. It's why I adore you so much. If you would just look upon me and not judge... Think past what you know and what you've perceived beauty and ugliness to be. See more. *Want* more. Please, Christine..."

The lacings were loose, yet his hand still kept the mask in place, his eyes bearing into hers with a desperation he knew she couldn't comprehend. Hesitating and wondering if she could feel his entire body shake with a rise of his own fears, he added, "Disgust is a perception, Christine, a learned aversion due to society's aesthetic principles. You don't have to be disgusted."

What was she doing? Christine felt herself nod her acquiescence before she even justified it to herself. Behind that mask was a horror; she had seen enough earlier to last her entire lifetime, and yet here she was encouraging him to reveal it again under a false hope that she could see the more he wanted her to. She was undeniably sure that he was giving her more credit than she deserved because she had *never* seen herself as strong. In the back of her mind was an incessant voice that asked, when she looked at him and only knew aversion, what would happen then?

Slowly, Erik lowered the mask, his eyes never drifting from hers as he exposed his flaws to her widened blue gaze. ...Vulnerable, yes, this was vulnerable. No words existed at that moment; he only watched her carefully, scrutinizing, and above all, needing one sign, just one...

This was different than the last time; that was

Christine's first thought. Her earlier encounter with his face had been followed immediately with a rage the likes of which she had never before been victim to, contorting already warped features into something beyond ugliness, ...terrifying at its essence. This... This was inciting pity, not fear. He was...corpse-like, scarred and disfigured, one side of his face skeletal. Whatever flesh it bore was drawn taut and thin over the bone structure, transparent up to his exposed scalp with the hairline far back and oddly irregular as it joined a normal setting on the other side. His green eyeball was deeply sunken into its socket of smooth bone and a very flimsy lid that did not appear as abnormal when shadowed by the mask's presence. Even staring solely into his eyes during their conversation in warm candlelight, she had not taken notice that he had no lashes and above, no eyebrow to frame. Bare, exposed, and as malformed as the swollen bulge of his upper lip, ...one more flaw on a demented palette. Her mind called it a face of death; without fire and fury attached, the devil was no longer even a faint consideration.

Tears were slipping free of the restraint he had been harboring and spilling over the damaged flesh as he whispered, "I don't see disgust in your eyes... I...I don't know what I see. I've never seen it before."

"It's compassion," she whispered back, "and empathy... You were born this way?" The subject felt taboo, and she was inclined to stifle herself from broaching it, but her inquisitive urge would not listen. It could be as powerful as her curiosity at times.

He tentatively nodded that corpse's head, and every motion intrigued her: the movement of his mouth when he spoke, every blink of his lash-less eye. It was odd to her, ...odd but not repulsive.

"Now do you see why I hold such little credence in God?" he demanded. "Did I deserve to be born with this face, Christine? Did I deserve to be shunned and tortured for it? You believe that faith and prayer can change anything; well, I prayed and prayed for a new face. I prayed for acceptance, and I never was heard... Perhaps if *you* pray for me, Christine, if you pray for mercy for my tarnished soul, I will know some peace. A prayer from your beautiful lips would be as lyrical as a symphony."

How cold reality could be! Her eyes caressed those misshapen features again and again, and all she could think was how unfair it was for her to be mourning her own loss. She had ignorantly never considered how she had hurt him in her initial response to his face, never considered beyond escaping his rage and his ugliness. She had acted no different than everyone else, and it made her feel guilty to realize he had been expecting better of her.

"Christine," Erik whispered, crying quietly, and on a sudden whim he could not deny, he leaned close as she watched with hesitant eyes until, taking a tremulous breath for courage, he set his disfigured cheek against the smooth skin at the top of her chemise.

He nearly sobbed with the first contact. She was so warm, so soft, so alive! He purposely refused to notice the way her body tensed and was petrified against him because she did not pull away in spite of it. She could have; his hold on her was minimal at best, but she stayed rooted to her spot, even as her un-patterned heartbeat and shallow, gasped breaths gave her away.

His tears were wetting her skin and absorbing into the silk of her chemise, but Christine's focus instead was riveted to the texture of his scars. It wasn't the same as touching and learning with fingertips; his cheek was laid to a sensitive expanse of flesh and the strange smoothness of it and its incessant chill were creating tingles down her spine. So timid and afraid, his arms weaved around her waist until he was delicately holding her, and though she went rigid to allow such a transgression, as the seconds ticked by, she gradually calmed until she relaxed in his grasp and allowed him.

Sighing against her, his breath danced across the surface of her skin and made goose bumps arise as he gently bid, "You can't imagine how it feels to have you so close, ...to hold you. It's all I wanted, all I've dreamt of. No one has ever...allowed my touch before..."

Erik paused, unsure he should say more, but he felt such an intimacy with her in that moment, one only enhanced without a shared gaze to raise question and doubt, and so he indulged himself and spoke freely, things he had never believed he would reveal to anyone. "When I was a boy, maybe three or four, I tried once to touch my mother... I just wanted to be held; I was only a child, but she...she could never tolerate my presence. She believed I was the devil incarnate, that she had given birth to the antichrist, and she never forgave me for it. ...All because of my face... She wanted me nowhere near her, and...she attacked me with a hot poker to remind me never to dare try again."

Christine listened in horror, hardly comprehending that he spoke of *his* life. It was too awful to consider, and yet he remained seemingly detached and aloof as he told it. Holding her with one arm, he raised the other and drew down the collar of his shirt at the nape of his neck. Cheek still to her skin, eyes still away from her reaction, he exposed a strawberry-shaped, upraised, white scar. She could already guess it was only one of many on his body, and she was glad he did not see how she cringed to behold it. As he brought his arm around her again, she dared to raise her own, and shaking in their path, her fingers trailed a soft caress across that scar, grazing skin just within his collar. To her surprise, he cried out and went stiff against her.

"I...I didn't mean to hurt you," Christine stammered, abruptly yanking her hand away. But realization cut her like a dull knife, and with tears suddenly gathering in her eyes, she instead insisted, "I didn't hurt you, did I, *ange*?"

"No," he breathed so softly she almost did not catch it.

"This...is foreign to you," she pressed. "I could be as gentle as it is within my capabilities to be, and you wouldn't know how to respond."

"Forgive me," he vehemently begged as if for the greatest sin he had ever committed. "I didn't know you intended to-"

"Sshh," she crooned, and with only a breath's pause, she again brought her fingers to the scar, noting how he tensed but did not draw away the instant her skin met his.

Erik was holding his breath, his entire body shivering against her. A willing caress, freely given; it was more than he had ever fathomed asking for. There was no threat there, no pain as a result. Pokers caused pain; fists and kicking legs caused pain. But her touch was tender, her fingertips as soft as every bit of her. As she grew bolder in her actions, she brought her hand from that scar up over his thin hair and down again, soothing him in the only way she could. And it was so pleasant that he longed to cry at the same time as he feared that if he did, she would stop, and oh, how he never wanted her to stop!

Christine shooed away the voice in her head that insisted what she was doing was wrong, refusing the pull of both it and her own modesty. Sense knew what he was and the past that truth implied, but she set it aside. He needed her; that was all she could rationalize at the moment. To be needed was such a consuming feeling, one she was eager to indulge and know because it was so much better than reality. In reality, he was a murderer; at the present, he was a broken man, and she was *his* angel.

"*Ange?*" she softly called after long moments of only tremulous breaths.

"Erik," he corrected gently.

There was a flash of a memory with the name in her head. He had told her during the commotion after her betrayal and the eruption of his temper that had followed, and yet much of that scene had remained a blur, shadowed by the seeming horror she had uncovered.

"Erik," she repeated and felt him shudder down the length of his spine simply from the sound of his name upon her lips. "Why did you lie to me all these months? Why did you pretend to be an angel?"

"You know why," he insisted back.

"Yes," she replied steadily, her caresses never ceasing, "but I want you to tell me anyway."

Releasing a soft sigh, his grip instinctively tightened on her before words would come, needing reassurance that she was there yet still terrified to look in her eyes. "Because you needed an angel, not a monster. You could have never loved a monster, never spoken so freely of your life, never opened your heart and soul... You would have held back a piece of yourself, and I wanted *everything*." Erik paused, momentarily terrified to go on so much that he had to collect courage and force himself to continue. "And you *did* love the angel, Christine; I know you did. ...Could you never learn to love the man beneath? ...Could you never see that beyond the monster, he can be the angel you want?"

"The angel I want...doesn't exist." No bitterness crept through her words; how could it when she was being held in his safe arms. ...It had to feel the same to be wrapped in an angel's white wings.

"He could!" Erik insisted passionately. "He feels the same as the man; both love you beyond anything in the world. I beg you to see it. Forget fear; forget what you think you know. Just *feel*, Christine. Tell me what your heart is saying."

She bit her lip, her brow furrowing with a greater weight than he could understand. "It's saying that I don't want to be alone again."

How could she promise beyond that? How could she promise *anything* to this man she barely knew? Yes, he had been the angel she had been so certain she loved, and holding her as he was, without a glimpse of that malformed face, she could almost pretend nothing had changed, that the voice she knew so well as her angel's was essentially that. Angels were perfect; he nearly had been, yet now that was lost and this was all she had left.

"You won't ever be alone again," Erik vowed, and she had the smallest suspicion in the back of her head that perhaps that was not a blessing at all. Perhaps it was the beginning of a nightmare.

"My...lessons," she stammered, shaken with her contemplations. "You will still teach me, won't you?"

"Of course. You are my protégé; there has never been a lie in the music. It was always only pure." Sadness pricked Erik's heart where hope had been thriving because he felt the wall she was establishing between her heart and his, a wall he worried he would never be able to break down. Love... It was easy for him to love her, but having her love in return, he realized, was something he could not force her to give. If he dared try, he would push her further from his grasp. The only way to get what he wanted was to earn it, and he felt determined at that moment with the mere taste of what it meant dangling before him that he would succeed and keep his usual impatience within his control.

With reluctance so great that he had to force uncooperative limbs to comply, he released her from his embrace, ducking his face low and beyond the candlelight as he sought his mask. He did not straighten until it was replaced and he was the regal phantom again, his very aura reestablished with its manmade presence.

Christine immediately missed his nearness, though she did not let on of it, drawing her torn gown closed with shaking hands and hugging herself tight. Her eyes were riveted to him, and she could hardly believe he was the same man who had only just held her. Allowing herself to be held by the Opera Ghost and murderer... No, she couldn't have permitted such a sin. Was it another trick and manipulation? ...Was her soul already tarnished for yearning to feel him near again?

"I apologize for my earlier outbursts," Erik was saying with a modicum of reserve. "You need not fear I will ever lay an unwanted hand on you again."

Unwanted... Her mind dwelled on that word. And if such a thing *were* wanted, would he touch her then? She felt angry with herself for the question as it flitted through her brain.

Passing one last long glance over her, he added, "I will come for you tomorrow at our usual time for your lesson, and if my presence is tolerable, we will begin to work down in my home instead. It is a safer situation for us both as I would not want your name connected to my reputation around the opera."

Secluded away in his home, the idea should have shaken her, but she could not deny that angel's voice; it would always be her undoing. "Tomorrow," she simply repeated, and with one more shared stare, she wearily walked back up the aisle toward the church door.

Erik watched her somberly, and before her hand reached the knob, he dared to call, "Christine?" His entire being lifted just to see her turn back and return those blue eyes inquisitively to his. "Would you rather I had stayed the intangible angel to you? With never a hope for anything more?"

Christine pondered his question a silent breath, unsure she wanted to know her own answer when it seemed such a blatant betrayal of her conscience. But then she earnestly replied, "An angel could never have loved me back, could never have touched me; you said so yourself. And at some point, intangible wouldn't have been enough. I would have needed more... No, Erik, I wouldn't have preferred you stayed the angel. I prefer you to be a man."

"Even a broken and ugly one?" he pushed, denying the temptation of hope.

Hesitating to muster courage, she whispered

back, "An angel couldn't have held me as a man could. Broken and ugly were inconsequential when your arms were around me..." Trailing off with a scolding from her inner voice, she kept his gaze one last breath before hurrying out of the warmly lit church, out into the night, the cold, and the storm, unsure which situation was truly more dangerous to be a part of.

Erik stared after her, unable to cease the rise of tears in his eyes as his body recalled the softness of hers and begged for its presence once again. She might not be able to give him love, not yet, but she *had* given him hope to push on and seek more. He was confident that in time she could love him. She had to; she was made for him.

Suddenly turning back to the overlooking eyes of an ever-present crucifix, he awkwardly bowed his masked face and dared to pray one single prayer: ...that she would be his.

"Choices and Perceptions"
Told from Christine's POV. Erik holds her to the choice she made.

I made the choice... I made the choice... The words repeated like a mantra in my head, over and over again, almost a monotone chant. Rhythmic, soothing in some constant way, they incited the gentle rocking my body had undertaken as I sat awkwardly perched on the edge of the canopy bed in my room in Erik's home, ready to leap to my feet the instant things changed. *Oh, weren't they bound to change...*

Chanting up my own courage only lasted so long, as sporadic thoughts continuously burst my trance and returned the tragically unaccepted events of only the past few hours. Hours? Dear Lord, was it really only *hours* ago that I had been preparing to perform that ill-fated opera? It seemed like years when so much of my very existence had been shifted. Opera roles and performances were suddenly mundane in the ultimate scheme of things. Had I actually wasted minutes of my precious freedom feeling nervous about singing onstage before a full audience? I wanted to curse my own naïveté, for it seemed that in solely the past few hours, I had gone from child to woman. Suddenly, life was in perspective, and the fuzzy innocence childhood gave was vanished to nothing.

"I made the choice..." I spoke the words aloud this time, wanting every one of my senses to pick them up and believe them. I *had* made the choice. I had determined the path I myself would now follow. Coercion was only a gentle nudge toward its end, not the basis beneath as I was certain everyone else was convinced. Yes, Erik had threatened to murder Raoul if I did not choose him, but surprisingly, it was only the final push my heart had needed to accept a decision that had already been made. As I said, no one else would have believed that.

Sighing desolately, I let my fingers idly caress the intricate beading on my skirt. A wedding gown;

yes, this was a wedding gown. Well, Erik certainly had not wanted his intentions misconstrued. He wanted me to know that my agreement was permanent and binding. ...Yet seemingly more comparable to a prisoner in a jail cell than a bride. Even if my prison was a bit more luxurious than most, it was a prison just the same.

Within seconds of a kiss that had practically shaken the foundation of the earth with its power, Erik had locked me in my room like an obstinate child, and I had not seen or heard from him since. My conclusion on the subject was that he had busied himself getting rid of Raoul's presence, a prisoner himself, though his cell had had the less pleasant distinction of being a torture chamber. And I was certain that Raoul would not have left calmly. No, he would have made a futile attempt to fight for me. Poor, foolishly misguided Raoul. He was fortunate that Erik was committed not to harm him because without a restriction in place, the Vicomte's life would have been as good as over despite my seeming sacrifices to save it.

So I wasn't permitted a goodbye to the love of my shattered childhood. I doubted I would ever see Raoul again, and under the current circumstances, I only knew a momentary mourning for our idealistic relationship, the same bereavement that I was indulging for my ended childhood. Raoul was a part of it, holding the heart of the little girl I no longer was. After tonight, we would have had no future even if Erik had released me from my choice. I was different on the inside. I doubted Raoul could have understood that. Our stolen goodbye was something I only accepted when looking at it with Erik's eyes. Surely what he perceived could only be a tearful farewell full of kisses and oaths of undying love was best avoided. I could hardly begrudge him that.

...*Where was Erik*? My mind asked the question again as my insides twisted in a mixture of boredom and queer anticipation. After all, I had no idea what was to come, what our life, one I had *freely chosen*, would hold, and yet I was convicted to my path. If I had still been the weak child, mourning lost love and freedom, perhaps in this time alone, I would have sought a means to take my own life. Wasn't suicide a better option than a lifetime with a monster? It would certainly make a glorious ending to a tragic opera if this tale were only a work of fiction. Taking my own life... Dramatic, poetic, the fitting finale to a tale of horror. But the ironic twist in my story that, strangely enough, made me stronger than that was that I loved the monster.

It was still odd to admit such a thing openly to myself when I had kept it buried in denial for so long. But it was true. I loved Erik. Albeit, not the version of him I had had to endure this evening, one bordering insanity and on the verge of murder. No, I loved the Erik I had been lucky enough to know before our world had come crashing down around us. Teacher, friend, mentor, ...the match of my innermost soul. Back before Raoul had reappeared in my life and had convinced me to see things his way, Erik and I had been so very close. We had delighted simply in one another's existence. It had been beyond the music, beyond even the awe I had always known for his genius. It had been a constant longing to be within each other's company, a need to be together. He had been closer and dearer to me than anyone in my entire life.

Why then had things imploded as violently as they had to lead us to this travesty of an ending? ...What argument could I make to justify the petty shallowness of an immature girl? Raoul had held my childhood heart, and weak as I was, I had let those fleeting wisps of feeling return and spring back to life. No, I had never loved him, but I had respected and trusted him enough to value his opinions about Erik and his supposed 'control' over me. My God, the Vicomte's charm! When he exuded it, he could have me believing anything he chose. He had twisted every detail around until it *had* seemed like I must have been manipulated. Raoul had even convinced me that Erik used his music to hypnotize me into feeling something for him!

Naïve fool! I shouted at myself now to recall it. And how I had ignorantly hurt Erik! It sickened me to consider it!

Suddenly as I sat there still ruminating on the past's mistakes, the click of the turned lock made me jump with a start and leap to my feet, terrified for reasons I couldn't find. Erik's eyes were cold when they sought me out, biting furiously beneath the replaced presence of the mask. Oh, how often did he hide behind that manmade barrier? More times than he probably realized. Now it was the face of the Opera Ghost, his alter persona and cruelest façade, who stared at me and ran bitter eyes over my appearance from head to toe for a long, disconcerting moment before he strode into the room, ...dragging with him a uniformed priest. So there was to be a wedding, after all... Did that make me happy or frightened? Even I myself wasn't sure of the answer when the Opera Ghost was my groom and the Erik I loved was far, far out of my reach.

The priest was practically heaved to the opposite side of the room, and as he scampered to his feet again, his wide, horror-stricken eyes landed on me a long second. And what sort of expression did I give in return to this scene? Solemn to be sure with a clear lack of surprise. No, nothing Erik did surprised me anymore.

"My dear," the Opera Ghost sneered with a modicum of spite lacing his golden angel's voice. *Dear...* Back when things had been pleasant, every endearment uttered had been saturated in genuine sentiment. Then, he had called me '*ange*' as if I were the angel he was supposed to have been. Now 'dear' felt as cold as an insult.

"Erik." I was ill-equipped at imitating such a tone, especially when the only resentment I carried was solely due to the fact that he was playing a part with me and refusing to give me back the man I wanted. Still, I was stronger in composure than either of us had expected me to be, and he showed his astonishment toward such a feat in one solitary moment before he hastily hid it away again.

Straightening his shoulders with that arrogant air that always besot him when he was the almighty phantom Opera Ghost, he explained with a certain amount of detachment, "I have taken the liberty of escorting your former fiancé home, and on my way back, I brought us a guest. Father Benedict will perform our marriage ceremony, a real, *legal* marriage. ...Does that surprise you, Christine? You did agree, and surely you couldn't have expected a spoken vow to be enough."

"I *did* agree," I insisted back. I could guess that he expected horror, shock, terror. None of which I gave. In fact, I remained stoic, defiantly holding his eye, and so I glimpsed the miniscule breath during which my strength rattled his composure.

"This is all a part of your game, isn't it?" he suddenly accused, and then tossing his hands up in the air, he gave a fraction of the maniacal laugh I had been subject to all evening. "Of course it is! You want to confuse and intrigue me, take me off my guard so that the first chance you get, you can make your escape. Well, I cannot argue against your attempt, futile as it may be, and you certainly have amused me. No tears and pleadings. It's...unexpected from you."

Unexpected... Dear Lord, how long had I let the child within me reign supreme? It shamed me to consider that he was right, that his seeming insult had validity enough to leave me inwardly cringing. But I let none of it show on my face. No, I didn't want Erik to know my regrets.

"I am playing no game with you, Erik. I made a choice," I emphasized every word, "and if you are ready, then let us marry and start our life together." I turned to the wary-eyed priest and nodded confidently, "Father, if you will."

The man looked as if he yearned to refuse, but was far too terrified to utter a word against us. And indeed, what could he say? We had both consented to marriage; Erik was *not* forcing me. The priest's only argument could have come in the form of being dragged here by mediocre force, for this was not a cowering child and deranged murderer standing before him. No. I was determined we'd never fall into those roles ever again.

My eyes slowly rose to my groom, and one solitary twinge of panic coiled in my stomach. And it wasn't even my own! Because for an instant, so quick that only a resonating echo told me that it was even real, I caught a flicker of fear in those mismatched eyes. *Fear...* Had I *ever* seen Erik afraid of anything? He was always so far beyond strong and completely poised at every turn, and had I looked at him in this current breath, fear would have never even crossed my mind. He had buried it away as if it had never existed, and I knew that for now I would have to do the same and wait to ask why. But my mind suffered, and over and over again, I pondered what he could possibly be afraid of. *Me...?* I could logically conclude little else.

Putting up a façade that my brain spun mercilessly behind, I extended my hands to him, my eyes holding his, secretly seeking those unpleasant emotions he never again gave away. Moving with a grace that captivated me as always, he strode the few lengths to stand before me. ...Did his hands really tremble in the second before they caught mine? I couldn't be sure.

His skin was cold, always cold, eternally and basely so. I had to wonder if moving out of the damp catacombs would change that, or if it was something built into him. ...Was all of him so cold? And yet wasn't it within mere moments that my own natural heat chased the edge of the chill away? Cold became secondary as I focused on his hands, on their shape holding mine. To me, they weren't the hands of a deformed murderer; no, they were the hands of a genius, a brilliant inventor, a virtuoso composer and musician. Not even after the events of this night did I look upon them and see a flash of blood or violence. No, I only saw Erik's hands.

At some point I did not notice, the priest joined us; I only gave recognition to him when his nervous jittering back and forth distracted my peripheral vision. At the same instant, both Erik and I looked away from each other and to his intruding presence, simultaneously giving him our full regard.

"Are you...sure?" Father Benedict stammered, and it was blatantly clear that the question was directed solely at me.

"Without a single doubt," I replied, meeting Erik's gaze, as it seemed to hold the same question in its depths. "Are you?" I dared to ask my groom as well, recalling that flash of fear I had seen.

Those mismatched eyes narrowed, his stare shrewd and fixed on mine as, disentangling one of our joined hands, he lifted it to draw away his mask, revealing that stark, mangled deformity with a posed challenge to me alone. I heard the little cry of horror our observer gave, knowing that Erik must have as well but gave no consideration to it. No, he was only concerned with me and my reaction to his pitiful excuse for a face.

"No doubts, Christine?" he dared to taunt, tilting that corpse's head to test me so brutally.

But my expression had not changed and neither had the conviction in my heart. If he had thought to shock me, such days were long over. I knew what that face looked like, not only from the times he had vividly put it on display mid-rage at me. I saw it on the blank canvases of my eyelids every time I closed my eyes. Its image was ingrained there so permanently and had been since my first encounter with it, stealing any shock value it had once had over me.

31

Holding those eyes, one sunken so deeply into its socket and so vibrantly emerald while the other shown perfect and blue, I replied resolutely, "No doubts," and I saw it shake him ever so slightly.

He left the mask off, and I would have had it no other way, wanting to *see* the face of the man I was marrying. The priest was the only one of us unnerved, but as his shaky voice resounded around us, Erik and I kept eyes solely on each other, everything else forgotten in the midst of a hazy backdrop.

I barely heard or understood a single word, surprising myself when the time to speak came and I actually managed to utter a committing vow. I was far too engrossed studying the man before me, my groom, my about-to-be husband.

How long had it been since the major rift between us? ...Six months, give or take. Six months... Six months of changes, six months filled with days that I was not the focus of those eyes, six months of thoughts through his head that I knew nothing about, ...six months of pain and loneliness that I had ignorantly caused. And in six months, though that face was the same as ever, the man and soul behind it were altered in ways I wanted to learn. ...Six months of separation, and yet we were ending together. Oddly enough, perhaps it was only due to his forceful, seemingly crazy actions that we had arrived at this point. If not for his ultimatum, I likely might have stayed the weak child at Raoul's side and suffocated my own heart in the process.

I had to wonder what Erik was considering as he stared back at me. His expression was unreadable, no smile in his eyes, no elation in his very aura. He remained so dignified in composure and yet gave off the faintest trace of apathy that absolutely grated on me. I *knew* he wasn't apathetic to this scene. I *knew* he loved me. And yet he seemed so determined not to show even a trace of it, making it seem like I could have been *anyone* standing there with him, marrying him, and it wouldn't have mattered.

As the traditional ceremony ended and we were now legally bound to one another as man and wife, I expected *something* from my groom, maybe relief at least. Instead, I was suddenly yanked to him by the grip he still had on my hands, and as a gasp I could not contain slid out, he kissed me hard. It was nothing like the gentle kiss we had shared earlier, one I had instigated to seal my vow and show him I had meant every word. This was forceful, bruising, an act of possession rather than love. I was his now, and he was making that abundantly clear.

When he let me go with an abruptness that made my head spin, he turned to the priest without even a flash of regard to my presence as the hurt rejection welled inside of me without my consent.

"I'll take you back," Erik said stiffly, and even though he tossed one single look my way, it was completely devoid of emotion. And that was all. No words, no explanations, not even a goodbye. Erik half-dragged the priest back out of my room, closing the door behind them and leaving me alone.

Alone on my wedding day. Practically rejected by my husband. Ignorantly bound to him for the rest of my life. Regret loomed, but really what *could* I regret? I had hurt Erik, and he was making a point. I couldn't regret going through with my vow and marrying him because I genuinely loved him in spite of it all. Regret... I regretted the past six months. *They* had formed the man I had just married, and now I would have to live with the consequences.

For about ten minutes that seemed *far* longer to my frantic nerves, I paced my room before I realized with a huff at my own stupidity that I had not heard a click. I was not locked in this time. Was that an iota of trust now that we were legally married? I would have thought so had I not ventured out into the empty house only to find the door that led out into the catacombs locked from the outside. ...What could I argue to that? He didn't trust me. Why should he? But being locked in the house was superior to being

33

locked in one room, or so a lingering flicker of optimism thought. But I squelched that optimism in my next coherent moment: squelched, stepped on, shredded to tiny, indecipherable pieces.

With a heaved sigh of discontent, I wandered the quiet rooms beneath approaching waves of melancholy. I had to wonder now that we were wed if Erik intended for us to remain underground. To my sun-starved mind, it seemed no way to live. Dark, dank, cold. I could already fathom catching ill quite frequently under such conditions. The house itself wasn't intolerable. Fireplaces in every room chased the brunt of the chill out, but it was still so...devoid of natural light. I liked the sun and the moon and the stars. Even cloudy days and rain were better to look at than stone walls and ceilings. I couldn't imagine never seeing them again.

Eventually with nothing to occupy myself, I ended up back within my own room, door closed, privacy established. What privacy, though? This was my wedding night. I knew a trepidation I hardly wanted to acknowledge that created frantic butterflies in my belly.

I was not ignorant on such intimate subjects, as most women my age were. Being a member of the *corps de ballet* would have taught me plenty and certainly beyond the basic actions. Those girls were well-versed and not shy to discuss even the most salacious of details, for surely in my quiet observance, I had learned quite a bit and vivid instructions on acts I felt certain only prostitutes performed. But in regard to the simple mechanics of things, I attributed my education to a father who was desperate that his only daughter would not be taken advantage of. My father had spent most of his career in and out of the theatre scene, and he had known its inner workings and how far performers often went to please patrons and managers alike. Preparing me for a similar career path, he had felt it necessary to instill in me a respect and reverence for my body and the act of giving it so intimately to another. Oh, Raoul had tried on more than one occasion to acquire such physical pleasures, insisting again and again that he loved me and it was only the natural progression of love, but I had never conceded to more than a few kisses. ...And how grateful I suddenly felt for the awkward conversation I had had to endure with my father! Otherwise I likely would have fallen into the same mindset as the other ballerinas and given in to Raoul months ago.

And now...tonight I would give myself to Erik, ...my husband. Quivering from head to toe with a nervousness that flushed my pale complexion pink, I suddenly had the urge to busy myself with something, *anything* to take my mind from the thought. It was too quiet in my room! In the house! Quiet enough for thoughts to reel in my brain.

I decided on a hot bath, determined to find calm after the extent of an overwhelming evening. *Calm, ha!* Relaxation of any sort would not come. I was tense even within the deliciously warm cocoon of water and fragrant bubbles. At some point, I even tried to sing and concentrate on the way my voice echoed off the tiles of my bathroom, filling up space. But thoughts kept bursting in, and finally, I had to give up, rushing from the water's embrace and grabbing my nightclothes on the wings of a sudden consideration that Erik could simply burst into my bathroom if he so chose and find me bare in my tub. He was my husband, and I couldn't and wouldn't deny him, but I had the irrelevant yet oddly necessary desire to make the moment special, more special than being found in my bathtub.

With shaking fingers, I dressed in a white, silk nightgown, the loveliest one in my wardrobe, and a lace wrap, hoping, even as I blushed to consider such a thing, that Erik would like it. I didn't even know if he desired me in such a way; I had never given thought to it until now. Back before our separation, there had been a few times when I had suspected that he wanted to kiss me, but the mask had always stood in the way. It was an obstruction; to kiss me, he had to remove it, and at the time, that had been an unacceptable condition. Now...well, everything was changed.

Sitting upon the soft blankets of my bed, I flounced the silk of my skirt and combed through my damp, loose curls with a growing sense of impatience. I had no idea how long I would have to wait, and as the determination swelled within me, I knew I was ready and sure. But the longer I sat, the more my apprehension re-flickered to life and the more insecure I grew. At some point, I even found myself concluding that my intrepid innocence would seem foolish to Erik, most especially if he had done such things before. Perhaps he would expect me to know how to please him, or at least not to be the timid mouse I suddenly felt like. If I was dealing with the Erik of six months ago, I could say with absolute certainty that he would have been gentle and understanding, but this new Erik... I wasn't confident to predict anything.

Minutes of further discomfort ticked by, long, almost unendurable. Then an hour, ...then another hour, and I felt I would burst from the waiting. Dear God, what was taking so long? Or was it simply that he didn't want to be here with me? ...Or, and this was a torturous thought to my addled brain, had something happened to him? I trusted his stealthy ability to blend with shadows and move about like the ghost they called him, but after tonight, too many people were out for vengeance. *Oh, Erik, where are you?*

I could remain still no longer, and with bare feet striking a thick layer of carpet that thankfully kept out the chill, I crept from my room with no more intent than to wander the house. Locked in, I couldn't very well go and look for him. ...Locked in, and I would die here if something happened to Erik. Funny that the thought only then occurred to me.

As I passed that prohibited exit, I halted in my

steps. There, hung by the door was Erik's black cloak, the very one he had been wearing hours before. He was here... He was home. And it astounded and perplexed me that he had not dared to approach me. Better judgment argued to leave things be and return to my room, but how could I? My life had been transformed this very day; he was my husband. I couldn't consider that we'd begin our marriage so rifted apart.

I sought him out and was summoned by the glow of the fireplace in the sitting room, bright enough to imply that it had been recently stoked. It was strange that it felt so welcoming when the image I got as I paused in the doorway was hardly that at all. Erik was seated in his throne-like chair, staring somberly at the hearth, mask hiding the vast depth of the pain that radiated from him in the way heat radiated from the fire. In his hand was a glass of some sort of alcohol; it looked as if he had barely sipped from it, a crutch to numb a pain he seemed more inclined to suffer.

Erik never looked away from the flames, never cast a single glance my way, and yet he suddenly commanded, "Go to bed, Christine."

This time my sense won, stifling any protest and snuffing each out before they could dare hit the air. My eyes ran over him one more moment. Dear God, he seemed so broken, and I was only vaguely aware why. One would have presumed he'd know an inkling of happiness to have been victorious; even a bit of his earlier arrogance would have sufficed, but all I felt permeating the room was sorrow.

And though it hurt me, I left him there and went obediently to my room, unsure there was anything that could be said tonight to make a difference. Tomorrow, ...yes, tomorrow when all of this seemed a nightmare, then I would mend the gap between us again.

*****

Optimism was a useless emotion to consider

when dealing with Erik. Had I conveniently forgotten how obstinate he was, or had he just grown worse in my absence?

A week passed by, torturously long and barely endurable, and my new husband hardly even acknowledged my existence or my presence. He put walls so insurmountable between us that I had no idea where to begin to dismantle them. I had one clear and vivid realization: his intention was to punish me by inevitably punishing us both. I had been naïve to consider that things could become as they had once been between us. Even tentative friendship seemed an unfathomable outcome. *Friendship?* By the end of that week, I would have been overjoyed with casual acquaintanceship, even a solitary nod when I entered a room, *anything*. But no. And any conversation I attempted was avoided with a muttered reply and an abrupt retreat.

Often, he chose not to be in the house's confines at all, disappearing before I awoke and returning late into the evening. We *never* ate a meal together, even as on a few occasions, I dared to ask for simply that. I had an inclination that his reluctance went beyond a wish to avoid me as I noted that never, not even in our more congenial days, had we eaten together. To eat, he would have to remove the mask, and since our wedding, he had been careful to keep it always in place. I couldn't say why beyond his desire to play a persona, to be the Opera Ghost at all times: cold, calculated, manipulative, aloof. If he fell into the role, then his heart wouldn't be allowed to care for me, ...and he couldn't be hurt. How could I change his mind when I had been the very person to cause that hurt to begin with?

During that hopeless week, trapped in the house as I always was, I learned the desolation of loneliness. I was in awe of Erik's strength for suffering such an affliction himself for so long. One week was far too much for me. I looked for anything to busy myself. My lessons and career in general had currently been put on hold, and I hadn't the heart to tolerate the rejection I felt certain I would get if I tried to broach the subject with Erik. So, instead, I spent long hours on neglected housework. Though Erik was tidy and meticulous with his belongings, the dusting and scrubbing tasks seemed to have been overlooked, enough so to keep me going.

When I ran out of idle cleaning, I took to rearranging my room and wardrobe for no real reason but to avoid boredom. And then...what *was* I going to do with myself? Was part of my punishment to include having no direction with my life? Maybe he wanted to break my spirit to nothing. When that happened, would he suddenly change his cold mannerism? Would that suffice for him? Or did he want me dead as well? ...How much punishment was enough?

Given too much time to think, I came to a blatant decision that left no room for argument. If I wanted him and his affections, *truly* wanted him, I was going to have to be the one to bridge the distance. And this was beyond apologies and penance; this was a restatement of our very relationship. It was a boldness on my own part, a willingness to hold my heart out to him and let him do what he would with it. I felt I had no other option if I wanted anything but a distant marriage for the rest of our lives.

Fortunately, one morning after that first agonizing week, I arose early enough to catch him before he abandoned me for the day. He was scuffling about his music room, leafing through haphazard piles of music with some intended target, and for a second, I lingered back in the doorway, still so uncertain how to approach him. I had little chance to ponder, for though I had given no noise to betray my presence, his eyes suddenly locked on me. It was as if he simply *felt* me.

Erik did not speak; he waited, hands halting mid-stack of music, eyes demanding what words did not. Flustered, I stammered, "I wasn't spying on you."

...And I cringed at how ridiculous I knew I sounded, watching his confounded expression.

Shaking his head as if he dismissed me, he left the pile without whatever he had been seeking and simply muttered, "I have to go."

Bravery, where are you? I demanded of myself, and as though it answered and took control, I found my legs scooting me to stand in the center of the doorway, blocking his exit. Of course, that had to make him stop and look at me.

"Wait," I commanded softly, desperate not to sound as nervous as I felt. "Do you really have to go out again today? Couldn't you...stay here with me?"

He was silent, and I felt his gaze measuring me up, probing deep into my mind and seeking something I was unsure to name. Most people would have cowered under such a penetrating stare and rightly so. It made me feel vulnerable and exposed, but instead of running from it as I had times before, I stayed firm and actually savored it. I *wanted* him to read my soul, to see exactly how deep my adoration for him was rooted. I was confident that love would be what he'd find, ...and yet his stone-set expression never softened as I hoped it would.

"I have to go," he repeated flatly.

Before he could try to pass me, I pushed, "Could you perhaps return early? Maybe we could have supper together. I can cook decently enough."

The refusal was in his eyes, about to strike the air, and I abruptly attempted a persuasive grin laced in every hope I felt in my soul. Could he really deny that?

"I...I'll see." He seemed flustered, off guard ever so slightly, but enough that he paused a moment more and just stared at me and a smile that was yet unwavering, before he slipped past my shape and left the house.

It wasn't a victory, and I did not count it as such, but it was a start.

...Was it surprising when suppertime came and

went, and he never appeared? I should have prepared myself for such a fate, especially considering how far apart we were from each other, but it still stung me harshly. I ate alone in the dining room, unwilling to indulge in threatening tears, and yet I never tasted a single bite of the food on my plate, moving mechanically with a head far too full to focus. I was already beginning to feel the hopelessness settle in, ...the defeat. *Was this all there'd ever be?*

Desolation dragged onward, and as the clock chimed a late hour, I felt restless and agitated like a suffering spirit caught in the world of the in-between. Clothed in my nightdress, plain and cotton, not the silk I had attempted on my supposed wedding night, I wandered idly through the empty house and finally ended up in Erik's music room. Over a week without singing or music in general felt like a lifetime. I was itching to practice, to sing, to learn, and even if the best teacher I had ever had did not want to teach me anymore, I was determined that my talent would not be squandered.

Standing before the ivory keys of the grand piano, I struck a chord, and taking a deep, opening breath, I began a simple vocalise. It took long minutes and various exercises to break my voice free of the tension it carried for my overburdened body, and when it was finally loose and able to glide on the breath, I beamed at my own accomplishment. And now I was ready to move on to a challenge, one I could conquer in the end and control through the chaos of reality.

Strolling to the bookshelves lining one wall, I scanned a multitude of scores and repertoire, unsure where I wanted to begin. Something new, that was a given, but what? I finally chose a Mozart opera. Italian. Surely that would prove to give the distraction I needed.

Taking the heavy score to the piano, I sat before the keys and opened to the first scene, exuberant in a way I had not known in months. Music often did that to me. How I loved to learn new music! When Erik had been my teacher, we had covered role after role as I devoured each one with an insatiable appetite. Such a thing had always impressed him; he had once told me so.

I was not a piano player. The extent of my skills came from my ability to read the staves and strike the notes I needed, so learning was a tedious process when alone. I went line by line, poking my pitches. Tedious *and* time-consuming. I truly didn't know how long I sat there, working, and I certainly didn't know that at some point, I had gained an audience. No, I didn't notice anything until laden with fatigue, I closed the score and rose, ready to give up and go to bed.

I nearly jumped out of my skin when I turned and came face to face with Erik as he lingered in the doorway, leaning casually on the wooden frame, watching me.

"Mozart?" he inquired, and I could only manage a wide-eyed nod, still thrown by his observing presence. "Ambitious, aren't you?" he continued. "Considering you're six months out of practice."

"But I was singing at the opera-"

"Six months out of my lessons then," he interrupted and sharply corrected.

What to reply to that... *'That's your own doing'*, perhaps? And yet such a bold accusation would not pass my lips. At the moment, I would have taken anything he had to give, in any tone, even a berating one, because in truth, it was the most words and most interest he had put towards me in over a week. Any pride I had left called it pathetic, but my heart dismissed everything but his eyes and focus upon me, ...*finally*.

"It may be ambitious," I stated back, "but I'll manage to learn it. I enjoy a challenge." ...And I had quite a few on my plate at the moment, didn't I?

His eyes were summing me up again before he gave a solitary nod. "Yes, you will rise to the occasion as you always have, ...but I would be a fool to allow you to do so on your own."

Yes, there was a hint of an insult there, an implication that I *couldn't* do it without him, but I chose to bypass its presence in favor of another more pleasant conclusion: he wanted to teach me! One memory of our lessons, of the elation I always knew when lost to the music with him, and I clenched my fists at my sides to keep control and prevent leaping up and down with glee like a silly child.

I created a skeptical look over features that yearned to smile and softly demanded, "What exactly are you saying, Erik? That *you* would be my teacher again?"

I was sure he saw right through my façade, even though his expression never altered, his eyes still penetrating me so deep. But I retained enough composure to meet his stare fixedly, hoping he acknowledged, somewhere in the recesses of that mind, that I was being strong and unwavering.

"Perhaps I shall," he replied after a long paused moment. "I devoted quite a lot to shaping that voice, molding it. I wouldn't want it destroyed...or underestimated for that matter. I have a suspicion that if I am not around to push you, you will never measure up to your true potential."

My eyes narrowed, but all I said was, "But would you have the time to be my teacher? You've been quite busy lately; ...you haven't been here very much." It was as close as I could get to an accusation of avoidance without causing his temper to flare. How well I knew this man to be able to predict such a thing and accurately so!

"I will make time," he insisted, crossing his arms over his chest haughtily. "But I will expect you to do the same. I will expect an unchanged level of professionalism and commitment to your talent, the same that I received the last time I took this role. Is that understood?"

I nodded slowly, again desperate not to seem

too eager. "When do we start?"

"Tomorrow after breakfast."

*****

Erik's idea of breakfast was sitting poised at the end of the table, awkwardly sipping a cup of tea and watching me eat. I tried not to show how uncomfortable he was making me feel, occasionally attempting conversations that never actually got underway or offering him food that he nonchalantly refused. I was grateful to finish and finally get to my lesson. Had I even slept the night before with the anticipation bubbling within me?

Unless one is a singer or musician under the tutelage of a very exceptional teacher, one can never understand the sheer joy and wonder of a lesson. It is not the same as book learning skills or school studies; it is not about adding knowledge to the brain or testing its capabilities. It is about talent and honing a gift that is inborn; it is about letting the very soul out even if only for a short time. With Erik, it was always ecstasy. He made me feel so special, as if my talent put me so far above the rest of mankind, as if because I had such desire, such passion for music equal to his, I was some sort of extraordinary thing. And to be his pupil, to see the extent of his genius and commit all of myself to his teachings, was an absolute blessing to me. I never held back, never avoided the silly, seemingly mundane exercises he would ask me to do because I knew he always had a purpose, whether he was after a specific sound, tone, or color. In the end, he was always right and drew out of me a beauty and fullness that I never could have dreamt of creating.

Over the course of the days and weeks to come, we were able to fall back into the roles of teacher and student as if we had never suffered a hiatus to our learning. Eagerly and without reservation, I was the awestruck pupil again, striving to make my teacher proud. How much did I savor every spoken word of praise, every nod of encouragement, every time he closed his eyes and seemed to relish a sound I was making?

We worked daily for hours on end, neither of us wanting our lesson time to cease because as soon as it did, the rifted marriage became our reality again, and we drew apart as if only the music could bring us together. We didn't know how to play the roles of husband and wife, but we were so accomplished at teacher and student; those parts were easy and required no real work. Those parts were favored. For now, I convinced myself to settle with that, to relish and cling to those few hours out of an otherwise distant day and pretend that, for at least that time, he loved me, too. ...It quickly became hollow and not nearly enough to satisfy my bleeding heart.

And wasn't that exactly how it felt? Bleeding... Like a gaping wound existed down the center of my heart. During our lessons, it mended and sealed but oh so temporarily, for as soon as we were back to our separate corners, it ripped wide open, never to heal, to bleed again and again, to leave me in an agony of loneliness for the vast majority of every single day. This wasn't the marriage I had vowed to. This wasn't a marriage at all.

A month had passed since that fateful night when my choice had sealed my future, and every bit of our relationship was at a stagnant standstill. A month... A month without seeing sky or sun, a month without interaction with any other human beings, a month without even seeing my husband's real face...

My lesson ended on a high note literally and figuratively, a glorious, resonant pitch that nearly shook the walls with its power, surprising both me and my teacher.

"Brilliant," Erik complimented with as much of a smile as he usually gave, not a full one but enough to say he was pleased. "That last section of the aria was flawless, and the cadenza flowed seamlessly."

My humbled grin and the blush that was attached slowly faded when I saw his hands closing the score before him. "Oh, ...are we finished?"

"For today. You did well, Christine."

I felt the walls on the verge of resurrection even before they rose, and frantically, I blurted out, "May I cook you supper?"

He looked at me oddly; neither of us had expected such an urgently spoken question, the very tone of my voice making it seem like some dire, life and death situation. To me, it was... But slowly, he shook his head. "I don't think so-"

"You won't eat with me because you can't wear your mask," I interrupted, surprised by my own boldness. Taking a deep breath for calm, I attempted again, avoiding his flaring expression and the anger I knew would come behind it, "Please. I want to share a meal with you, a real meal that doesn't constitute me eating alone, and I find your reasoning to deny such a simple thing ridiculous. I've seen your face; why do you feel so inclined to hide it?"

The temper stirred to life in his cold stare so vividly that a chill crept along my spine, but I did not regret my words and held my ground. "Why?" he spat back at me. "Why, indeed! You can be so utterly naïve! There is a decisive difference between looking upon this face and sharing a meal with it!"

Maybe I *was* naïve, but I couldn't help to reply, "I don't understand."

He huffed his annoyance. "Yes, I realize that! And how could you? It is beyond your ability to comprehend, which is why I don't expect such things from you. I leave things be as they are; why can't you do the same?"

My own temper flickered at that; never did I indulge it with Erik, his being more than enough to deal with and often frightening me and keeping me from fighting back. *Strong*, I told myself; I needed to be strong if I ever intended to get what I wanted. "Because I am your wife," I stated with the edge of anger's bite.

"*Wife!*" The word was heaved right back at me like an insult. "Really, Christine? Is this the

46

discussion you wish to start right now?"

"If not now, then when? We've avoided it for a month, and you'd likely have us continue to do so for the rest of our lives!"

His mouth dropped wide and agape. It amused me to consider that he had assumed I would follow his lead forever; it equally intrigued me to know I could shock him so deeply.

"*This*," he pointed between us, "is *not* a marriage! *This* is an act of domination! This is a means of exploiting you, of making you prisoner and prize and one of my very possessions in this house! Another pretty trinket won by my skill and prowess."

Tears choked the back of my throat, destroying my bravado as I whispered blamefully, "You're lying." It was a weak accusation at best, and as he leapt to his feet and came to stand before me, I remained frozen in place, lacking strength to do much else when the wind felt so knocked out of me.

"Why must you push me?" he demanded coldly as my weary eyes lifted to meet his. "I have not laid a hand on you; I have done nothing to hurt you. For the most part, I have let you be in the time you've been under this roof. You should be grateful that I *haven't* treated this like a marriage!"

"Grateful," I repeated the word distantly. Dear Lord, he was the only person who could hurt me so completely and break me so irrevocably, and the worst part of all was that he was unaware of my pain. He thought he was being merciful.

Proving his own point, Erik went on, explaining what didn't need to be said. He really did consider me a naïve child, and how I wanted to scream at him that I wasn't! "I could have forced so much of you, Christine! I could have demanded that you *be* my wife! You have no idea what you have been spared!"

"Then why?" I whispered, courage down to a solitary dying ember. "Why did you insist to marry me?"

I saw something in those eyes, something akin

to a tenderness from long ago, but he quickly pushed it back and only answered, "I don't know."

With that, he suddenly turned and stalked out of the room, slamming the front door with his escape. I heard the lock click into place and wondered if he believed I would try to run away after our little confrontation. He didn't even seem confident to know I wouldn't.

But hope was thriving yet within me. ...Because of his answer. If any of his previous rant had been true, he would have sought to hurt me, to insist again that I was only a prize. I knew he was lying then as I knew it now. And if nothing else, it encouraged my heart onward.

*****

It was very late when Erik finally returned to the house. I was lying awake in bed, my door opened a thin slit so that I would hear him as he quietly entered his own bedroom. As usual, he assumed I was asleep, and on any other night, he would have been right. Tonight, however, I wasn't going to rest until our conversation was finished, and I certainly wasn't going to let him flee midway again. No. I waited patiently a little longer until I knew he must have been seeking sleep. Then I left my room and silently padded down the hallway to his.

Erik's room was one I had only entered twice upon my perusal of the house. In fact, it was odd for me to place him within its dark walls because he was always awake before me, asleep after me. Considering him lying beneath the satin sheets of the over-sized, black-framed bed was an image I couldn't conjure up...until I actually saw it blatantly on display as I snuck into the open doorway of the room. Did he leave it ajar to hear me in case I got up? If so, his intentions were pointless. He was quite asleep already.

A smile I could not conceal creased my lips to see him beneath the hazy faint glow of the bedside lamp he kept lit. Erik, *my* Erik, teacher, angel, Opera

48

Ghost though not my favorite of his personas, lay peacefully asleep in his bed, clothed in black, silken nightclothes, mask-less and vulnerable and yet still so very powerful in aura alone. I couldn't breathe for that moment, terrified any noise or movement on my part would destroy the scene before I could appreciate it. *I love him*: that was my one, transcending thought, reinforcing my plan when a good part of me would have been content simply to gaze upon that scarred face.

Still lingering in the doorway for fear how he would react to my intrusion, I called in the gentlest tone I could make, "Erik?"

He stirred immediately, and first thing, his hand darted to the bedside table for his mask, his fingers hasty as they replaced it. "Christine? What? What is it?"

"I...can't sleep." The instant his mismatched eyes were on me, I felt my weakness threatening to return. It made me tremble on my feet and hesitate before the words I wanted would land upon my tongue. "May I...may I sit with you for a moment?"

At first, he didn't answer, and I prepared my next line of pleading in my head, ready to be called upon if needed. Finally, he let out the breath he must have been holding and said, "Just for a moment."

My knees wobbled beneath my weight as I crept the few steps to the vacant bedside and tentatively took a seat upon the soft mattress. On the opposite side, he sat upright, watching me expectantly, and keeping his stare in mine, I dared to lift the covers and slide my legs beneath, resting their edge at my waist as if I belonged in this scene with him. It was awkward, and yet neither of us drew attention to that.

"Why can't you sleep?" he asked after a moment, eyes never leaving mine.

He seemed to want to talk, which both surprised and delighted me, urging my honesty. "I was bothered by what you said earlier." Pausing, I gave him the chance to deny his claims, to state things correctly and tell me the truth, but he remained pensive, forcing me to broach the topic myself. "Do you regret this, Erik? Do you regret marrying me? ...Is there even anything to this for you?"

A huffed sigh escaped him after a moment, and I hoped he was not about to snap at me in a rage. How could he? I had asked so gently without even the hint of a threat.

"You have no idea, Christine," he finally replied in a soft tone, one I hadn't been privileged to hear in months. "You have no idea how things have changed for me, how the seemingly mundane to you is just so new and so thrilling to me. You, here... And everything you do. Just to come home to somebody's presence, to feel life in this house. ...Sometimes I'll linger in the sitting room late into the evening, and I'll hear you singing while in the bathtub. To you, it is a trivial, unimportant detail, something you just do without thought behind it; to me, it is *everything*."

I felt the depth of my blush like fire under my skin as I stammered, "You...you hear that? ...Me?"

He smiled with amusement, genuinely so, and I was so stunned and enamored that had I been standing, my legs would have given out on me. There was even a flutter of a *chuckle* in his voice as he replied, "It's quite an eclectic array of tunes you favor. I find it entirely intriguing. You will flow seamlessly from a French art song to a Swedish folk song to a parlor piece I've never heard before. Those parlor songs are certainly nothing I've ever taught you; you know how I feel about such popular tastes."

I nodded matter-of-factly and replied, "Music that is watered down so the general public can understand it." I could remember a drawn-out rant he had once gone into on the subject. Dear God, the memory was so long buried! He had been Angel then, not even a man, and ignorant child as I had been, enchanted by him even then, I had sought to learn every detail he would give, including his preferred tastes in music. Parlor songs had been an inquiry and had sparked so much more than the yes or no answer I had expected.

"Exactly," he agreed. "But you sing them so lovely that I forget not to like them. ...Of course, all of this I hear in echoes and through barriers, eavesdropping if you will, but such things are precious to me right now. Ridiculous as that seems. They remind me that I am not alone... I've been alone for so long. I'd gotten used to quiet and the usual void it leaves." He hesitated, holding my stare so somber as he stated, "I don't regret marrying you, Christine. I just wish I had done it for better reasons. You asked me earlier why, and I didn't give you an answer. I'd almost rather lie to you than admit the truth because it's so...pathetic, horrible even."

I felt sure he was about to avoid that very truth again, force it aside before I could learn its details, and I was desperate not to allow him to do so. I had only a split second to consider how far I could push before he would leap to anger's call. With Erik, it was never far. But I had to take the chance and softly whispered across the chasm separating us, "Tell me. Why did you marry me, Erik?"

I could read the disgust in the sneer that crossed his masked face. "I might as well give you one more reason to think of me as a monster; it doesn't matter anymore anyway. Selfishly, I married you so that the Vicomte couldn't. I married you to have a viable hold on you, to keep you here, ...and to hurt you. I knew I was taking away your future, the one you wanted, and I didn't care. So go on. Tell me you hate me, and things can continue on as they have been. I'll teach you, if you would still like, and that will be all."

Listening to him speak, one could almost believe he was apathetic toward what he had done; he played detachment so well. But I knew better. And suddenly I understood why he was determined to avoid me and keep distance between us. It wasn't to punish *me*; it was because my very presence was punishing *him*.

"That isn't a fair proposal," I said after a moment, careful to keep my inner thoughts as my own. "I married you expecting a marriage, even if a slightly unconventional one. And maybe neither of us truly knows what that means, but you have decided for both of us that we won't even try to figure it out. I don't want to hate you, Erik; I *don't* hate you. And I definitely don't want this separation between us for the rest of our lives. Doesn't it affect you even a little?"

"Of course it does!" he declared with vehemence in every syllable. "It's killing me to be so cold toward you. You were once my only friend in the world, ...even in my life. Do you remember? We used to be so close... I've never trusted anyone the way I trusted you."

I wanted to leave things there, for that to be all that was considered and spoken of. But I knew he couldn't. And the rest of the story was the part I longed to forget and knew he never would.

"And then...that boy came." There were wisps of rage skirting his eyes with the very mention of Raoul, but pain dwarfed them, vividly on display, vibrant to its core. He had always concealed it with anger and cruelty. How often before realization had come to me had I neglected to see that at fury's center, he was only a man with a broken heart? And how often had I refused to face my own hand in his creation, refused to lay blame on myself, and instead chose to accept Raoul's persuasions?

"Erik," I feebly attempted, "those things are past us now-"

"They aren't; they can't be," he interrupted solemnly. "Ask yourself the same question you asked me, Christine. Why did *you* marry *me*? And you will see just how integral a role every bit of those agonizing months has played to put us here and is still playing now."

"No," I argued back, not as convicted but only due to a lingering deficiency in courage. "*I* made the choice. I chose to marry you. ...And I don't regret it."

He didn't believe me, so certain of my supposed ulterior motives, but before I could force my protests upon him, he pushed me back altogether. "It's quite late, Christine, too late to be dueling out our past and its faults. Far enough has been laid out tonight. Go to bed."

A furrow creased my brow, but what could I truly argue to that? He was pulling away, and I knew the pointlessness of striving for more that way. I'd only end up angering him and damaging every miniscule bridge I had just built.

So rather than push, I instead opted for a fraction of the boldness I was growing, and timidly under the pink of a blush, I asked, "May I sleep here with you?"

The shock in his eyes amused me for the instant he allowed it to be seen. Then regaining composure, he bypassed an answer and posed another challenge. "Since you are so keen on making choices, you decide what you will do, Christine, of your own free will without coercion attached."

Rising to the occasion, I held his stare and scooted lower beneath the covers, laying down and curling on my side facing him. It was so delightfully smooth under those satin sheets, and yet I immediately attuned my senses to his nearness, to the heat growing and fluctuating between our bodies, to the very scent of him lingering on the pillow my cheek was pressed to. It surprised me how comfortable it felt to be with him this way without even a flash of our previous awkwardness. No, this felt too right.

Tentative yet, he imitated my actions, eyes always with mine, facing me on his side so hesitant and cautious. I had to wonder why. Once again, I bore the thought that he was afraid of me. ...*Was he?*

Silence extended, yet neither of us seemed to blink as we gazed at one another. Finally, I was the one to break its shroud. "You know, there was another question that you earlier would not answer. ...Why would it be so terrible to share a meal together?"

I wondered if he would still employ patience with me or if this was too much, and when he gave a small huff, I prepared for the brunt of his temper. But his voice was devoid of any hinted anger as he answered, "Your inquisitiveness gave you the answer already. I can't eat with the mask in place. It is one of the very few things I must do without it. ...I am uncomfortable to be so exposed and won't subject you to such a thing. The mask exists for a purpose, Christine. It gives me some semblance of dignity over the things I can't control."

"You married me without it," I gently argued with a memory of the priest's abhorred reaction and Erik's lack of regard to it at the time.

"Cruelly, I was hoping to shake you," he admitted. "I was so sure you were playing a role and that your determination was a façade. I wanted to remind you *what* you were marrying."

Cruel, ...yes, that would have been cruel had he been correct, only as we both knew, I had proven him wrong. Shaking my head against the satin of the pillow, I insisted, "And you can't sleep with the mask in place either. So you will take it off and sleep beside me now."

"But I will turn the light out, so you won't see it."

I felt a childish pout threatening. He left me no room to argue on the subject, a subject I truly thought ridiculous at this point in our relationship. I had to remind myself that to him, it was the absolute cornerstone of his life; to him, his face and his deformity had *made* his life exactly what it was.

"A compromise," I suddenly declared before he could end the conversation. "One meal like a real family at the table, and if I make you feel uncomfortable even for an instant, you can replace your mask and I will never ask you to remove it again."

"You think very highly of your tolerance level," he accused. "You are overly confident in this situation without the right to be. As I've said, *seeing* this face isn't the same as what you're asking."

Overly confident? I felt I *did* have the right as I justified with one fact. "I've kissed that face. Kissing is another act you can't indulge with your mask in place."

Silence followed, and Erik grew meditative; it surprised me to know he had to formulate an argument. Usually, he could think faster on his feet than anyone I'd ever met. To know I had actually stunned him to contemplation was a minor victory for my hopeless plight.

When he finally met my stare again, there was a touch of amusement within him as he conceded, "One meal. We'll put that confidence of yours to the test and see what comes of it."

The grin I gave him was exuberant; it was triumphant. Yet I dared to confirm. "And you won't change your mind, will you? You won't disappear like the last time and leave me disappointed and eating alone?"

"I may not have eaten with you, but I have been here every morning for breakfast for weeks now. I can't risk leaving and potentially missing your lesson. It is, after all, the one high point of my day."

"Mine, too," I admitted plainly. "Then breakfast it is, and we'll eat together."

"It's settled."

Before I could reply, he reached over to the bedside table and turned out the light, and darkness stole his image from my eager eyes. My ears caught the shuffling of limbs, as I felt sure he was removing his mask again. I knew the irrational urge to extend my hand to him, to find those scars he still wanted to keep as his own and caress their irregular shapes, but I did not dare give into the fierce temptation. *One step at a time*, I insisted to myself. This was already quite the turning point. Slow was better where Erik was concerned.

"Erik?" I called gently across the darkness.

"Yes, Christine?"

"Goodnight, *ange*."

I heard the breath escape him in a soft sigh at my chosen appellation, unused in far too long. Angel... He was *always* angel to me.

"Goodnight," he breathed in a whisper, and I shivered in spite of myself. It was as if every letter, vowels and consonants, had touched me and caressed me. *God, that voice!* It *was* ethereal and oh so powerful, and how willing I was to surrender to it again and again.

When I fell asleep that night, I was deliciously content. In more than a physical sense, Erik seemed within my reach now. I felt sure that we both wanted the same thing in our hearts and souls, and it therefore had to be the inevitable outcome. Yes, it just had to be...

*****

I could feel myself beaming when I entered the dining room the next morning and found breakfast laid out beautifully, ...*two* plates and an assortment of delicious food. Erik sat at the head of the table, sipping his tea and seeming already uncomfortable even though his mask had yet to be removed. But the instant his eyes landed on me, I saw the expression there soften and grow into something beautiful, something I had so missed and longed to see.

Like a silly little schoolgirl, I had taken extra care to dress and ready myself that morning, choosing a pink gown with a chiffon bow in the back and lace trim, my favorite from my wardrobe. My dark curls had been tied half-back in a similar ribbon with shorter tendrils I had tirelessly twisted and re-twisted around my fingers perfectly framing my face. *Perfection...* Yes, I was after perfection, and it overwhelmed me as Erik's eyes ran over every nuance of my appearance and gave his delight away. For a man who often kept a wall between his emotions and outward expression of them, any inkling of visible sensation meant he actually felt quite a lot more.

"You look lovely," he said before regretting it with a mental lashing that I saw in a cringe, wall abruptly rebuilt.

But I acted unaffected and only beamed brighter at the compliment, hoping my reaction would encourage more as I took my seat beside him. "Did you cook all of this?" I asked, gesturing to a table brimming with platters. Surely there was enough food for three breakfasts!

"I've been awake for awhile," he justified, "and...I needed something to keep busy."

Nervous, my mind concluded. He was nervous for every bit of this. But I was as resolved as I had been the previous night, unwilling to allow doubt to exist, even when his apprehension tried to inspire mine to life. It was just a face, and the sooner Erik could understand that, the sooner we could actually have a marriage.

"Well, ...shall we eat then?" I posed lightly and watched him expectantly all the while. I knew he yearned to change his mind and perhaps launch into a rage instead, anything to rid himself of the situation, so I kept a reassuring smile in place and did not push him to be ready.

His hands shook as they rose to the mask. It astounded me that he was actually afraid. How many times in our past had he thrown that face on display to try and terrify me? But, I guessed, when using something like that as a weapon, it had power and purpose. Now he was attempting to use it to be something ordinary, performing an ordinary task, and it just wasn't.

I caught the briefest echo of his harshly-taken breath the moment he lowered the mask, and then his eyes desperately sought mine, searching for some sort of approval. I just smiled, proud to see such bravery from a man I had never thought could be lacking in it.

"Now, shall we eat?" I asked again as if there wasn't a veritable corpse sitting next to me at the table. With a face like his, he was just that, and I loved him even more for it. I saw in that mangled face what others never could. I saw the soul of it. It was in the light of that sunken emerald eye, in the thin, luminescent coat of skin across a hollow cheek, in the nonexistent nose. It was tarnished, and it was twisted, but it was brilliant.

Erik hesitated, his eyes still searching mine for what he had obviously presumed would be there, what he had *planned* to be there. "You're...sure, Christine?"

I nodded adamantly. "Yes, of course I'm sure. Why does that surprise you so much?"

He didn't answer. Slowly, tentative in every sense of the word, he reached for the plate of eggs, serving himself and yet casting me glances at every opportunity. I didn't let him know how much his constant suspicion affected me as I imitated his actions, taking the plate from him as though all of this was the most normal thing. And wasn't it? For us, it was; new and different, but this was our version of normal. And I was determined that in a few weeks' time, none of this awkwardness would be remembered. We would just eat together like our own little family, and the fact that my husband was mask-less wouldn't cross either of our minds.

To me, this was the beginning, and the only end I wanted was one without a mask altogether, one where my darling Erik would display his face proudly to me, one where I could kiss my husband whenever I wanted without having to first undergo suspicion that it was all a lie. ...I really hoped he was realizing that I wasn't that good of a liar.

All right, to be honest, there was a bit of strangeness to watching Erik eat, ...more like *spying* on Erik while he ate because I couldn't bear for him to misunderstand my intrigue over the entire process. With such a transparent layer of skin on his disfigured side, the workings of his mouth were prominently put on display at every bite, the movement of his jaw, the chewing of his teeth. It caught my attention at first in the way a science experiment would: the inner mechanics of the mastication process. Then as I considered that was how my own mouth likely looked behind a skin barrier, how *every person's* mouth looked, the novelty dimmed until it didn't seem unusual anymore. I was exceedingly careful to hide every bit of this from Erik, terrified to give him the failure he was seeking from me, most especially with my condition attached: that I would never again see his face. There was quite a bit of pressure always in the peripheral. I *couldn't* fail; it was inconsiderable.

"Erik," I called, though his attention had been in a constant shift between me and his plate every moment, "everything is so delicious, and..." I smiled, hoping and praying he saw the depth of my emotions in my gaze. "I am enjoying sharing a meal with you so much. Are you? ...Is this really as horrible as you thought it would be?"

Setting his fork alongside his plate, he pondered as he slowly and blatantly chewed and swallowed, testing me I knew, but my eyes were only on his. *Thank God the novelty had worn off!* "Not horrible," he conceded after a moment more. "No, not horrible. You surprise me."

"How so?" I pushed, regarding him with a tilt of my head and a fraction of a light playfulness I had not indulged with him in ages.

"You're stronger than I remember you being," he replied honestly, and I thrilled to know he was *finally* seeing it. "I had thought this whole situation would have broken you by now. But instead of falling and weakening, you...blossom even down here in the dark, ...even with me."

"Maybe *because* of you."

Those misshapen lips, ones I tingled to consider kissing again, curved into a slow, timid smile, so many questions, so many doubts in the background but held at bay.

"So?" I gently questioned. "Does this mean we can have our meals together from now on? Or must I talk you into each and every one?"

Again, his fixed stare probed mine, and not finding what he wanted, he demanded, "Tell me honestly, Christine. Does eating with me bother you? Why does it not seem as grotesque a sight to you as I know it is?"

"It isn't," I insisted. "Haven't I proven as much?"

A lingering skepticism plagued the nodded answer I received, but he softly replied, "All right, we will eat together from now on."

*****

If it had been left up to me, he wouldn't have replaced the mask for my lesson, but on some level, I could understand his need to be the proper teacher. He was no longer the Erik I had shared breakfast with, and I was not the Christine full of encouraging smiles. Months of practice made it easy for us to make a distinction, imperative and integral a part as it played to being loyal musicians. Everything else had to be put aside.

It was with a slight air of discomfort that Erik chose not to leave the house after my lesson, to remain and work on his music, which I knew was how he had usually spent his afternoons before I had come to live with him. I kept out of the way, knowing how engrossed he became once lost in composing, but from the other room where I had taken up a book, I could not keep from listening and delighting in the sound of the music filtering through the lonely house. It left a constant smile on my lips.

Supper had only half of breakfast's uncertainty, and with each bite, it dwindled further away as Erik's trust in me grew. Even conversation flowed smoother, almost with an air of friendliness to it, and dear Lord, I couldn't stop smiling still!

Afterward when all was straightened up, my

confidence was solidified enough to lead me to where Erik sat before the hearth, mask in place and making me miss his scars. I wondered how oddly pleasant they would have appeared with the inviting light of the fireplace to illuminate them: ...unthreatening, beautiful maybe.

"Is something wrong, Christine?" he asked to my pensive expression.

"No, ...I wanted to ask for a favor." I hesitated beneath an awaiting stare that gave none of his inner thoughts away. "Could we perhaps take a walk up to the roof? I haven't seen the sky in weeks... There will be stars out by now and the moon. I would love to look upon them even just for a moment."

There was a flicker in his eyes that told me that he suspected something else, and it hurt me to consider he would mistrust me so much. What did he think? That I would run as soon as we were beyond the catacombs? I hadn't asked to go out into the world. If escape were my intent, why would I confine myself to the roof with him? And why could *he* not reason that?

"The roof?" he posed, and surpassing the denial I felt certain would come grew a challenge. "All right, Christine. A walk up to the roof. Get a cloak. There will surely be a chill in the air."

There already was, from what I could tell. Yet again he was testing me. He *wanted* me to attempt to run, to forget the fact that even if I tried, I wouldn't get anywhere. He wanted to give himself the reason he needed not to trust me and prove that all my endeavors at reaching out to him were manipulative at their core. It left me resolutely determined to make him sorry for his every unjustified doubt.

Our journey through the catacombs and up into the world was a silent one, but when we emerged through Erik's hidden entrance onto the rooftop, the cold night air and its refreshing crispness made me forget all else. Had I really lived without fresh air for an entire month? I had forgotten how delicious it was! And the night sky filled to excess with moon and stars was a veritable work of art to eyes that had been in the dark for so long.

Tossing my head back and arms out as if I meant to embrace things that were virtually untouchable, I laughed with delight and purposely paid no heed to Erik's constant stare. He could consider me dramatic and ridiculous, but I was too engrossed to care, savoring every detail for fear of how long I would go without them again.

"Don't you miss this when you're underground and buried away all the time?" I asked, gesturing to the twinkling stars above our heads.

Erik lingered back, simply watching me with arms crossed over his chest. "Nature's beauty shrivels in comparison to the ugliness of humanity. If avoiding the one means I have to give up the other, it is a meager sacrifice to make."

I knew I had no right to argue when his past was an unspoken vacancy neither of us wanted to put words to. I didn't need details to know it was awful, unfathomable even. "And I have given you little reason to think differently." My own mistakes were as guilt-ridden as his, and I cringed beneath their weight as I wearily sat down on the ledge surrounding the edge of the rooftop.

Erik shook his head and corrected, "You've given me the *only* reason to think differently. Even amidst the bad times we've endured, the good ones far outshine any in my life."

I didn't reply right away. To me, the bad were shameful and unforgivable. It astounded me to realize the capacity for cruelty I possessed, especially when I had previously considered myself a compassionate person. But I was little better than the many persecutors and tormentors Erik had been subject to at every angle, ...worse because he cared for me.

Sighing softly, I kept my eyes on the stars as I revealed, "I've known loneliness before. When my father died and I found myself utterly alone in the world, I barely believed I would survive the void left behind. But then I came to the opera, and an angel taught me to sing and filled every empty space in my life and in my heart until I felt whole. These past months when we were apart from each other, I realized that I had only known loneliness' shadow before. I was...lost, walking around hardly alive in the world. ...But the worst of it, beyond that even, has been this past month. Living with you but being further from you than ever and not being able to reach you."

"Christine, stop." His voice was saturated in a pain I was sure he didn't want to show but could not conceal. Raising my eyes to him, I felt it hit me with blunt force to the gut, creasing the features of the unmarred side of his face in a way I was sure was reflected across scars as well.

"Erik," I could not keep from trying, even as better sense protested and fought with me. "I have to make you understand. I married you because-"

"Because you had to, because I would have strangled your lover if you hadn't." He snapped the words bitterly. "Your reason was noble enough. You sacrificed yourself to save the man you loved. I understand it perfectly well; now leave it at that!"

"I can't," I whispered, feeling tears I did not want clog my throat. Dear God, I didn't want to seem weak now. "It isn't true."

"Christine!" he warned sharply. "I have not the patience required for this discussion! Leave it be!"

But I couldn't and wouldn't. I had already incurred his rage and likely caused another rift in everything I had accomplished. I had everything to gain by this and nothing left to lose. Forcing away tears, I snapped back, "Why did I kiss you then, Erik? Have you not considered that at all? If my intention was only to save Raoul, I could have committed myself with a word. Why did I kiss you?"

His answer was quiet and yet it tore a hole

through me as if an entire orchestra had struck a loud and violent crescendo. "To hurt me, of course."

I couldn't breathe, and the gasp I managed an entire minute later burned its way into my lungs, as I demanded, "What?"

The confidence in his conclusion was unwavering. "I hurt you, and you wanted to hurt me back, to taunt me with what I wanted most of all and what could never fully be mine. ...I could have forced kisses on you since then, more than that even, and everything would have been as much a lie as that first kiss."

"No, no," I miserably whimpered, the tears coming in silent paths. "A...a lie... How could you think that? How could you...?" For one more breath, I was lost, and then with a suddenness that surprised us both, I leapt to my feet and stalked toward him. "I'll prove it! I'll prove it! I'll kiss you right now. No coercion, no Vicomte, no choice to be had. I'll kiss you because I *want* to kiss you."

"No, Christine!" His hand rose to halt my approach. Did he think I would tear his mask away on my own? ...Would I? I was certainly determined enough in my plight.

"Yes!" I shouted back, his temper no longer a factor. Let him rage at me. Little could deter my conviction. "Take off your mask, or I will do it for you."

My challenge did not hold the same power that one of his did; if anything, he scoffed a bit in disbelief.

When he made no move to comply, I accused, "Are you more afraid that you will be right and I am lying, or that I'm telling the truth and I genuinely want to kiss you?"

"Afraid?" He spat the word as if it were the most heinous of insults. "I am not a man who fears many things in this world."

"Yet you fear me." How often had I thought it and not said it?

"*You* are *destroying* me!" Fire flared brightly

in those eyes, his hands clenching in fists before me as if seeking control, but I never moved away, rooted to the spot yet never considering myself foolish. He wouldn't hurt me; I knew that as confidently as I knew he loved me. Even at the height of his rage, he would never lay a hand or fist upon me.

"Take off your mask, Erik," I calmly commanded again, even staring into the face of a hellish anger.

"And if you cower, shall I force you, Christine?" he retorted, leaning close to establish his valid threat. "Shall I force myself upon you, *as is my right*? And bed you like the monster you believe me to be? Shall I become the man I was on the night I forced you to marry me, the one on the very brink of insanity's grasp?"

"That wasn't you," I insisted sternly.

"It was! And it was *you* who drove me to it! You and your naïve little games with my heart! *You* created that love-starved madman!" His hands only then opened from their fists to catch me by my upper arms. "Do you know how ashamed I am whenever I consider that night? How it sickens me to know what I did and why I did it? I let loving you and hating you come together to become a powerful drug that consumed me." His unmarred features were as contorted with rage as those hidden from my sight were by default. "And now, *now* you come before me with your innocence shining like some tempting beacon, and you wave in front of me the very object of my obsession. A kiss... One kiss. How I have dwelled on that one act for weeks! Desperate for answers to the exact questions you put before me tonight! Can you not understand that I had to make it a lie? I had to or be completely lost again to you and to a heart that has suffered enough. That is why I beg of you, let it go! Let all of this go! Leave my broken heart and the scant bits that are left of me alone!"

Tears streamed down my cheeks; I felt their cold descent without even acknowledging that I was crying. I had destroyed this man... Only now did I understand what that meant. It was something I was still ignorantly doing, and I wondered if he was right, if giving up on every one of my failed endeavors was the only way to salvage him. I would have done it, about to give a slow nod of consent, but he suddenly changed the game.

Releasing one of my tightly held arms, he removed that mask, that damnable barrier, and exposed his scars. With a pleading in his eyes that took my breath away, he begged as if for his very life and existence, "Go on, Christine. Show me it wasn't a lie. Prove me wrong... *Please* prove me wrong."

I did not pause a single second, did not give consideration to the concluding consequences. No. I pressed my lips to those bloated, misshapen ones, pouring passion like salt on the gaping wound in my own heart. He still had one arm in his grasp, and with my free hand, I dared to cup his scars. Never before had I touched them, never before learned the oddities of their textures and shapes. Now I practically melted from the first contact, letting my fingertips graze that sunken eye cavity so tenderly.

He was crying...or I was; all I knew for certain was that tears smeared both our cheeks. I could taste them as I moved my lips against his, coaxing him to follow, shivering delight when he did. He was far more tentative than I, always a question in the background, and as I continued to explore his scars with eager fingertips, he moaned against my lips and abruptly fell headfirst into the kiss.

Never before had I kissed or been kissed with such rampant fervency. It was *my* tongue that slipped between the seam of those misshapen lips and tasted him, *my* desirous whimper escaping unbridled when I felt him shudder. Even as I relished every instant, I drew back to press fevered kisses along the bloated arch of his upper lip and then feather-light ones to those oddities of features, lingering just above the place where his nose should have been. Kiss after kiss, and I tilted my face to nuzzle my bare, flawless cheek against his mangled one, wet tears captured between.

"Oh, Erik, Erik," I whispered desperately, "this is no lie. Please don't call this a lie..."

As abruptly as it began, it was over, and he jerked back and away from me, his eyes wide and wild as they met mine. I shook my head urgently, bidding, "No, no, Erik, please..."

It was beyond shock; it was some aghast form of horror I couldn't understand, feeling so sure he had felt what I had. Tears shimmered in pools in emerald and sapphire eyes, those misshapen lips parted still as they had been when mine were there, and as his stare went between me and the mask clutched in his hand, he suddenly turned and fled from the rooftop and from me, escaping into the darkness of his passages and leaving me alone in the moonlight.

*****

Alone, yet still my options were minimal. What hurt most was that he had left me, unknowing if I would make an escape and be gone from his life entirely. And I could have. I knew the way out of the opera house; I could have used it, could have made the last month no more than a nightmare. But I didn't. And it was for reasons that far exceeded the legal bindings of a marriage.

Alone, I wandered the dark catacombs on a path I knew well, a path home it now was, and I found the house just as we had left it...and lacking of Erik's presence. I hadn't really thought he'd be there, but hope can cruelly draw conclusions on its own. *He'd be back*; only that thought soothed me.

I took a hot bath to chase out a chill that was beyond skin deep, prepared for bed, read a little, and still Erik did not return. It was late. After the emotionally exhausting day I had suffered, my eyes were heavy enough to begin to drift closed without my consent, and I knew I'd never be awake when he finally arrived. So giving up my vigil, I decided to go to sleep...in his bed. Bold, yes, but he would have to come across me and hopefully wake me in the process. Even a verbal lashing for my indiscretion would be welcomed.

Sinking beneath the satin cocoon, I deeply inhaled his longed-for scent into my lungs, intoxicating myself on it as my mind imagined him lying beside me as he had the previous night. Just knowing he was near had been enough to calm me then. Tonight after kissing him and touching his face, how could such a minimal pleasure ever suffice?

At some point, I slept. I cannot say how long, but my next coherency came in the form of a cold yet gentle pressure against my mouth. *Erik...* Was I dreaming? I must have been, but his lips felt so real: swollen and smooth, a texture all their own, and that chill that dulled the longer they were against mine. It was when they tenderly moved, enough that his tongue was grazing my lips and tasting me that I knew it was real and I was awake.

My arms disentangled from the blankets to encircle his neck and caress his mask-less face as returning consciousness took note that he was stretched out beside me atop the barrier of the covers. His skin was frigid, breaking into the growing spirals of desire assaulting me to insist he had been outside. Dear God, had he simply wandered the city all night? That agonizing idea made me draw back and look at that scarred face in the dimly lit bedside lamp.

"I didn't lie," I pleaded for him to believe me. "I didn't lie."

"I know," he softly replied, bending near to rub his scarred cheek against mine, nuzzling my warm skin and stealing some of that heat. Turning, he let the empty hollow and two holes from which he breathed graze my small nose, and I eagerly tilted my face upward to kiss the very spot. "Christine," he breathed, laden with such an immeasurable depth of emotion that I ached to hear him repeat only that, my name just that way, forever.

My trembling fingers tugged the edge of the blankets, and he drew them back to climb beneath with me, immediately pulling me into his arms, the only place I wanted to be. Cuddling into him, I savored every hard plane of his body, every muscle and limb, desperate to be lost to every one.

Erik's hands gently combed through my hair, his lips laying kisses to the crown of my head as he bid, "Go to sleep, Christine."

I was too exhausted and too blissfully content to protest. No thought of tomorrow needed to be considered, no worries over our future. Not tonight. No, tonight my dreams would only be delightful.

*****

The week that followed was almost my dream brought to life, ...*almost*. Our relationship had re-grown its roots of friendship, returning the sense of comfort, camaraderie, and trust we had once had. We spent time together, talking, laughing, learning, close as ever. Our every meal was shared, and removing the mask was without a second thought even if he still wore it the rest of the day, my next challenge to be had. In the evenings by his own suggestion, he took me for walks through the city, our arms joined like a courting couple. At night, I slept in his bed, in his arms, pleased to peer up at his mask-less face every so often in the lamp he left lit. He wasn't hiding anymore, and I wasn't turning away.

Yes, things were settled and pleasant, and wasn't it petty and a bit childish on my part to want more? Erik was keeping a barrier between us that, though flimsy and nearly transparent, was unbreakable at its source. Physical contact was limited to those arm-in-arm walks and the occasional idle touch, always innocently chaste. The only taste I was ever given of the true extent of passion brewing and thriving in his veins was at night as I eagerly went into his arms and he lifted away the mask from hindrance. Then he would kiss me goodnight in a way that made every pore in my body come alive and sing with need. One kiss, always only one, and he would pull away and smile so tenderly at me that I would lose my will to argue and beg for more.

The first nights I assumed he was holding back for my sake, perhaps waiting to make certain that I wouldn't shy away. But as things instead fixed into a standard routine, I grew impatient and restless. He was my husband, and I wanted him in a way that almost terrified me with its uncontrollable power. If not for the identical reflection I felt in that single kiss every night, I would have concluded, and with great disappointment, that he did not desire me in that manner. But no. I had an intuitive hunch that the desire in him outshone even my own, but whether he was afraid to indulge it because of me or because of himself, I did not know and was apprehensive to ask.

One afternoon at the end of the week, I was bustling about the sitting room, dusting end tables and straightening up; I preferred to keep occupied when Erik was out, which thankfully wasn't so often anymore. Just as I was finishing and deciding which room to move to next, I heard the door open and rushed to the foyer with a welcoming smile on my lips. To my surprise, Erik's smile far exceeded mine. Had I ever seen him so blatantly excited about anything?

"What?" I asked with the smallest giggle of delight.

"Come here. Come here." Catching my elbow in his palm, he steered me back into the sitting room and had me sit on the couch as he declared, "I have a surprise for you, something I think will please you very much."

My interest was piqued, and my brows arched curiously as he withdrew from the inner pocket of his jacket a rolled-up paper. Beaming still, Erik glanced between my awaiting expression and the paper as he opened it and laid it out on my lap. ...And I gasped!

It was a house! Or a diagram of one, plans drawn to precision of exterior and interior with measurements scribbled here and there in Erik's handwriting. I knew without a doubt that he had designed it, recalling his stories of being an architect in Italy for a stint, and surely every detail about the house's created façade had an Italian flare intermixed with some indiscernible factor that was purely Erik.

"This is... This is...," I stuttered, searching for words enough to say what I felt.

"Our future home," he filled in for me, "...if you like it, of course."

"Like it? Erik, it's beautiful!" My fingertips traced the front porch railing with its curved spindles as my head envisioned it in full dimensional form. "Did you design this for me?"

"Down to the most minute detail," he proudly answered, eagerly taking a seat beside me and adjusting the drawing to rest equally on both our laps. "See, the porch will extend all the way around the house, whose back will face the setting sun, if I've arranged it correctly. We can watch the sunset every night over the horizon, watch the stars appear since you are partial to such natural wonders."

I felt tears in the back of my throat, making their presence known as I lifted grateful eyes to my elated husband. "That's...perfect," I softly reveled, adoring him in my gaze.

"And," Erik excitedly continued, "these plans can be altered to whatever you wish, Christine. They are not set and final yet. So, more rooms, less rooms, anything. Name it, and I will do it for you." Gesturing to the interior diagram, he rested his fingers on the upper floor. "Right now, measurements taken into account, the upstairs is laid out for four bedrooms. I know that is a lot, but we can make them anything we'd like. They need not *be* bedrooms, you know."

In my head came the fleeting image of children with sweet cherub faces, and even though I mercifully pushed the pictures away, the want remained. Could I be blamed for harboring a natural instinct to be a mother? It was a desire I doubted my husband would understand or share.

I grew silent with the thought, and urgent to regain my smile, Erik continued, "And if you'd like, you could have your own bedroom, as you do here, to decorate and adorn to your whims."

What he thought would please me only enhanced my melancholy. My own room... The one down the hall was solely used to house my clothing as of late. I no longer even liked its existence; it laid a way out always there, a means to recreate distance instead of solve problems. ...And now Erik once again wanted to give me that escape, thinking so wrongly that it would please me to know I had it, ...a chance to change my mind.

"Christine?" he called gently, genuine concern in that golden voice. "What is it, *petite*?"

With desperate hands, I pushed the thoughts away and as far from my expression as I could, smiling with feigned elation. "It's just...overwhelming. The house is so beautiful. I know you don't favor that world, and the fact that you would be willing to make your life there for me is... Oh, Erik, it's amazing."

"You *are* my life now," he insisted vehemently, daring to lift a trembling hand to cup my cheek.

He saw it as solace, but it only drove the sword deeper into my gut. A touch when I wanted so much more, wanted to *give him* so much more. Again I was reminded that this still was not a marriage. There was love, but reined in so tightly. Neither of us had spoken the words; both of us were holding hearts at arm's length from each other. It was a love trapped by boundaries, barriers, and locks that I did not know how to break down.

In the vein of my very thoughts, he lowered his hand after a moment and rose with the diagram in his grasp, and I felt the extension of more than just physical distance between us.

"So," he went on, "I've purchased the land. The final papers were signed just hours ago. It is a lot outside the city with enough acres attached to give us privacy from most of the world. As soon as the ground thaws, building can begin. I am calculating six months, and we will be able to move into our future. ...Would you like me to find us something to rent until then, something above ground? I know another six months down here must seem abysmal."

"No, no," I replied, glancing fondly about the sitting room. "This has grown to feel like home to me. In some way, it will be sad to leave it. ...Our story was written here."

"Mostly the conflict in the middle," he corrected with a somber shake of his head, his fingers grazing the design. "Our happy ending will be written here, above ground, in the sunlight."

I did agree with that. It was just what I had always wanted for my future, a real home, not an underground prison, ...even without the amorous affections of the man I had married.

*****

Time went by, and soon enough to Erik's delight, construction began on our new home. As usual, he threw himself fully into the project, overseeing every step of his elaborate design, and I was proud of his initiative, interacting in the world he hated, trusting no one but himself with the task of overseeing his hired workers. He even brought me a few times to see the progress, and although to my untrained eyes, it was just a basic foundation or a dug-out cellar, I mirrored his enthusiasm to show me, impatient only on the inside to see a real house instead.

Leading the development meant Erik was gone for hours every day, and I could not help but feel lonely, having grown accustomed to his presence in the next room composing or setting the table as I finished preparing supper. Those mundane things constituted the makeup of our marriage, and without them, the true meager inadequacy of it was coming through to taunt me.

After that first month of construction, the

melancholy weighed heavily on my shoulders, and luckily, Erik finally took note of it on his own. We had just finished a relatively quiet breakfast, and lost in thought, I didn't realize that Erik was attentively watching me until he spoke and shattered my reverie.

"You've barely taken a single bite," he commented, and I idly glanced at my full plate, having nearly forgotten it was there.

"Oh... I guess I'm not very hungry this morning," I stammered. I should have assumed he wouldn't believe such a flimsy excuse.

I never was interrogated, never had to admit that something was upsetting me; as was often the case when he took the time to attune his emotions with mine, he could accurately conclude the problem.

"I've been considering something," he began with an arching of brows and a pensiveness I enjoyed seeing across his features without that infernal mask. "As you know, I still have a box at the opera, a secluded, private box that no one sees me enter or occupy. And tonight there is a performance, albeit one that won't be anywhere near as glorious as it would have been with you in the lead. But...we could attend."

My eyes widened, my head reeling with the possibility as I battled the childish urge to squeal in delight. "We could? Oh, Erik, could we really? I would love that so much!"

He smiled with earnest exuberance that was the result of simply making me happy. He seemed to take so much joy from spoiling me. "Then we shall go. It will almost seem the outing of a normal couple."

"We've never been skilled at normal," I teased, delighted when he chuckled in reply.

"No, we haven't, but tonight we'll pretend. I'd much rather act the role of gentleman than be the Opera Ghost when I have you on my arm."

"I concur with that." Married to the Opera Ghost... The thought had never crossed my mind even though it was entirely valid. I preferred to just consider myself married to Erik.

The term 'Opera Ghost' never again appeared in my head when we were clothed in our best and ready to leave our underground sanctuary. How could it refer to the same man I adored with my stare? The mask was in place and yet not even a consideration; it took nothing away from his handsomeness in my eyes.

His gaze was constantly on me from the time we departed and all during our ascent with a flickering smile and appreciation that thrilled me. My formal attire was deep blue with silver trim, low-cut, cap sleeves, a ruffled bustle in the back; it was the most elaborate in the wardrobe. Determined to appear the fine lady and play my role in this little game of pretend, I had taken great care in arranging my curls, sweeping them up and pinning them in place with enough pins to be sure they couldn't move. I wanted us to be the vision of an artist's portrait, a painting brought to life with that idea of *normal* as our reality.

Capturing Erik's eyes as they roamed me again, I blushed beneath my timid smile and prompted his honesty. "And why are you examining me so intently?"

"You are exquisite, Christine," he remarked with a sincerity that brought goose bumps to life along my skin. Those golden tones could overwhelm me with a word; if only, in his attentive regard, he could see that!

Box 5 was just as Erik had said, private, secluded by the presence of thick curtains on either side and seats set back and out of view of anyone else. It was a relief of sorts. Too many people knew me and had heard exaggerated versions of my story. And Erik was practically a legend that was as eager as I not to be put on display.

From the moment the overture began out of the pit below, I knew a resonant, reminiscent thrill run through my body that quickly became a dull ache. I longed to be on that stage in a way I had not acknowledged that I felt. So long away from performing, and theatre life had begun to feel like a distant dream. I had forgotten how natural it had always been for me to be an integral part of it.

"You know," Erik softly said, leaning across the armrest between our seats, "I could easily have you put back on that stage. You belong there, Christine, in the spotlight. You were born for it."

Reading my mind again, I concluded, and yet I turned a grateful smile in his direction. "You know me too well."

"Well, yes, but the longing in your eyes says it all."

"I thought you liked me confined to the house," I teased with a grin, and yet he was entirely solemn in his reply.

"I like you to see happy far more. So? Would you like to be on the stage again, *ange*, to dazzle them all with your brilliance?" Just as he asked, La Carlotta began her opening aria, and Erik cringed so dramatically that I hid a giggle behind my hand. "And the sooner the better for the entire world of the arts."

Giggling still, I nodded consent. "All right, but can you try to do it with as little deceit as possible this time? Your Opera Ghost notes used to cause a lot of trouble for me among my fellow cast mates."

"Connections, my sweet *ange*," he reminded. "If you know people in high places, you need to take advantage of that. Besides I may be the very vocal Opera Ghost, but I'm also the silent owner, so that makes me in charge legally as well."

I couldn't argue when he brought up that point. He *was* the opera house's owner, legitimately but secretly and had been for years. The Opera Ghost was only a means to run things his way and remain unknown to his associates. He had learned long ago that his mask would pose a barrier even in the world of the rich and elite.

The opera itself was pleasant enough. A few times I could not help but mirror Erik's grimace when

La Carlotta overshot a high note or butchered a cadenza I had sung perfectly for Erik in my lessons. Sensing my thoughts through my cringe of disappointment, he reached over after the fumbled passage and squeezed my hand to draw my attention.

"I hear *you* in my head," he softly said, leaning near my ear. "And you just sang it flawless as ever."

I stared at him in absolute wonder at the uncanny ability he possessed to make me feel like a sacred idol being reverently adored. It was in that heavenly voice and the light in his mismatched eyes. It was love as sure as if he had said the words, and my heart responded with a flutter.

Though he took his hand away after that one contact, it was set near mine, and without a second thought, I slid my fingers along his palm to intertwine with his cold ones, holding his intent stare all the while. He did not draw away, and within minutes, his hand was no longer cold, matching my warmth so perfectly.

For the rest of the show, our hands remained entwined on the plush armrest, and every so often, I could not help but glance away from the drama onstage to regard them. Everything about it was innocent, but it meant something so powerful. It was strength and unity; it was the edge of the something more I yearned for, the very threshold to its path.

As the opera ended and applause rang out, Erik met my eye, and lifting my held hand, he grazed his bottom lip along my knuckles. It was as much of a kiss as he could give with the mask's obstruction, but I savored it, closing my eyes beneath a blushing grin for a brief and blissful instant.

...And then everything was shattered before I could cling to it and try to keep it intact with a sharp gasp from the box's entranceway behind our seats.

Glancing over my shoulder in surprise with the roar of applause filtering about and bows being taken onstage, I leapt to my feet and flipped around to face our intruder, wide-eyed.

"Raoul." His name passed my lips lacking real sound, my stare locked on him without breath taken into my lungs. I felt my stomach fall as realization struck. Raoul, ...Raoul had snuck up into Box 5 and had caught us.

And Erik... Ripping my eyes from my aghast former fiancé, I saw my husband on his feet beside me, leaning casually back on the thick brocade curtains. His Opera Ghost persona was in place and unshaken in his haughty regard. How I hated every detail of it!

"Christine," Raoul gaped, recapturing my primary focus. "It's you. I thought...I thought I imagined it."

"Imagined?" I stammered, glancing back and forth between the men. "How did you even see us up here?"

"I didn't. I saw a shadow in this box from my own, and I thought... Well, I hoped it was you, and... My God, I'm so relieved that you are all right."

"Why wouldn't I be?" I demanded with a flicker of annoyance. As always, I was the supposed weakling, damsel in distress, and it was unthinkable that I could take care of myself.

"Yes, de Chagny," Erik taunted in his arrogant façade. "Why wouldn't she be all right? Hers wasn't the neck I was hoping to break; that was yours, if you'll recall correctly."

The look I shot Erik was where I directed all my perturbation for both of them; it saturated my glare and fumed as brightly as his temper, and it would have stayed as his had Raoul's audacity not jerked my attention back with his boldly thrown retort.

"Fiend!" the Vicomte hissed. "I have been terrified to consider what she has been subject to at your monstrous hands!"

Erik gave a sharp, mocking laugh and asked me bluntly, "Would you like to tell him, or shall I?"

I knew what he implied, but I only shook my

head miserably. How had such a lovely evening come to this? Once again, I was the prize set between these two aggressive competitors, wondering if they would destroy me before they finally managed to destroy each other.

"Tell me what?" Raoul's voice bore a waver, as if he could already guess just how much he was going to like this news, and it only made Erik stand tall and proud with his victory.

"Christine and I are married," he triumphantly declared, and for the first time in months, I knew a genuine wave of hatred and resentment toward him, ...not *him* but the role he felt he must take on. *This* was not Erik; this was the madman who had once been determined to manipulate me into staying with him, the one who could kill and destroy. This was not the man I loved.

Raoul's face was aghast and ashen under the news, the idea an absolute horror to him. "You...forced her, you disfigured freak! She'd never wed you unless you tricked her into it! Did you use the same ploy you used to get her to stay with you? Threaten *my* life knowing she'd do anything to keep me safe?"

"Get out, de Chagny! I'm bored with you and your pathetic drabble." Only I could have known how much Raoul's accusations stung Erik, playing on the very real fears he had harbored for so long. Only I could see the slightly lower carriage of his stance, hear the dimness in his threats, and only I could have set him to right again, but I was too annoyed over the entire situation to want to encourage either of them.

"Christine," Raoul suddenly begged, "say the word, and I'll come for you. I promise. I'll get you out of this devil's lair."

My eyes grew wide. *Foolish Raoul!* Still in love with me, or at least in love with the girl he thought I was. And he would get himself killed once and for all because of his inability to face the truth.

"I married Erik by my own choice," I declared

adamantly, meeting my husband's intent stare yet never softening my own. "He did not force me into anything I didn't want. Just leave it at that and go, Raoul."

"Christine," the Vicomte attempted again. "And now he has you lying to protect him! Bastard!"

"Get out, de Chagny!" Erik raged again, so loud that I suspected people leaving the opera below must have heard the echo. "Or I will complete the job I should have the last time we saw each other and end your waste of a life! I told you then that if you ever came after Christine, I would kill you; you can count yourself lucky that I don't follow through on the threat and do it now!"

"Go, Raoul," I urged, knowing Erik's restraint was minimal. "Just go."

He looked at me one last, long breath, his reluctance vividly shown, but he had no choice but to comply with death threats dancing in the air, leaving the way he had come, his footfalls echoing back to us with each heavy step.

My angry gaze settled on my husband, who would not even look at me as he opened our private exit along the wall of the box and coldly commanded, "Come on."

Not a word was uttered on the tedious journey home except for the detailed rants playing in my head if only to convince me that I had every right to be upset. Erik had his reasons, but as I well knew, every emotion, including the hurt ones attached would fade to anger. Wasn't that heart always protected by his temper, hiding behind its wall of fire and brimstone?

I expected a tirade when we arrived home and was unsurprised and unflinching when he slammed the door so hard that I was shocked it did not fly off its hinges. But the shouting did not materialize. He just stared at me, holding my eye without giving away one solitary emotion for a long moment before he stalked down the hall to his sitting room, leaving me alone and confused in the foyer.

Two minutes, two unendurable minutes and, of course, I pursued him, halting in the doorway to observe his dark shape in his throne chair, his eyes staring blankly at the fire in the hearth. ...And I waited.

"Say it," he suddenly commanded after a long moment of stillness passed. "Say it, Christine. Tell me that you're angry with me for taunting that boy. Yell at me for threatening his perfect existence. ...And please, God, tell me that I have no right to feel the way I do right now. That my feelings are unjustifiable and ridiculously presumptuous. ...Please just tell me in the way you do that I am wrong."

I knew what he wanted to hear, but all I could manage to say to pacify him was, "I don't love Raoul."

"But he loves you." Those mismatched eyes averted to me then, and I could hardly believe how the pain outweighed the anger, his every word laden in disgust. "He desires you. It was written across the urgent longing in his eyes. The way he looked at you... Had you not been present, I would have killed him with the jealousy in my soul as my inspiration." Scoffing disbelief with the mocking bit of a laugh attached, he continued, "He thinks so certainly that I forced you to marry me, ...because you couldn't possibly have *wanted* to be with me. Oh no, of course not! That is inconsiderable to the likes of him! You're *supposed* to want the dashing Vicomte, ...but you don't, do you, Christine?" The uncertainty created a betraying waver in his tone. "...Do you desire the Vicomte?"

"No," I answered immediately, stalking into the room to halt before his chair. Even if he denied my words, he had to see the truth in my eyes. He just had to! "Erik, no, I have *no* desire for Raoul."

"But why not?" he pushed somberly. "He is perfection, Christine. Rich, flawless features, a real god among men. Every woman *must* desire that."

"I don't," I insisted again, shaking my head desperately. "Erik, please stop this. You're the only one I want."

"Do you?" He shouted the question, the fire flaring in his eyes brighter than the one in the hearth. "Do you indeed! Because your ex-lover seems convinced that I must subject you to horrors of the flesh! And who can argue against gallant Raoul and his gentlemanly pledge to avenge your honor?"

"Erik," I strove to interrupt, but he was on his feet, pushing past me to pace before the hearth. "Erik, please."

With a suddenness that made me jump, he halted and faced me, roaring, "He desires you, and it is acceptable because of who he is, what he is! But I...I must have forced you if I would ever expect desire from you! I must have *raped you* to get you in my bed! Repulsive freaks like me aren't meant to feel and know desire! But the handsome Vicomte can put it openly on view, even coveting another man's *wife*, and it is wanted!"

"I don't want Raoul!" My volume did not equal his, but the power was there, the rage flaming to match. And I was not done. "I married *you*, Erik! I want *you*!"

"You don't know what that means," he bitterly accused, "what *any of this* means!"

"I do!" So many things to say that I felt them jumble and muddle my brain. All my arguments, though, really boiled down to one. "I married you, knowing what was expected of me, what a real marriage is, but you don't want that. You don't want to love me or to desire me."

Before I could go on with too many pent-up thoughts, he suddenly lunged, catching my arms and twisting them tight behind me against the small of my back as he dragged my body to his. "Pity that I do then, isn't it?" he hoarsely demanded, eyes so full of unrestrained passion that I felt myself trembling all over. Never had it been so prominently shown to me, always held at bay and leashed. Now it was a raging inferno. "Don't want you?" he mocked the words. "If only I didn't! Then every bit of my existence would be so much simpler! Look at you right now. You're afraid of me; you think that I *would* force you just as the Vicomte does."

"I'm not afraid," I stated as calmly as I could. And I wasn't. Nervous, apprehensive, but *not* afraid. "You *won't* force me; I know that without a doubt."

"Oh, do you?" He took it as a challenge, pressing my entire length flush to his, and as I felt the throbbing ache of his desire so hard and blatant against me, I knew I was right as my insides melted. *Forcing?* He wouldn't need to *force* anything!

I could feel my breaths becoming shallow, like my lungs were suffocating themselves, and I didn't care, tilting my face upward toward his, sure he would see the hazy need in my eyes. Erik stared at me a long, frozen moment, searching my emotions, trying to decipher and understand what obviously surprised him to know existed.

Finally, in a husky tone I barely recognized as his, he insisted, "I am not the Vicomte, Christine."

"I know that. You're my Erik, my *ange*, my husband, ...the only man I've ever wanted or desired." I was so honest that it took an effort to push the words past modesty's lingering barrier.

And for one blissful minute, I was certain he believed me. Then just as abruptly, it vanished, and he released me, recoiling back and out of my reach with a shameful expression leaping to life in his stare. He was disgusted with himself and what he perceived to be an indiscretion, and desperate to convince him otherwise, I took a step closer, reaching to him.

"No!" he suddenly roared. "Leave me be! Can't you see what you're doing to me? You're a poison in my blood!"

I leapt back, staring at that tortured figure through horrified eyes. A poison...? Was I? But wasn't he the same to me? Poisoning me, stealing everything I was; the only difference was that I was his *willing* victim.

Though he refused to grant another look my way, I lingered there a moment more, part of me futilely hoping he would regain enough sense to affirm the truth in his mind: that I *did want* him. *Pointless*, I told myself, and with a sheen of tears crowding every vacant space in my eyes, I turned and fled the sitting room, fled desire as a whole.

At some point as I readied myself for bed, I heard the front door slam shut and knew he was gone. A fleeting concern raced my brain that he wouldn't return, but my heart could not bear to dwell on such a horror. Well, when he *did* return, he would find that I had chosen to sleep in my own bed, taking the pre-offered escape this time. For two people who couldn't even manage to apply the term 'love' to their situation, maybe it wasn't such a terrible thing to have. When everything felt like a jellied mass beneath my feet, ready to turn to liquid and drop me at any second rather than solidify its construction, distance was preferred if it could salvage.

In my last aware thoughts before sleep wrapped solace around me, I realized I had never once put a notion to Erik leaving here to do something wrong and amoral, something from his Opera Ghost days. I never once considered that if he wanted, he could have gone after Raoul and taken his pain and anger out on him. I knew without a doubt that he wouldn't. It amazed me to be so confident in that belief, but I trusted him that completely. It was a shame he didn't know it.

*****

Erik didn't return to the house that night or the entirety of the day that passed. For the first time in months, my lesson time came and went, and even though I chose to work alone rather than forgo it altogether, I had a deep void in my chest that wouldn't ease its torment. It wasn't right; it didn't *feel* right.

Maybe I would have broken down and cracked, cried until my tears ran dry or something to that extent, but this separation wasn't intended to punish me. Just like before, he was using it to punish himself, and I was just the unlucky casualty to his masochism.

Miserable and lonely, I soaked for an indiscernible amount of time in a hot, soothing tub before settling into bed, though I doubted sleep would come easily. My head was far too full, and for hours, I suffered for it. At some point, tears came, finally breaking through my self-inflicted façade, tears that mourned the heart I wanted and yet couldn't seem to reach. Perhaps I was wasting my own in the process. Perhaps *this*, this semblance of a marriage, was all I was meant to have with him. Could that be enough for me? ...And if it wasn't, then what?

The door gave a soft creak, and I lifted my tear-stained face from my pillow to see his dark silhouette outlined against the intruding light from the hallway lantern. *Erik...* My heart wanted to fly, to go straightway to his, but I caught it with merciless fingers and held it down, clinging it to my chest.

As he approached my bedside, every footstep utterly tentative, I caught the reflection of tenderness in his eyes as they ran over me, a gentle softening of his masked features that only made my tears threaten to fall faster and harder.

"I thought I'd find you in my bed," he said, so hushed, and only hesitated a moment before lightly sitting on the edge of my mattress.

Forcing tears beneath a blanket of apathy, I lifted myself onto one elbow, my loose curls a tangled mess around my shoulders and matched his tone as I replied, "I didn't want to torment you further with my presence. You made it abundantly clear last night that you don't want me, that I am 'poisoning' you. I was only seeking to set things right between us again."

My words made him cringe, and that abhorrence he always seemed to know for his very sense of self resurfaced. "Christine, it isn't that way..." Silent a pondering breath, he seemed to decide upon a different tactic as he asked instead, "Are you happy here with me? Are you happy with our life?"

"Yes," I answered immediately without thought. It seemed an absurd question because being with Erik *was* my happiness.

"Well, I am happier than I've ever been in my life," he admitted earnestly, his eyes bearing so firmly into mine. "You can't imagine what it is to suddenly gain a future and a reason for living, ...to not be alone anymore. I adore every moment and wake up anticipating every day to come with you in my life. You have to understand then that I never want to do anything to jeopardize such a blessing or risk losing you. After this time together, that is an unbearable thought."

Gentle as could be, I pushed, "But what about more than this, Erik? What about the *rest* of it?"

I saw his jaw clench, his eyes coming to rest on his fisted hands atop his knee. "What the Vicomte dared to insinuate last night hurt me more than I wanted you to see or to know. I have been so desperate to act the gentleman with you, never to *be* the monster you bore witness to the night I forced you to marry me."

"You didn't force me-"

"As you've argued," he interrupted but without the sharpness I would have expected. No, he actually smiled. "Either way, coerced or not, I was determined that I would never do it again and never manipulate anything from you." With adamancy firm as stone, he declared, "I would never force you, Christine. And last night even just to taunt you with the concept sickened me. I knew from the night we married that I would never demand that of you. How could I want you to come to my bed solely because I had to power to make you do so? To have you there out of a sense of duty and loyalty to a vow and a threat that I had laid into place myself?"

I listened intently to his every word and watched the torture on his features and in his eyes. It amazed me that this held so much weight to him. He saw it as being the damning act between making him a man or a monster when to me, his dubbed sense of wifely duty had been my excuse to let what I desired be acceptable. Yes, I would have given myself to him that first night because I felt I must, but at the same time, I *wanted* to even then.

"Christine, why are you crying?"

Was I? ...I hadn't realized my tears had slipped free of my control. Perhaps because everything felt like such a hopeless mess, perhaps because I was frustrated and didn't know what to do next, perhaps because I realized right then that though I was happy, this *wasn't* enough for me and never could be. I'd be lying to say it was.

"I promise you," he went on, and I could see that he was desperate to pacify me. "I will *never* be the monster the Vicomte made me out to be. I will *never* force things on you. My behavior last night was barbaric, and I apologize vehemently for it...and everything I said. If you are poisoning me, then I pray you do so completely because I'd rather be intoxicated by you and lost in you forever than lose you from my life."

My hands darted out from beneath the blanket to cover his mouth and silence him, part of me terrified my timidity would quell the miniscule flame of courage I was desperate to keep lit. Holding his eye fiercely so that he would understand my seriousness, I demanded, "Tell me honest and true, Erik. ...Do you desire me?"

I slowly lowered my hand, but it trembled midair as it lingered in its suspension. Every part of me shook with a sort of terror that was soul deep because I knew that if he said no, he'd be lying, and I wasn't sure I'd ever be able to have the ending I wanted if he lied to me now.

"A ridiculous question to be sure; you already know the answer to that," he stated with a huff and a touch of a smile that made the light in his eyes dance. "Why must you ask such things?" Then with a suddenness I had not expected, he grew serious and solemn, his gaze piercing mine. "Especially to a man who's only known desire for one woman in his entire lifetime, who's only...*loved* one woman ever... Questions like that are irrelevant; they only remind me what I can't have."

I stared, lost in those eyes, utterly speechless when I *needed* words on my side, and I watched him slowly, wearily rise and turn from me, leaving my bedroom in heavy footsteps that dully thudded with my heart's beat. *No, no, no!* Things couldn't be left this way! Tomorrow, everything would be as it was days before, as if the past conversations and passionate outbursts were unimportant dreams. Erik was so good at repressing the unwanted parts of his life; this would become one more. And God, how I would suffer for it!

But I had to wait, to recollect my failing bravery, to take pause and consider a valid course of action.

The house was silent beyond my door, and I concluded that Erik had gone to bed, though I felt sure he would be as awake and tortured as I was. So on bare feet, I made the trek I hadn't needed to venture in months and entered his dimly lit room. This time it was he who lifted his head to observe my approach, his welcoming smile unhidden and scars awaiting my eager touch. He raised the edge of the covers, and I immediately crawled beneath and into his open arms, swallowing back a sob at how deliciously whole I felt the instant his firm grasp had me, my face pressing to his chest as I breathed him in. Kisses were laid to the crown of my head, and I savored each one. He thought he was forgiven and all was as it was before, and I *almost* went along with it if only because of how content I was to be this close to him. But no, ...I couldn't. It wasn't enough; it *couldn't ever be* enough.

Slowly drawing back, I met his eyes with mine and saw such a depth of emotion that I yearned to have it always as my own. In a hushed whisper, I said, "You called my question irrelevant and said I already knew the answer, but I want to hear the words. ...Tell me that you desire me, Erik."

"Christine," he attempted a feeble argument, but my arms around him prevented any form of escape; there was nowhere to go, no place to run and hide.

"You're afraid of it," I accused yet again. "And you're ashamed by it."

"How can I not be?" he passionately insisted. "My God, Christine, I desire you with a fire so powerful that I don't think I can control it. And then what happens? Then I become the monster; then I take what isn't mine."

"But it *is* yours," I protested. "It's *always* been yours."

"You felt it last night," he reminded, searching my eyes for confirmation. "You felt the effect you have over me, the sheer ache you cause within my body at every turn. Didn't it frighten you, Christine? To know that I am burning so intensely, that if you tempt me, I won't be able to resist you? I barely did last night!"

I shook my head, meeting his stare without fear. "It made me melt. I'm not afraid, Erik; I've never been afraid. You're so certain that I'll run from you again, but how could I ever...when I want you so much?" Plainly stated, entirely straightforward, now if only he believed in what he was yearning to deny.

"You want me?" Releasing his hold on me, Erik offered his hands freely to the air between our bodies. "You want these hands, stained in the blood of many as they are, ...a *murderer's* hands on your body? You want them to touch you in your most intimate places, to slip so deeply within you and tease you so mercilessly?"

His words and the images created in my head from them were encouragement enough for my willing consent, and catching both of those sinful hands in my own, I guided them to my lips and pressed kisses against their palms, studying his reaction close enough to see the wave of desire flow through him.

"They are not the hands of a murderer to me," I justified, keeping them trapped with entwined fingers. "They are the hands of my husband, hands I *want* to touch me."

The breaths escaping his lungs were shallow and gasp-like at their edges as he hoarsely demanded, "And you want this face, malformed and distorted as it is, kissing your flawless body across every inch? These bloated lips caressing your silken flesh?"

Quivering, I leaned close enough to graze my own lips over his...once, twice; my tongue dared to add a soft lick across the swollen arch of his mouth, and I felt him shudder down his spine. In a breathless whisper, I agreed, "Every inch."

A moan escaped him, so unbridled that a flush of heat swept through my veins in response, making me writhe and scoot urgently closer. I could tell he was barely keeping restraint to intact as he demanded, "Christine, and you want this body atop yours, joining with yours as one being, never to be separated again, making you mine in every way possible?"

Breathing was impossible and nearly forgotten in the shadow of desperation for those very things. It astounded me just how powerful a need it created, one that once ignited, burned so intensely that nothing mattered but finding the way to put it out. It surely wouldn't die without some sort of overwhelming culmination. And dear Lord, how I wanted it!

"Yes, yes, yes," I gasped breathlessly to the identical flames searing through his eyes. Catching his scarred cheek on my palm, I let coherency peer through to be certain he understood me clearly and absolutely. "I desire you of my own free will, not because I have to, and I am not in your bed out of obligation or duty. I want you, Erik. I'm *burning* for you."

My attention caught on the tremble of the hand he brought to entwine possessively in my curls, the caress saying something contrary to the hesitation in his stare. "I don't want to hurt you."

I knew enough to know such a thing was inevitable at first, and since I couldn't lie and promise he wouldn't, I whispered with a blush I could feel warming my skin, "I want to be one with you, Erik, to be yours. Please...don't push me away."

His breath escaped him in a sigh. "I don't think I can. Oh, Christine..." Catching one of my hands within his, he slowly guided it between our bodies, all the while holding my eye captive with his trepidation. "But tell me this does not frighten you."

My hand was pressed to his hardened manhood, and I sucked a harsh, forced breath of air into starving lungs. The brief instant I had been held flush against it the previous night had only hinted at its sheer size and strength. And now to feel it, to curve my fingers around its thickness with only a few flimsy barriers between skin... I was in awe.

"Are you afraid now?" Erik pushed, his voice so hoarse and nearly breaking with the forceful waves of his ache. I could see it like a ravenous hunger within him. "Are you afraid of what you just claimed to want? *This* inside of you. ...Tell me, Christine. And will you now run from me and destroy every illusion of happiness I've ever had, punish me for my wanting?"

My answer was to pull my hand free of his hold, but before he could assume his fears were valid, I dared to slide my fingers within the waistband of his pants and seek a real touch. He gasped and shuddered with fervent surprise, moaning deeply the instant my fingers closed around him. Modesty begged me to retain some limits, not to let wanton emotions take control, but the feel of him, so hard, smooth, and warm in my hand made my insides quiver and desire reign supreme. I wanted him! Dear God, did I want him! Fear seemed trivial, and nervousness was shoved to the background.

He was the one to end my eager caresses after only a moment more, disentangling my hand from within his clothing, and I knew a momentary panic, worried he had found regret. But amidst my surprised cry, he caught my lips in his, kissing me hard and demanding, his mouth lacking gentleness as it moved hungrily against mine, and I succumbed completely, wrapping my arms around his neck and arching my body against his, aching to be closer and closer still.

One of his hands entangled in my hair, snaking a path to the nape of my neck to splay wide and grasp me firm to his vehement kiss while the other sought the ties of my nightdress. He no longer hesitated in any endeavor, and unlacing that meager binding, his hand stole within and found my breast, cupping its weight in his palm while his fingertips dared to graze the hardened tip.

I shuddered violently down the full length of my spine. Had any single touch ever caused such an uncontrollable reaction within my body? *That* almost frightened me as I wavered a bit in my conviction. My innocence was coming through. I didn't know what to expect from my own body, feeling suddenly ignorant and inept. But the more he teased with his fingers, the more I felt reluctance and apprehension fading, and my sudden fears became a pleading within my very core. *Give up control*, it begged, and I did. In that moment, I would have eagerly accepted death at his hands if that were the ending to come, anything as long as he didn't stop.

Those misshapen lips departed from mine so that they could begin a trek along the side of my throat as I whimpered. Only once did I receive a question of permission in one shared look, but my hazy stare must have pleaded for me because he did not pause again. Lips and tongue both teased my sensitive skin as my small cries surprised my ears. His hands parted my nightdress, and before my clouded mind could deduce his intentions, he captured my nipple between his misshapen lips. Shivering and whimpering, I dug my fingers into the thin hair on the back of his head, clutching him to me even though I lacked any real strength of limbs anymore, all bones and fibers feeling weak and liquefied. I was left with one semi-coherent, marveling thought of how passionate Erik was, how incredibly overcome with desire and yet still so gentle with me. As always, he put my wants and needs first; how could he ever call himself a monster then?

His hand descended the curve of my hip and along the side of my thigh, and catching the material of my nightdress in a fist, he began to bunch it up until his skin, warmed now by mine, could touch me. I could already fathom his purpose, and when his hand entered the final barrier of my pantaloons, I parted my thighs, moaning softly with my urgency.

His first grazed touch brought a groan that escaped his mouth where it was buried against my breast. I already knew I was wet and aching, and to realize how such a fact overcame him and made him shudder against me only made me wetter. The tips of his fingers stroked while my hips arched nearer, nearer to that craved touch. He controlled every bit of me in that one caress, and I surrendered without lingering fear, fisting my hands in his hair as I cried out.

All at once, his lips and hands left my body, and I nearly whined in disappointment, craving and unfulfilled.

His eyes met mine, and it astounded me in my dizzy haze how clear and rational he suddenly was when I still felt like I was falling without a net. In a husky voice, he bid, "Do you love me, Christine?"

It never occurred to me that I hadn't actually said the words aloud. He might have been avoiding their syllables as well, but he *had* said them before and established the depth of his emotions. I had been the one to run from that.

"Yes," I whispered fervently. "I love you. I do, Erik."

"And you want me? And a real marriage, a future together with every detail that includes?"

"Yes," I repeated, caressing his scarred cheek with gentle fingers.

"No doubts?"

"Not a single one."

Nodding as though that was all he needed to hear, he reached for my nightdress and casually lifted it over my head. My pantaloons followed under my attentive stare as I fought to read his mind as he so often accurately read mine. His eyes trailed languidly over every inch of my revealed skin, and I felt myself blushing. How funny that reddened shyness was to come up even when I longed not to appear the timid, little girl! It betrayed my innocence in blatant hues.

When his eyes found mine again, he grinned and teased, "So nervous! And pointlessly so! You are such glorious perfection, Christine." His fingertips grazed an idle path from the top of my shoulder down between my breasts to splay wide across my flat stomach, the sheer length of his hand and fingers covering every bit of my flesh with its span. "Beautiful, so very beautiful," he breathed as he leaned close to press a lingering kiss to my collarbone.

And how he made me *feel* beautiful! It was in the sheer reverence of his expression; it was something that made me feel unearthly to my essence, beyond mortality, greater than its limited boundaries. I was not a vain person. But Erik, my darling angel, had always sought to prove to me that I was exquisite. And how deeply did he believe his own sentiments and endearments? So much that I felt like a worshipped goddess as his eyes again took a roaming path over my body, the fire in his stare searing me with every brushing.

"I am aching so much to have you," he huskily whispered as his fingers moved over me. "And yet at the same time, I am terrified to let this moment end."

"Why?" I demanded back, catching his wayward gaze in mine. "You seem so certain it will never come again. Don't hold the doubts I don't have, Erik. I want forever, and as such, this is only our beginning."

Though he was still clinging to a solitary hesitation in the background, I left it there. This was a man who needed proof, and I was determined that over the course of our life to come, he would have just that. And every doubt would seem ridiculous then and unwarranted.

As my fingers sought the buttons down his shirt, I urged with conviction, "Make love to me, *ange*. Make me yours."

I saw that possessive streak take control of him. Had he been anyone else, even Raoul in our courting days, I would have hated him for it. But as deeply in love with him as I was, I savored it, wanting in some strange way for his mark to be upon me, to be claimed as only his. Some would call that pathetic and dependent, weak even, but I knew that loving Erik was what made me strong and I was unashamed to admit it.

He did not let me finish with the buttons, jerking the half-open shirt up and over his head, and with a sigh of delight, I pressed palms and fingers to that exposed expanse of skin, tracing and adoring every carved muscle of his chest and stomach. Even as I touched him, he was ridding himself of the rest of his clothing, baring his body boldly to my curious regard. And yet in spite of his feigned bravado, I could practically feel his flash of trepidation, his search for some sign of approval. It amazed me to realize how alike we were!

Trailing my hand in a timid descent, I dared to touch his hardened manhood as I had earlier, shivering up and down my spine to hear his uncontrollable moan. Softly, teasingly, I inquired with an innocent raise of brows, "Does it make me brazen to enjoy touching you like this?"

95

"No, no," he practically gasped, his hands twining in my hair in an attempt to steady himself. "Not brazen."

"Yes, but I find I like it all the more because it is arousing you so much. That *must be* brazen. I like knowing how much I'm making you ache." I admitted it plainly, but I left out the fact that in equal amounts I delighted in how simply my spoken utterances caused him to shudder. He liked hearing me say the words, which, though so innocent, were also tentatively provocative.

"Need I remind you," he replied hoarsely, his hands continuing necessary paths over any bit of my flesh they could find, "that I am your husband. Brazen doesn't apply."

"No?"

"No, it is sensual and tantalizing, not brazen." His fingertips were between my legs again, caressing my wetness as he shuddered violently. Edging close enough to nuzzle his scarred cheek against my hair, he admitted urgently, "I don't think I can wait much longer; I have to have you. I *need* to be inside of you."

I trembled at his words and did not hesitate, reluctantly ending my caresses but as eager for the rest of it as he was.

Erik closed the bit of distance remaining between our bodies until we were pressed skin to skin, and I could hardly believe how warm he was, not a reminiscent chill anywhere. *God, how delicious it felt!* His flesh, so different from my own in texture, so *Erik*, flush to mine, and the hardened length of him urgently nudging my body, his eyes holding my stare all the while. He hesitated only an instant; I wasn't sure for my sake or his. And then I felt him hold his breath as he suddenly thrust deep into me.

I froze. Pain... Yes, there was pain, one I had only partially prepared myself for. I knew it had to get better; it had to fade, but betraying tears rimmed my eyes without my consent. I wanted to hide them and tried to duck my head, but Erik was too close, too perceptive of my emotions as always, and catching my chin with his knuckle, he forced me to meet his worried stare again.

"Christine," he whispered tenderly, and his free hand rose to brush the tears from my cheeks. I knew he was exercising control, as frozen in his place as I was, and how I loved him for it! "Say the word, and we'll stop," he insisted firmly. "We need not do anything else. I would be content simply to hold you in my arms."

Humbled yet again, I knew that he meant every word. The longer I lost myself to those brilliant, mismatched eyes and marveled over him and everything he was, the more the pain became only a dull ache. "I don't want to stop," I whispered, caressing his scarred cheek. "Please, Erik, ...don't stop."

The concern never left his features, but rather than move and continue, he slipped his hands between our bodies. I never questioned him, and when his fingertips began to tease me once again with determined caresses, I knew he was doing it for me. How I adored him!

Erik took great care and ample time to reignite my waning desire, every expression passing between our shared stare telling me how much it delighted him to draw the fervent cries he was getting from my lips. Only when I had fallen back beneath a haze of passion's power and was beginning to restlessly arch my hips, overcome with the fullness of him within me, did he slowly begin to move. I felt the shudder run through his entire frame, the tremulous breath he seemed afraid to take, and willingly moved with him. It was a gentle rhythm, a graceful thrusting in and out of my slick body, and I clung to him with fisted hands against his shoulders. I wanted more, I thought mid-passion, and as if reading my mind, he thrust deeper, harder, making small whimpers slip past my lips.

"Erik," I breathed desperately. In that moment, nothing existed in the world but him. Desire was a cloud in my brain, stealing a rationale I eagerly gave up and raining fire along my body. I knew pleasure was coming, something so necessary to every fiber of my being that I willingly relinquished every ounce of control to its power. And then in an unrestrained shout that left the recesses of my lungs, I became its willing victim. Ecstasy washed through me, starting from the place where our bodies were joined and branching out through every limb, seeping into every cell. I nearly sobbed to succumb so powerfully to its spell, and to glimpse the way Erik savored knowing he had caused it made me eagerly find his lips with mine, kissing him with a mixture of love and gratitude for this one blissfully perfect moment.

Beyond pleasure, the best part surpassed my own bliss. To gaze upon my Erik, to feel him move within me with only wispy fragments of passion left so that awareness reigned, to delight in every tingling sensation along every inch of touching skin, those things made the love within me so strong and unbreakable. His palms caught my hips between them, his need driving him to fiercer motions, and in awe, I watched ecstasy overcome him, watched those mismatched eyes close to the shudder that racked his entire being, heard and savored the guttural cry he gave, so far from his golden, heavenly tone but equally as beautiful. It amazed me that only I would bear witness to this, that only I, for the rest of our lives, would have this passionate side of him. It was something that was completely mine. Had I ever been given such a wonderful gift?

Silently smiling, I witnessed reality's return across those disfigured features, relishing his weight atop me, his body still joined to mine as if we were inseparable. ...And weren't we just that? Everything felt changed, altered at its innermost core, solidified finally.

Before he could utter a single word, I whispered urgently, "Please don't regret this." A terror gripped me, sudden and raw, that he would now force me away from him, and I kept my arms firmly around his torso and arched my hips to savor the sensation of his throbbing, satiated body within mine.

But Erik leaned closer yet and pressed kiss after kiss along my hairline, vowing fervently, "I love you. I love you so much, Christine."

Relief. Oh, the joy of such exuberant relief! Relaxing my grip, I gently ran my hands up and down his back, molding us so perfectly together. I had never imagined such exquisiteness could exist in the living world, sure that only heaven could create such sensations. If nothing else, it assured me a million times over that I belonged exactly where I was, in my darling angel's arms.

A strange thought occurred to me, and made oddly bold by our union, I dared to ask, "Had you done this before?"

He actually *chuckled* at my question! "What an absurd thing to ask!" But my expression made him hastily answer. "Of course not! I was not exaggerating to say you are the only woman I've ever desired. It was not some sweet endearment. It was entirely true. I am not the sort of man to have swells of amorous attention toward every female I see. And...with a face like mine, I never believed any woman could desire me in return."

I immediately caressed that mangled flesh with a tenderness I saw him savor. How much it hurt me to consider all he had endured, some of it by my own ignorance! And how fortunate I was to be in his arms right now, being loved and cherished by his beautiful heart!

"I desire this face," I made it a point to say, "in a way that I've never desired anything."

"Truly, Christine? And you have no regrets then? ...You just gave yourself to me so openly, so completely."

"I love you," I said as if that was justification

enough. "And I love this face; it is the face of my every dream, the completion of my very soul."

When he bent close to kiss me, there were tears shining in his eyes, and they were still present a little later when he made love to me again, clutching me to him as though we'd never be parted. And with a lightness in my heart, I believed him.

*****

If I had presumed to know desire's definition and associates, the next week taught me that I had previously only touched its corners. *My God, desire!* It was a hunger and need that became as necessary to my existence as breathing. Erik was as surprised as I was, and yet it was he who pushed for more, he who brought me beyond passion's boundaries to ecstasy in ways that I could have *never* imagined possible. And Erik... He never tired of seeking new ways to make me melt. It seemed like he derived more pleasure from pleasing me than anything else. We were like children learning something new and previously undiscovered. To us, there were no limits, and shyness evaporated that first night to Erik's passionate insistence. How he amazed me constantly! And to consider that he had believed he would never know these physical pleasures, to consider that fervent spirit laying dormant his whole life and then realize that it had just been waiting for me to have and hold as my own! At times, I felt undeserving of such a blessing.

I was happy, content, excited with the prospect of a future laid out the same beneath our feet. We finally had a real marriage and finally were everything to one another, and as Erik kept declaring exuberantly, once our house was finished, our new life would be complete.

Every day he left early to oversee building and returned in the evening to have supper with me, one I had the privilege of playing the domesticated wife to prepare. Then as we both exercised patience, my lesson followed, now with purpose to each step as Erik

100

insisted that I would be the star by the start of the next season. He was only teacher then with his ever-present expectations that he forced me to exceed with each day's work. But then as lessons ended, he abruptly transformed into husband, grabbing me often before I had my music put away and carrying me to bed while stripping clothes off at every step. It was overwhelming, and it was my dream come true.

One night, I had been half-dragged, half-carried to his bedroom, my gown in a pile someplace in the hallway and various other articles of clothing strewn at random spots when I made him cease with a provocative gleam in my eyes. Only my chemise was covering me, resting with a thin layer of lace at mid-thigh, and he was desperately groping for its hem.

"Not yet," I teased, sidestepping his hand as he groaned his disappointment.

"Cruel, Christine. I've spent all day shouting at incompetent workers, longing only to be here with you, and now you propose to make me suffer further?" he asked, raking desperate eyes over me as if his stare alone could devour for him. "Must I beg?"

"Oh, you will be before I'm through with you," I promised, guiding him toward the bed with an inviting, crooked finger. He did not hesitate to follow, shoving off his already open shirt on the way. "You might as well disrobe entirely."

His brows rose with a delighted question that lit every disfigured feature but was never spoken. With eyes that remained on me as I climbed on the bed and knelt on the mattress, he quickly unfastened his pants and rid himself of everything else so that his aching manhood was exposed to my eager stare. I adored that body; I adored learning its every nuance even more than learning my own. And to have his arousal so blatantly and proudly on display made me ache with an intense emptiness needing to be filled.

"And now?" he posed, chuckling lightly with amusement. "Or were you just intending to ogle me all night?"

My blush shown through my boldness, but I did not let it deter me as I commanded, "Lay on the bed, ...but keep your hands to yourself or I will take my time with every moment until you are sobbing with want."

I could tell the idea wasn't nearly as unappealing as I would have liked it to seem, but he obeyed without complaint or deviation, laying on his back beside where I sat with a tempting tilt of his head that challenged me for more.

I knew I blushed yet; I couldn't help it, but I scooted to sit beside his head, bending to graze one simple kiss along his misshapen mouth.

"Oh no," he groaned. "A gentle kiss to start. You must intend to be merciless with me."

"You'll have to wait and see." Slowly, I began to crawl down the length of his body from his head, laying idle, upside-down kisses on my way. Imitating my game, he dared to capture one of my breasts between his lips, wetting the thin material of my chemise as it passed, but I abruptly jerked beyond his kiss.

"Cheater," I taunted, glancing over my shoulder to see his seemingly innocent expression.

"You practically dangle it in front of me, and I'm not supposed to respond?" he demanded as if the idea were absurd.

"A little restraint, *mon amour*," I chided before I continued my game, laying teasing kisses along his chest and then his belly. I was so brazen! *He* made me brazen! He drew it out of me like it was some hidden talent, and I never fought it. How could I want to resist its power when the sight of my husband squirming beneath my ministrations was so appealing?

My legs and arms were on either side of his body as I edged lower until with one last look over my shoulder to delight in his anticipating, wide-eyed expression, I took his hardness into my mouth. He moaned deeply at the first second of contact and arched his hips up toward me, but at such an angle, he had very little control, unable to grasp my curls as he often did when I kissed him there and guide my rhythm. No, I had complete control and knew with a blush so fierce that I would torment him.

Drawing back so he slid completely out of my warm mouth with his moan of disappointment resounding, I began to press tiny kisses up and down the length of him, occasionally adding my tongue and making him jolt with delighted surprise.

"Christine," he gasped, and I threw him a suggestive look over my shoulder before suddenly taking all of him into my mouth again, still deliberately gentle and reserved in my actions.

At about that time, it seemed he tired of playing my helpless victim, and to my cry of surprise, his hands caught my hips and jerked my body downward so that his mouth could find my heated womanhood, bunching my chemise out of his way. I wanted to protest, but he knew exactly how to use his tongue to make me shiver with surrender. *Oh, he would not change my game to his advantage!* Without pause, I decided to make him as overcome as he was making me, and I began to suck and tease him fervently, mercilessly as he moaned against my body.

Such passionately erotic endeavors could only last a minimal time when we were both already writhing, and to my mew of need, his strong arms lifted me until he could break free and drag me up into his embrace, his wet lips finding mine in a violent kiss that I met without pause, tasting myself when his tongue dove into my mouth.

When he finally took me, tearing off my chemise without a single care, we were both so lost to desire that hands fisted and nails clutched urgently frantic at one another. His thrusts were harsh and rough, but I only met him, nearly sobbing when release came and pleasure erupted within me so powerful that I shuddered fiercely in his arms.

"God, I love to make you explode like that," he

hoarsely gasped against my ear, creating more tingles along my spine.

Words were still a jumble of nonsensical letters in my mind, and coherency evaded me as his hands caught my hips and held tight with his own pending climax. An unbridled shout and a raspy growl, and his weight crushed me into the mattress beneath him.

I pressed kisses to his sweat-covered shoulder, running my fingers through damp hair, and with a flutter of a giggle, I asked, "Are you all right?"

"I will be momentarily," he managed to reply, searching for his breath, "when I regain the ability to move. My God, Christine, how did you come up with *that*?"

"Are you complaining?" I teased, arching my hips with his satiated body still inside.

"Lord, no! I'm just...amazed by you yet again." His hands combed my curls away from my face, and with a wry grin, he declared, "Ah, I know! Your ballet days and the tawdry tales of the ballerinas must have inspired you."

"How do you know about that?" I demanded in a whine of embarrassment.

"You should have realized by now that there are not many things that go on under my roof without my knowledge." Tucking my hair behind my ear, he stared at me with such unfathomable love in his eyes and said, "And wherever you were, I was usually there as well, hiding in the darkness, wishing only to be a part of your shadow forever. It's ridiculous to consider now that that would have ever been enough. To never actually hold you or kiss you. ...To never be so deeply inside of you after the most incredible lovemaking ever known to mankind... Christine, I am so blessed to have your love. I am entirely undeserving of it, and yet I am selfishly determined never to let it go just the same."

"You better not," I warned, leaning near to press my flawless cheek to his scarred one. "I love you, Erik."

His arms enfolded me without an inkling of space between us, and I closed my eyes to savor something so wonderful that I could hardly believe it was real and it was mine.

*****

The next morning, I stood before the mirror in my room, pinning my hair back from my face. Even as my fingers performed the task, my mind was elsewhere. How could it not be fixed on Erik? And how could a blush not be lighting my cheeks a soft pink hue with every recalled image in my eager head? That blush and the secretive, introspective smile attached gave me away.

"Do I even need to ask the subject of your thoughts?" Erik inquired teasingly as he came behind me and met my eye in the mirror's glass. "Or may I assume that *I* put that beautiful smile there?"

"*Every* smile is your doing," I corrected, but sweetness faded to passion as he leant down to brush his misshapen lips along the sensitive side of my throat. In a whimper of longing, I demanded, "Must you leave me already?"

I felt his smile against my skin. "Considering that I've already been delayed once by you this morning and am presently late, yes, I fear I must. But when I return, I will thoroughly devour you to make up for every second apart."

Memories of the previous night bled into memories of just an hour before, and the warmth of the blush on my cheeks grew. Well, he was right to say *I* had been the one to stop him from leaving, ...shamelessly so, and any complaints he might have given were only moans with my very first attempts.

"Oh, all right," I reluctantly conceded, watching in the mirror as he rose behind me and covered that face I so adored with the mask. Immediately, my fingers tingled with the urge to rip it away again. Its presence seemed utterly unnecessary and unwelcome now, and I knew a swell of amazement at how quickly that had come to be.

Smiling at me in the glass, Erik brushed a gentle caress down my cheek, and then he was gone and I missed him in my very first breath taken on my own. Oh well... Another day of tinkering about the underground house, seeking things to keep busy or go mad from the silence. It certainly left me impatient for our new house to be completed. Then there would be a garden to tend and sunshine to provide bursts of delight. Then there would be a home of our own. ...And, although the detail had only been implied with the choice of a real marriage, children...

My mind was a haze of plans with images of tiny fingers and toes to enchant me when walking toward the sitting room, I received my first impression that something was wrong. It was a sensation: a peculiar, unsettling feeling that twisted my stomach. A perusal about gave nothing to ease my mind but nothing actually out of the ordinary either.

And then I heard a noise come from outside the front door in the catacombs, ...scuffling footsteps. It wasn't Erik; I knew that instantly. It was someone unconfident in the dark, stumbling, awkwardly on guard, ...and en route to the underground house.

I had little time to consider a plan, fear twisting my heart and preventing the most logical reasoning from being more than a jumbled mess. Had I had a clear head, perhaps I would have hid or locked myself in the secret confines of my room, but my thoughts came down to one: this was my house, and I wasn't about to be frightened in it.

Courageously defiant, I strode right out the front door and into the darkness without pause, scanning every shadow. Again footsteps, but they were louder now, echoing about, nervous, uncertain with every motion, ...and then a familiar voice.

"Christine?"

"Raoul!" Seeing the Vicomte de Chagny emerge from the shadowed passageway in his pristine suit was far more shocking to me than seeing him at the opera over a week before. My expression was something akin to horror. *Raoul here? ...Why?*

Raoul came to stand before me within the light cast from the open doorway, his smile laden with relief and renewed confidence now that he was beyond the dark. "I saw that monster leave, and I knew this would be my only chance."

"Chance for what?" I demanded curtly. How could I return his friendly smile when his presence felt like a horrible intrusion? "What are you doing here, Raoul?"

"I came to rescue you, of course."

"Rescue me?" I scoffed at the very idea. *Absurd! Ridiculous! ...*And yet so very like the gallant Vicomte and his self-proclaimed nobility.

Without permission or consent, Raoul suddenly caught my hand, his grip firm when I tried to pull away. "Ever since I saw you at the opera, ...saw you with...*him*, I haven't been able to stop thinking about you. My God, what a fool I was to have left you here this long! I should have come for you no matter what threats he tried to lay into place! I should have stolen you away months ago! And instead I ignorantly let you suffer!"

"Suffer?"

"Yes, my poor darling, to be forced to marry that monster, forced to...," he grew pale before the words even left him, "take him to your bed. What you've been through, I can't even imagine. But everything will be all right now. I'm going to take you from this place. We'll go away where no one will find us."

I was fighting his grip, desperately trying to yank my hand free as I contemplated his words. He thought what he was doing was right! "Let go of me! You can't just carry me off! He's my husband!"

"He's a murdering freak!" Raoul shouted back. "What's wrong with you, Christine? You should be grateful that I'm here. Your nightmare has finally ended!"

"Nightmare?" I practically shrieked, my voice

resounding off the stone walls. "I love him, Raoul! *I love him*!"

"The bastard's obviously using a spell to make you think such things," Raoul justified, his free hand grabbing my waist as he sought to pull me toward the dark passageway. "Come on, Christine! Once you're free of this place, you'll realize he's been tricking you. You poor child! This whole time he probably had you convinced that you *want* to be here with him. That's why you never tried to run and get to me, isn't it?"

"Let go!" I shouted, but my will alone could not break me loose of his unyielding hold. "*I* chose Erik, Raoul. *I* chose to stay with him. *I* made the choice! And I chose to marry him because I love him! Now let me go!"

"Christine," the Vicomte insisted tightly, refusing to concede, "I'm doing this for you!"

I screamed as he dragged me deeper into his hold and fought to lift me off my feet, struggling with limbs and nails. This was *not* happening! I was not going to let it happen! He would not take away my happy ending!

"Stop fighting me!" Raoul yelled as I elbowed him in the stomach, but his grasp still would not loosen.

And then I felt him being yanked back and away, his arms releasing me, and I fell in a heap of limbs and skirts to the hard, cold floor.

I nearly cried in relief. Erik was there with a noose clamped tightly around the Vicomte's neck as poor Raoul clawed at its binding and fought to breathe.

"Are you all right?" Erik asked, his relieved eyes perusing every inch of me, though his hold on my attacker never slackened.

I beamed at him with a quick nod, rising quickly to my feet, and though my mind argued, I dared to beg, "Don't kill him, Erik."

"I should!" he sneered, purposely yanking the rope to cause Raoul to gag. "Breaking into my home, assaulting my wife and nearly kidnapping her. And yet now we are back in our predetermined roles in quite a familiar situation: your neck in my rope, your life in my hands. My instincts are just begging me to strangle the breath out of you."

He wasn't going to do it. His eyes met mine, and I knew without doubt that he wouldn't. Perhaps a few months before, such a thing wouldn't have been so clear to him, and the Vicomte would have already been a dead body on the ground. But my Erik had changed. *I* had changed him.

One more tug on the rope to cut off the Vicomte's lungs, and Erik suddenly dropped him, rope and all, to the floor as the Vicomte gasped for air, tearing fiercely at his binding. An eye always on his struggling adversary, Erik stepped toward me, his hand reaching for mine, and I scampered to his side, clasping that hand and the arm attached and adding a grateful kiss to his shoulder.

Raoul staggered to his feet, the rope tossed carelessly to the ground, and backing away from us step by step, he was wide-eyed and white as a sheet. "Christine," he stammered as he shook his head in reality's bewilderment.

"If you ever lay a hand on my wife again," Erik growled hastily, "I will not be so generous as to let you live! Now get out!"

I ducked my head against Erik's jacket, tears in my eyes that I could not control, and all I heard were the Vicomte's running, scuffling footsteps as he fled our world, a place he couldn't belong or hope to understand. When quiet was all that could be discerned, Erik was the one to guide me back into the house, his arms so warmly secure around my trembling body. I caught the click of the lock on the front door, precautions suddenly necessary, but he did not speak or release me until we were in the sitting room and he was drawing me onto the couch with him.

It took a coercion of every cell in my body to let

him go so I could meet his intent yet unreadable stare. "How did you know?" I asked in a shaky whisper. "You were gone."

He shook his head, and his fingers brushed my tears away. "I have alarms all over the catacombs. I knew someone was lurking about. I never left you alone."

"So you saw all of that?"

"Unfortunately, yes." Only then did he let his real terror appear, giving me the glimpse I wanted into that soul.

"He thought he was doing the right thing," I weakly justified. "But, ...oh, Erik, what if you hadn't been here? What if he had taken me away?"

"I would have come for you, of course," he confidently answered. "You should know quite well by now that I'll never let anyone separate us."

"And we're married. That's binding." I caught the edge of his mask and yanked it away, needing to see that face.

"It's so much more than that now." Though I was curled to his side, it wasn't close enough for him as his strong arms drew me onto his lap and into his embrace. "I wouldn't have come for you because by law you were mine, a possession if you will. I would have come for you only because I love you and I know you love me as well."

He knew, and that meant more to me than anything he could have said. After all this time, he trusted my heart. He knew that when I said I was happy and I loved him, I wasn't lying. *Finally!*

Smiling even as tears fell again from my eyes, I pressed my cheek to his scars and curved my fingers in his hair, breathing him in and yearning to be lost in him.

"You know, I'm not going to leave you alone again," he warned. "Not until we are safely in our new home away from this place and this life."

"I have no complaint to that," I replied. "However, the Vicomte will always be a part of our lives if the opera is. There is no escaping that."

"Then he better have learned his lesson." I felt the tightness of welled rage within him. "Let him try to cross me again. I wasn't exaggerating my threat, Christine. *No one* hurts my family."

I couldn't contain a smile as I nuzzled my nose against his sunken cheek. "I know, my love. You are my guardian angel, after all, and I and the children expect you to take care of us."

"Children?" He abruptly drew back and met my eye, and I giggled with amusement. He, the mighty Opera Ghost, looked suddenly terrified. "I think... I mean... Isn't that a discussion for another time?"

I shrugged innocently. "Maybe, maybe not. The things we've been doing lately, ...*frequently* doing, tend to have that ending result, you realize. And I don't think you'd want to give such things up..."

"Certainly not!" he exclaimed, trailing his fingertips along the neckline of my gown. "And...the new house would be large enough, I suppose."

I nodded my encouragement. "It would indeed. Home, family... Erik, that's our future."

His grin matched mine when he brushed a kiss against my lips and set his forehead against my brow. "I love you, Christine. You gave me the future."

Future...and forever attached.

*****

Are some people born particularly luckier than others, or is it all in one's perception? Many would call me unlucky to love a man with a corpse's face. But I consider myself luckier than anyone else in the world for that same reason. Supposedly, Erik's face is some unfortunate tragedy, but to us, it is a blessing that drew us together. Perception as a whole is an interesting, unclear opinion at best, lacking a distinct right or wrong path. It is contingent on each and every individual, and if one is lucky, then one is just happy, no matter the circumstances or the details attached.

So I call us lucky and happy, and by such a perception, our ending will be perfection, full of love and bliss. It is my dream come true, and all because I made the right choice...

"A Heartbeat"

Told from Erik's POV. As a certain peace prevails after the unmasking, he attempts to teach Christine about the essence of his music.

I often stare at her when she sings under the pretext of teaching. That is my role, isn't it? Teacher, angel, tentative friend. She will be mid-aria, putting all of herself into tone and technique, presuming I am watching to correct any folly, but my mind will be far from where it is supposed be. It will be full of observances of the seemingly mundane: the interestingly deepened blue of her eyes this day, the tinged hue of her cheeks that one, the ever-present freckle near one temple, almost invisible to casual regard but never to my desperate examination. I often contemplate everything that is her, intrigued by the bits of soul I can always discern, the way that when she is genuinely happy, that soul peeks out from her eyes as if seeking my own and saying, 'Here I am, all for you'.

Yes, I am convinced without a doubt that she is meant to be mine, that our very souls previously mentioned are mirror images of one another's, hers lighter for lack of sin than my tarnished one, but the same in makeup and essence. Despite the minimal amount of time I have spent amongst the world, I have come to realize how rare an occurrence it is to find the other half to one's soul. Too many mistake desire for destiny and end up unhappy and broken. Is it any wonder then that I am so desperate to hang onto this other half of mine? Neither of us could be happy without the other; it may seem presumptuous of me to argue that, but it is a blatant fact and reality. I argue what I *know* to be true.

This particular day, we were having our daily lesson, moved down to my home since I had been found out, and she was singing me a snippet of a Swedish folk song from her youth. I often picked her brain for inspiration, influenced by every aspect of music that I could get my hands on, and beyond that,

I simply delighted in hearing her. She could sing me anything, and I would fall as a willing slave at her feet. Her eyes twinkled as she came to the chorus. I read in those depths memories and nostalgic attachment, wondering which of her parents had taught her the song and what detailed images played in her mind's eye. To me, such a connection to one's past and childhood was unfathomable, my own such a cruel endurance, but watching her now and whenever she'd speak of hers made me wish for a time like that to cling to. Perhaps if I had had one of the pleasant sort, I'd write happier music, know happier emotions. But then again, perhaps I'd have ended up in a different place and would have never known Christine, and just as quickly as I pondered it, I re-embraced my own wretched existence before her. Every bit of it mattered and was glorious in its awfulness if it meant I'd end with her.

As she ceased her song, she smiled so brilliantly that I felt the glow of it like sunlight striking my masked face. She was stunning when she smiled, and oh, how I adored her playful moods. I counted myself fortunate to still have them as mine. For too long after she had learned I was no angel, she had denied me of them, acting reserved and unsure constantly in my presence. Somewhere along the way pushed by my insistent hands, we had resurrected our relationship and had found the seeds of the friendship that had been thriving. It wasn't what I wanted, but it would do for now.

"Well?" she demanded, her dark brows rising inquisitively. "Did you like it?"

I was seated on the piano's bench watching her where she swayed in the bow, and I nodded slightly. "It's certainly different than what I considered 'folk song' to be."

"But...did you like it?" Always seeking my approval. And it was not that she sought appreciation for the song itself; it was *her*, always her. And how I doted on her! I was never one to deny her an abundance of compliments, most especially on the voice I was shaping.

"Yes, Christine," I replied, my expression as light as hers had been. "You sang it lovely."

Her grin brightened all the more, and I was in breathless awe, staring wide-eyed as she giggled. As always, it was a most exquisite sound to my ears. "You know me far too well," she stated the very thoughts in my head. Was there truly any doubt that could be considered then of our connection?

I shrugged off her comment even as it thrilled me, feigning nonchalance when the tinge of a smile I gave betrayed and revealed what I hadn't shared.

"So what are we working on today?" she posed, leaning toward me with her little fingers curled against the wood of the piano. "*Faust* again? ...Something a little more...undisclosed perhaps?"

I knew exactly what she was getting at. For a couple of weeks now, she had been pushing to sing some of my own composed music. It had been my fault for putting the concept in her head with an idle comment of how beautiful she would be able to sing the heroine's role in my opera. *My fault*, I repeat, for I had bypassed the stubborn streak in her, the acutely vivid memory that kept her recalling every utterance I made. I had known no peace since then.

"Soon," I promised, receiving a disappointed pout that on any other subject would have broken me. "Remember, *petite*, you are working with the composer on his very own work. It requires a bit more on your part than your usual roles. There are a few concepts you have yet to learn."

"Teach me, *ange*," she bid, tilting her head as her curls tumbled over her shoulder and caught the focus of my eye with their silken shapes. "Whatever I have 'yet to learn', I can; I promise."

Yes, she would. Such a musician with the hint of a perfectionist within, not to the extent of myself, thank God, but enough to keep her pushing herself.

"Today's lesson will be our starting point," I

115

told her, delighting in the flare of excitement she openly gave. "But you must trust me and do as I say without protest or questions."

"Don't I always?" Her brows lifted so sweetly innocent, and I was sure we both wanted more at that moment; we both wanted our meaning to extend beyond a lesson in music and vocal technique. *If only...*

"All right," I conceded, rising slowly with my confident air of teacher in place as I strode around the piano to face her. "Our lesson today will be on the importance of silence."

"Silence?" she dared to utter before clamping her hand over her mouth with an apologetic shrug.

I didn't need to scold her misstep, so I continued. "Silence is music in its own right. It is the point from which music flows...in the silence. It is a beginning and an ending." I stood close enough to her that the delicious fragrance of vanilla wafted my senses; intermingled with her own scent, it intoxicated me as always. In a gentle voice, I bid, "Close your eyes, Christine."

She did not hesitate to comply, and her blatant trust was humbling to behold. Anyone else, knowing who I truly was, the phantom and Opera Ghost in every regard, would never so willingly put their life and well-being in my hands, but she did so on a daily basis.

I was shaking, glad she didn't see it; that was something she would not understand. My hand slowly reached for hers, catching it, overcome when she willingly wrapped her fingers around mine. It wasn't common for me to touch her or to dare cross the line of propriety, but she gave no regard to that, never once opening her eyes, never appearing apprehensive or afraid. If anything, I caught the tinge of a grin still existing on her lips.

As I lifted her hand, I studied it as I often did when she wasn't noticing, reveling in the small, slender fingers and graceful arch of her knuckles;

116

every bit of her was a work of art. I guided that beautiful appendage to myself with a tremble that raced through my body and pressed her open palm to my chest at the place of my heart.

"Can you feel that, Christine?" I whispered so as not to cause too many ripples in the quiet hanging peacefully in the air.

She nodded, her smile growing. "Your heartbeat," she whispered back, eyes still obediently closed.

"Exactly. A heartbeat is the first music, first rhythm, first sound a baby learns in its mother's womb. For every single person, it is an initial inspiration, calming, soothing. Everything, Christine, every sound in the world is a form of music: the bird in the tree whose song is interspersed with rustling leaves as percussion, the pounding of ocean on shore, the quiet peace of a snowfall, the cascading trickle of raindrops. Music exists beyond the sphere of instrument and voice, of aria and symphony. It's in the air we breathe, in nature and world, playing incessantly at the start of the first heartbeat."

I was telling her all of this so softly and watching her intently. These were my thoughts, my own musings that I had never had any notion to reveal to anyone, but she sparked impulses within me to share everything I had ever given pause to consider. I wanted her to understand me as fully as I already understood her and feel my own inspiration in her veins as well.

I continued to speak at the level of a whisper, "Listen, Christine. Feel my heartbeat and find its song. Only in silence can you hear it." My free hand found her other one still at her side, and less trepid this time, I guided it to her chest and matched the pose we had with mine, so that her palms were pressed to both of our beating hearts. "Two hearts beating together make a more beautiful music than any ever heard."

The moment I said the words, I regretted them,

terrified to push her and have her learn my feelings at the same time as I longed for just that. I had frightened her away from me once before and was determined never to do so again, even if it meant keeping to these roles for as long as we had to.

So though she gave no reply, save the still-existent smile on those full, pink lips, I put aside any romantic notions and went on, reluctantly drawing her hand away from my heart. "Listen to your own song, Christine. It plays within you, in your very soul. Too often it gets overlooked in the chaos of the world around us. Only in silence can you find it again... It is inspiration and creativity, and it is the stem of all music, the root, the starting point."

Though I would have loved to keep touching her even if it was only against the smoothness of her hand, I slowly drew away and instructed, "Keep your hand against your heart and your eyes closed. I am going to play something, and all I want you to do is listen within yourself. Let the music enter you and seek your soul. *Feel it*, Christine. Don't think or make a sound. Just feel."

I sat before the piano keys again, my eyes only on her as I began to play. It was a beautiful, lyrical aria from my opera, and I watched and saw the wonder of it crease her pretty features, knowing that she knew it was mine. The smallest sigh fell from her smiling lips, her entire body instinctively leaning toward the piano as if in some strange way, it yearned to crawl inside and become an integral part of the melody. If only she knew she already was. I had composed every bit of this opera for her, from emotions I felt *only* for her. The piece I played was intended for her to sing, composed with her voice in my inner ear. In some way, I thought sure she knew it; the bliss on her beautiful face was amazing to me, the subtle flickers of emotions the melody brought to life that were genuinely real.

As I played, I contemplated my next move in this lesson, pondering for the hundredth time if she could handle what I was about to lay before her. For while this particular piece was solely beautiful and innocent, the opera itself was hardly that. It was...sensual; it was intimately erotic in a way I knew my sweet Christine had yet to fathom. Hence why I had never shown her my music. I wrote from a place of desire and sexual frustration; attribute it to a lifetime denied the fulfillment of such urges and a more recent present of learning their true extent with my first glimpse of Christine. Every desperate need, every fervent arousal, I had poured into my opera, and I was entirely certain that just as she had been able to feel the sentiments in this innocent aria, Christine would be able to feel the driving desire of the next piece, this one a passionate duet I had written with the intended performers being her and myself. It was absolutely brimming with provocative lust in a most primal vein, and I was terrified how she would accept it, *if* she even could.

With one last long look at her heavenly face and a resolution that this was a lesson she very well needed to ever fully be mine, I modulated the key and flowed seamlessly into the next piece. The very first chords shook her; I saw it in a shudder that racked her entire body, her smile fading away. She never opened her eyes, likely not wanting me to see what she was feeling, but the eruption of a pink blush across her skin gave it away. Her fingers curled into the palm against her chest, her elbows suddenly drawn into her body and arms wrapping around herself tight as she shivered. I didn't know if such a reaction was out of terror or desire, and she was determined to keep the answer hidden.

I continued to play with the music seeping into my own veins as well. It was always the case. I could never detach myself from it or the emotions I had felt upon composing it. What began as a tingle through my limbs rapidly became a dull throb, intensified all the more by her nearness. *She* was it, the object of my lust, the craving in my veins, the temptation of my every desire. And she was so close, practically within my grasp. If I reached out, if I succumbed and took her in my arms, she could be mine...

My hungry gaze trailed her face, noting how she bit her bottom lip, lines creasing her flawless brow, and I could see every erratic, trembling breath she took. My God, she was aroused! There was no denying it and no denying that my music was the cause. I couldn't decide whether or not to hate myself for that reality. My pure Christine was having her very first taste of passion, and I was far too humbled to be allowed to witness it to berate my own deceptive hand in its presence.

On the wings of desirous flames, I hoarsely demanded, "What do you feel, Christine?"

I almost thought she wouldn't answer, jolted by my voice and blushing furiously even though her eyes never opened. Finally, in a quivering tone, she answered, "I...I don't know."

"Tell me, *petite*," I huskily breathed.

She grew even redder, her arms hugging her body. "I...I've never felt anything like this..."

"Does it frighten you?" I dared to ask, my eyes never leaving her and my hands still playing despite the near fever I could feel upon my skin.

She nodded. "Yes, ...it terrifies me."

I knew I should end things there; rationale begged for it. The last thing I wanted was to scare her away. But didn't she need to learn and understand? I was too encouraged by the sheer fact that she could decipher desire so vividly in my music, and I reminded myself that she could never truly accept me if she shied away from such things.

"Open your eyes, Christine," I commanded gently, never ceasing the provocative tune.

She was reluctant; I wondered if she would refuse, but then those lashes fluttered and blue depths met mine, hazy with desire and yet laden with such trust in me that I wondered if I deserved it.

Crooning tenderly, I bid, "Come to me,

120

Christine," and watched her timidly walk around the piano, hesitate, and then sit on the empty space of the bench beside me, shaking so hard that I could see it.

I never stopped playing as I explained, "This is my music, Christine. It is raw, and it is intense; it will inspire within you new sensations you never fathomed could exist. I need you to understand that, to truly listen and let it into your soul if you are ever going to sing it." How much more lay beneath my words? How many of them pleaded for acceptance of my very self? "I am letting *you* into *my* soul by playing this for you. If you think it is too much for you, then we will stop and never speak of it again. But if not, if you can push beyond fear and uncertainty, then you will receive more than you ever could have imagined."

I knew what her answer would be before she even gave it, already aware of how desperately she wanted to please me. Our trust was as much a blessing as a weapon I would have to use against her if only to win her heart.

"I will sing it for you, *ange*," she whispered. "And I will try to make you proud."

To my absolute shock, meeting my eye one tremulous moment, she suddenly laid her head against my shoulder as I continued to play. I almost stumbled over the passage, too overwhelmed, glancing down at the top of her dark head with tears threatening. My sweet child... And here I was practically assaulting her with my music's potency! I could feel the shivers her little body suffered, her gasped breaths and racing pulse. It terrified her, and yet, for me, she willingly endured it without question or protest, trusting me with her protection. And though I desired her to inconceivable heights, I loved her so much that I modulated my sensual duet back to her beautiful aria. She relaxed within moments, sighing with returned bliss and all the while keeping her head delicately upon my shoulder.

When at last I ended the song with a flicker of sorrow in my soul, I told her, "We will begin to work on this piece tomorrow. Now I'll take you back to your dressing room."

Smiling her excitement with such a promise, she was jovial again on our journey above, everything else forgotten. If she noticed my despair, she pretended she didn't, practically bubbling when I left and vowing to meet me after rehearsal ended as always. And I knew she'd be there; she would never deny me...

I never played my duet for her again. I let her indulge herself with the aria, hearing so much potential for the more that I wanted but could not have. She wasn't ready... Perhaps she would be someday...

But before I could learn our ending, the Vicomte appeared in her life, and my dreams of love, acceptance, and desire shattered to shards of crystalline glass at my feet. He would be the one to convince her that such passion, no matter its valid existence and blessing, was a black and evil manipulation on my part, and my innocent Christine would believe him and deny what her soul was singing in every silent hour. Our ending would be tragic instead of happy, ...and all because I loved her too much.

"A Beautiful Lie"
In an effort to earn her happy ending, Christine accepts Erik's
proposition and learns love through pretend.

A sea of masked faces whirled around the makeshift dance floor on the stage of the opera house as the string ensemble played a brilliant waltz. It was the night of the annual Masquerade ball. Paris' finest were in attendance, boasting their generous patronage to the arts. Though they were masked, the most affluent made certain their presence was known, prepared to reap the benefits of their stature.

One such aristocrat, the Vicomte Raoul de Chagny, was recognized immediately. No mask could hide his flawless, handsome features, but even as the opera's managers attempted to fawn over him, the young Vicomte shooed them off to devote all his attention to his lovely companion for the evening.

Christine held his arm as they meandered through the crowd, making their way to the dance floor. She was poignantly aware of the gossip and blatant stares she was receiving. If only those busybodies had any idea that she was secretly engaged to Raoul! That would certainly give them something worth talking about! The very thought brought a fleeting smile to her lips, and she suddenly felt the weight of the diamond engagement ring dangling on a chain around her neck and tucked beneath the neckline of her gown.

It was foolish that they were hiding the news. Raoul wanted to shout it from mountaintops; it was she who was so adamant about keeping quiet for the time being. It would cause a stir in both their worlds, but she hardly cared about that; it was someone else's world that she wanted to avoid stirring, someone whose retaliation to such news would be far worse than biting comments and sharp stares...

Pushing morbid thoughts aside, she did not allow her smile to waver as Raoul began to lead her in the dance steps. No, no dark thoughts tonight. They would still be there waiting tomorrow.

Christine's feigned bright countenance lasted well into the night as she spent dance after dance in Raoul's arms. Laughter fluttered from her lips; she was such a wonderful actress when she chose to be that no one suspected her exuberant expressions and doting smiles were far from real.

After awhile, nearly exhausted, she wandered to stand on the sidelines as Raoul reluctantly abandoned her to converse with a fellow patron. Her feet ached in her pretty little slippers, and realizing that she was likely disheveled from too many turns about the dance floor, she smoothed her gloved hands over her pale pink skirt and adjusted her lace-trimmed mask.

Glancing through the many faces seeking Raoul, her eyes came to rest on the elaborate staircase, a part of the scenery for the current production that was being used by the partygoers this evening. At the top of the stairs, the crowd parted and revealed someone dressed as the Red Death.

Someone... She knew who it was immediately, and like a moth to a flame, she was drawn to him as the eyes behind the skeleton's head sought her out. She felt a shiver race the length of her spine the instant his gaze found her, bearing into her as if he could see every secret on her soul. A wordless command seemed to resound over the noise of the crowd and the orchestra, and she automatically began to approach as he descended the staircase to meet her.

Christine felt like a sleepwalker, wandering the plane of dreamscape without acknowledgement to reality pirouetting about her; nothing existed but a beckoning voice somewhere in her subconscious. Her only motivation was to get to him, her angel, her captor.

At the foot of the staircase, he came to stand before her, holding her eyes mesmerized in his. Erik knew the sort of power he had over her, knew it was unethical to exploit her in such a manner, but he could not help himself. She was so beautiful, shining with youth and innocence. Torturously, he had watched her spend the night in the arms of the Vicomte, longing to be the one in his place, to hold her, to feel her against his heartbeat where she belonged. And now there was no Vicomte to destroy the illusion; now she was his.

Erik trailed eager eyes over her, taking in her flushed cheeks beneath the edge of her mask, the tendrils of baby curls clinging to her temples, but as he observed and sought to memorize every nuance, his gaze abruptly halted, his expression darkening.

"What is it?" Christine heard herself ask in a breathless whisper as if the voice were no longer her own.

He did not answer. Following the path of his locked gaze, she saw what he did, and her heart leapt in her chest. *Her ring!* During the dancing, it must have escaped, and it was now on display for everyone to see, ...for *Erik* to see.

"Erik," she stuttered, fighting to devise some sort of plausible explanation.

But before she could realize what he meant to do, his gloved hand caught the trinket as it glinted off the stage lights, and with a harsh tug, the chain around her neck broke free, dropping the ring into his palm.

She gasped, her hand clutching her now bare throat. She could feel the sore indents from the fierceness of his actions, and their telling presence surprised her. For all his temper and rages, Erik had never laid a hand on her with the intention of causing pain. But there was no question of his intent at present as his eyes shot fire.

He nearly growled at her with the intensity of his anger and desolation, and with a sudden swirl of his cloak, he vanished from her sight as if he had never been there at all.

Wide-eyed, Christine stared at the open place where he had stood, her hand grabbing at her throat, missing the heaviness of her necklace. She was shaking from head to toe. Never before had she seen such a look in his eyes; it frightened her.

Hardly taking a moment to consider her actions, she darted into the crowd, rushing for the edge of the stage. Before she could arrive at its escape, a hand caught her arm, and she gave a terrified cry as she flipped around.

"Christine, what happened?" Raoul asked, worried by her frantic expression.

But she could not answer as she yanked out of his hold. Shaking her head in wordless apology, she turned and hurried back on her intended path, hearing him call her name after her as she lost herself in the vast crowd.

Making sure that Raoul did not follow, she disappeared down the long corridor of dressing rooms. It was dark and empty now; no one was around to help her or find her. But she refused to consider that as she stumbled into her dressing room, locking the door behind her and barring out the world.

She hesitated only long enough to light an oil lamp, and then mustering every ounce of courage she possessed, she faced her mirror.

"I know you're here," Christine said confidently, pleased that her voice did not tremble as her body did. "Come out."

Her reflection in the glass began to fade as the hidden doorway opened to her trepid eyes. The Red Death himself stood stoically framed by the mirror's base, his powerful gaze piercing her like a lance.

Straightening her shoulders and insisting to her lackluster courage that she was not afraid, she demanded, "Give me back my ring."

Apathy was his chosen demeanor as he strode into the room, ignoring her command. "The Vicomte will be quite worried when he finds that you have so carelessly run off. He will think that you have encountered some terrible misfortune."

Christine stifled every instinctive urge that

begged her to move away. Extending her palm as she fought not to quiver and cower, she again demanded, "My ring."

Erik regarded her bemusedly. "Have you lost something?"

"You had no right to take it from me."

"Your ring? I haven't seen it." Erik glanced at her bare throat and cringed at the marks his fierceness had left on her flawless skin. ...Heartache was a powerful emotion. "Your fiancé will be sore when he learns that you have lost your engagement ring."

The bitterness in his voice stung like a harsh slap, and Christine stammered, "It...it isn't like that. I haven't given him a definite answer-"

"Don't you dare lie to me!" Erik snapped. "I will not tolerate lies! I deserve the truth!"

Shaking, she lowered her eyes to the carpeted floor. "I...I was going to tell you..."

"Were you? Or did you plan for me to learn the news *after* the wedding perhaps?"

"Erik, please." She couldn't look at him; the pain in his voice was so raw, so real. She had not considered how much she would hurt him, preferring to think of him only as the villain standing in the way. Now there was no denying that even villains had hearts as Erik's seemed to spill its secretive contents in every beautiful tone.

But a pause had him reining emotions again, every one that should have been called unacceptable, and replacing them with a malevolent sneer, he chose cruelty as his weapon. "You deceived me, played with my heart like an ignorant child. I have killed for far less."

Christine's eyes darted to his. *He couldn't possibly mean to...*

Erik laughed aloud at her assumption. "Killing you wouldn't be beneficial to me." Leaning back on her vanity, he bridged his fingers thoughtfully in front of him, studying her in the dim lamplight, and finally contended, "I have a proposition for you."

"A...a proposition?" She could not help but be on guard.

"You want to leave here, to marry the boy, to have me permanently out of your life. I can give you all of that...for a price, of course." He pondered a moment, though he obviously already had his plan in mind. "I want one week, one week with you...as *my* wife."

"What?" The color drained from her face, pooling out with the arrival of terror, and her brow furrowed beneath the weight of her thoughts as she fought to understand.

"I realize that I can never have you in the way I wanted, not with that boy constantly tugging from his corner. All that will result is an ending of pain and death if I choose to ignore your wishes and force my own on you, so I am willing to settle for one week to live the life I should have had."

"I...I don't understand what you mean. I cannot be your wife."

"No, but you could pretend. You are the most wonderful little actress I know. How many of your contrived smiles for the Vicomte lately have been fraudulent?" Erik tilted his head, running eyes over her as she shivered under his powerful gaze. "I want one week with the woman I love loving me in return, being my wife with all the duties and privileges that title brings, ...even if the emotions behind it aren't real."

Christine shook her reeling head and demanded in a hushed tone, "How can you ask such a thing of me? I am to marry Raoul."

"Yes, poor handsome Raoul. You do realize that if we continue on our current trek, *he* will be the one to suffer. I may have said that I had no intention of killing you, but the Vicomte... He has stolen what should be mine. He must pay for that insolence. Choosing to do this could save his life." The more Erik spoke aloud of his random idea, the better it seemed. Christine, as his willing wife in a fantasy that for one week would be his.

"I...I couldn't possibly," she stammered. "What you are asking is too much."

"Is it? I am offering you your fairy tale ending and your handsome prince charming, the life you so adamantly claim to want. All I want in return is one week."

"As your *wife*." She said the word as if it were an insult.

"You have a choice to make," he retorted sharply. "And I advise you to consider well. Your future happiness and that of your precious Vicomte are at stake." Stepping toward the mirror, he called over his shoulder, "I expect your decision tomorrow. If you are here awaiting me after rehearsal, then you have agreed to be my loving, devoted wife; if not..." He trailed off, shrugging nonchalantly. "The Vicomte's welfare is of no concern to me."

With that, he left, retreating to his darkness as she stared wide-eyed in his wake.

Once behind the mirror's glass, Erik lingered, watching her, wondering at the thoughts in her head. He was disgusted with himself for the way he had treated her and the ridiculous proposal he had made. It wasn't what he wanted, but then again none of this was. It was immoral to force her into the role of his wife and cruel in a manner that he had never wanted to be towards her. Part of him hoped that she would refuse, but the other part... The other part wondered if it would really be so terrible to fall into the dream.

In the dressing room, Christine had hung her head low, her expression hopeless. Gently touching the boundary between them, Erik wished he could touch her instead, but barriers existed as more than glass plates when he knew he was the cause of her current sadness. As it was, they each had their roles to play, and yet tomorrow, they could be reversed and scripted into something new; tomorrow hope could be a dream instead of a nightmare. Tomorrow...

*****

The next day, Christine felt like she was in a daze. Her mind drifted in every direction, causing her to trip through rehearsal, fumbling entrances and notes. No matter how many times she went over an impossible ultimatum in her head, she was afraid that her choice had already been made for her. All she could do was accept it.

One journey would seal her fate. During lunch break, she escaped the confines of the opera house with a purpose, hurrying through the Parisian streets. One visit, one lie, and no one would seek her out; no one would know what she'd shamefully committed to hold as her decision. She told herself that it was for the good of everyone, that her sacrifice would ensure happy endings. ...But she didn't truly believe it.

Later as Monsieur Reyer ended rehearsal for the day, Christine wearily staggered to her dressing room. Her entire body trembled with the invisible weight in every step; she felt as though she walked to her own execution.

Nearly the instant she entered the room and closed the door behind her, the creak of the mirror's hinge caught her ear, and her eyes darted to the secret doorway in time to see the almighty Opera Ghost wander inside. He was obviously wasting no time claiming his prize when she recalled so many days where he wouldn't dare emerge from the dark and step into her light. Perhaps he didn't want to risk the chance that she might change her mind and flee, shattering his illusion before she had ever let it begin. His seemingly confident air angered her as it permeated off him in a glaring smirk; it was as though he knew that she would give in to his proposition.

"Good evening, Madame," he greeted. *Madame, his wife...*

She cringed with the thought, and he immediately scolded, "Ah, ah. You are to be my devoted, *loving* wife. Not one abhorrent expression if you want to preserve your future happiness."

It took every ounce of effort within her to wipe the hateful look from her eyes and replace it with a sweet smile. Biting back any retorted comments that yearned to break free, she instead said, "Good evening, *mon époux*. I was anticipating the moment when I would see you again."

Excitement bubbled within Erik. Even if this was all a lie, to read such a kind sentiment and see a smile on her lips was blissful. When was the last time she had bestowed a smile upon him? ...He couldn't even remember.

"I trust rehearsal went well," he stuttered. He was not the sort of man to fumble for words, but under the swelling emotions within him, he was nearly overcome.

"Not particularly," she replied. "I was distracted, ...thinking about you." It might not have been true in the pleasant sort of vein, but it wasn't a lie.

"I am delighted that I am the subject of your thoughts, but I wouldn't be a good teacher if I didn't say that I don't wish to interfere with your talent."

"Always the teacher first and husband second," she commented, feeling oddly sure that her assumption would be entirely accurate.

There was adoration beaming in his eyes, and it was so sincere that it shook her. She fought not to be influenced by his fantasy, to cling tight to the world as she knew it to be, but he seemed to desire the illusion, so desperate for her love that it fuzzed the distinct edges of reality and made her suddenly terrified what that would eventually come to mean.

"Well then," he broke into her muddled thoughts and with only a slight fumble to insist that it was anything but a natural gesture, he offered his arm, "shall we set out for home?"

She hesitated in spite of the game, knowing that going with him ended any chance to change her mind. She had to do this...for Raoul and their future. Swallowing back her fears, she smiled at him, her expression her own mask to hide behind, and slid her arm through his, laying her palm on his sleeve. It was the closest to a touch she had granted him since becoming aware of his true face.

Their journey was spent in uncomfortable silence. As the boat sailed them in view of Erik's hidden lair, Christine momentarily forgot her trepidations to admire the warm glow radiating out from the cracks of the door, welcoming her from the damp chill of the catacombs.

"I have dinner awaiting us," he told her, his voice jolting her back to the present. "You needn't worry about clothing; there is a wardrobe full of gowns in your room."

Her room... He had shown it to her once before, that first night she had come to this house when his guise had been that of an angel. Never had she explored it or stayed in its canopy bed, though its presence had been inviting.

Erik watched her carefully at every chance, urgently trying to decipher the thoughts in her every expression. Daring to break the fantasy for a brief moment, he asked the question that had been bothering him since they had left her dressing room. "What sort of explanation did you give the Vicomte for your absence?"

Her real discontent overcame her; she did not try to hide it. "I went to see him during lunch. I told him that I had an aunt in the country who was very sick and that I must go and attend to her for the week."

Bitterness twisted his stomach. Here she was at his side, but hours before she had been in the arms of the Vicomte, making vows of love and devotion to *him* instead. Almost sharply, he declared, "Your superior acting skills likely made him believe you."

Was he speaking of Raoul or himself..., Christine wondered but did not dare ask.

Succumbing to the lie once again before she could learn the truth, he lightened his tone and smiled at her sweetly. "Welcome home, my beautiful wife."

Erik helped her out of the boat but did not release her, keeping her hand captive in his gloved one. Still his eyes went to hers, asking permission without a word, but she only smiled with her actress' air and curled her fingers around his palm.

This was heaven! Erik had never known what happiness felt like. Lost in the dream, he ushered her to dinner in his elegantly decorated dining room, casting furtive glances at her between bites. Conversation was pleasant and seamless; he told her a story about one of the many misfortunes he had caused for Carlotta in such great detail that she laughed. He actually made her laugh!

As she finished the last bit of food on her plate, she said, "Supper was delicious. You are a wonderful cook."

"One of my talents that you were unaware of." He teetered a glass of red wine in his hand, making the liquid spin before he took a sip, always careful to avoid hitting his mask.

Christine suddenly wished there was still an entire plate of food in front of her. If dinner was over, then...what next?

Erik could sense her rising unease as she shifted anxiously in her seat. Setting his glass down, he suggested, "Would you like a hot bath? I know how chilled it can be here. A hot bath will help."

"That...sounds wonderful," she replied with a silent sigh of relief. Some sort of escape. Even if it was only delaying the inevitable...

"There is running water in your bath chamber and nightclothes in your armoire."

Christine nearly leapt to her feet. "Thank you. I will return soon." With that and a quick forced smile, she fled the dining room for her bedchamber. She did not hesitate to lock the door behind her, unsure what her *husband* would expect. Did the title, even if feigned, mean that he could enter any room uninvited? She was loath to find out.

*****

A little while later, Erik sat in his living room, studying the fire in the hearth absentmindedly when the sound of soft footsteps caught his ear. With the hint of reluctance, he turned his head and watched as Christine tentatively entered the room. His eyes took in the vision of her in her nightdress and wrap, but any pleasant thoughts died when he read the fear in her gaze, blatant despite her fake smile.

Slowly, he rose from his chair and took note with a stab of remorse how she jumped as if startled. Pretending he did not notice, he gently called, "Christine, come here. I have something for you."

She was dubious. He read suspicion amidst her reluctance to comply, but on shaky knees, she wandered closer to the hearth and halted a seemingly safe distance from him.

Erik stepped to the mantle and opened a trinket box set atop. Withdrawing its contents, he faced her but did not dare approach. He simply held out his hand and waited until she hesitantly took what he offered.

"A wife needs a wedding ring," he told her, but the ring she held had captured her attention.

She had never seen anything like it. The stone was large and pale purple, glinting and shimmering in the firelight. On either side of it were two smaller diamonds, pure and clear and dancing light like prisms.

"It's beautiful," she breathed, twirling it in her hand so that she could watch it sparkle.

"I purloined it during my stay in Persia. I never thought I'd have anyone to give it to."

Christine tore her eyes from the continuous glisten to regard Erik. "I can't accept this. It's yours."

He shook his head even as she held it out to him. "You are my wife, and I want you to have it. It's meant for you."

With a hesitant nod, she stared transfixed as she slipped it on her finger. "It fits perfectly."

"As I said, it is meant to be yours."

The sadness in his voice affected her. It was disconcerting that it brought such an overpowering urge to comfort him, an urge that she quickly denied.

Erik took a step closer, and she instinctively recoiled before forcing herself to remain in place. Her mind spun a web of thoughts about what was to come, but she tried to be brave and remember why she was doing this. *For a happy ending... Yes, this was for her happy ending.*

As she waited for her fate, to her surprise, he simply pressed a feather-light kiss to her forehead and then moved away again. She would have thought she imagined it, but his lips left a cold chill behind, invisibly branding the surface of her skin in memory.

"Goodnight, Christine," he bid as he strode back to stand before the hearth.

"Goodnight," she echoed with confusion creasing her brow. She knew and understood her wifely duty... Why was he denying it? Wasn't that what he wanted all along in proposing this game?

She pondered asking but quickly thought better of it, scampering to her room lest he change his mind. She would count herself lucky. Maybe this experience wouldn't be as awful as she had thought.

Erik listened to her leave but did not cast another glance in her direction. All he could do was wonder why he had begun this when it could only result in pain. Things would never change.

*****

The next day, Christine found it much easier to retain her jovial mood. Without the previous night's pressure, acting as Erik's wife was little more than being kind and congenial. As the minutes went by, it was to her own astonishment that her fake smiles became more and more real and anchored in her heart.

Refusing to let the hopelessness of the situation affect him, Erik chose to fall victim to the dream. He spent the day with her as he had always imagined: a shared breakfast, her lesson with him as diligent teacher, then reading together, telling each other snippets of text and discussing. After dinner, he even suggested a walk by the river, which she eagerly accepted with a grin he thought might be genuine.

As they emerged up into the world, Christine was suddenly aware of how deeply she missed it when hidden away underground. The air, though cold, was fresh and delicious against her skin, the dark evening sky alight with endless stars. She halted a few steps ahead, gazing upward in awe. Were the stars ever so bright?

"Don't you miss the world when you spend all day locked away from it?" she asked over her shoulder as he came to join her.

Erik shrugged. "I have seen little good come from this world you so love. It is no loss to me to be without it." His hand instinctively pulled the rim of his fedora lower as though it could hide the stark glow of the mask.

"But look at the stars, Erik. There are so many; it is amazing."

"For all the beauty God created, mankind is so intolerably ugly," he commented flatly. "It is a cruel reality." Before she could make a reply, he offered his arm. "Shall we?"

Nodding and smiling in return, she looped her arm through his without hesitation. It surprised Christine that she could become victim to this game as much as he was. It simply called for living in the present moment and pretending that this was the outcome to all the pain they had both endured.

Her eyes drifted to the glistening ring adorning the hand set atop his arm. *His ring...* With this ring, she was his wife. It left her to wonder if this was how their life together would have been if it were true.

Their walk was spent in silence but comfortably so. The breeze off the river blew frigid, and Christine leaned near to Erik, ignoring her mind's warnings as she savored the sensation of his body so near. It was so pleasant that she was disappointed when he finally led her back to the opera house and the catacombs, wishing for a few more minutes of such closeness.

Later after a hot bath to warm her again, Christine sought him out as she had the previous night. There was a lingering apprehension knotting her stomach that she could not be certain was unnecessary.

Much like the night before, she found him in the living room, standing near the fireplace, staring into the flames.

"Are you warm?" she asked, her voice breaking his reverie as he flipped around to face her.

"Oh," he replied, trying not to show how she had startled him. "The cold does not affect me. I am accustomed to it." A bit of his sadness returned with his tumultuous thoughts.

"Are you all right?" she asked, concerned in a way that did not need to be acted.

He nodded with a forced smile. "Yes, ...fine. It's getting late. You should go to bed."

"All right," she replied softly. She was about to turn and go when his voice stopped her.

"Christine?"

"Yes?"

Erik hesitated, not daring to step closer as he softly asked, "May I... May I kiss you goodnight?"

Her heart leapt in her chest, her voice trembling as she answered, "A husband does not need to ask his wife for a kiss."

Shaking his head, he told her, his eyes fiercely solemn, "I am not asking you as my wife. I am asking you as Christine."

She was strangely moved by his words, and without a word, she nodded her reply.

Hardly able to breathe, Erik approached as she tilted her face upward expectantly, watching him with nervous eyes. He ran his gaze over her, studying her face and parted lips. Never in his life had he felt more uncertain or more afraid.

Bending slowly, he only brushed his lips over hers, so gentle that a shiver raced his spine in sensation's wake. Then almost abruptly, he backed away again.

"Goodnight," he softly bid, dragging his eyes back to the fire.

Confusion formed deep wrinkles in Christine's brow. Was it wrong for her to want more? It had to be... But as much of a relief as it was that he did not ask more of her, she felt a queer sense of rejection and disappointment.

"Erik?" she called gently.

"Hmm?"

He would not face her, and without thought, she came to stand beside him, waiting until he turned to her. "May I kiss my husband goodnight?"

Erik stiffened, wanting to refuse, wondering if she was only playing well at his game, but all he did was give a single nod, his body's desire far too potent to fight.

Lifting her hand as her ring sparkled in the firelight, Christine cupped the unmasked side of his face in her palm, holding his fearful gaze. Her lips met his lightly at first, testing, careful to avoid the barrier of the mask. Gently, she began to move her mouth against his, coaxing him to respond, delighted when he did.

As his every detail consumed her senses, she grew lost in the strange foreignness of kissing him. She had only ever been kissed by Raoul, and never had she dared to take the lead as she now was. Erik's lips were different, cold as the catacombs and yet seeming to warm from contact with hers. ...Even as she kissed him, her body whispered that it wanted more.

Erik made no attempt to hold her, keeping his hands in fists at his sides even though they tingled with the need to touch. He imitated the motions of her kiss, unfamiliar with such an act but yearning only to please her. His entire body quivered with the swelling urge of desire, thick and heavy beneath his skin as he fought to keep control. But its fire was too bright and potent.

Abruptly, he burst out of her spell and jerked away, cringing beyond her reach. "Go to bed," he ordered, cold and inarguable.

Hurt shown in blue depths, so sharp that he bore its reverberating sting, but without protest, she obeyed, only casting an anxious glance back at him as she fled for the sanctuary of her bedchamber.

As soon as she was out of earshot, Erik succumbed and fell to the tears that had been threatening, sliding into a heap on his throne-like chair. He pressed his fingertips to his lips where hers had been, missing their softness and warmth. She would never understand how bittersweet every moment with her was considering his future of loneliness. Why had he ever started this accursed game?

In her room, Christine collapsed into her bed, but her mind was alert with visions of the past moments. She had been playing a part, hadn't she? The dutiful, loving wife... And yet why did it hurt her so much to be commanded out of his presence with desire left to feel like something worthy of shame instead of the exhilaration it had been only moments before in one solitary kiss? Everything about this was wrong, and yet had she ever felt more like herself than this past day spent with Erik?

What was she doing? She wanted to scream at her ridiculous mind. *Raoul* was her fiancé; he was the man she loved. All of this was an act, a role like so many others she had played. It would secure the future she wanted, the future she was determined to have. ...And yet more and more, she was forgetting that future. It was fading away with each smile she gave to Erik...

With a tormented sigh from her troubling thoughts, she buried her head in her pillow and prayed for sleep to take her away.

*****

The next morning, Christine awoke to a light rapping on her door. Pushing her bedraggled hair back from her face, she quickly leapt out of bed, smoothing her nightdress with suddenly nervous hands and scurrying to answer.

Opening a crack, she peered out with sleepy eyes.

"Good morning," Erik greeted, fully clothed and smiling cheerily.

"Is it morning?" she asked, her voice still thick with sleep.

"It is very early, but, yes, it is morning." His eyes traveled over what he could glimpse of her disheveled appearance with consuming tenderness. "As always, you are enchanting, no matter the hour."

She could feel her cheeks redden under his compliment, grateful the shadows hid it from his notice. "Thank you, but why, may I ask, are we awake at this early hour?"

"Actually," he began, "there is someplace I want to take you, and we need to have an early start to reach it. Dress warmly and meet me in the living room."

Nodding her consent, she watched him hurry away with a twinge of amusement. Had she ever seen him so excited about anything?

Quickly, Christine prepared, selecting a light grey, woolen gown with a thick, black cloak. Her long locks were weaved into a single braid that hung heavily against her back, simple yet pretty. She took an extra moment to regard her appearance in her vanity mirror, smiling at a girl who smiled back. That girl seemed genuinely happy, her blue eyes glowing with vivacity. She wanted to argue that it was a stranger, but it was *her*, *only her*, and how disturbing such a reality was!

Christine found Erik waiting impatiently in the living room, a travel bag in hand.

"What is that?" she asked curiously.

"You will see when we arrive." With that, he ushered her out of his home and to the world above.

Their first stop was the opera house stables, housing horses used mainly for show onstage. Without explanation, Erik sought out a lovely white horse, which neighed happily when it saw him and eagerly approached.

"He knows you," Christine declared, amazed.

Erik stroked the horse's long mane fondly. "Oh, Samson and I are old friends."

Cocking her head playfully to one side, she demanded, "Do you steal him often?"

"No, I *borrow* him often," Erik corrected with an innocent grin. "What does it matter? This poor animal hardly gets enough exercise as a stage horse, so in reality, I am keeping him in shape."

She just shook her head and watched as Erik saddled the horse and loaded him with his pack. When he was ready, he turned to her with a tinge of hesitation.

"Do you mind riding with me on Samson? It is much easier than saddling another horse, especially considering that Samson is as gentle as a lamb. I cannot say the same for some of the others."

"I would be happy to ride with you," she replied. "I haven't ridden since I was a child."

"Don't be afraid. I'll hold onto you." Meeting her gaze, he assured, "I won't let go."

"I know." There was something far deeper flashing between them: a vow, a loyalty, a devotion, and flustered, she looked away, busying herself with climbing onto the horse.

Erik swung on behind her, and immediately, his senses were assaulted with her: her scent wafting his nostrils, her soft, warm back pressed so firmly to his chest, wispy curls that had escaped her braid tickling his skin. Every detail brought memories of the previous night to the surface and made him ache to keep her as his forever.

Christine was grateful that Erik could not see

the tumult of emotions in her eyes. She wanted to scold herself and her betraying heart. What was wrong with her? Why could she only concentrate on his erratic heartbeat against her back and his shallow, tremulous breaths? Why was her every urge begging her to lean into him? She fought to focus her mind on the feeling of being horseback instead and the lack of stability as Samson adjusted to their weight, but as Erik tentatively brought his arms around her to hold her in place, her concentration was lost again.

Determined to keep control, Erik clicked to Samson to go and busied his attention with the task of riding. They left the stables and the opera's grounds and traveled by sideways and alleys through Paris. The sun had only just risen hidden behind a thick layer of grey clouds, and yet to Erik's eyes, so unaccustomed to natural light, even veiled sunlight burned and blinded him until he finally adjusted.

Everything was quiet, not many people on the streets at such an early hour, but he still took the byways, staying out of sight until, at last, the city ended and open land began.

As they picked up speed, Christine's eyes wandered the landscape, fields full of browning grass with dormant trees scattered sparsely about. Ahead of them, the trees thickened, and Samson's hooves crunched brown leaves as he entered thicker brush.

The ride was long. They went from forested areas to open fields and back again, occasionally passing a lavish estate house. Christine had no notion where they were and wondered how Erik could tell when they passed nothing that could be considered any sort of landmark. The air around them held a mid-fall chill as the sun fought to brighten up grey clouds, but cold was inconsequential. Christine did not even notice its sting with Erik so close as their bodies seemed to create an impenetrable heated barrier.

After awhile, deliciously warm and content as she was, Christine dozed off, her head leaning gently against Erik's chest and cradled by his heartbeat.

Erik gazed at her in silent adoration, studying her as she slept, her features beautifully peaceful. His eyes were drawn to the lovely line of her throat, and he had the urge to press kisses down the length of that creamy column, to burrow his lips in its crease and taste her skin. He could fantasize such a scene into existence: an outing with his lovely bride, over-laden with eager caresses and kisses, the very libretto of a couple in love... By his own game, he should have had the right to act it out, yet still he hesitated. How could he take such liberties with a constant fear that in the backs of blue eyes, disgust ran rampant and would never fully diminish? The fantasy in his head was preferred to the fantasy in his arms...

It seemed all too soon when they finally arrived at their destination. Erik pulled Samson to a halt, the motion rousing Christine as with a flush of embarrassment, she sat up straight and tall in the saddle and tried to create as much distance as she could.

"I'm sorry," she stuttered, casting flustered glances over her shoulder. "I guess I fell asleep."

"No apology is necessary," he replied, hoping she wouldn't catch the disappointment in his voice. Swinging down from the horse's back, he told her, "We're here."

A chill overtook her where his body had been keeping her warm, and she missed its branding imprint. But forcing her eyes to scan their surroundings in a lackluster attempt at distraction, she shook her head in confusion at the vast number of leafless trees in every direction.

"And where exactly is here?" she asked skeptically.

"Patience." Lifting his arms to help her down, Erik half-expected her to refuse, but she didn't, setting her palms atop his shoulders and letting him aid her descent. Taking it as encouragement, he did not pose question as he caught one of her hands in his and began to lead her forward. "This way."

"But the horse," she protested, glancing back at the idling animal.

"Don't worry about Samson. He won't go too far. It always seems inhumane to me to chain him up."

She nodded her understanding, but words fled her as he brought her to a clearing ahead.

"What is this place?" she breathed, gazing in awe. What stood before her were the remnants of what appeared to be a medieval hall. The basic stone walls stood covered in vines, weathered with age; in places, they had corroded completely, leaving open holes that extended up to the roofless sky as daylight and cold poured in around them.

"I found this when I first came to France," Erik told her, watching her take it all in and pleased with her astonishment. "There are many such places all over the world; you would be surprised. They are the remains of a bygone age, lost amid nature."

"Was it a castle?"

"A small one, probably belonging to a lord or count." Gently tugging on the hand he still held, he led her through a long crack in the front wall and into the castle.

It was just as Erik remembered. Before them was a stone staircase leading up to a platform, all that remained of the second floor. Everything else between decaying stone walls was open with sparse patches of grass and bushes growing about. The leftover castle had become a part of the forest itself.

"And no one knows this is here?" she asked, incredulously scrutinizing every feature.

"I'm reasonably sure that it is forgotten. Of course, I haven't been here in years." Releasing her hand, Erik wandered into the middle of the small room. "I used to come here and write music with my violin. Every piece was so ridiculously melancholy and wallowing."

"Wallowing?" she asked with a smile. "Was

none of it happy?"

"I don't think I wrote a happy note until I met you. It's impossible to write about happiness if you've never known it."

"After our wedding, you mean?" she teased, thinking he was playing the game.

But his expression was cast in solemn seriousness. "No, I mean the moment I first saw you and was overcome by your beauty."

His honesty made her uncomfortable, and shifting back and forth nervously, she avoided his stare and changed the subject. "I didn't know that you played the violin. Why have you never played for me?"

"I haven't played in a long time," he replied, "but if you like, I will play for you when we return home."

It was surprising to her that she knew so little about him, and yet she realized that she had never taken the time to learn. She had spent every moment running from him, being afraid of things that didn't seem to be real anymore. How could they be real in this fantasy game of make believe?

"Christine," Erik called, drawing her mind out of her thoughts, "sing."

"What?"

"Just sing."

Raising one dark brow with another unspoken question, she complied with his command. Taking a deep breath, she let her full soprano pour forth. Her first note startled her as it resounded crystal clear off the stone walls, and she jumped with surprise. But at Erik's encouraging smile, she began again, this time expecting the resonating echo that followed.

Erik leaned against what remained of a stone stair rail, his eyes feasting on the vision of her as her beautiful tone drew him under her spell. She had chosen Marguerite's Jewel aria from *Faust*, and as she glided effortlessly through the notes, he felt a shiver rack his body. Had any earthly sound ever been so exquisite?

She landed on her final high note, and the full pitch bounced around them, her smile brilliant and beaming with her achievement. How he longed to be a part of the scene!

Before the magic was lost, he sang a line of recitative from *Faust's* final act.

Christine felt goose bumps arise at the sound. It was no wonder that she had once mistaken him for an angel. No mortal man could possess such golden tones. He had not sung to her since he had been her angel, and hearing him now made her realize how much she felt a loss without his music.

With never a hesitation, she replied with Marguerite's answer, falling into the role as he then began their final duet in the opera, singing to her:

"Oui, c'est toi je t'aime..."

Erik did not approach; he stayed at the stair rail, but his gaze bore into her as he sang, his voice weaving around her. She stared back, almost mesmerized, and when it came time for her to sing, he heard her voice quiver before becoming strong, her expression laden in awe as if to insist she hardly felt worthy to sing with him.

How he wished that this were not a game they played, that her sung words of love had true sentiments behind them!

As the song ended, Erik began another, delighted when she smiled with genuine pleasure and continued to sing with him.

They did not cease their musical interlude until much later when they had sung through half a dozen songs, their voices intertwined in a brilliant beacon of sound. Then almost reluctant to end, he brought his travel bag up the staircase to the remaining platform at the top and revealed to her excited eyes a large blanket, which he spread atop the stone floor and a packed lunch. Lounging, they ate as grey clouds passed above their heads in the nonexistent roof.

Sipping a glass of wine, Erik told her, "I have

dreamt of bringing you here for so long; I knew you would appreciate such a place."

"It's beautiful," she replied, clutching her own glass in both hands. In her mind, she contemplated the previous night for the hundredth time, wanting to voice her thoughts and ask the questions his behavior had incited. But instead, she chose another difficult topic and hesitantly asked, "Erik, if I asked you a question, ...would you give an answer and not be angry with me for it?"

His brow furrowed, but he said, "If I can, I will tell you anything you'd like to know."

She paused, sipping her wine before softly putting her curiosity into words. "What happened...to your face?" Once it was said, she could not look at him again.

Erik's entire body stiffened. His impulse was to snap at her for daring to ask such a thing, but he commanded every inkling of self-control to stay calm. He reminded himself that she was not trying to hurt him, that she couldn't realize. Swallowing back his pride, he attempted to sound detached and aloof as he said, "I don't know... Can we find a more pleasant topic of discussion?"

"No," she insisted, made confident by his lack of anger. "You keep saying that there are so many things I don't know about you. Well, I'm trying to learn, ...and as your wife, I think I deserve to know the truth."

He felt inclined to argue that fact, but clenching his jaw tight with repressed emotion, he reluctantly revealed, "I was born this way... My mother said that I was marked by the devil."

Christine wanted to touch him and give him some form of solace as she glimpsed a pain he seemed disinclined to share, but she kept still as he continued speaking, his gaze focused on his glass.

"I never considered myself marked by the devil; I believed I was just unfortunate or that perhaps God cursed me with this face that so disgusts you as a cruel joke. From what I have seen in my lifetime, He isn't a very fair God."

Shame crept with a pink blush over her skin as she remembered the way she had condemned and run from him after stealing his mask away. She had only considered *herself* at the time and her fear; never had she thought that he was just a man whose fate had been thrust upon him, who suffered far more than any human being should for something that he was born possessing.

"Erik," she called tenderly, her hand timidly setting atop his, "it is a face, nothing more. It is skin, muscle, bone; it is not you or your heart or soul. Those are the things that shine through, and they are beautiful."

"Don't," he commanded, pulling from her grasp. "Don't play my wife now and give me honeyed lies. I can't bear it."

"I'm not lying-"

"You were repulsed by what you saw!" he nearly growled at her. "You told your perfect fiancé that my face was grotesque and deformed, a *monster* you called me."

Cringing, she felt tears threaten to well up at her own guilt and cruelty. Only now through his eyes did she see how ignorant she had been. "You're right. I did say those horrible things to Raoul. But I regret every word. I'm sorry, Erik. You are *not* a monster; you are a good man."

"Stop, please, stop," he suddenly begged, and the desperation in his voice silenced her. He looked as if he would cry. "I can't dare let myself believe you. Go back to pretending, Christine. Play your role as my wife, and don't say anything else about that."

"Why?" she whispered through her own tears.

"Because I can't accept it to be true. Because if it is, then all I am left with is the question of why you chose *him*, of why I wasn't good enough for you..." Abruptly, he forced composure and hid the extent of his pain as he coldly demanded, "Play your part, or I will have to go back on my word and end this game and the Vicomte."

His threat wasn't valid; Christine knew that he wouldn't follow through on it, but she gave up anyway and with only the sheen of tears in her eyes to reveal the truth, returned to his game.

Unspoken thoughts and fake smiles shadowed the rest of the afternoon. She was grateful when they finally returned to the opera house, and she could have some time alone. In the solitude of her room, she was finally allowed to let her tears overcome her.

It was quite late when Christine emerged. She had attempted sleep, but could not find it, tossing and turning until she finally had to rise. She wondered if Erik was still awake and was almost pleased when she saw the light of a fire coming from the living room. Its warmth called to her and drew her in as her bare feet wandered silently across the carpeted floor.

She didn't need to make a sound; he seemed to feel her approaching presence, turning to regard her as she paused in the doorway.

"Couldn't sleep?" he asked gently.

She shook her head. "Neither could you, it seems."

"I had a lot on my mind."

Christine shifted back and forth and softly asked, "Me?"

"Always you. I don't think I ever have a thought that isn't about you."

With the hint of a smile on her lips, she entered the room, lingering a fair distance from where he stood near the hearth. "Earlier, you said that you would tell me the answer to anything I asked."

"Yes?" Erik probed with an inkling of reluctance as he recalled her last question.

She couldn't say why she needed an answer or where she found the bravery to ask, but the words tumbled out of her mouth. "Why did you send me to bed last night like a disobedient child?"

"Christine-"

She could tell that he meant to dissuade her from her train of thought, so she quickly went on. "I came here and agreed to your terms under the impression that I would be required to fulfill the duties of a wife, and yet you haven't taken what is rightfully yours to take."

"It is rightfully your *fiancé's* to take," he corrected sharply, "when you become *his* wife."

"I am not his wife," she protested. "I am yours."

Snapping his fingers, he pointed at her. "And *that* is exactly why I sent you away. Because this is all a game to you, albeit a game I started, but a game just the same. I do not want you in my bed because you feel you must in order to save your precious Vicomte's life. I want you in my bed because you want me, because you choose me, ...because you love me..."

On shaky knees, Christine slowly closed the distance between them, coming to stand before him. Her voice trembled as she bid, "Pretend that I am your wife, and I will pretend that I love you."

"Christine," he breathed, a flash of tears in his eyes at the very idea.

Lifting a hand to trail her fingertip over the outline of his lower lip, she whispered, "I love you, my husband."

That was all she needed to say for Erik to eagerly fall into the fantasy again. Perhaps he just yearned to believe in it so badly, but it was easy to block out reality and the rest of the world.

Before she could realize his intention, he captured her lips with his in a fierce kiss, refusing to listen when common sense begged him to hold back. This was the way he had wanted to kiss her the night before: passionate, deep, fervent. His arms wrapped around her soft body, pulling her flush against him, encouraged when her arms encircled his neck.

Christine's head was swimming. Never before had she felt anything so powerful. Liquid heat coiled in her belly as she felt the hard maleness of him pressed firmly against her; it coursed through her veins until it settled with a dull throb between her legs.

Suddenly, he yanked his lips away, unable to release her from his embrace as his hands clutched the soft fabric of her nightdress.

"Tell me what you are imagining," Christine breathlessly gasped, gazing at him through darkened eyes.

"Imagining?"

She nodded. "Yes, today we were married in a beautiful ceremony in a church...," she trailed off, waiting for him to continue the story.

Erik immediately understood. "You wore a gorgeous gown of white with lace trim, and I cried when I saw your beauty as you walked down the aisle. I vowed to love you forever beyond life and death, and when we sealed our love with a kiss, it was magic, so perfect, so eternal. And all day long, I envisioned our wedding night and showing you how much I love you."

"And now it is our wedding night," she urged, lost in his words.

"Yes, and I will make love to you as I always dreamt I would." His voice was husky with the desire burning his body, but suddenly, he shook his head and protested, "No, ...no, this isn't real."

"It's a fantasy," Christine agreed, her palm cupping his masked cheek. "And I want to be lost in the fantasy with you. Please, Erik, let the fantasy be real."

How could he deny it when he ached for just that? As his eyes bore into hers, he swept her into his arms and carried her to her bedroom. He didn't want to consider anything beyond this moment when her eyes told him that she truly wanted him as well.

Setting her on her feet in the center of the room, Erik acted out the fantasy in his mind. Taking great care, he unbraided her beautiful curls, letting them fall free and loose over her shoulders. Then patiently, he undressed her, not touching skin until she was completely bared to him.

She blushed under his ravenous gaze as he studied every inch of her, but he glimpsed no shame or regret, only a shyness that made his heart ache with adoration.

With the most delicate touch, he began to explore her flawless skin. It amazed him to watch his stark white hands with his long fingers, details he had known as his for his entire life, and then contrast them with hers, her creamy, smooth flesh, every nuance fragile and perfectly cast. Her eyes closed beneath heavy lids, her breaths echoing around him, and it was the greatest delight to know *he* was causing such feelings in her. When his fingertips found her so wet and ready for him, a groan rumbled in his throat.

Hardly able to wait for patience to catch up, he carried her to bed and laid her atop the mattress, quickly undressing beneath her fevered stare. When at last, he was bared and towering over her, she parted her legs, never a hesitation in the depths of her blue eyes.

Erik tried to be gentle as he entered her, shuddering as her wetness surrounded his aching body, but she cried out and clung to him with fisted knuckles.

"Sshh," he crooned, pressing penitent kisses to her forehead as he held still within her. "The pain will subside in a moment."

Christine nodded with wide eyes, trusting him in a way she never had before. And when he began to move within her, she knew no pain, only desire.

Erik was tender with her, relishing the delicious sensations as they built within his body. There was no rush; he wanted her to find pleasure first and was only too happy to give it. Only when she lost all control, crying out his name as her body spasmed with ecstasy did he seek his own and a bliss he never wanted to end.

Afterward, neither of them spoke. They lay

under the covers as he held her, but he was unsure what to say, what to feel and believe. Eventually, Erik felt her drift off to sleep, and laying a tentative kiss to her brow, he watched her until his eyes grew heavy.

*****

A little later, Christine stirred from her slumber. It was Erik's sleeping form beside her that returned reality, and a slow smile curved her lips with the memories flickering in and out of focus. As her eyes studied him, taking in every detail of his masked face, she called gently, "Erik?" She had to wake him; she couldn't help herself.

"Hmm..." It was a long minute before he opened his eyes, but finding her beside him made him jump into a seated position with surprise. "It...it wasn't a dream."

"No," she replied, "not a dream, but not quite real either."

His fingers pressed to her lips to quiet her. "Don't talk about reality yet; it's still night."

Only too willing to comply, she smiled at him and reached up to trail her fingers over his mask. "What happens next?"

"What do you mean?"

Sighing contently, she explained, "Now that the wedding is over. What will happen to us tomorrow? What is our future?"

Never had he believed he would hear such words from her; it made him happily fall back into the dream. "Tomorrow we leave on an elaborate honeymoon, a tour of Europe with all the luxuries money can buy. When we return, you will sing in the opera, and I will write music in our lovely little house outside of the city."

"Is there a porch on this lovely house?" she asked with a blissful grin.

"Of course, with white spindles and a swing. We will sit on it every evening to watch the sun set and another day end." *If only...* He wanted to treat it lightly, but his heart ached with desperate disappointment.

Her fingers were still caressing his mask. Softly, she said, "I want to see your face."

His limbs went numb with the very idea, his head shaking a firm refusal as words failed him.

"You are my husband," she insisted with determination. "May I not look upon the face of the man I love?"

"Christine, ...you needn't do such a thing as penance for the words you said to the Vicomte. I do not expect you to find my face as anything but repulsive; you need not pretend otherwise to ease your conscience."

"In playing this game of pretend, we have had to forget the past and all past indiscretions. That is what I am asking of you now." She could see another refusal before it crossed his lips, and she continued, "You don't want to remove your mask because without it, you are vulnerable. Baring your face is a more intimate and frightening act than baring your heart. But, Erik, I've already seen your face; I see it still in my dreams at night. It doesn't disgust me. It is *your* face. It doesn't change who you are to me." She spoke a truth that had been present far longer than she realized.

"You are playing your part in this deception," he accused bitterly. "I can't bear to continue this now; I can't bear to have you look at my face and lie to me. Please, Christine, ...it would hurt too much."

"This is no game, and this is no lie. Let me show you that your face doesn't matter, that I am not repulsed by you. Trust me, Erik. Please, I am not lying to you."

His eyes raked her face, searching for the telltale crack in her pretense, but he couldn't find it. He yearned for her words to be true and needed to believe her. If his face didn't matter, it gave him hope.

His hands trembled as he gave in, and watching her intently, ready for the disgust he was so sure he'd see, he removed his mask.

Christine broke their shared gaze and shifted her attention to his scars. This was the first time she studied his face. The only other time she had seen it, she had cowered in fear and refused to look. It shamed her to remember that now. How quickly had she shunned him simply because of his appearance, something he had not caused and could not change.

Keeping her actions tentative lest he stop her, she lifted her hand and lightly traced the myriad of scars marring his cheek. It was skin; it was just skin. The texture was slightly different, the color slightly darker than the rest of him, but that was all. It was nothing to recoil from in disgust. It was only a face... It was ridiculous that *this* had stood as the barrier between them.

Erik shivered under her soft touch, tears welling in his eyes. "Stop," he gasped out. "Please stop."

Jerking her hand back, she worriedly asked, "Did I hurt you? I didn't mean to."

He was lifting the mask back to his face, but she caught his hand in hers and held it tightly.

"Wait," she protested frantically. "I'm sorry. I won't touch you again."

"You didn't hurt me," he replied, pulling free, but before he could replace the mask, she grabbed hold of his hand again, unwilling to let this end so easily. "Let go, Christine."

"Why? Why do you want to hide your face? I haven't given you any reason to."

Erik's gaze held hers furiously. "I accepted your feigned love; I will *not* accept your feigned compassion as well."

"But it's true-"

"The last three days have been nothing but lie after lie: every smile, every laugh, every kind word. I asked for lies, and you gave them to me. And this is one more."

Her hands clutched his to keep him from acting and hiding his face, and her eyes locked fixedly on his mismatched ones, staring deeply. "This is not a lie. And neither is this." With that, she leaned close and pressed her lips to his ravaged cheek. It was a long kiss, delicate, her lips soft against flesh that had never known the pleasure of any sort of human touch. Turning her face, she laid her smooth cheek against his scarred one, releasing his hand so that she could wrap her arms around him.

Erik was overcome with the desperation to believe this was real. How he ached and wished for it more than anything in his life! Crying softly, he nuzzled his cheek against hers, embracing her as if terrified to ever let her go again.

Drawing back after a moment, she smiled tenderly and asked, "May I touch you, or will it hurt you?"

"It doesn't hurt," he managed to say. "Your touch is blissful."

Once again, Christine lifted her hand to his cheek, holding his eye with a silent question as she caressed him. This time, he did not pull away, watching intently, studying her every expression as if terrified to know what she was feeling.

Softly, he said, "I am not a handsome man."

Her fingers moved with a careful ease as she replied, "That is arguable."

"I am not your handsome Vicomte."

"I never asked you to be." Her fingertips outlined the swell of his misshapen mouth, her mind matching realities and deciphering that these were the very same lips she had received dozens of kisses from only hours before. With the mask in place, they could almost be misconstrued as perfect.

Shuddering with rising desire, he replied, "You deserve a handsome man like the Vicomte."

"And you deserve to be loved." Her words were a hushed whisper, her gaze concentrating on her task and avoiding his. "Will you kiss me, Erik?"

Eagerly, he complied, finding her lips with his. His eyes closed, but hers remained open, taking in the sight of his true face as her hand brushed up and down the scars, her fingers growing accustomed to the texture.

Erik was aching with the need to possess her again, his hand drifting beneath the blankets to cup her breast. Drawing his lips away, he hoarsely whispered, "I want to make love to you like this...as myself with my true face."

Christine could only nod, arching into his touch as his fingers brushed over her nipple. She could feel passion swelling to life within her again. It overwhelmed her in a way she could not deny. Her lips found his scars with kiss after kiss as his caresses grew more fevered until the rest of the world was fading away to only desire.

*****

As day dawned, Christine awoke alone in her bed. She was shivering, missing the warmth Erik's body had given her, the pleasantness of his weight beside her. Slowly, she sat up, clutching the blankets to her chest, her curls tumbling down her back to dangle in messy coils around her. Her head felt hazy, her memories of the previous night flashing in rushed snippets. An image of him leaning over her, his eyes hungry with desire just before he had entered her, flickered in the forefront and caused her entire body to tingle in reply.

She needed to find him, needed to see him and know that he had similar thoughts and feelings. In a flurry of movement, she arose and dressed in a pale blue gown. It delighted her that her skin carried his scent, as though she had been marked as his, and a secretive smile tugged the corners of her lips upward and her heart with it.

Pausing at her mirror, she fluffed her thick bun of curls, beaming at her reflection before leaving the room. As suspected, she found him standing near the hearth, lost deep in thought. It was a sharp disappointment when she saw that he had replaced the mask, hiding once more behind its security.

Erik lifted his gaze as he heard her enter the room, his eyes bearing the sadness in his heart.

"I...I wondered where you were," she stuttered. A new sense of nervous awkwardness hung thick in the air between them. Nothing would ever be the same, ...and yet she wasn't sure that she wanted it to be.

Without a word, he held out his hand, offering what he held in his palm, and hesitantly, she took it, her hand barely brushing his.

"My ring?" she asked, a tremble in her voice as she studied the Vicomte's engagement ring.

"Go back to your fiancé," he replied, his voice tight and bitter. "This ridiculous game of pretending is done."

"W...why? The week isn't over-"

"You needn't worry. You have played your role superbly. I don't think anyone else could have been more believable. It was just as I asked, and now I want you to return to the Vicomte. You are free of me and my world, and as promised, I will let you go and have your happy future."

Christine shook her head, her fist clenching her ring without notice. "But I haven't fulfilled my promise. I was to give you a week as your wife-"

"Why can't you understand?" Tears resonated in his eyes and his voice. "I cannot keep pretending. It is a beautiful lie, but believing in it is tearing my soul apart. I can't hold you and love you for the rest of my life. I have to let you go to another man, the one you truly love..." He trailed off, taking a breath as sobs threatened. "You gave me so much, far more than I could have imagined, and I am grateful. Last night was the most wonderful night of my life, but it was only a lie..."

"No, it wasn't," she protested.

Erik couldn't look at her anymore, turning to stare apathetically into the flames. He had to be unfeeling; he couldn't let her see how deeply he ached. "We have to stop pretending. You are not my wife.

Return to the Vicomte and marry him, and don't look back."

"But, Erik-"

With a fierce flash of anger, he rounded on her and shouted, "Christine, this is killing me! Go! Leave me now before you destroy me to nothing!"

She shrank back, tears filling her eyes, and with a sudden cry, she turned and ran from the room, from the house, from that horrible underground world and the disfigured angel who longed to be her husband. Her heart stung, but its inspiration was *his* pain.

Christine didn't stop running until she emerged into the daylight, her eyes burning and squinting in the brightness of the clouded sky. Her mind was reeling with torturous images of the agony in his eyes.

A lie, he called it a lie, and it *was*, wasn't it? The previous night was a part of their game... *No! No, it wasn't!* And it tormented her to consider that he thought so! She had been a coward to hide behind a game of pretend, to use it if only to let herself learn to *feel*. A lie had existed in the beginning, but somewhere along the way, it had become real. She had given herself to him because she wanted to *love him* and know what it would be like to be *loved by him*. He had to know! She had to tell him! But first...

*****

The Vicomte de Chagny was more than pleased to hear that Christine was awaiting him in the library. He hurried down to meet her, his eyes gleaming with adoration when they fell upon her. ...His happiness quickly faded.

"Christine, what is it? What's wrong? Is your aunt not well?" He caught her hands in his, gasping at their coldness.

She shook her head, her brow furrowed as she admitted in a whisper, "I lied to you, Raoul. I shouldn't have, but I thought it was the only thing I could do."

The Vicomte was desperately trying to comprehend her broken thoughts. "Lied? What do you mean?"

Opening her palm to him, she revealed his ring. "I can't marry you, Raoul. I'm in love with someone else."

"Christine, ...what are you saying? ...I don't understand."

"I am so sorry," she replied with genuine compassion as she regarded his pained expression. "I thought I was pretending with *him* when really, I was pretending with *you*. I pretended to know what love was, but how could I when *he* was the one to teach it to me? ...I can't marry you, Raoul."

Raoul still fought to understand, but her resolve was unshaken and her conviction true. "Don't do this, Christine. I love you."

"I'm sorry," she repeated and set the ring into his hand. "But I love him."

She ran, her hard soles echoing on the cobblestone streets as she weaved between crowds that stared after her as if she had lost her mind. She wasn't entirely sure she hadn't.

It seemed a never-ending journey back to the underground of the opera house, but finally, she was there, throwing open the door and yelling, "Erik! Erik!"

Erik was startled by her frantic calls, hurrying to meet her in the hallway as she sought him out. "Christine, what's wrong? What are you doing here?"

Her eyes drifted to the suitcases in the living room doorway and the dark cloak resting upon his shoulders. "Are you going somewhere?" He only nodded, and she demanded, "Why?"

"Did you truly believe I could stay here with memories of you in every room? And then to consider you with the Vicomte, marrying him, starting your life with him? ...I have to leave and find a new place far away from here."

"You can't!" she shouted desperately. "Erik, you can't leave me!" She suddenly threw her arms around him and hugged tight, pressing her face to the curve of his shoulder. "I love you! I love you!"

Erik stared down at her dark head, wondering what had gotten into her. "Christine, I let you go to the Vicomte. I promised that you would be free to marry him. What else do you want of me?"

"Just you," she replied and then repeated softer, "Just you."

Catching her wrists in his hands, he pried her loose, pushing away. "I told you that I couldn't bear to play this game any longer. Why must you torment me with more lies?"

"I am not lying; I never was. Erik, please you must believe me." Tears filled her eyes. "Last night, what we shared, every word, every emotion, it was all real and honest."

"It was a fantasy."

"Then I want to be lost in the fantasy with you and not for a week, for the rest of my life..." Tentatively, she stepped close again, and when he did not back away, she lifted her hand to remove his mask. With hazy eyes, she traced the scars as she had the night before. "I love you; it is the truth of my heart, and if I must prove it to you a million times over, I will."

Tears gathered in his eyes as he wrestled with his thoughts, wanting to believe her with a desperation that twisted in his soul. "Prove it to me right this moment."

"How?"

"Marry me without reserve or hesitation; marry me because you love me." He was so certain that she would refuse and prove the shoddy design of every fabrication, but to his surprise, she smiled brightly.

"I will, with all my heart and soul," she replied.

Swept on the tide of the soaring emotion in his veins, he suddenly caught her in his arms and kissed her, all the more lost when she met his lips feverishly, willingly opening her mouth as his tongue tasted her. He lifted her off her feet, never ending their kiss. He meant to make her his bride that day, but first, he eagerly succumbed to the passion flaring within, receiving only a whimper of desire from her as he carried her to the bedroom.

In the fervent melding of bodies, he let the depth of his love and adoration, his utter happiness overwhelm him, losing himself in her as she clung to him with wild abandon. And all he could think as he came crashing back to earth was that if it was all a lie, then as long as they both believed in it, it would always be true.

Afterward, Christine held him in her arms, his tortured face pressed to the flawless skin of her chest, and she whispered fervently, "I love you, Erik."

He did not look up at her, only clutched her with desperate hands, unwilling to ever let her go again.

A beautiful lie, he thought to himself as he drifted off to a dreamless sleep.

"To Look With Blinded Eyes"
Told from Erik's POV. After holding her to her vow, Erik seeks to
teach Christine how to love him.

I should have let her go... Love really does
make people do foolish things, things that logic
proclaims don't fit into the realm of reason. It blinds
us to the truth and makes us look for loopholes when
none exist.

Christine made a choice, and she was fully
aware of every consequence such a binding
arrangement implied. Love dulled the razor sharp
edges and transformed reality into a fuzzy dreamscape
where her choice was a product of her heart. No
matter the fiancé dangling by a noose feet away or the
incessant tears in her blue eyes, tears I'd been half-
mesmerized with all evening that transfixed my
addled head at every turn of phrase on their
meandering descents. No, I let love wipe clean the
slate of truth and write me a new story, one where
those tears were evidence of elation and relief instead
of horror and pain, one where Christine's heart was as
awake as mine in that predestined moment that our
lips met. Love convinced me that I was doing the
right thing, granting her what she wanted when I
freed her former fiancé and forced him on his way
alone. Love washed away every image that did not fit
into my script. Tears, desperate eyes, hopelessness,
the miniscule fractures lining the heart I told myself
must be mine. A terrifying notion that I might have
spent the next decade or two equally as ignorant,
composing a libretto for the girl I wanted and
manipulating her into acting it out with me. Yes, I
was a fool. I must have been to be so sure Christine's
every thought and feeling were synonymous with my
own, as if we were created of the same fibers, two
broken halves of the same whole instead of a
contradiction of water and oil.

Her lips were lies. Every product from their
perfect pink sanctuary: words, kisses, smiles. Can I be
blamed for wanting to believe things so beautiful, for

yearning to make them a viable part of my ugly world?

Lie and choose me, but her body was her betrayer. Within the hour of the Vicomte's departure, Christine took ill. A fever. It struck her hard and fast.

I had only just finished cooking a quaint supper, determined to push us onto the path to our future and celebrate this very first night of our fairytale ending. I laid out the table with such nervous precision, urgent to please my new bride. ...*Bride*, I was calling her that in my head despite the absent formality of a proper marriage ceremony. Oh, what did it matter? We would never be a volatile part of society anyway. Let us call ourselves wed; no one would dare contradict it.

Humming contently beneath my breath, I went to collect my little bride from her room where she had retired after the evening's exhaustion. My steps were uneven and uncharacteristically clumsy, but I was apprehensive. I'd never played the role of bridegroom before, not even in fantasies. I was oddly unconfident to portray its nuances. Before Christine had left months ago, we had been acting a different play altogether, and I understood my role of captor and villain. Now...well, I felt awkward. A bridegroom... And would it be suitable to enter her chamber uninvited, to go to her bedside, to perhaps kiss her awake...?

My stomach quivered with anticipation at the mere idea. A kiss... and I'd kissed her once already. One kiss that was all mine, one kiss as the precursor to a lifetime more. It didn't have to be only a single, fleeting memory. No, because she was mine, my bride, my Christine. She had chosen me...

As I said, love blinds us to the truth, and at that moment as its willing victim, I smiled, *smiled* because my damaged face was bare, mask-less as it had been all night, and my little bride hadn't shunned it and wouldn't ever again. ...*Yes, I am a fool*...

Smiling yet, I entered her bedchamber. No knock, no calls of announcement. ...My little bride, how I couldn't wait to share my smile with her!

Lips lie, but a body burning with fever does not. No, no... That was my first dose of reality, cold and numbing while the skin of my unconscious beloved was searing and hot. She still wore my chosen wedding gown, white and lace, and her flesh was a vividly clashing pink against it, her dark curls clinging to her damp temples and only a nuisance when she shifted about so restlessly. They tangled their locks and stuck in haphazard chunks to her cheeks with every motion.

Fever... It was an obvious diagnosis, and while instinct bid me to touch her and confirm, I couldn't, fisting my shaking hands at my sides. My first conclusion, as illogical as it seemed, was that I had done this to her. *That kiss!* The one I had only just recalled with such euphoric bliss. Of course! I must have contaminated her, must have given her whatever disease I was half-sure I carried in my soul. Yes, my atrocity must be contagious! The guilt tore at my insides. One kiss, something I'd lived my entire lifetime without, and as gentle as it was, as beautiful, it had destroyed Christine! I was so sure of it, and not even rationale argued against me as my trembling fingertips dared to touch my misshapen mouth.

Ugly! Hideous! An abomination! My mouth was a bloated disaster while hers was exquisite perfection! Her illness was my punishment for believing I had any right to touch my lips to hers.

My obedient, little love, finally acknowledging in her heart of hearts that she could love a monster like me, and now I would lose her! To have her stolen away not by her arrogant Vicomte but by God Himself! I would have seen it as fitting penance for my crimes if not for the fact that Christine did not deserve to die simply for possessing an open and loving heart!

No, this couldn't be my fault; I decided it with relief, and as I dared to inch closer to her bedside, I tentatively grazed my fingertips to her heated cheek.

Well, of course she was sick, rationale finally posed. Life and death choices, months of separation and having to play a role for her Vicomte. I noticed at first glimpse tonight that she had looked pale and lacking her usual light. Too much! It had finally caught up with her.

My resolve to take care of my bride only increased tenfold. I knew I must tend to her, to keep loyally to her side and do anything to make her well again. And in my head, gullible as I now believe it was, I concluded that Christine would be grateful, that she would awaken and grin at me and tell me how happy she was to be home and safe in my care. Soon enough this would all be forgotten on the path of our future.

Fevers are a funny thing. When they are awful enough and they rage out of control, they can steal a person's sense and ability to comprehend through their fury.

Christine was moving fitfully upon the mattress, muttering random unintelligible words and phrases. To watch her and know she was suffering broke my heart. How I wished it were me instead! I felt so sure I could conquer any illness, even Death, now that I had Christine in my life. But she was such a small creature, so fragile, her every feature its own tiny porcelain piece of art. I was terrified as I watched her. If I lost her now... No, I couldn't even bear the thought!

My agitated eyes raced frantically over her bridal finery. Too many layers, too much fabric and undergarments to restrict breath and comfort. I knew I must remove them, but still, my hands were shaking and terrified. To undress her... It didn't feel like my right despite this game of bride and groom I readily indulged. I had only entertained notions of such behavior in the caverns of my mind. There, I was the same as every passionate, virile man, yearning and aching for desire's fulfillment. And of course, I intended for more than chaste kisses in our future to come, but...not like this, not stripping the only woman I'd ever wanted without her knowledge or consent.

But...I was a husband now, and I needed to put my bride's welfare first. I needed to take care of her.

Hoarse whispers echoed in the air about her parted lips, more words I could not decipher, but I pretended they were the approval I wanted and yet didn't have as I gently caught her shoulders in my palms and guided her to her side to find the clasps down her back. For all their quaking, my fingers were diligent and barely touched more than metal hooks and satin material. Parting the gown to her waist, I carefully guided it off, drawing it away and trying not to stare. Detachment, I yearned for its apathy, but when I had never before seen some of those glorious curves and had never been fortunate enough to have inches and inches of creamy skin spread like an artist's canvas before me, my eyes had their own agenda and memorized every vision.

Stockings, slippers, corset, petticoat: every layer uncovered a new terrain of smooth, flawless brilliance. She was still whispering nonsensical syllables, and in my mind's longing, I could string them together and make them into something I wanted, into words of love and desire, into a soft beseeching for my touch. Ridiculous, I know! But I allowed the bittersweet fantasy to tease me, and as she lay stretched before me in only chemise and pantaloons, I traced my fiery eyes over discernible details, never, *never* touching. A touch, no, I couldn't be allowed such a privilege. So I pretended and used eyes as fingertips to outline her every shadowed curve and womanly feature. And I ached alone and hated myself for it.

Uncomfortable yet, Christine stirred, and as her dark lashes fluttered over heavy blue eyes, I went numb, petrified in my place. Oh, the indiscretion! Surely, she would be ashamed that I had dared! But though her eyes stared, they never saw beyond the picture show occurring simultaneously in her head, and after only a moment of more muttering, she closed them again.

I did not hesitate this time as I bound her in blankets, no more ravenous ogling and unfulfilled wanting. The little voice of optimism in my head insisted that there could be more later, that the next time it would be as she lay aware and wanting as much as I was. Ah, optimism! How cruel that persistent voice could be! I only wish I could have lost it years before. Its subsequent inspiration of hope was only another cruel tragedy in a life full of far too many.

While it became my goal to make her well, it seemed that her body's was to succumb to illness. Her fever raged despite my every attempt to break it. Years in a Gypsy camp had taught me the particular combinations of herbs to concoct a crude form of medication. Being alone for so much of my life and unlikely to seek a doctor if I ever took ill demanded an exactness to every brew, so I was doubtless that they worked. But though I so carefully measured and mixed and tenderly gave them to my sleeping love, they did nothing. It was as if she *deliberately* chose to remain ill and unconscious. Preposterous as that seemed to me!

Medication failed, I resigned myself to delicately sponging her brow and the small features of her face with cool cloths. The adamant shadow at her bedside, I barely left for even a moment, terrified she'd awaken without me when my presence would surely be a necessary comfort.

As I watched her with unfailing adoration, I pondered what our future would hold once she was well. I harbored dreams of a house in the sunshine, of my wife curled to my side as we watched sunsets, singing for me as my constant muse, kissing me to sleep every night as I held her in my arms. Optimism again, but I couldn't find the desire to argue with it. And I never let myself recall our past or the darkness that had tainted every detail until now. None of it mattered anymore. I was determined that everything would be different. Yes, it *must be* if her heart was mine.

Hours went by the same, and Christine shifted and whimpered in her restless unconsciousness. Thoughts of the future were shackled to the present. I couldn't look beyond her suffering, and my heart ached in my chest. I wanted to cry simply because I felt so useless, so helpless. I was supposed to be the strong one. Let death and damnation pose battle with me, but let none of it dare even brush a finger to my love!

She whispered again, and from those flustered lips, I heard the softest sound, "Erik."

My name! *Mine!* In the midst of her delirium, and she called for *me*! In such a horrific situation, happiness should have been impossible, but I could not halt its sweeping possession.

"Christine," I whispered back, and lowering the cloth, for the first time I dared to grant a caress from my eager fingers, grazing her jaw and then her cheek. I poured adoration into every touch, determined never to take a single contact of skin to skin for granted. "Open your eyes, Christine, and see your devoted husband who loves you so. You are my whole world; it stops without you. Please, Christine, return life to me."

I whispered every word in passionate echoes, praying that she heard, that my voice could penetrate the fog and find her.

Those lashes fluttered again, parting to reveal shades of blue beneath, and a timid smile touched my lips, my hand yet outstretched and lightly resting against her chin. "Christine."

Her stare was unfocused, and I wasn't certain she even noticed my presence at first. Then so suddenly that I hadn't the chance to react, her little hand darted out from beneath the covers and caught mine, grasping tight and firm.

"Don't leave me," she gasped desperately, tears

welling at the corners of her eyes. "Oh, please don't go."

"Never," I immediately vowed, shaken to my core. She wanted me! Well, of course, as always, I was her constant.

The hand on mine was sticky and hot, the fever exuding from every silken pore, but it was determined and never loosened its grip as it pulled me closer. I went willing and eager, never regarding even my own modesty's insistence as I took a tentative seat perched on the edge of the mattress. It was strange and odd to consider that in some mundane way, we were sharing this bed, as near to one another as we'd ever been. How silly to dwell on such a point when we were barely indulging even a touch!

"Stay, stay," she was muttering, her frantic eyes glancing idly from my shape to random places about as if they could not settle.

"Always," I vowed and brought my free hand to graze her cheek. "Always, Christine. I'll never leave you."

She seemed to relax a bit at my words but within a gasped breath, was tugging my hand again as if to draw me nearer still. In hushed consonants, she bid, "Lay with me. Oh, please hold me."

My muscles went rigid with merely the thought, and I wasn't sure I could make them comply. *Hold her...* I had only dreamed of such a pleasure.

But she did not allow me time to ponder the logistics of such a feat or to plan it out in my head, as I would have preferred. She was pulling me again by my captured hand, drawing me down to her, and left me no choice but to be awkward and ungraceful.

Had I thought it out, I would have known exactly how to go about it, where my arms should go, where to rest my hands, but instead I was clumsy, desperate to learn and please her with fumbling appendages that for the first time in my existence felt lanky and oversized to perform such an intimate task.

Hold her... I wasn't permitted to fathom my

own inadequacies, for in the instant I stretched out beside her, she did the job herself and weaved willowy, pale arms about my torso, pulling me the rest of the way to her. My Lord, she could be so strong when she was convicted and wanted to follow its path. Lost to a fever, she could not seem to recall hesitation or apprehension or the very real fact that she'd never embraced me before. The closest we'd come was that single kiss, and it had boasted our usual tremors and quivers of fear at every nuance.

I was half beneath the blankets, never fully cocooned, but the heat radiating from her was what struck my attuned mind first. The fever! It stole inhibition, but it also left me to wonder how much of this she believed was a dream. Her arms fitted about my shape, her little hands pressing against my back, and as soon as I settled into her grasp, she burrowed her dark head against my chest.

My Christine... I wasn't sure what to do or how to behave. Was I permitted to grip her back, to touch her, to perhaps lay a kiss to her damp crown? I had no basis for comparison and had never practiced my role of bridegroom to be certain. Dear God, but she was so soft, so *tangible* against me!

Typically in my existence, I denounced instinct and second-guessed every impulse. How could I not when I'd learned years ago to keep a guard always in place? But this time instinct was all I had, and at its insistence, I wrapped my shaking arms around her and twined my fingertips in her silken curls, relaxing in an exhalation and settling in her hold.

She nuzzled her cheek against my erratic heartbeat and scooted closer as if she could not bear an inch of space between our bodies, and desire became a poignant reality dragged to the forefront. The half-dressed love of my life was arching her soft, feminine curves against my untouched body... It almost frightened me to consider that my body's reaction was a natural impulse so far beyond my usual control. *Desire...* It shamed me to realize that I could do nothing to hide it, and I prayed her fever made her ignorant to its proof.

"A nightmare," she suddenly mumbled, her restless fingers tautly grasping my jacket in their kneading motion. "It was all a nightmare."

"Sshh," I crooned as gently as I could. "The nightmare is over, and you're safe, Christine, safe...in my arms. I'll never let you go."

She calmed at my words, and as I went stiff against her, she turned her cheek to set the sweetest kiss to my flustered heartbeat. I wanted to cry again, but tears kept back until her next words hit the air.

"I love you," she breathed, and a sob shook my shoulders. My hands fisted in the silk of her chemise at the small of her back, and I crushed her in a desperate embrace, finally daring to lay that kiss to her crown.

"Oh, Christine," I whispered amidst tears that were tumbling into her dark locks with their fall. "How I love you! How I've *always* loved you!"

Kiss after delicate kiss I pressed into her web of curls, and she was acquiescent, never shying away or refusing a single token of my devotion. It was my very dreams brought to life, every tantalizing scene that optimism had dangled, ...and in the next moment, it became misery.

"Don't let go," she whispered again, pressing to my every plane and feature. "Please, Raoul, don't ever let me go again."

Numb...and then sharp pain piercing a heart that had only just learned to beat. Raoul... My delirious, little bride had just given away Love's deceptive allure. Love had convinced me that she knew who was in her bed with her, holding her, loving her, but Love was a fickle liar who appreciated playing games with the hopeful. Raoul..., she thought my arms were Raoul's, my kisses, my tears, my adoration. It was bitter and cruel and left me momentarily stunned in my spot.

She was the one moving between us; she was

the one clutching tighter with more fitful hands while I might as well have been the corpse she had once dubbed me: unresponsive and empty. I felt as if the life had been drained out of me and left nothing in its place, every dream snatched from my own fitful hands. She was grasping the dream in her addled head; evidently, I was doing the same. Fever made hers linger. I suddenly wished I had a viable infection to blame my idiocy upon, for when tomorrow she could say she lived a dream in delirium, I could only call myself ignorant.

The pain of the heart is a consuming emotion, worse than any other I've ever carried. For a man like me who never accepts defeat or weakness, it left shame in its wake; I was disgusted with myself for my own gullibility, for wanting too much, for believing I could have it. I knew such self-hatred that it boiled like a venomous brew and left every bit of me as lethal as a viper's bite. Toxic, my touch was toxic, my love, every good emotion I'd ever tried to offer. *I* was the contamination, not the ugly lips I'd wanted to blame and pin Christine's sickness upon at first glance. *Me*, my heart, my love. They left a stain upon anyone I offered them to, and Christine suffered, suffered because I loved her.

I was poison, but though I abhorred myself for it, I abhorred her equally at that moment. I hated her because she didn't love me, because she yanked my every dream out of my hands with her vain heart. Foolish, foolish girl! I ached to hurt her back, to punish her for her cruelty. If she weren't so cold and callous, she would have opened her heart to mine instead of building me dreams to love in her stead.

My frantic eyes glanced down at her dark head, her silk clad, half-bared body flush and molded to my own. No, she was *mine* now. Whatever the musings of her inconstant, immature heart, she had made a choice, and the choice was binding. I was a possessive creature indeed, and I would not give her up even as sense repeated again and again that I should have let her go this night, that I never should have held her to stay. To that rationale, I insisted again that she was *mine*. Mine now and forever.

As such, I suddenly acted without reasoning, and catching her chin with my shaking fingertips, I jerked her features upward, tilting her face to my inspection. She was lost somewhere amidst fever dreams, her blue eyes half-closed and distant, and without impetus, I abruptly forced my lips to hers, sculpting perfection with my own distortions. She didn't respond; I didn't expect her to. A kiss earlier had been a fantasy; this kiss was claiming possession.

I wasn't gentle, not when part of me ached to punish her so badly. I moved my misshapen mouth fiercely against her heated one, kissing her in a way I had never even imagined. No, all my musings had included tender adorations; this was practically damning.

With a growl of self-loathing, I drew back and stared at her flushed face with a peculiar, masochistic thought. I could take her like this, on the cusp of reality with never a protest to be had. After all, she was my wife by her own free will, and it was my right to have her. I could lay claim to her body, take her virginity, mark her in some way so that she could never leave me. It wasn't a transgression when in my mind, we were already wed.

My hands dared to race a path down her back, delving between a silken curtain of curls to find her curves and trace the gentle arch of her hips. She was so beautiful, so perfectly cast. As I stared at her dazed visage, I allowed indiscretion to rule my mind with the perverse urge to trail my misshapen lips over every feature of her glorious body, to learn what perfection felt like to the touch, ...to tarnish it with my ugliness and make it undesirable to anyone but me for the rest of eternity.

I hated myself with the thought. I might dub myself a monster, but I certainly did not have to behave like one to prove a point.

With a resigned sigh, I ignored the instinctual pulsations of a desire that would continue to go unfulfilled, and I chose to return to the bittersweet inclinations of a shattered dream. Weaving my arms around her body and cradling her to my chest, I could so easily pretend that this was my happy ending. I could pretend that I was holding my bride, and she was holding *me* in return, not the lost lover in her heart.

As minutes ticked by, Christine relaxed against me into a less restless sleep, her mutterings quieted and heart a steady beat with my own. I stroked her curls with my fingertips and dared to lay another kiss to her brow, yearning to my very bones and suffering alone. Was that all I'd ever do?

*****

A sharp gasp stirred me from fantasy and unceremoniously returned me to reality. Opening my eyes, I gazed into the horrorstricken expression upon Christine's face, her muscles rigid and tight against me. Pretending was pointless when feverish delirium had passed, and all she could see was the disfigured murderer asleep in her bed with her.

As if abruptly recalling the ability to move, Christine darted out of my arms. She scooted to the opposite end of the mattress, only more agitated as her urgent eyes took in her flimsy state of dress. Accusation bit me from her stare, yet never made its appearance on her lips as she wrapped shaking arms about her own shape.

I didn't offer apologies or explanations. What could possibly be said when we had so flippantly been tossed back into our original roles? Not for the first time in our sordid relationship, I dragged hurt beneath a façade of apathy and rose to stand at the bedside with a calculated coldness to every motion.

"I trust your fever has broken since you suddenly seem to recall that you were sleeping with the devil," I emotionlessly stated. "I will not beseech forgiveness for my rights as your husband. The days of having me knelt at your feet, begging for your favor have come and gone. I don't care if you love me or not now that you are mine."

"H...husband?" she stammered, trembling violently before my glare, and the fear in her eyes, her utter, unavoidable shudder stung me so mercilessly that it was easy to choose anger and retaliation.

"What did you think when you chose to stay? That we would continue on in our prior circumstance with barely a touch allowed, never a kiss, my repulsive hands kept as far from your body as possible? You wore my wedding dress, Christine; surely the point was clearly made." My words only enhanced her unease, and before pleadings could be made, as I was sure they would come, I insisted, "I have brought you back from the brink of death, and you are further indebted to me for my care. I will consider your gratitude in the form of a kiss."

I watched her pale at the mention, and yet I remained un-swayed. How easy it was to fall back into my hated role of captor and manipulative monster! It was *not* what I wanted, none of this was, but if I had to play the game to win affections that should have been mine, then I was not above doing it. I had once tried tenderness with her, and it didn't work; it only made me a creature worthy of pity. Being a monster inspired fear, but at least her fear I could control when her heart was full of lies anyway. I would not lay my own vulnerably before her again. No, I'd almost done that the previous night, and look where it had gotten me!

Tears rimmed Christine's big eyes, but I never let her see how they shook me, holding my ground instead of breaking. Her entire frame was quaking, arms fitted tight about her waist as she huddled low enough to conceal many of the feminine silhouettes I had absorbed the previous night. She couldn't know that their grace played in my mind's eye in spite of her meager attempts, or that their memory only encouraged me onward. They made me want.

"Erik, please," she muttered desperately, shaking her head so that those dark curls bobbed in their springy spirals.

"I will not be swayed, and I will not leave without my kiss. Your precious Vicomte's life was worth such a sacrifice, but your own is not? I spent the night as your dutiful husband, nursing you back to health, and will I have nothing for it? A single kiss, Christine. I advise you to concede and do this of your own free will. It will not be pleasant if I must force it upon you." I was reminded that I already had, but that would be my secret to bear.

She hesitated a moment longer, those wide eyes traveling between my conviction and my awaiting, disfigured lips as if unsure which scared her more. Never masking her reluctance, she unraveled her limbs from her torso and edged tentatively across the mattress, closer to where I stood.

I watched her with an undeniable flush of anticipation. My love in her white underclothes approaching with the intent to share a kiss. If only she could know even an echo of the longing I did!

The tears were still in her eyes, hanging suspended so beautifully yet never falling as she raised herself on her knees, tucking disheveled curls behind her ears with quivering fingers. I did not make it easy for her, did not meet her halfway or adopt a less severe expression. I stayed rooted in my place, eyeing her with a hunger I could not fully control.

"Well?" I demanded impatiently as she lingered upon her knees as if contemplating what the demanded kiss could entail.

She shyly licked her lips, and I was captured in that unwittingly provocative gesture with the perverse yearning to know the sensation of that little pink tongue along my own lips instead. I might have denied myself sensual opportunities, but my mind was an erotic fantasy when I chose to let desire run free of its boundaries. Music demanded such a connection to passion's power and a release of inhibition. I could think anything I liked, even if acting seemed unfathomable.

But I was determined not to frighten my innocent, little bride with even the suggestion, and I kept my hands hanging loose and unthreatening at my sides, my body unmoving and awaiting. Awaiting but staring eagerly as she lifted herself high upon her knees, her curves on display again but never acknowledged as she reluctantly closed the meager distance between us. I saw poorly-hidden disgust, wondering if it had been the same the night before, and I had simply refused to see its truth.

But I didn't have the chance to dwell, not when in my next breath, those sweet lips delicately touched mine, feather-light at first and then with more and more gentle pressure. Ah, to feel her kiss! It was so different than trying to force it the night before in her bed. Her lips, warm and soft, puckered in a pretty rosebud shape and growing firmer with her confidence.

I allowed her without movement of my own, keeping passive and pliant. My only telltale that I ached for much more was in my hands as they unconsciously made fists to retain control. I wanted! How I wanted!

One kiss, and as she drew back, her eyes nervously flitted to mine, as if to prove that she'd taken my challenge. I considered her a fool. Tempting my temper when I could have demanded so much beyond a single kiss? Perhaps she didn't understand the extent of the fire in my veins. Perhaps she fancied herself in control of my pitiful emotions, as if should she comply and surrender to the mundane details of a kiss, she could twist my heart about her fingers and have me as a willing slave instead. How it infuriated me!

So sudden that she never had the chance to refuse, I caught her upper arms with hands I had to pry out of their fists. Deafening my ears to her small cry, I pulled her off the mattress and set her on her feet, ignoring how she swayed with residual proof of her illness. No, I wouldn't let her fall should the vertigo overcome, not when I intended to hold her. I clasped her firmly against my body, the way I had held her as she had slept, but this time my desire was a reality and revealed. I wanted her to know it, to recognize it, to understand that I was not the same pathetic freak she had left six months before, pining and wallowing in her wake. I had been prepared to adore her and let desire be a blessing between us when I thought love ruled her heart. Now...well, now I would not play games.

Christine shook in my grasp, but she did not fight. She acquiesced and was a yielding mass of warm curves against my aching body. I would not allow reality to shake me. No, I needed to be strong and powerful. I already knew she didn't love me.

In a voice that was husky with the need throbbing through my bones, I stated flatly, "Welcome home, my bride."

That was it. No gushing of eternal devotion or concern for her health after her illness. Those were my thoughts, but I refused to make them into words. Let them remain trapped in my head and in a heart with a locked door. I pondered kissing her again, claiming, but there was horror in her eyes. Horror for her disfigured husband, the monster who'd stolen her life and her freedom. It was something I was unsure I'd ever be able to assuage.

Rather abruptly, I released her, missing her shapes at the first breath of separation, and my only pause was to make certain she was stable on her feet. I'd never let her fall...

But the next moment, I fled her room, slamming the door in my wake and abandoning the only place I longed to be.

*****

I didn't expect to see my little bride again anytime soon, not until I gave up my silent vigil in the sitting room to seek her out on my own anyway. So it was an unexpected surprise that shook my confident façade when I caught the sound of approaching footfalls. I had been sulking and brooding, lost to an empty stare with the fire in the hearth that a few times had boasted tears. Thankfully, they had not been a reality when Christine joined me. They would have dented my armored veneer.

She brought sunshine with her appearance in spite of every unfavorable emotion in her aura. Beautiful, graceful, not even the lingering dark circles shadowing her eyes or hints of weakness from her bout of fever dimmed her internal glow or the way it radiated around me and sucked me into her charms every time. I was as much obsessed with the spirit as I was the girl; every bit of her, and she should be mine.

Christine shifted nervously on her feet in the doorway, and I did not try to calm her by quitting my intent scrutiny. No, I wanted to look at her. Was I not even allowed that privilege without suspicion? She was properly clothed now, wearing one of the gowns from her wardrobe, this one lilac, and while I missed views of curves and skin, my mind's eye redrew them for me in my head. Memories, ...yet they were a disappointment if I couldn't tear fabric away and touch as well.

"So you do not intend to be the uncooperative prisoner locked to starvation in her room?" I had to taunt if only to hide the transgressions in my thoughts. "I was half-sure you preferred your own death to a life with a monster."

"Why would you say that?" she dared to ask, and I shrugged apathetic shoulders.

"Well, that fever of yours obviously had an intended outcome. It probably was a disappointment to wake and realize you were still alive. ...I'm sure that was only one in a list of disappointments. Isn't that so, Christine? Opening your eyes to glimpse the disfigured atrocity of your husband's face was likely another and the most horrific of them all. Yes, ...you must have believed you were having another nightmare."

My disfigured face, and I hoped the guilt I glimpsed in her was genuine because since I'd left her room, I had made it a point to locate my mask and replace it over my face. I had foolishly hoped never to need it again, not after she had chosen me. What did I care if she was the one to look at my face? If she could stomach and accept the sight, the mask was unnecessary. But...well, another ridiculous, optimistic blunder.

Christine's eyes fluttered to the mask, but she only said, "I made a choice. I intend to honor it."

"And live as my wife?" I couldn't help but push, and though she was somber with the blatant truth of her future, she gave a single, dull nod. "Say it," I commanded with a snap, my hands clutching the armrests of my chair in their unease.

"Yes, ...live as your wife," she softly obeyed. It might as well have been a calling for her own execution: sadness, regret, disappointment, all things that should not factor into a future of bliss and love.

"Then come and sit with your devoted husband. You need not linger in doorways in your own home, Christine."

Her footsteps were trepid and light, but she apprehensively approached my throne-like chair, questions uttered in every motion. Halting and breaking her eyes from mine, she anxiously knelt at my feet, her skirts a pool of purple about her small shape. We had indulged such a pose before, months and months ago, equally as tentative but with a growing comfort in each other's presence. How often had she sat at my feet after a late supper, neither of us speaking as I still felt un-eloquent when her blue eyes were upon me? We would simply delight in each other's company. And now...I had an unuttered wish for it to be the same, for it to be even more than that.

"Will you...," I began, watching her eager eyes raise before I cursed myself. No questions, I shouldn't have to question; I should be able to demand if I wanted. "Lay your head against my knee," I ordered instead and yet my voice was telling and soft, cajoling in a way I had not intended.

Though she hesitated, I saw no fear as she scooted closer and timidly set her cheek against my knee, gazing at me all the while. I seemed the only one fearing at that moment, for my hand shook as I brought it to her and grazed an uncertain caress to her brow.

She tensed, and I dared to report, "No more trace of fever; you are well." It was a flimsy excuse when the truth was that I just wanted to touch her. A husband who needed excuses. It didn't seem fair.

"A wife who shuns her husband's every caress." I stated it emotionlessly even as the truth of it cut to my locked heart, and proving my own point, I attempted another touch, idly stroking her hairline.

She stiffened against me, eyes wide, but she stammered in return, "I will not shun you, Erik. You may touch me if you wish. ...You are my husband."

Liar, I wanted to speak the word, but instead made it blatant and undeniable, racing my fingertips along her cheek to her jaw and feeling her fight an urge to recoil. "Should a wife tremble so to bear her husband's touch? It hardly seems acceptable."

Her cheeks tinged pink beneath my fingers, and her eyes would not meet mine. "A wife who has never born the touch of a man would tremble. Innocence and modesty would justify its source."

"And yet I must wonder, would you tremble the same if the Vicomte were in my place?" I asked and feigned apathy. "Would innocence and modesty account for anything if these were *his* fingers against your skin?"

"Why does that matter?" she suddenly demanded, shaking her head against my knee. "Raoul is *not* my husband."

"But I must wonder such things, you see, because I've never touched a woman. I cannot say if your trepidation is appropriate. If it is a result of modesty, I should feel humbled and treat you all the more tender because of it. ...But if it is only because you are disgusted by the man you've chained your existence to and vowed to obey and adore, then I must be disappointed." I paused long enough to lay my fingers to her cheek, and I watched her lower shame-filled eyes as I dared to tell her, "I've imagined cherishing you as my wife because you want me as your husband, but if I must, I will force such desire upon you and punish you for pretending it already exists. ...Well, I suppose my touch is punishment enough, isn't it? My hands upon your virginal body... It's practically an abomination in words alone."

Blunt, inarguable, and I knew why she still would not meet my eye; her red-stained cheeks revealed it for her.

"I've only ever been a gentleman with you," I told her, carefully restrained in every emotion I set forth. "Perhaps you thought I would remain the same and ignore every one of my unacceptable desires, that simply your word to stay would be enough. But I demanded a wife, Christine, with every trapping that accompanies the title. I may not be able to force your heart to beat to my liking, but you are a superb actress when you choose to be. Perhaps if you play the part, it eventually won't become such a hardship to endure and you won't shudder every time I attempt even to caress your cheek." I formed the blasphemous touch again, trailing the backs of my fingers from her cheek to her lips and back again, and though she did not deny me, her eyes kept distance in their unfocused blue pools.

"You're asking me to lie to you," she softly stated as if that were the greatest sin in my words, and only then did she look at me, seeking confirmation.

"You *always* lie to me," I replied equally as steady. "I am only seeking to control your façade this time. Yes, lie, but I will know that I chose the game and that beneath it, your heart is as cold and unattainable as it ever was. I'll know, and I'll stop making myself the fool in futile hope of capturing it. ...And perhaps if you lie, I'll stop feeling as if every attempted touch, every kiss is a sin. I'll cease to curse myself and my ugliness for ever daring." I could not keep emotion detached as I told her in candid honesty, "I abhor myself, Christine, every detail of my accursed life and my accursed face, but your constant rejections and disgust convince me that I am beyond detestable, that I am as condemned as the devil in hell. *You* are the one to make me a monster, and I will *not* endure our marriage under that epithet. Don't make me take on that role and force you to my bed as no better than a common rapist. You chose this life; pretend you actually wanted it. I'm not asking for overdone melodrama and a love that cannot breathe; I'm simply asking to be able to touch you without constant revulsion in your eyes. I feel it's a reasonable compromise."

Christine wouldn't meet my eye again, and abandoning my tactic with a heaved curse, I abruptly got to my feet and stalked away, nearing the dancing flames in the hearth in hopes that their motion would hypnotize my mind and take my thoughts far away from here. Every one of my previous dreams was already shattered. What good did this place hold anyway? I had gone from having a consenting, *loving* bride to existing with a stranger who couldn't even endure the graze of my fingers upon her sacred skin. After holding her the previous night, this was a bitter reality to face. Once again I pondered that I should have let her go and left myself the fantasy for comfort instead.

I had wittingly put her out of my attention, preferring my silent melancholy to a longing I no longer wanted, so it was a bit of a surprise when I felt a small, tentative hand upon my jacket sleeve. Jerking my eyes to her, I wondered when exactly she had risen and come to stand beside me, how long it had taken her to collect courage enough to dare a touch. Perhaps it was minutes, and yet I hoped for seconds.

I didn't speak, didn't ask; I simply stared at that hand, at its delicate construction and deceptively-concealed deadliness. She could kill me with a touch; she wouldn't know that, but it was true. One willing touch, one *wanted* touch, and the monster before her would crumble to dust, dead and destroyed, and only a man who adored her wholeheartedly would be left, the prince ready to fall at her feet. One wanted touch, and not even the ugliness of her noble prince would matter; only the heart beneath would exist, and it was beautiful despite its abhorrent shell.

"I chose you as my husband, Erik," she softly said, her voice little more than timid whispers. "I do understand what that means and what you expect of me. I...I'll give you what you want, and I won't be disgusted."

I didn't pose my doubts. Instead, I raised my unclaimed hand to my mask and diligently removed it, watching her steadily all the while. She didn't flinch, not even when I felt firelight playing on my scars and illuminating their distortions. Those blue eyes gazed pensively, and then slowly closed as she tilted her face upward, as if expecting a kiss.

A kiss... But I slowly shook my head. "You won't be disgusted," I repeated her vow with a bite, "yet still you close your eyes."

Her lashes fluttered again as she abruptly attempted a denial. "No, Erik, I-"

"Lie, Christine," I ordered coldly, unable to consider listening to a single excuse, "but at least do it convincingly."

That was all I could endure. With a growl of my uncontrollable annoyance, I stalked past and left her standing there with frantic eyes. I had asked for lies, hadn't I? Lies to feed the cruelty of an internal enemy called Love. Lies to convince me that every detail of this wasn't the sin my conscience was starting to dub it. But lies could never be enough. I wanted love; I *deserved* love, ached for it. Why when I went to such extents to earn it, did reality mean she wouldn't love me in return? I could play every trick I had, go to great extremes on every plane of life, but I couldn't change her heart. And it infuriated me to be so weak!

*****

I am a man who has survived every hardship and cruelty the world can offer, who has been consumed by every dark power, every bitter emotion, who has been omnipotent and played God at whim. And yet despite it all, I've come to learn that the root of the heart is that betrayer of an emotion called Love. Every other sensation, action, desire, means *nothing* without Love's effulgent intensity. Love is the greatest purpose of existence and makes our lives have meaning. To touch another life is to matter.

Long ago I realized I'd only be remembered for the damage I'd caused, the lives destroyed by my devices. And I hadn't cared because I hadn't known Love's consumption. I hadn't been infected yet by its bite and left to long and envy.

Love takes two hearts, willing and eager. I could love all I wanted, but if I didn't have her love in return, it was meaningless and wasted. It was forgotten. Two open hearts choosing each other. That was the greater purpose behind existing. I could desire it, but I could not force it to be mine.

As I paced my room with uneven steps, I pondered my situation. Christine didn't love me; she would live with me as my wife with every advantage I wanted to include, but in her heart, she would pine for her dashing Vicomte, perhaps fantasize him in my place and compare our life with a perfection that likely wouldn't have been real anyway. Love's blinding periphery made the Vicomte into prince charming and me the villain keeping them apart. Logic insisted that the intelligent course of action was to release her from a coerced vow and let her have the life she truly wanted even if it was an idealized dream that would leave her as disappointed as I myself currently was. Yes, the intelligent course, before Christine twisted every detail and transformed her acceptance into hatred for her captor husband.

But...well, I had a mind to rewrite the story altogether. Why should there by only two choices, and why should her heart have already made a decision without ever giving me a chance? I was suddenly determined to carve us a new path altogether. If she were willing, I could alter her every perception and make our future a blessing rather than a curse.

I let my ideas form their meandering nuances, desperate not to allow optimism to make me hopeful, ...not again anyway. Once I felt confident in the course that was laid out, I replaced my mask and surrendered my solitude, seeking out Christine. My doubting nature wondered if she'd spent the afternoon searching for an escape. Perhaps she'd found a way out; perhaps she'd abandoned me, silent and stealthy, while I was engrossed in forming ideas to keep her. Perhaps she was already gone, protected by her Vicomte and vanished from my life...

The very thought had me suddenly rushing my steps with suffocating impatience. *Oh God, I shouldn't have left her alone!*

My hasty footfalls halted abruptly outside my sitting room. *Christine...* Her blue eyes lifted with a start at my flustered appearance from where she sat before the dwindling flames in the fireplace, a book spread in the bed of her purple skirts.

"Erik," she anxiously greeted, closing the book with trembling fingers and setting it aside. "I...I was waiting for you to come out. I was starting to worry. Shall I go and fix supper?"

Supper... The dutiful wife, and her façade was intact and cemented firm as ever. It would have been almost too easy to fall into its perfect deception, to forget that her heart could have a contradictory beat and believe it was only mine. But...I had other plans.

Careful not to give any emotion away, I joined

her before the fire, hesitant as I lowered myself to kneel on the carpet beside her.

"Erik, ...are you all right?"

"No, ...no." I was reading her intently, searching for some reason to forgo my idea before I ever even suggested it. Perhaps if she were a stronger girl, more secure in her convictions, less likely to be swayed by the rest of the world, then I'd have no chance. But how often had I wondered if Christine truly wanted the Vicomte or if it was only the idea of him that enticed her? The acceptable man society would approve of, ...the man her father would have approved of...

In a tone that didn't allow argument, I said, "You don't love me, ...but you could."

"Erik, what do you-"

"I'm not an easy person to love, Christine; I realize that. I do not follow standard principles of what is suitable or desired; I have a difficult heart, ...but I could teach you to love me."

"Teach me?" she repeated with an uncertain arch of her dark brows. I took it as encouragement because there was the faintest hint of intrigue in blue depths.

"I've taught you so many things, Christine; music, the very soul of it. You loved me in the music; I've no doubt of that." I knew she could not deny, and as I continued to study her beautiful features by the glow of the firelight, I explained, "We love with our eyes first and foremost. Your heart might have loved mine, but your eyes could never allow the face of a demon. Your eyes looked for beauty, for something acceptable to love instead, and they chose the Vicomte with his perfect face. Your eyes made the choice for your heart, and even now they will not look past what they deem ugly. ...My face is an abomination, and you can never love it this way."

Her attention fluttered to my mask and its necessary presence, but she did not protest a single word.

188

"Your eyes have dubbed my face as repulsive," I continued without sway, "and it is. It's a horror, but...if you could look beyond its malformed canvas, you could love the man beneath."

"And...how would I do that?" she softly breathed, and I almost broke my emotional wall and smiled. Almost... It was practically an instinct because I glimpsed curiosity from one always so curious, and it gave me hope.

With flustered fingers, I withdrew a dark scarf from my jacket pocket, holding it to her inspection. "Will you trust me?" I asked when I knew I didn't have to. And stretching the scarf horizontal, I gave her an indication of what I intended.

She was apprehensive, catching her bottom lip between her teeth. I savored that sweet gesture and its natural impulse, and after a moment, though doubt lingered in blue eyes, she nodded.

My hands shook and fumbled in their usual grace as I lifted the scarf to her. I watched her lashes flutter closed and delicately laid the makeshift blindfold across her eyes, blocking her vision of a man in a mask whose predominant talent was driving her heart away. No, I could be more; I could be everything if she would let me.

The scarf was carefully knotted and would not fall loose. Only when I was sure did I reach for my mask and remove its barrier. Paranoia looked for an impossible reaction, so accustomed to her automatic need to recoil from something so hideous. But she was kneeling, unshaken and peaceful, waiting for my guidance with a trust I had never been granted before.

Quivering down every fingertip, I tentatively captured both her hands in mine, pleased when she did not refuse or protest. She only tilted her blinded head inquisitively, not even a tremble as I lifted those small hands in my larger ones. Between our kneeling shapes, I slid my fingers up her smooth palms until they could press to every match, fingers and thumbs, knuckles misaligned by size, palm to palm. I was conditioning her to the touch of my hands, teaching her to allow and not fear in that one gentle contact.

"Are you afraid of me, Christine?" I dared to ask in a breathless whisper as my eyes memorized every detail of this sweet moment.

An idle shake of her head, and as if to prove herself, her fingers inched to weave between mine, bending to clasp instead of simply caress, her fingertips a gentle pressure against my knuckles. Pairs of hands joined, and with only the briefest hesitation, I lifted them, the terrified one between us, as I brought them to my eager face. Always careful, I disjoined entwined fingers and set her hands from satiny palms to small wrists against my cheeks.

I didn't know what I expected when I had devised this plan and hoped to be courageous enough to carry it through. I had not dared to fantasize this moment for fear it would only fail. Sense told me that there should be shaking or tension, something to indicate that though she did not see what she touched, her mind recalled and remembered its disgust. But Christine didn't give anything away, pliant and permissive to my hold, and when I lowered my clasping hands and left hers, she did not pull away and sever contact as I anticipated. To my shock, she curved her fingers against the abnormal planes of my face with a firmer touch.

In theory and contemplation, detachment was easy. A thought, an idea of convincing her through touch that disgust was irrelevant. Her hands upon my face... Ideas didn't bring feelings and didn't prepare me for the overwhelming sensation of her skin to mine. My face had never before been touched by any hands unless violence was involved. Punches, strikes, and I was the one between us to tense, my skin half-recalling pain and readying for it. But there was no pain in the caress of those small, warm hands. There was curiosity, perhaps an odd fascination, a captivation I hadn't fathomed, and no curses or cringes of revealing revulsion.

"Are you...afraid of me, Christine?" I asked again, unable to distinguish any other coherent words when I was so overcome. My voice caught, a little skip in constant sound, and I prayed she did not realize it was with an attempt to curb tears.

"I'm not afraid of you, Erik," she softly bid. Her fingers moved, making tender caresses as she timidly explored, and I held my breath. I was terrified if I gave her one recollection that it was *my* face she willingly touched, that *my* body was mere inches away, close enough that our knees brushed, one memory would remind her to pull away and end this.

So I kept still and silent, and focused on a touch so longed for that it sent tremors down my spine. My eyes fixed on her blindfolded face, on every smooth line and feature, crafted so precisely and contrasting from the ones she touched. Her hands made identical caresses upon each of my cheeks, one cheek so close to normal and one so demented that I was in awe that she dared. Perhaps in her head, she made comparisons, but nothing shook her resolve, not even the dented place where a nose should have existed. No, her fingers caressed it all the same.

And it was too much! I couldn't bear it! I, who had begun this game! I was the one to end it just as abruptly as I shrank back beyond the sweetness in her hands, ducking out of their reach and leaving them to grasp emptily at open air.

Christine made the softest sound, and I didn't want to let myself believe that it was laden in disappointment. No, I wouldn't even consider it as I reattached my mask with trembling fingers and hid my deformity from sight the instant before she removed the blindfold.

"Erik?" she softly bid. I could barely look at her and certainly not her eyes. Dear God, they held a hurt! As if I'd rejected *her* this time!

"I...I'll go and prepare supper," I awkwardly stammered, stumbling to my feet and fleeing her presence while those accusing eyes followed my every movement.

What was I doing! *I* was the one who longed to tear down walls and yet just as quickly, I was also the one to resurrect them. It didn't seem fair that beneath my every desire lurked so much fear, enough that I could not seem to pin it on trust and believe that when she touched me, she wasn't cursing me in her mind. No, her thoughts were a mystery, and they terrified me!

Supper was silent. We barely shared a glance, and if I looked up and caught her gaze, it filled me with such shame that I had to cower and turn away. She had touched my face; I had manipulated her into it, and as far as I knew, she was as regretful as I was. Regret and shame: I was coming to know such emotions so well lately.

Evening faded with the flames of the hearth as I stared dully into their sanctuary. *I should let her go*; it was the most unpleasant thought twisting my brain, and yet I knew it was the right one. But how could I possibly find the strength to crush any fragments I yet possessed of dreams and watch her go to the arms of another man?

"Erik."

Her voice was as lilting as a symphony; every time she said my name, she convinced me how unworthy I was of her. No, my name was not beautiful enough to grace her sacred voice. She should be speaking the wonders of heaven, not the appellation of the devil himself.

I was tentative as I lifted my eyes to her approach, and my attention caught on her hands as between them, she held my dark scarf, idly twisting it in her grasp. "Christine, ...what do you intend to do with that?"

Without a word, she knelt on the floor in the same place as earlier, watching me until the scarf blocked a view as she lifted it over her eyes and tied it into place. Sight gone, she lifted her little hands toward my presence, inviting me to her, and I wondered what she thought to gain by repeating this experiment. Did she consider this another lesson from her once teacher; did she perhaps hope to prove something to us both?

I should refuse, or so said my lingering rationale, but there was too much temptation in the room. Those little hands extended yet, and all I could do was recall how soft and warm they were against my skin. I wanted them upon me so badly that desire clenched tight in my gut and left me to follow its pull as I tentatively lowered myself to the carpet with her, creeping close inch by inch until I was within her reach.

The softest smile tinged her full lips as she heard my approach. I felt unworthy of its curves. But I surrendered to her request and hastily removed my mask, gazing upon her all the while. I edged nearer and into the produced embrace of her hands, losing an unbidden sigh as they found my cheeks between them.

Neither of us spoke a single word as if any concrete sound would only be an intrusion, but touch muttered its own volumes of intimate musings. Her hands upon my face... I never let myself consider that they didn't want to be there of their own accord. No, because she still smiled, encouraging and lovely, and never trembled as her fingertips found the misshapen arch of my mouth and traced its abnormal shape with diligent precision.

I couldn't stop impulse, and as those fingers followed the seam between my lips, I dared to kiss them. Soft, beseeching, reverent. It was gratitude and wanting and every emotion my heart deemed necessary. And her smile never dimmed. It was so beautiful that I wanted it for my own.

Her palms cupped my face, and suddenly unable to stop myself, I crossed the lingering gap between us and dared to kiss that brilliant grin.

All our kisses thus far had seemed transgressions in their way, whether they were coerced or stolen unaware. This was the first contact between us that felt requited. I couldn't find regret because she didn't shrink back or tense. She hesitated one instant of surprise, and then her perfect lips were returning the caress and kissing me back.

Dear God, such exquisite sensation! Her touch was firm and demanding, molded to the malformed shapes of my face. She could not see them or know disgust; her skin was acquainted with mine already and sure in itself, and she kissed me without a single trace of unease. She kissed me because she wanted to. Her lips moved in synchronization with mine; I did not even have to coax her to follow. As passion made me braver and encouraged more, she shocked me with her uninhibited reply, with fingers that delved into my hair and grew taut in an unshaken hold, with a soft sound like a whimper that escaped in the instant I dared to part her willing lips with my tongue. This was a desire I'd only fantasized into existence, and it breathed and writhed between us like a living thing. ...And I was suddenly terrified to consider what it meant.

I only tasted her, enough to let her delicious sweetness tingle my taste buds and leave me addicted and yearning for more, and then with reluctant disappointment, I pulled my mouth away, fighting against her surprisingly protesting grasp. She even tried to kiss *me* again! She leaned her little face close, arching near, but I broke away and wouldn't concede, watching her hands reach and grasp at nothing in my place.

"Are you afraid of me, Erik?" She demanded my earlier question with flustered desperation and a slight hysteria as if she had to speak lest I flee her presence.

But I extended a shaking hand and caught the scarf about her eyes, untying as I pulled it free. "Look at me, Christine," I commanded. "Look at this pitiful excuse for a face and truly see it. Is it what you envisioned as you kissed me back in its every horrible detail? Or is it just so easy to forget with your eyes covered, when it is a seeming dream between us?"

Her gaze showed her anxiousness, and I chose to make it worse, grabbing her hand as she jumped with surprise and abruptly bringing it to my mangled cheek. She was tense, tense all over despite the touches we'd shared, but I ignored it and forced her hand back to my disfigurement.

"Still disgusted," I taunted with the unavoidable flare of my temper. I was as angry with myself as I was with her. I should have known better.

"No," she quickly insisted, but her hand was shaking in mine. "And I've *never* been disgusted."

Her bravery would have surprised me if I weren't so certain she was lying. "And yet every time my face is bared to you, you shun its hideousness as if it would taint you as well."

"No, not your face," she protested with an adamancy I'd never seen from her. "*You.* I shun *you.*"

Growling my anger that she would dare such an argument, I caught her shoulders with my hands and pinched tight. "What?"

Her hand was yet against my cheek, and though it quivered, she did not pull it free. "You want so much of me," she suddenly accused. "Every time you look at me, you beg for every bit of myself, Erik. And I could vow it to you, but it won't be enough. You'll always doubt because I couldn't love you as you wanted from the start. I rejected you the same as the rest of the world, and you'll never forgive me for it."

"You reject me still-"

"I chose you," she interrupted when I expected her to back down. "Why is it not enough that I agreed to live as your wife?"

"Because you love the Vicomte," I stated as my reason.

"I feel *safe* with the Vicomte," she countered. "He doesn't long to rip me apart and take the very heart of me. He makes it easy while you expect a love that is going to change the foundation of the world beneath our feet. And if I can't give it to you, how long until you resent me for it?"

I was staring at her so intently, reading every emotion as it played along her face and believing her every admission. Because she was afraid. Because she was holding my eye with never a flinch and keeping her palm to my mangled face until it steadied. Because I knew she spoke the truth.

"You said you'd teach me how to love you as you want," she reminded, calmer now that the words were in the air. "You were to show me what it means, and yet I'm not sure that you know it yourself."

"I know love," I protested, and yet my voice had dulled of its sharpness. "I *love you*. You are the one who chooses the fancies of a rich aristocrat over what I offer at my every breath."

"Why do you keep insisting that?"

"Why indeed," I spat, and renewed irritation became despair as the hand at my cheek opened its fingers and splayed wide against my skin, burning me inside and out. Yet still I spoke accusations. "You had the fever, Christine. You begged me to hold you; it was not by some absurd transgression that you woke in my arms. I held you as you wanted, only in your delirium, it was not the arms of your devoted Erik about you. You pleaded and spoke your eternal love to darling Raoul. He was the invisible presence in our bed, and truths came with his intangibility, it seems. ...You said you love him, and you destroyed my every dream for our future in your selfish, little hands."

"Love," she repeated in a breath, and yet her eyes were bearing into mine all the while, so transfixed and intent. "You're to teach me to love you," she insisted again. "You covered my eyes and took my sight. You believed you had to go to such lengths to convince me to bear your touch, and have I now shown you that such a thing is ridiculous? It's a face, Erik, and I am not cowering from its unordinary construction. I am touching your face, and it is the same as I envisioned it in my mind's eye when you kissed me. Is that what you wished to know?"

"This face, Christine?" I posed doubtfully.

And she shocked me to a gasped breath as she suddenly leant forward in my hold and set the gentlest kiss to the swollen arch of my upper lip. I couldn't bear it anymore, half-certain I would grab her and clasp her and never let her go despite her lingering trepidations. And it scared me so much that I abruptly released her and got to my feet, refusing another glance.

"Erik? ...You ask for love, and yet you won't accept it."

"Ask for love? Force love upon you, you mean," I corrected with disgust I could not conceal. "I've pushed my heart to yours since the first day, and you're right. I expect a love that transcends every detail of my world. Perhaps you could have given it to me of your own free will if I'd let you, but I tried to manipulate it from you, to force your world to alter as inextricably as mine and weave our lives together in permanent union. But...no, it makes me a monster; in seeking your heart, I nearly damaged both of ours irreparably." I shook a miserable head, suddenly so weighty with its spiraling realities, and before I could think better of it, I met the protests in her eyes and said, "Go back to your Vicomte, Christine. I release you from your choice. Go and find the life you truly want and clasp it with both hands. Never let it go again."

"Erik-"

She was starting to rise from the floor, her hands reaching to me, and before she could clasp, I escaped the future I wanted but wouldn't have, the bride attempting to appease with her touch, the house where dreams were supposed to be coming to life but were only hollow shells. And I didn't have to regret it and insist to sense that I should let her go because I already had.

*****

197

I am quite good at sabotaging my own happiness. Maybe in some vein of utter self-hatred, I feel I don't deserve it and seek to punish myself by taking away every chance. I wanted Christine, ached for her, adored her with every fiber of my being, and yet I wouldn't let myself have her. And why? ...Because somewhere along a meandering path laden with evil crime and sin, I had grown a sense of morality, a sudden need for penance and redemption, a realization that I couldn't just take what I wanted. I had to earn it. I was not a god separated from humanity because I was so far above it. As much as it pained me to admit, I was a part of it, the same as every other of its species.

And Christine... I could pine for her all I liked, but plenty of loves went unrequited. There was no written law to say she must love me back because I loved her so hopelessly. No, it had to be her choice if I was ever going to have her as mine.

Coming to these conclusions was the easy part; following through was another story. I wandered the cold city in the dark, step after adamant step until my desire dimmed and I felt certain that if I went to the house and found her gone, I wouldn't pursue her in a fit of rage. I offered her escape. If she took it, I had to let her go. As I said, it was a feat that was easier said than done when it meant that I went from having a willing if unhappy bride to nothing but an empty house again.

I was nervous as I returned home, wondering if there would be anything left of a shattered dream, even just fragments that I could meld back together. The fire was lit in the sitting room hearth and cast shadows out into the foyer to welcome my presence. It meant little, answered no question, but I still followed its glow with a twinge of hope I couldn't deny.

And there she was... I thought I dreamt her image at first. Peacefully asleep upon my couch in her white nightdress, obviously awaiting my return. She could have been gone, could have been in the home of the Vicomte right now, sleeping in his arms. But no, ...she hadn't left me. And it meant so much more than the first time she'd chosen me because I'd let her go without threat or consequence. I'd let her go, and here she was with me still.

"Christine," I breathed to myself as I dared to kneel on the floor beside her, gazing upon her as she slept. With only the slightest hesitation, I bent and gently rested my head against her heartbeat, savoring its music. My Christine... She was the greatest gift I'd ever been granted.

I felt her stir, the subtle shift in a constant pulse, the breath released in a soft sigh that ruffled the hair along my brow, and as I reluctantly lifted my head, I was shocked to silence to watch a slow smile light her lips when her eyes met mine. Had I ever received such a welcome?

"Erik..."

And when walls threatened, I wouldn't let them be built. "I've never loved the way I love you, Christine," I told her, genuinely honest without a temper to make endearments carry the weight of threats. "I never knew such feelings could exist, and...they terrify as much as they consume. I thought to teach you to love me when the truth is you must teach *me* to love you. ...To love you in a way that won't destroy our hearts at its culmination."

She seemed to meditate upon my words, but her little hand reached for my mask. I allowed her with a certain amount of intrigue, watching her remove it without even a tremble and expose my distortions. "This is a man I could love," she revealed. "One who offers me his heart and lets me choose how I will hold it. Beneath your mask is a soul, Erik, and it is so brilliant when it shines. It makes this face beautiful. But how often do you deny its power with your desire to control? You want to *force* my heart to beat for you, but if you would let it be, it could play a duet *with* yours instead. Two equal parts of a whole."

Her fingers caressed my cheek, and I dared to turn and graze a kiss to their warm softness. "I love you, Christine."

"Trust my heart to love you back," she bid.

"Why did you stay?" I could not help but pose. "I thought I was giving you what your heart truly desired."

"My heart is already where it desires to be. The night I chose to stay I was afraid, Erik, because I saw no trace of the angel I once knew in the madman tossing ultimatums at my feet. I was half-sure he was gone, and I regretted the choice I'd made if it meant I could never have him back. But now I see that heart bared to me, laid beside my own, and I want to be nowhere else."

As she spoke those beautiful words that brought unbidden tears to my eyes, I allowed impulse to guide me and gently touched my fingertips to her cheek, astounded when she did not recoil. "I would love as gentle as a lamb if it meant I would have you forever in my arms."

"No," she said with a hinted smile, "I adore the fire in you too much. Teach me not to run from its possession, and I will teach you not to run from your own surmised doubts."

Fire... Yes, with her, it could burn with flames, and how often had I used desire's power to create more walls and lose what I most wanted? I desired her so much, and I was equally guilty of turning it into a seeming sin in the process. It didn't have to be that way anymore, not if she were willing instead of afraid. *Fire, there could be fire.*

"And...are you still afraid, Christine?" I asked as I made my fingers move along her cheekbone and down to her upturned jaw. "You tremble still when I touch you. If it is not disgust, ...is it fear?"

Her small, timid nod left me to consider how often she'd avoided my touch, how often I'd selfishly made it about my face, never considered that she bore her own reasons for hesitancy. How right she was! I created doubts and things to run from and never let her simply love me as she would.

"I won't hurt you," I vowed, "and I won't force you despite what I've let you believe. Make it your choice, Christine. You've chosen to stay as my wife; you decide what that means."

I could see that my words surprised her and cursed my own transgression to make her think otherwise. I had presented my desire as a *punishment*. I hated myself for such a thing!

"My hands upon your body," I muttered more to myself in my self-chastisement. "I was the very one to make you fear and denounce it! I made desiring me into a sin!"

"So...teach me something different," she insisted, and her free hand came to clasp my own to her cheek. "Show me that your touch and the way it feels are not something worthy of fear. ...I don't want to be afraid of something I want so much, but it pulls me under its waves and drowns me in its power. And is it any wonder why I ran to the Vicomte when he makes me feel *nothing* like what you do?"

"You love him," I protested and tried to keep the bitterness from my tone.

She shook her head against the couch pillow. "What I feel for Raoul is too easy to be love; it isn't attached to the heart. What I feel for you... It overwhelms my every sense and steals my soul."

"But is it love, Christine?"

"Don't doubt, *ange*," she reminded. Her palms cradled my face between their softness, scars never considered. "And if I simply say the words, will it put you at ease? Can you not see their letters in my eyes? Everything I feel is so blatantly put before you. Can you not see my heart, Erik?"

But I did. To know she held my face as if it were any other ordinary face and wanted me, that she chose me even with freedom in her grasp, that in spite of her lingering trepidation, she yearned to be mine... All of those things spoke volumes to love.

This was our starting point. I had to trust in what she freely gave, and she had to let go of fear to love me. For once, every one of our mismatched emotions was perfectly aligned.

As my answer, I kissed her, shivering to feel her *smile* against my mouth as if this kiss was all she wanted. Her lips pressed to mine, love in every contact. It was my dream brought to life, even more brilliant than fantasy because it was real.

And so I won my heart's desire. I could have been doomed to an eternity alone. I could have let her go and broken both our hearts in my blind hastiness, forcing feelings upon her shoulders that didn't exist. I could have been the cause of destroying what I longed for most. It was a tragedy only steps away, and I was fortunate that it wasn't mine.

Our path wasn't carved out before us; it was formed as we went along its meandering trail. It wasn't perfect or without foibles as we learned the true nuances of love and desire. It was a life evolving. But Christine loved me; I saw it in every detail of our life together, and I adored her doubly back. She changed me and made me a man worthy of her heart. And I counted myself blessed because she taught me what love truly was. She was my inspiration, and love was our dream together. Two parts of a whole heart.

"Monsters and Masks"
After six months of separation, Erik attends the Masquerade
Ball, desperate for one touch.

Erik loved to watch her dance. The lithe, graceful movements of her agile body, the pure elegance on her feet. Such details had been the core in desire's awakening. Back in days of ballet slippers and tulle, his eyes had been drawn to every curve of her woman's body. He'd learned the potent power of wanting, possessed through rehearsals spied from Box 5 with images he could not escape. Pirouettes and plies, every gesture, every motion had taken her beyond the broken child he'd sheltered under his wing and reminded him that she was not a little girl seeking his tutelage and praises; she was a full-grown woman. Her naïveté often made him forget that very real fact. A woman's body, and lusting from his hidden regard, running feverish gazes up expanses of bare legs and along attributes too well-defined by scant costumes, he had been awakened to the baser yearnings of the human body. Before her, such urges had ending points and were trained in denial. *She* sparked them into uncontrollable infernos. She...with dance as her weapon.

Dancing in a room full of masked patrons and cast mates was not the same. The steps were conventional, the costumes formal and overdone. This was not the opera ballet being practiced to only his furtive spying, and Christine was not one in a gaggle of tutus, shy of her talent, nervous to stand out. Layers hid improper views of shapely calves and thighs, and when a mask stole a need to be oneself, it was simple to fall into a role and play a part. He'd never had that excuse.

Masquerade, to ordinary people, meant make believe and fun. He took it as an insult, as if they were taunting *him* and only *him* with their little game of dress-up. That was the reason he avoided this yearly mockery, confined himself below and pretended not to know that the opera house above him was filled with noisy people treating masks as favored accessories. It *sickened* him.

So why attend this year? Because he longed to see her dance. Months without a single glimpse of her had taken their toll. At first, separation had been necessary. He'd dropped their precious chandelier with a rage so intense that it had frightened him, all inspired to life by her betraying, little heart. And so, he had locked himself underground with music as his only ally in penance. Six months lost in melodies and lyrical lines, and yet it had been *her* voice singing in his inner ear. He had turned desire into a fierce hunger to compose, pouring its telltale yearning into his opera and giving lust its own song. But...when it was finished and the notes ran out, he had nothing left and nowhere else to steer a need, and so here he was, back to watching her dance from the shadows.

Standing on the upper landing, hidden in the rafters, he gazed down at the couples whirling across the dance floor. Christine stood out as if a beacon light shown upon her. Her blue eyes were aglow in the brilliance of her soul, her smile genuine and blissful. He recalled days when such a look had been his. ...Or rather, an *angel's*. She'd *never* granted him such luxuries. No, they were stolen away with a mask, and when reality had carved itself in pictures, smiles had become only tears and fear. An angel's smiles had found a replacement, and *he* currently matched her grin for grin with his perfect face only half-concealed by a pathetic excuse for a mask. Erik should have known a Vicomte would not want to hide his flawless features like everyone else at this charade. No, he'd want to flaunt and distance himself from being a man in a mask.

Sneering disgust, Erik refused to waste thought on the Vicomte and returned his attention to Christine. *His* Christine, dancing in the arms of another man, giving grins meant to be Erik's. Her lace and silk mask covered most of her precious features, and he had to wonder if in wearing it, she gave a thought to him. Was he a forgotten nightmare somewhere in the background, or did she think of him even for an instant in the midst of this melee? But...she looked too happy, and he had never brought her happiness. No, ...no, she must have forgotten. Six months without incident *would* have such an effect...

Erik's eyes drifted along the exposed line of her jaw, down the column of her throat to one bare shoulder exposed by her low neckline. Such perfection, like a sculpture crafted by God's own hands. His memory teased with recollections of silken skin, so warm and soft. He'd had only fleeting caresses, too few to imprint the texture on his cold hands. Fingertips tingled with a need to steal a touch. Just one. To touch her skin and remember what it was to *feel*. For months, he'd suffocated every emotion and every craving in the music. Now they burned their brightest and insisted one touch would calm their addiction. One graze of skin too smooth to be real, too flawless to ever be entrusted in his care. Oh God, if he touched her, it would remind him that he was *alive*.

With great stealth, Erik dropped down into the wings and ignored the crowd as he slipped within its boundaries. He was masked and for the first time, an equal. No one knew he had *reason* for his 'costume', that the skeleton face of the Red Death he'd chosen was satire and as close to reality as he dared go. He *was* that veritable corpse, but they looked and saw another willing participant in their make believe world. To his disgust, a few ladies even attempted to catch his eye! Hussies! And let them peel away his mask and then see if they were still so shameless! Only one person in the horde had the potential not to scream in horror and run, but she was too busy denying her heart of its rightful beat to learn to be brave.

And there she was. He stood on the outskirts of the dancers, letting her image fill his view. *Christine...* How easy this would be! She was bumped left and right by too many people crammed on the small dance floor, so many others unwittingly blessed by touches they could not give proper reverence to. All he had to do was approach and take the offer freely given.

He waited until the orchestra ended their piece and couples were about to split and scatter. Just as the Vicomte took his accursed hands from her and gave release, he ducked between bodies, focused on only one, and rushed close.

A single touch. It was an obsession because it was so attainable. One would quiet the yearning. It *must*, or he would go mad!

He was near enough to see the lights reflected in her curls, adding strawberry hues in a sea of dark. More temptation. More touches he could steal. But as he rushed past, he settled for the one he was after, brushing her bare shoulder with the pads of his fingertips.

Immediately, a gasp tore from his lungs. Oh, the ache! She was as silken as remembered, warm and soft, her skin a template for passions he longed to bestow. One touch, and it seared the surface of his fingers and shot a rush through the limb, down his torso, racing his bloodstream until it settled with a dull throb so intense that he trembled on his feet. One touch..., but no, one wasn't enough. One was a tease, a prelude to greater and better things. One was a *disappointment*.

The next dance was about to start, and quivering with the rapid spin of his plotting mind, he made an impulsive choice. He was an equal in this room, masked, unrecognized. He should be entitled the same liberties as everyone else when a face was no longer a hindrance.

The Vicomte was about to claim her again when Erik came behind her and dared to brush his fingers through her hair, shaking to be so bold.

"A dance?" he lowly muttered, disguising his one revealing betrayer with whispers, deep and concealing. He was behind Christine, out of a direct view of blue eyes that would have rattled his pretense, but he dared meet the Vicomte's stare with firm resolve. Well, of course, he was just another man asking a dance with a masked lady. The Vicomte could pose no argument as long as the guise was in place.

And yet Erik kept wary beneath his bravado, on guard with an undying fear to be identified. But the Vicomte reluctantly nodded, his disdain obvious and unhidden as he gave Christine's gloved hand a fond squeeze and walked away with arrogance in every step. The puffed-up peacock, not wanting to show defeat! It was as if he boasted that Erik may have won the battle, but Raoul was determined to win the war.

Christine laughed. Erik heard the sound, and it tickled his eardrums with its longed-for timbre. It was a precursor to the wave that struck as she turned to face him, her supposed dance partner. He had to lower his mismatched eyes, hide their colors behind lash-less lids with a sudden terror that she would *know* him in a single look.

He focused on layers of pale pink and lace instead, on the way her gown hugged her curves, fitted snug the way he longed to fit her in his arms. Dragging an anxious gaze up, he trailed womanly graces, now so close that they were within his reach, the swell of her breasts beneath a low-cut neckline. ...And the gold chain sitting so unthreateningly upon the pale skin of her chest, its pendant tucked under a lace edging so prying eyes would not see. Others would think it a family heirloom, a necklace, possibly fake if they recognized her as cast, but Erik knew what dangled from its fettering cord. It was humorous that the Vicomte claimed Erik held Christine to him using music as his chain when the *Vicomte* had chosen a literal chain, proclaiming ownership every spot it touched her skin. Damn him!

No longer willing to play timid, Erik captured Christine in a dancer's pose and began to whirl with her about the dance floor, following the paths of other couples. She was surprised with his abruptness, stumbling a bit to match his steps, but she went willing, convincing him that she had yet to realize *who* she was allowing to hold her.

Rage fueled the dance; it was the fire beneath his feet, encouraging him to take her harder and faster around the dance floor. And she...she saw it as a *game*! She laughed delight beneath her breath and fought to keep up, probably thinking him a half-drunk patron or another cast mate. A night full of make believe and pretend! Of course, *danger* couldn't touch her in such a magical setting! Of course, she *must be* safe from any monster and his yearning clutches! Ah yes, because she wore proof that she belonged to another and was already taken; her dearest lover would keep her safe! Erik had the urge to rip the chain from her throat if only to free her.

She was yet laughing, that delicious sound that he longed to bottle up and steal, and daring to race his stare over her masked face, he savored the smile, the glow in her blue eyes, the *happiness*. Why was it a sin for this to be his? He'd treat it like a blessing much more than anyone else ever could. It was beautiful.

So engrossed in his fantasy, he faltered a step, cursing his uncharacteristic clumsiness and blaming it on her, and as she stumbled with a small cry, he did not hesitate to catch her bare shoulders between his hands to keep her upright. Dancing ceased as abruptly as it began, and he felt his palms and fingers burn at first contact and shake despite their firm hold.

Skin! So much skin! He'd longed to touch bare shoulders, and now they were searing his flesh from his bones as a consequence he eagerly permitted. He ached to beg for her to burn his entire body the same. He was so cold, but she was a flame. He would burn alive willingly in her hands.

Perhaps his chill gave him away, or maybe it was the harshly gasped breaths he could not keep quiet or just the meeting of blue eyes to mismatched ones full of feelings he could not hide. But he felt her tense in his hold, all laughter a distant memory as she stared with slow realization and aghast horror.

"No..." The word left her in her exhalation, soundless and yet heavy, and his fingers instinctively tightened, taut and digging into soft flesh he'd just blessed until he saw her cringe.

"Was I forgotten all this time?" he dared to taunt, choosing anger over the pain her terror inspired. "Speak my name, Christine. Let me know I am still a thought in your head."

"Erik," she muttered miserably, tears crowding the corners of her eyes. He wanted to tell her not to cry, that tears *stung* when they were caught beneath a mask and held to skin. She wouldn't know such things. Maybe she needed to learn them herself.

Before her gallant hero could spot tears and steal every opportunity, Erik released her shoulders, wincing to see a discolored imprint left behind, and catching her gloved hand instead, he dragged her with him through the crowd. She didn't struggle or scream, only cried softly. He wasn't sure he could take that as hope.

Out of the throng and into silent corridors, and he pondered his options as her whimpers deafened his ears. This was unintended, uncalculated. He hadn't considered taking her with him tonight, but...just the idea of the Vicomte playing savior and filling her head with more fear and terror, cursing the reappearance of the Opera demon, making Erik's love sound like a degradation and appalling sin... No. This was *his*. Too long without her, and he was dead and hollow in between. Now life flowed anew, and he'd be damned if he'd let it go so easily.

Erik drew her to her empty dressing room, pulling her inside and locking the door behind. Still she yielded with never a spoken protest, unless tears could be counted. Darkness engulfed once out of the dimly-lit corridor, and when a small cry left her lips, tainted in fear, he released her if only to light lamps and give her solace. He knew her so well, knew she had an irrational fear of the dark and its secrets. Maybe that should have been the point to make him realize why she could never be his. He *was* the dark.

But candlelight stole the blackness with warm comfort, and Erik kept back and watched her in tentative apprehension as she wove shaking arms about her waist and sobbed quietly to herself. As always, a part of him ached with her. How he hated to see her cry! Something so lovely should never know sadness. But he forced himself to recall that she knew sadness because she was with *him*, and compassion faded to ash.

"You foolish girl," he muttered lowly. "You brought this upon yourself, Christine. You and your cursed innocence. Did you truly believe it was over? That six months apart would cure me of my obsession? No. It is a disease, an affliction of flesh and bone, a poison in my veins. Did you think my love was frivolous and fleeting, that it would burn out with time apart? It burns more brilliant now than ever. You, you, *always* you. Like an elixir I must consume or die without. And *why?* I have no answer for such a question. Why *you?* Why an immature, spoiled child who refuses to see beyond her homemade illusions of the world? Why a girl without compassion or pity who spent so long running from my love and blighting it to her lover? You are *cruel* and *heartless*, and I love you still!"

She flinched with every word he spat at her, tears tumbling faster, and with a suddenness that made her start, Erik closed the distance between them and clasped her shoulders in a brutal hold, fingers fitted to their previous marks.

"This is *your fault!*" he shouted and refused to falter to her cries. "You could have left this place and never looked back. I *let you go!* An intelligent girl would have grasped such an opportunity with both hands and fled the madman in love with her. But *you!* You stayed in Paris at the opera! You cruel child! You love knowing that you have my heart at your feet and the power to trample it and destroy me."

"No," she whimpered, shaking her head miserably, but she would not meet his fiery glare, and it only convinced him that he was right.

"No?" he taunted. "Why didn't you *go*? You wanted me to *fail*, to crawl back into your life, pathetic and pitiable. You wanted to hurt me."

"Hurt you?" she stammered. "No, I didn't... I..."

But Erik extended one tensed hand and grabbed the chain about her neck. With barely a graze of silken skin, he ripped it free, ignoring her cry of surprise and dangling the glistening diamond ring hanging from its cord between them.

"How...how did you know?" she sobbed. "You were gone. All this time, you weren't a part of my life."

"Yes, because you chose to forget me. You went from one game of pretend with an imaginary angel to the next with your noble fiancé, never a care for anything else. Merciless child," he hissed again and waved the ring before her eyes. "You wanted me to see this and mock me with what I can never have. Any consequence is *your* fault for being here with your valiant Vicomte to hold you in his arms, ...for being so *beautiful* and making me *want* you in spite of it all. Damn you, Christine! You have destroyed me!"

Tears had never ceased their fall, and yet he caught guilt in their sparkle and an empathy he hated her for feeling. And as she gently spoke his name, he tossed the ring from his hand and caught her shoulders again with a fierce growl, shaking her hard.

"Damn you!" he shouted. "You have taken a god and made him mortal and worthless. I am supposed to be the legend, feared and obeyed. I earned that place, but you have made me *pathetic*. And I wallow and cry because I can't have your love! Because I want you so much that my own body has become my enemy! It's *your* fault! The devil tempts with sin, Christine. He places it before man and urges him to fall and take. *You* are sin. The devil wants me to possess you and fully condemn myself to hell. *He* made you beautiful and sensual; *he* created *you* to arouse my desires and make me hunger this way. And perhaps I *should* give in. You brought it upon yourself by remaining. You could have left this place and been done with the nightmare!"

"Erik, you're hurting me," she whimpered. "Please stop."

"Why? Because if your fiancé sees bruises, he'll tell you I'm a monster? But you already know that. He's poured *his* beliefs into your head and made them yours. I wasn't a monster before, not to *you* anyway. But now...well, masquerades mean pretend, don't they? Being someone or something you are not. I'll be a monster and *take*. And you, Christine, ...you play your part. Be the victim. Cry and beg me to stop. It will fuel the flame."

"No," she suddenly cried. "I don't want to play pretend games anymore!"

A cold chuckle left his lips. "No more pretend? But you came here in a mask ready to play like the rest. Another role, another part. Play the game with me now. I'll let you *choose* your character. Will you be a victim and beg for mercy, or will you be a coquette and pretend you want me instead? It's funny that we are allowed to be something we are not tonight because a *mask* makes it so. Why am I not permitted that excuse everyday? I can fluctuate between monster and man but cannot blame it on a mask. No, it's only seen as a failure in my soul. There is no *joy* in wearing a mask, and yet everyone at this Masquerade laughs and flirts, plays dress-up like overgrown children. When a mask can't come off at the end of the night, make believe no longer applies. Perhaps that is why I can't have you: because you can play make believe and I can't. I am only allowed reality, and a mask is my *life*."

"I...I'm sorry," she whispered, and while a part

of him longed to believe it, the rest could not. She was a child of fairytales and sugarcoated illusion. She needed truths and harsh realities instead. She needed to *see* or she would never be his.

Christine gazed at him with fear quivering her limbs. This night was supposed to be about bliss and excitement, ...fun in a mask. She suddenly called herself ignorant for never considering anything else. But...Erik had been no more than a memory for six months, and her world had spun onward without him. Was she to be blamed for never considering he would appear at the Masquerade? ...She'd been half-certain he was gone for good.

"Erik," she attempted to sound gentle and soothe him. "You're right. We need not play games in masks. It...*is* cruel. I never realized-"

"That you can remove yours when the last dance has ended?" he snapped with that unpredictable temper that always left her nervously on edge. "That tomorrow you will be only *Christine* again and carry on in the world as ordinary as every other?"

With an abruptness that shook her, he jerked the lace-trimmed mask from her face. She felt oddly exposed without it. Holding it up to inspection, he waved its flimsy material with never a care for delicacy. "What is this? An elegant accessory? And look what lies beneath. Beauty, perfection. No scars. Not a single one. You are as breathtaking as ever. If you wore scars, everything would make sense. But you don't; you *choose* to be masked with this decoration."

Tossing it to the floor, he glared at her hard enough to make her shiver on her feet as he decided, "And now I will play your equal. Games of pretend are over and done, and now the masks come off. And what shall you find? Not *beauty*. Of course not. The same horror as ever before. I would have kept it hidden, but *you* don't want pretend."

He still had one hand upon her shoulder,

keeping her in place with a forceful hold, and though she trembled to watch him, she did not look away as he reached for his skeleton mask and tore it free. The masks were off... And reality wasn't the beauty and elegance of a Masquerade Ball. It was ugly and scarred. *That face...*

She hadn't seen it in consciousness since the day she'd stolen his mask and shattered the illusion. Dreams were its confines now, a place where she could never fully study its nuances, where she could not touch or inflict more damage. And in some strange way, six months of only envisioning it had left a sting of disappointment. Reality awakened here with this vision. It was...horrible and disturbing, but it was *real*.

Her breath came in soft gasps; she could not control such a natural response as he stood exposed and vulnerable before her. It felt...intimate, and she wondered if she should consider it a betrayal to Raoul that she did not scream or fight, ...that she did not *fear* or *recoil*. No, she stared and let her gaze wander as she hadn't been allowed the first time. The masks were off, ...and the bravado and persona with it. A man stood before her, nothing but a man.

Erik seemed upset that she *didn't* respond with terror, and as he shook his head in uncertain confusion and fought to accept her silent curiosity, she saw every crack in a veneer. Opera Ghost evaporated as quickly as a mask and left him nothing to hide behind.

"Cry," he suddenly commanded with firm adamancy. "Scream, Christine. Tears, I want *tears* and fear! Cry, damn you!"

She jumped with his pinching hold, but she refused to obey. Her voice wavered with a flustered and uncommon bravery, as she demanded, "Why? You said no more pretend and no more roles."

He was urgently trying to read her; she felt the penetration of a stare so intense that it sought secrets beneath skin and carved into bone. He looked for lies, but she showed him none, and it only seemed to enrage him.

With a frustrated growl, he yanked her to her mirror's glass. She kept pliant, unsure how far she could push his temper. She wanted to believe he would never hurt her, but she'd seen him lash out before, seen him drop a chandelier and shatter it to pieces like his broken heart when she'd run in fear the last time. The symbolism was not lost on her; she had to excuse the horror if only for the truth. His heart, just as delicate and beautiful as that chandelier, and she bore the blame for its destruction. But...considering he could have come for her, shattered *her* instead, it left an inkling of trust as he positioned her before her reflection, lit by her mediocre lamp that cast only warm gentleness in its glow.

"Erik, what...?" She'd been prepared to be taken with him, dragged into the passageway and to his home. She was ready to go, unconsciously waiting for this day for six months. Surprise came to be released before her image with him moving like a shadow behind her.

"Look and see. Truly *see* this, Christine. I will not play a game back and forth with your inconstant heart any longer. *Understand*, foolish child. For once in our sordid relationship, I *need* you to understand what I am."

He spoke in broken phrases so full of his uncertainties that they kept her wary, and to her astonished gasp, he lifted his discarded mask, the skeleton's visage, and held it over *her* face. One hand kept it there while the other clutched her shoulder and kept her body before his, his unmasked features nothing but shapes above her shoulder.

The breath left her lungs in a gut-wrenching sigh. The weight of the world in one piece of manmade material. It was...uncomfortable, hard and pressing to her soft skin, ...*warm*. Warm because it had just cradled *his* damaged features. The idea alone brought tears to her eyes, and she gasped air into suffocated lungs, the mask stifling every inhalation and *hurting* her. It wasn't beautiful or fun. It wasn't anything like the one she had spent the evening wearing. This was *real*, and staring at her reflection, her face hidden by its barrier, she shuddered and quivered, the tears coming faster and getting stuck and smeared to her skin.

"What if this was *your* reality, Christine?" he lowly bid, and she heard tears in his voice as well, the hands upon her trembling as hard as she was. "A mask, every minute of every day. Hiding yourself from the world. Met with horror at every turn. What would that mean to you? To have *no one* bear the sight of your face. It isn't a game, Christine. It's never been a game for me. But you...you think life is a fairytale, and you've cast me as your villain. In a fairytale, the villain never touches the heroine; the hero always saves her. ...I don't want to be the villain. Is it this face that has given me my part without my choosing? Because I'll give you one to mask, and then we'll be the *same*, and you can stop running from me."

Tears came faster, and a sob made her lightheaded as the breath was trapped and swallowed in the next. A skeleton's features over her own... A corpse's face like Erik's... And *that* was the only way he thought he could have her.

Erik was crying; she felt a sob leave him and shake her with its intensity as he choked out desperate words. "Sometimes I wish you were ugly. I wish you were so damaged that no one else would love you. *Only me.* You'd truly be mine then. I wouldn't have to battle the world simply to touch your shoulder." Shaking his head, he admitted, "I thought to scar you once. To *make you* as undesirable as I am, but... My God, Christine, I could never hurt you."

She calmed with his words because she knew they were true, and without a thought, she edged inches closer until her back was to his chest and his breaths were hers by proximity and desire. Why did it feel necessary to breathe with him? To feel his body close and savor every second? Months apart, and *this* was what she'd longed for. In the deepest recesses of her heart as she had played her part and put on a figurative mask for Raoul's sake, *this* was what she needed to fill the hollow hole within her. Just to breathe with him, as if his life were hers. ...She hated herself to admit it and to realize that the horror of a mask held to her features faded away with his nearness. It meant *nothing* if he were the one to keep her grounded. Perhaps that was the essential core of this lesson in tolerance. Two hearts beating in succession, two breaths shared the same, and nothing else mattered.

"You...you asked why I didn't leave," she softly whispered and felt him hold his breath. Anticipation? Fear was more likely the cause. "Because I was waiting for you to come back."

His exhalation was so harsh that she shivered with him, but in husky words, he commanded, "Prove it to me."

"How?"

"Return to the party with me like *this*. Without the Vicomte's bauble claiming you as *his*, but with my mask claiming you as *mine*."

He stated it so simply as if carrying through would be easy and wouldn't take more bravery than she possessed. *Erik's.* Hadn't she run from him once to avoid that fate? And why? The reason felt silly now. He'd already vowed never to hurt her, and his face was exposed and couldn't hold weight. So why was she determined to reject this place once before? Perhaps because it wasn't just *loving* Erik involved; it was being brave enough to stand at his side, not caring what the world said and how it viewed her for committing herself to the Opera Ghost. Following the acceptable route was easy. To be envied and adored for being on the Vicomte's arm instead of ridiculed for being on Erik's. He was an admitted murderer with a temper that carried its own trepidation; loving him meant going against everything she'd ever been taught and believed. Loving him meant traveling the untaken path... She wasn't sure she was strong enough for that.

"But...if Raoul sees you, he will come after and try to hurt you."

"If Raoul sees *my face*, you mean," he taunted sharply near her ear, and the shiver that traveled her spine was from more than fear... Fear, what fear? It tingled her body and made her press a little tighter to him when sense told her to pull away. "You don't want your precious Vicomte to glimpse what lies beneath my mask and know that *you* chose such abhorrence over perfection. It's degrading, isn't it, Christine? To want an ugly man? You're ashamed. ...But you *do* want me, don't you?"

For as confident as he sought to sound, she heard anxiety. He didn't believe his own claim, and yet the hand at her shoulder made a timid path, snaking about her waist and pulling her tighter still to him.

Oh God... She stared fixedly at her masked face in the mirror's glass and saw herself overcome. But...to feel him, his desire so much more than words, a *threat* against the small of her back whispering wanting with a throb and an ache. She was afraid of it, and yet she *wanted* it with a responding thrill that traveled her limbs and made her gasp.

"Do you want me, Christine?" he demanded again, more intent when she was certain her own body gave a definite answer. And it became an uncontrollable whimper slipping from her tongue as he dared to bend and press his bare, damaged face against her bare shoulder. This should repel her, *repulse, disgust*, make her sick with abhorrence, but...it *didn't*! It made the ache deeper, pulling within her and spinning reality out of focus. She forgot scars existed! How could she possibly? She *forgot* that his face once brought terror to life. It was disfigured, and Lord help her, she wanted it pressed to her skin! To feel its every abnormality against her!

Misshapen lips found the curve of her shoulder and set a tentative kiss against it, oddly shy when his erection was boldly put forth and arching against her to insist its strength.

"My masked beauty," he whispered, every husky consonant lifting goose bumps upon her skin. "But tell me why you shiver and quake. ...You came with me *willing*, away from the Masquerade and your supposed fiancé. Why, Christine? Is the fairytale over and pretend at its end? Can the villain finally possess the heroine?"

His lips pressed more reverent kisses to her shoulder, each its own question, and answers were nothing beyond gasped breaths. Letters could not move past her lungs; they were suffocated in sensations ebbing from the abnormal swell of his mouth and its branding mark.

But he seemed to *need* words, and with a frustrated huff, the arm at her waist turned her until she faced him and every scar she'd forgotten. He lowered his mask from her face, gave her nowhere to hide and no place to look but his fiery mismatched eyes. The thick longing creased his ugly features and made them a vision that tightened her stomach. His lips... They were malformed, the upper swelled and distorted, and yet as she considered that they had just kissed her shoulder, that they had been against her skin, she shivered.

Trembling hands removed her gloves, one at a time, desperate to be as free from their encasement as from a mask. With all the tenderness she possessed, she lifted a touch and trailed one fingertip along the abnormal swell of his upper lip, outlining its distortion and learning its soft texture. She felt him shudder, so violent that it reverberated against her fingertip, and those demanding eyes flamed and flickered with fervency amidst avid surprise.

As her finger grazed the seam of his lips, he formed desperate kisses that gushed a gratitude she

didn't comprehend. To be so thankful for one touch…
It seemed like touch was the right of every human
being, not a privilege. A blessing? One touch from
one finger? …It made her long to give a million more
simply to overwhelm gratitude and watch it become
elation instead.

"Tell me you want me, Christine," he bid, his
breath tickling the pad of her finger. "Make a choice
and end this game. Say that you're mine."

One short syllable, and it hung upon her
tongue, dangling between consciousness and desire.
Before it could be uttered, a sharp knock echoed the
room and made her jump.

"Christine? Christine, are you in there?
Christine!"

"Raoul…" His name fell without sound from
her lips as she glanced between the door and Erik's
rage. The Vicomte loved her, adored her, …would
break down any door to get to her. And as if sharing
the thought, Erik grabbed her forearm in a vicious
hold and yanked her to the mirror's glass, opening his
secret doorway and heaving her inside with him. He
closed the world out, but light permeated through, a
window between worlds with the Vicomte's frantic
calls echoing and bouncing off stone walls.

A kick, a crack, and as the dressing room door
gave way and let the Vicomte inside, Christine
watched from the mirror's protection, terrified even to
breathe.

She felt Erik creep behind her before she ever
dared peek at his murderous eyes and that uncovered
face. One glimpse, but he edged close, his lips
hovering at her ear. "Go on, Christine. Scream and
call his attention. Beg him to save you. Go on."

Every word was hissed into shadows, and his
arm caught her about the waist again and pulled her
back against his hardness, arching it firm to her body.
His misshapen lips pressed sudden kisses at the
crease of her neck, and she swallowed a gasp as
passion was too great to bear, coursing through her

veins in ribbons of sensation. Desire whispered its secrets and urged her to imitate his motion, to let him clasp her hips between his palms and keep her flush to him.

"Call his attention," he ordered coldly, and to her horror, he purposely edged her forward until she had no choice but to catch her balance with palms set flush to the mirror. If she pounded fists, she'd call focus; she'd bring notions of ghosts and haunted rooms to life. And if she called for Raoul, he'd know where she was. He'd burst through mirrors as he'd burst through doors. He'd save her, but...did she truly want to be saved?

Erik's mouth was at her throat, his malformed lips parted so his tongue could lap delicately at her skin and make her writhe back against him and swallow more urgent sounds from fleeing her lips. Silence. Not a word to give it away.

The Vicomte had found the discarded masks, his terror plain to be seen, but Christine couldn't bear to glimpse his perfect face. She was betraying his love and a vow, and she *didn't care*! Closing her eyes, she shut out his image and concentrated on Erik's mouth devouring her shoulder's bare curve as if it were the most glorious detail imaginable.

"Scream," he taunted again, hissing the words into her ear. "Call the hero, Christine. Or choose *me*, want *me*. Stop playing games."

His words stung a path through her veins. No more games.

He bent to her throat again, but before his misshapen mouth could burrow in its crease, she turned and met it with her own, finding his disfigured face in the dim shadows and kissing him hard. Her attempt was obviously unexpected. She felt him tense and shudder, fight an impulse to pull away as his body inched back. Every shuffle of a shoe resonated deafeningly back through the corridors, but she did not falter in her intent. She *kissed him* and found his swollen lips pliant to her assault.

One stumble, and Erik regained composure. His Christine, her sweet mouth voracious in its claiming seal. A kiss he'd never predicted or thought to feel as his. He nearly forgot to kiss her back. He was too astounded, allowing her control and following the motion of her demanding lips. He couldn't reason what it meant and simply let desire be desire, finding his footing and kissing with more pressure and fire to match and exceed.

His arms weaved about her small body, jerking her to the planes of his, arching against softness and making it supple to his whims. He wanted this, ached for this. It was a hunger denied for far too long. Gathering her to him, he urged her back to one stone wall, pinning her to its cold shape and thrust hips with more force and necessity against her.

Pulling lips free, he kissed a frantic path along her jaw and found her ear to restlessly insist, "Do you feel this fire, Christine? You *must*. It is searing flesh with its flame. Tell me you feel it."

Every word was hoarse, muttered to her ear between more kisses, and as she shivered and fisted her hands to his shoulders, she gave a slight nod. It was enough. He had the urge to gloat his achievement, but arrogance had one question that demanded an answer.

"And...does your gallant Vicomte make you feel such things?"

She hesitated, stiffening muscles with her obvious unease, and rage gnawed at his insides and made him clasp her tighter, forcing her firmer to stone.

In a low growl, he demanded bitterly, "Does he *touch* you this way, Christine? Does he press his desire against you? Do you kiss *him* with the same fervency that you just kissed *me*? Tell me!" He hissed the command against her ear, his stomach turning with possessive jealousy.

"Of course not," she replied in quiet whispers, and pushing him back, she dared to meet his eye and make her reply more honest. "Erik, please."

"*Please*? The masks are off, Christine, and this is just *you* beneath all the layers and pretenses. You are the same passionate creature that I am. How dare you deny that we are meant to be together and carry on with that pompous buffoon? As if *my* heart cannot account to his? How fair is that? And now I ask you to state your choice, to shout it to the world, and you *can't*. It is acceptable for such perverse yearnings to breathe in the shadows, but they must not see the light of day. Isn't that so, Christine?"

"Erik, it isn't-"

But he pulled her away from the wall and made her face the mirror again, this time without a reflection. No, this time it was a *window* that showed her just as many realities. On the opposite side, the Vicomte was searching corners, looking for clues as he clutched Christine's gloves in a fist, his mask as discarded as the rest of theirs.

"Christine," Raoul called, scanning with desperation. "Christine!"

"And what will you tell him?" Erik muttered. "Will you say a monster took you, put his hands all over you? Will you make it a sin when I felt you come *alive* in my arms? Another mask, Christine. Who between the two of us will keep playing make believe?"

Christine dragged her focus from Raoul and his love-fueled quest to her companion in the dark. Compared to the smooth elegance of the Vicomte's features, his pristine suit, his boyish charms and soft locks that grazed his forehead, Erik was truly the nightmare monster. His deformity was half-shrouded, the faint traces of permeating candlelight granting more crevices to abnormal skin, more spots light was not allowed to caress. He was the corpse, walking the earth dead, and yet hadn't he just kissed her with all the passion and virility of a mortal man? He said he'd felt *her* come alive in his embrace; she thought the same of him. *Alive.* No longer the creature denied every emotion, every gift living bestowed. And she was overwhelmed to know *she* was the one to inspire him.

Something inside begged her to touch his face, to feel such distortion and unacceptable atrocity and make it worthy to *be* a face. One touch... But before courage could catch up, Erik huffed and coldly concluded, "Come on. I'll return you to your Masquerade. You can chase down your Vicomte and play your innocent façade again, tell him you were there all along and his worrying was for naught. Save us all the drama of your lackluster strength tonight. Lord knows, I am quite tired of being its victim."

Christine stayed silent and ducked her eyes to hide a rise of tears. Of course, tears! And they made her seem weak. Always weak, the fragile little girl in need of protection from her own heart and its desires. When would she be strong? ...Would she *ever* be strong?

Not a single word passed between them on their trek through dark secret corridors, and with the taste of intimacies shared yet on her tongue, Christine took silence as rejection. She'd hurt him because she couldn't carry her heart with the same confidence that he did. She wondered if she'd only ever cause him pain. It seemed her curse.

Erik halted before what her eyes dubbed another wall. She was doubtless it was a doorway instead, a threshold back into the fairytale when for the first time, she wanted to stay in reality.

"I pray you remember tonight," he told her, and she heard his reluctance, the disappointment, the longing for more that she matched but did not reveal to him.

"How could I forget it?" she posed back.

"You're going to need to draw from every desire you just embraced. You cannot run from them again. They will be the inspiration for your character."

"Character? Erik, what do you speak of?" She sought an answer, and even though shadows veiled, she studied the details of that face and yet was incapable of reading him. He was always his own mystery.

"My opera, of course. This sojourn in the public world tonight was not just for *you*." His sharpness pierced her heart and brought a hurt she didn't want. "I finished my masterpiece and delivered it to the managers' office. They will find it tomorrow, and if they are wise and they *must be* after the chandelier incident, they will schedule its performance. You are the heroine, of course, but...well, your usual roles are so pure and innocent, and Aminta grows to be anything but. You cannot portray her without a sensuality I was unsure you could possess before tonight. She *is* temptation. It will be your greatest challenge to show the world what you just showed me."

"Erik, ...I hope I won't disappoint you." She meant her words. How much weight his opinion still held to her! She wanted to please him just as much as she'd once sought to enamor an angel with her talent.

His gaze had been cold as he'd stated his plans, but she saw it soften. With a gentleness that surprised her, he lifted a trembling hand and cupped her cheek in its curve. She glimpsed his trepidation and timidity, an uncertainty to even grant one touch, but *he* was brave enough to travel the distance, to expose vulnerability and *try*. Why couldn't she seem to do that?

"Sing it with the passion you just displayed, Christine, the raw desire, the flames and absolute possession. If you can do that, if you can stand on that stage opening night and give that to me, ...then I'll know your choice. I'll know you are *mine*."

The title alone made her shiver. And she understood. The masks were off, and he wanted her to expose *everything* she was, to make her choice and leave it on the stage. It was a starting point for a bravery that felt unstable and easy to falter.

"Make a choice, Christine," he commanded

again. "Decide if you want me or if you want him. Stop cowering behind *your* mask, the innocent little girl afraid to *live*. Sing it for me and show me what *you* want. Show me the real fire in your soul."

Christine gave a single nod, unable to decide that she could be that bold, but for the first time, she *wanted* to be. If for no other reason, then for the man standing before her with his heart as revealed as his face. He showed her everything he was in one look, and she knew that if she gave it up, betrayed his love, never knew the sensations he inspired again, she wouldn't *be* alive. The fairytale was suddenly boring and unfulfilling when compared to the truth in the darkness.

"Go," he commanded, drawing away before she had anything to keep as hers, and yet before he released her from his world, he hesitated long enough to touch her shoulder one more time. One touch. "Proof that I am nothing but a monster in your eyes or that I am a man possessed by passion. The decision is yours alone."

She glanced and saw what he did, marks left by a fierce grip upon her skin, fading but evident enough to call attention. Her mind flashed memories of being pressed flush to his desire, of fingers digging firm into her skin with taut wanting, and she had an undeniable yearning to bear his marks over every bit of her body. The surface of her flesh branded forever in his possession. Monster? No, she only saw proof of lust and an ache that left her empty inside.

With a heavy sigh, he drew off the red cloak from his costume and set it upon her shoulders, concealing bare skin and its telltale marks. It was as claiming as Raoul's ring had been, and yet she gave no complaint as she cuddled beneath its silk and felt it tickle flesh that was sensitive and charged with need.

"Go," he reluctantly ordered again and opened his doorway, letting wisps of light inside. She gave his shape a final glance and etched the distorted face into her mind's eye to recall later when alone and given time to relive every last minute without judgment for what she desired.

Dutiful and yet afraid, she left the darkness and heard the doorway close her out from its delicious embrace. She regretted it at first breath beyond its world.

Christine found herself in the far wings just beyond the loud clatter of the party. Before she made a decision to rejoin its lies with a heart that still beat in the dark, a voice halted her.

"Christine! My God, where have you been?"

Raoul came from the direction of her dressing room with terrified eyes as he rushed and pulled her into an embrace. He was shaking, and she hated herself for causing his fear and making him worry, ...for betraying him and wanting only to do it again. This embrace was...uninspiring, devoid of *anything* Erik's had made her feel, and in some manner, she resented Raoul for *not* bringing such wanton emotions out of her.

"Christine!" Raoul drew away and spoke in frantic phrases. "I thought *he* was back, that he'd taken you away with him!"

"Of course not, dear boy," she assured and saw him calm with her forced smile as she replaced an invisible mask she hadn't realized she'd been wearing until tonight. *The innocent little girl afraid to live.* "I went to my dressing room to get a cloak. I was...cold."

She had a feeling he'd believe anything she said when he equally did not want to face the truth, and she was right. He grinned his usual beaming elation and dared to touch her cheek, and all she could do was long for another's hand.

"I found masks, and I thought the worst," he gushed and never questioned the skeleton face discarded on her floor. "And...this."

He opened a fisted hand and revealed his ring on its chain, and she feigned surprise, lifting a hand to the spot it had once rested. "Oh, the chain must have broken... How lucky you found it!"

Taking it in her hand, she tucked it into a pocket of Erik's cloak and hid it away from view.

"Well, ...perhaps that is a sign that you should make it official and put it in its proper place around your finger," he replied, setting his hand to her shoulder. She stiffened, wearing Erik's mark beneath and considering the Vicomte as trying to take something already claimed.

"No, ...not yet, Raoul."

"But when, Christine? We've been engaged for months, and you still refuse to speak of it to anyone. It makes me worry that you aren't happy."

"After the next show," she impulsively decided. "Then I will announce to the world what *I* want, and no one will dare question it again."

"Christine..."

"Can we go home, Raoul?" she inquired with her sweetest smile. "I...I've had enough make believe games."

Desperate to please her, the Vicomte nodded and slid his arm about shoulders that did not belong to him as he guided her though the throng and out of the opera house.

Christine went willingly, but she felt...*changed* as she climbed into the awaiting carriage with Raoul. One night, one touch, one kiss, and her entire world felt transformed. Her eyes were open, and it seemed ironic that a night of masquerading and pretending to be someone else had shown her who she truly was. She knew what she wanted...

And as the carriage returned her to another role and more pretend, she was convicted that this would be the last mask she would ever wear. She'd learned the truth behind monsters and masks tonight, and she was about to destroy every illusion without regret. It was *her* choice, and she was entirely certain that it was already made. Sing for an angel. Wasn't that the grounding point of every desire? Sing for *her* angel, and make her decision known. His opera awaited and a role she was born to play if she were

228

brave enough to claim it as hers. And she knew what to do...

"Something Like A Promise"
Told from Erik's POV, as trust is rekindled, Erik learns the gift of hope.

I am an impatient man; it is only one among a list of flaws. But I am working on it...for her, only for her. I would do anything to keep her, even if that includes an overhaul of every characteristic that displeases her. Many would call me a fool to go to such lengths, especially for a woman who once denounced me and ran from me in terror and disgust. But then again, most people have not met us or would try to understand our unusual situation. She is my obsession, and I am hers. Foolish of me to make such an assertion, isn't it? I am not the only man in her life, but I know I am her destiny even if she doesn't. She will learn; I am confident of that.

One afternoon, I was desperately practicing my attempts at patience as I awaited her arrival in my underground home for her daily lesson. The new production was in its preliminary stages of rehearsal, so I knew it couldn't account for her tardiness. ...That left only one plausible explanation, and jealousy twisted in my gut. *Jealousy*, another flaw to work on.

Huffing in self-loathing, I idly ran a few unnecessary scales at the piano, needing somewhere to displace an over-focused brain. It wasn't working. Scales took no real thought on my part, leaving the wheels of imagination to spin free and weave every unwanted situation.

Finally, the smallest creak of the front door announced her entrance, and I sat up tall and straight, jerking my hands from the keys. I couldn't tolerate having her think I was minimizing my talent to play simple scales. Selfishly, I wanted her to think better of me than that.

With a gust of sweetened air, she strode into the music room, her smile genuinely bright and betraying nothing of her previous whereabouts. Of course, I had no proof to my assumptions, and she was a good enough actress to trick me if only to avoid my temper. *Temper*, that was number one on my flaw list, and so, thwarting its possession, I acted congenially with a grin to match hers.

She was so beautiful. It made me sure God existed because only a heavenly creature could have created something so exquisite. And the most wonderful part of all was that she didn't know it. She had no idea how men stared lustfully after her, and that naïveté made her so sweetly humble and innocent.

"*Ange*," she bid gently. How I adored hearing her call me that; it gave me such hope. "I'm sorry to keep you waiting for me."

"It's all right, *petite*." I knew she expected an interrogation, and though I longed for just that, I denied my urge. *Impatience, jealousy, temper*, I couldn't be their victim and give her reason to hate me and run to the boy. "Shall we begin?"

The skepticism that lit her eyes was a sharp sting to my determination to change, but I reminded myself that *I* had been the one to put it there with too many angered outbursts... Not as many lately. I hoped she took notice of that.

Christine took her place facing me in the bow of the piano and awaited instruction like the dutiful pupil she was. These roles were easiest for us: teacher and student. We always fell into them wholeheartedly and without the reservation that characterized the rest of our relationship.

As we began our usual vocalises, I no longer regarded her as the woman I loved; no, she became another instrument, one I had to tweak and adjust to get the tone and sound I wanted. It was a rare occurrence that I saw beyond my set task when teaching, and yet today, I took note from her first pitch that she was distracted. It was affecting her well-learned technique, her breaths too shallow and not supporting a voice that almost seemed too large to come from such a tiny girl. It took me only a brief consideration to guess part of the problem.

"You're wearing a corset, aren't you?" I demanded a question that in any other situation would be an unacceptable breach of propriety. But the rapport of teacher and student was intimate in such a different way than the rest of the world could understand.

She didn't even blush; no, her expression was apologetic with her attached nod. "I'm sorry... I was already late; I didn't have the chance to take it off."

Patience, screamed my inner voice when I had the desire to snap my annoyance, so I only pointed to the hallway, and understanding the unuttered command, she ran out of the room and to the bedchamber I kept specifically for her use to rid herself of it.

Corsets... Society demanded their presence, even in the theatre where proper singing required real, deep breaths. I *never* allowed her to wear it when we worked, insisting from the beginning that when she was the diva, she would have her way without argument. Then they would all bow to her and never speak a word of scandal if their prima donna denounced such nonsense.

A few minutes later, she returned, still pleading forgiveness in her stare, and took her place again. I hesitated and broke my own rule then. I observed her as if it were necessity, taking in her real curves. How much more beautiful they were without the artificial shape of iron and boning! It was inconceivable to me that they should be stolen away and remade into a standard pattern.

Again she could have blushed with my gaze so intimately perusing her, but to my surprise, she didn't, giving the smallest smile on tentative lips. Could I take that as encouragement? I had to wonder...

"We'll start again," I told her, and at her nod, I gave our first chord. Still, her breaths were shallower than I preferred. A day in a corset's confinement, and she was still suffocating herself at every breath.

Damn society!

Stopping with a suddenness that made her eyes widen, I got to my feet and stepped around the piano to her side, inquiring lightly, "You don't want to breathe today, do you?"

"I'm sorry," she said again. I knew she meant it and that the flicker of disappointment in her blue eyes was genuine. She was always eager to please me, hanging on my every word and compliment with greedy hands, ...at least in this setting.

I knew that what I was about to do was uncommon; I usually avoided touching her and wasn't sure she wouldn't shy away with modest notions, ...or possibly disgust. I couldn't fathom that she'd find my hands any more appealing than my deformed face. But even with the prospect of revulsion, I took the chance.

Holding up my hands defenselessly first, I explained, "I want to get your breaths where they belong. Is that acceptable to you?"

She was accustomed to my obscure teaching techniques by now and could pose no argument considering the outcome. She trusted me as teacher; I could see it clearly in her eyes and her unhesitant nod. It was a provocative reality to consider that I could do anything to her when in this role, and she would permit me with open arms... Provocative but unthinkable, not when her heart was what I wanted most of all.

Attempting to detach myself from the situation, I brought my hands to her torso, cupping my palms around her small ribcage. In spite of my determination, I felt my body respond, my attention drawn first to the delicate shape of her, the soft material of her gown, the scent of her so close and intoxicating my nostrils, the fact that her breasts were almost grazing my fingers. But one look in her blue eyes staring expectantly at me, and I forced at least part of my mind to my intended purpose, reminding myself that this wasn't supposed to be an attempt at masochism.

"Breathe into my hands," I commanded, praying she gave no regard to the harsh edge on my usually brilliant voice.

Complying without question, I felt my hands fill with her lungs and separate from each other with inhalation. "Better," I commented. "Now blow the breath away."

She obeyed, and I felt it tickle my skin deliciously, ruffling the hair at my temple. I wished for the briefest instant that the mask were gone so that I could feel her exhalation along my face.

"And take another." *Teacher, be the teacher*, my sense reminded. I attempted focus to parting rib-bones, and yet even as I did, I felt the most peculiar thing: her heart skipped every few beats, and her body trembled in my hands. I didn't know what to make of such reactions! She couldn't possibly be...*enjoying* my touch, could she? ...Maybe I'd found the revulsion I had been seeking.

As she finished exhaling, her eyes suddenly avoiding mine, I commanded, "Now the scale. On an 'ah' please."

Still, she would not look at me, but she began to sing with my hands in place. Her breathing was improved, and though I knew I should let her go, I couldn't seem to listen to myself just yet. So I stayed as she went from scale to scale, raising pitches by the half steps I usually gave on the piano, and I stared at her, even though she wouldn't look back.

"Keep breathing into my hands," I instructed, giving an excuse, *anything* to justify my presence.

I only remained until she ended the exercise, and yet it was to a chorus of her erratic heartbeats that I released her and feigned a nonchalant air as I returned to my piano bench.

"That's much better now, Christine," I told her as she finally met my gaze, hers showing things I'd never seen before and couldn't understand even as I tried. I contemplated apologizing for my forwardness, but I was, after all, her teacher first. My actions were acceptable if they were meant for her improvement, ...weren't they?

Our lesson continued from there per our usual routine, our roles back into play and not again breached. I was reluctant as always to end, and she mirrored my sentiment with a pout of disappointment with my last instructions.

Collecting disarrayed music across the piano, I cast suddenly uncomfortable eyes to where she leaned on the bow, watching me expectantly. Often when we finished for the day, she would linger, and we'd play our hand at congenial conversation, growing better at it with each day that separated us from our breaking point. But today, she seemed to have a purpose and was tentatively approaching it in a way that told me I wouldn't like what she meant to say.

And I didn't. "Don't you want to know why I was late?" she asked softly after a moment more.

"Not particularly."

"Why not?"

A huff of annoyance I could not stop passed my lips, but all I replied was, "I don't want to be angry, and I have a feeling that whatever you say will *make* me angry. You don't like my temper, remember?"

Her brows arched in surprise. "I don't, but... Can I tell you where I was anyway? And will you avoid anger until you hear everything I have to say?"

"You're making this very difficult for me." I attempted not to sound as frustrated as I was.

"Please, Erik."

Dear God, whenever she said my name, I felt as if choirs were singing blessings upon me. I had always considered any appellation a curse unless the title meant power like 'Opera Ghost' or 'Phantom', but she made me feel like my name was the most fantastic word in recorded language.

With another huff, I reluctantly nodded, plopping back down on my piano bench and fisting my hands with the futile hope that such an action would remind me to keep control of myself. "Go on then."

"The Vicomte came to see me." Guessing my rising temper, she held up her hands. "Now wait and breathe and let me finish." Only she could have spoken to me in such a manner without consequence; I foolishly even found it endearing in its way! "He invited me to a party at his estate tomorrow night. Ignorantly, he posed the question before my managers who made it quite clear that, as the Vicomte is our primary patron, I must attend."

André and Firmin, those damn fools would do anything if a monetary value were attached to the task! I felt the unmistakable urge to become the Opera Ghost and extract my vengeance, but I reluctantly kept it within as Christine went on.

"I know how you dislike Raoul, despite the fact that I've assured you again and again that I am not involved with him in any way beyond a shared childhood. *And* you've made me promise, more than once, I remind you, that I would avoid and ignore him, which I have done as best I could. *And* as my teacher, you must consider the importance of keeping on good terms with the patrons as well as my managers to further my career-"

"Your point, Christine?" I couldn't help but snap, even as I tried for calm.

"My point is that I *have to* attend Raoul's party tomorrow night, therefore breaching my promise to you. *But* I have a compromise to this situation..." She hesitated only then, lowering worry-fringed eyes to wringing hands. "*You* could take me to the party."

"What?" I nearly shouted the word under a malaise of thoughts, and she jumped with enough of a start to make me force a deep breath.

"Raoul said I could bring a guest," she softly muttered.

"Yes," I argued, "and he likely intended the young Giry or one of your other comrades of the female persuasion, someone to make you comfortable in a den of strangers."

"Exactly," she tried to agree, lifting desperate eyes, "and *you* make me comfortable."

"Let's make no mistake on this; the Vicomte wants you there because he is infatuated with you, ...*romantically* infatuated, Christine." I felt the twisting fist of jealousy as it gripped my heart. But to consider my Christine amidst those aristocratic vultures who would look down on her because of her profession and lack of wealth or title! That selfish bastard Vicomte had likely never given a thought to the vicious insults and biting glares Christine would have to endure; he only cared about the fact that he wanted her!

"I realize that," she replied with a fraction of my sharpness. "I'm not a fool. But, Erik, I *have to* attend. I haven't a choice in the matter. Isn't it better if you are there with me so I may prove my loyalty?"

Her posed plan was preposterous. "I *can't* go with you," I retorted without lingering care to gentility. "You must realize what you are asking of me."

"I do."

"Oh, do you really? Do you know how often I deal with that world?" I glared at her, but to my surprise, she didn't back down. "I thought you had collected enough information about my prior life to realize how I am treated by *that world* and how 'eagerly' they accept someone like me."

"Erik-"

"No, Christine," I interrupted her appeasing tone. "How could you ask such a thing of me? I am the 'Opera Ghost'. I am hated and denounced and have endured quite the repertoire of derogatory insults in my miserable lifetime. Why would I ever willingly put myself back into that spiteful, vicious cesspool called humanity?"

"For me," she stated softly, her eyes beaming with compassion I didn't want. God, I wanted so much more than pity from her! "I am utterly senseless to argue with you; I haven't endured anything that could compare to what you have and can't promise that you won't again. But I beg of you, Erik. Come with me. And then let them say what they will because neither of us will notice. I will be on your arm and smiling at you, and no one else will matter...to either of us."

My resolution was shaken with those few words. Hope was such a cruel form of masochism. To *hope*, to know that uplift of spirit and let it create fantasies and potential futures...and then endure the agony of their inevitable demise. It left no one to blame but one's self. And yet at the next instant, hope could be re-sparked to inconceivable, insurmountable heights, ready for the pain all over again. I was a fool to be its victim. But glimpsing within Christine all I longed for, my brain was already creating a scene whereby my beautiful angel gowned so elegantly blessed me with beaming smiles, making everyone including the arrogant Vicomte jealous beyond comprehension, leaving them to wonder how such a disturbing figure as myself could have the attention of one so fair. It was a surreal, optimistic vision; it wasn't a conceivable reality. It couldn't be for me, but hope dangled it like a possibility.

"Christine," I tried again, but she could nearly claim victory under my weakened conviction. "I don't..."

"Please, Erik, *ange*." She tilted that beautiful face so that loose curls that had slipped from their pins tumbled over her shoulder and made me want to touch them. Every bit of her was a constant temptation. The blush I had been seeking and anticipating during our lesson appeared only then as she softly said, "I want to dance with you."

My breath caught in my throat, strangling words for a long pause. *Hope*, I didn't want it, yet there it was. I didn't let myself dwell on the unstated reality that I would not be her only dance partner; no, I would not allow one consideration of the Vicomte to spoil my illusions. And so, going against better sense's protest, I replied, "All right, Christine. I will accompany you."

It was the smile I got in return, triumphant and glowing, that I kept in my head as argument to every second thought that threatened during the rest of the night and the next day. And there were *many* instances for its appearance to be sure. Even when she closed herself in her bedroom in my home to get ready, I fought the desire to beg her reconsideration with promises to take her any place else, halting a few times nearly at the threshold of her door. It was far too late for that now.

In my finest suit, I awaited her in the sitting room, pacing before the hearth with growing anxiety. It was a bad enough situation to have to take her to my rival's home, but added to that the undeniable presence of my mask, I was *actually* nervous! I could recall so many times when the mask had become my enemy, standing between myself and any societal prospects I could have indulged. I was fortunate that Christine had grown accustomed enough not to stare idly as she had done before. The first lessons in my home after she had learned who and what I really was, she had kept a riveted observance to it, sometimes seeing only its stark image. I could never say if it was simply because it had been something different or if she had been envisioning what lay beneath the entire time. Now to consider dozens of unwanted eyes on my masked face, I was sickened with the thought alone.

"*Ange?*" Christine's sweet voice halted my pacing mid-step as I averted all my attention to her. She was an absolute vision that took my breath away. Gowned in pale pink, one of the selections from her wardrobe here, she gave a shy twirl as if modeling for my regard, and I took that as permission to peruse her as I liked, taking in the abundance of creamy skin exposed at her neckline and the childlike curves of her bare arms. Her dark curls were gathered intricately atop her head, elegant and so like an aristocratic lady. Completing propriety, she wore a corset, and I knew a pang of disappointment as I envisioned the gentle curves of her waist from her lessons. Then again, it was almost a pleasant idea, that only *I* got that intimate, revealing image. Everyone else had contrived and boring perfection. ...I suddenly didn't hate that infernal contraption anymore.

"Do I look...acceptable?" she softly asked, furrows in her brow, though I was sure my expression revealed my admiration.

"No," I insisted with a shake of my head. "You far surpass acceptable... You are the most beautiful vision I've ever beheld."

Blushing, she ducked her head under a shy smile, making her all the more endearing to my eager heart.

"Shall we go?" I asked, and gathering courage, I dared to offer my arm as a gentleman. I had to wonder if she saw how it shook in the air the moment before she looped hers through it, steadying me with her nearness alone. Though I knew it was further a push to my masochistic hope, I could not keep from dwelling on her lack of hesitation, ...as if she *wanted* to touch me.

I would have preferred walking that way all night, with her like a gleaming star from the heavens on my arm, but too soon, we arrived at the de Chagny estate. This was, in all actuality, my first glimpse of their wealth; I felt it was merciful that I did not ask Christine if she had been there before. *Jealousy*, I didn't want to know it now with her at my side.

The mansion house shone with a welcoming light from every window, the noise of crowds filtering out before we even arrived at the front door. If we had been an integral part of that world, it would have caused anticipation, but for me, it only brought dread.

From the instant the butler opened the door, I was reminded why I avoided people as a whole. He cast a disdainful look at Christine first, but within the breath as his gaze met mine, she and her inferior status were forgotten. He could only stare at my masked face with widened, appalled eyes.

"We are here at the Vicomte's invitation," Christine stammered, noting the butler's stare and dragging worry-fringed eyes to me. Her concern was my saving grace, keeping my temper in check with one glimpse at it. *For her, ...for her.*

The butler cast another disapproving look before ushering us into a relatively empty foyer, the noise of company filtering out from the adjacent room.

Christine paused our trek, raising blue eyes to mine, and to my astonishment, as she disentangled our looped arms, she slid her hand into mine, weaving fingers together. I went numb a long, held breath, overcome by the warmth of her small fingers, the smoothness of her skin. ...Was every part of her so silken?

"Don't leave my side," she bid softly, and I felt that infernal twinge of hope clasp at my gut.

"I wouldn't dare," I replied, granting her as much of a smile as I could, unaccustomed to feeling exhilarated, most especially considering our current whereabouts.

Nodding under her own smile, she kept our hands clasped between us and led the way into the party.

My sweet, naïve Christine never could have guessed the true ignorance of society. In her trusting mind, the idea of lavish parties and people in fine, silken clothes in elaborate mansions was a child's dream, a fairytale. And though those things were laid out before us exactly as her imagination could have created them, the biting glares and whispered gossip attached were an inconceivable reality. Thankfully, my mask drew the brunt of their regard, and I would have had it no other way. Let them talk about me, insult me as they chose; *she* did not deserve that brought on herself.

As implied, we were quite out of place in that group, the hushed musings beginning almost immediately upon our entrance. It was degrading, and yet one glance at Christine, and I was awash in pride. She met the stares head on, keeping her pretty shoulders defiantly raised.

Within seconds of our arrival, the Vicomte rushed to meet Christine. Dear God, that boy! I hated him so much that just his perfect features and flawless attire made rage burn within my body. The only reason I kept control was the fact that Christine never released my hand, as if we were a set pair, molded together and unable to separate into two. I was actually eager for the Vicomte to see that! And when he did, I almost laughed in mocking delight at the dejection creasing his perfect face.

"Christine...," the flustered Vicomte stammered, "who is...your friend?" His eyes only then found my mask, too occupied by our hands at first to take notice, and I cringed in spite of myself.

"This is Erik," she replied, meeting my eye for a brief instant. "He's a composer and an architect and a musician... I don't think there are many things he doesn't do."

Shock must have been clear as day across my face for all to see in spite of the mask's obstruction. But I could have sworn that I heard *awe* in her voice! And as she glanced at me again, I caught the shy smile and faint blush meant for my regard alone.

"Oh, ...well." The Vicomte broke our intense stare, and I was doubtless that he did it on purpose. "Well, monsieur, I am the Vicomte de Chagny. If I am taken aback, I apologize. When I mentioned to Christine that she could bring a guest, I wasn't expecting...you."

I would have replied with something convivial even if it was contrived, but we were interrupted as another gentleman joined Raoul with a pat to his back. "Raoul, your friends are drawing quite a bit of attention."

I felt Christine's rising discomfort at the blatant regard the man gave her and had to reel in the urgency to snap his aristocratic throat for daring.

"Christine, you know my brother Philippe," Raoul said before adding, "the Comte de Chagny."

She scooted the smallest step towards me, and I ached to wrap my arms around her and comfort her fear. But under too many stares, I could only squeeze her hand and hope she understood.

"Mademoiselle," Philippe greeted with a provocative grin. "When my brother told me that he invited you, I insisted you would ignite quite the scandal. Appearing with another man and especially one so...odd, perhaps is the kindest term, is absolutely odious." His grin never faltered as his amused stare met mine. "You *do* know this is not a masquerade, don't you, monsieur? Masks aren't typically the fashion in high society."

I was unmoved by his words, my concern for Christine alone. Let them torment me as they would. "Not yet," I replied nonchalantly. "Perhaps I will start a revolution, and masks will become a favored accessory."

The brothers were staring suspiciously at me. I knew the odds of them connecting me to the Opera Ghost were minimal; that story primarily circled the ballet rats. But a man in a mask was disconcerting enough on its own.

"Maybe you should take it off, monsieur," Raoul insisted with a sneer. His attention kept shifting to Christine and my entwined hands every few seconds as if desperate to break them apart even if by forceful measures.

"No." Christine was the one to speak up, and I arched surprised brows at her attempt. "Leave him be, Raoul. Erik's mask is his own."

But Philippe's interest was piqued, and he pushed without waver, "Take it off, monsieur. What have you to hide? It's ridiculous to conceal yourself when you are among friendly acquaintances."

Friendly! I could already guess the way things would go, sighing as I determined the outcome in my head. It could only be wretched.

"I would rather not," I sternly insisted. "And as a supposed guest, I would say it is *my* decision one way or the other."

"You're ruining Christine's reputation," Raoul retorted bitterly. "Everyone here is gossiping about her because of *you*."

"Bad enough to have an opera tart in attendance," Philippe sneered. "But the fact that she shamed my brother and his affections by bringing some kind of freak is disreputable. Take off the mask, monsieur, and let her salvage some of her reputation."

"Perhaps we should leave," Christine suddenly declared.

"No, Christine, don't go." The Vicomte stepped toward her and insisted in an appeasing tone, "Maybe it's best if your *friend* leaves, but I entreat *you* to stay."

"If he is not welcome, then neither am I." She squeezed my hand, and I adored this flash of courage in her. If she had sought to prove loyalty to me with my presence tonight, she had done it tenfold and only exceeded herself with every sweet glance in my direction.

"Christine," Raoul tried, and it was in the commotion of his approach that I felt my mask torn from my face.

I went numb before rage or shame could arise. Part of me had been waiting for it to happen, and as predicted, Philippe stood there, holding my mask, his agape expression matching the Vicomte and an abundance of faces on spying guests all around. God, how many times would I have to endure similar scenes in my miserable lifetime?

Though I was enraged with a fire that seared my belly, my focus was abruptly drawn to Christine. I had little care for what the others thought about my deformity, accustomed to being unwillingly stripped of my dignity and the disgust it brought.

Lifting seemingly apathetic eyes to meet hers, I gasped aloud. In her blue eyes, ones I knew and could decipher as well as my own, I saw a mirror of my pain, pain I had been careful to avoid displaying. How well she could read me to know it was there!

Without pause, she came to stand before me, and as I watched wide-eyed, she lifted her little hand and pressed it to my scars, cupping my cheek and concealing it from observance. For a moment, she held my eye, acting as my mask without reluctance or a single flicker of disgust, and in depths of blue, I saw compassion...and something deeper, something that created more hope, ...something like a promise.

Keeping her hand protectively in place, she held out her other to Philippe, and he gave her my mask without protest, his revulsion still on display. It was she who replaced the mask over my disfigurement with trembling fingers, fitting it into place as if she'd done so before. But no, the last time she'd only taken; this was the first time she'd given instead.

I wanted to meet her eye and see those feelings I was fighting to understand again, but taking my hand in hers, she turned to the de Chagny brothers with a rash anger I had never seen in her.

"Goodbye, Raoul," she stated in a flat tone that thrilled me.

"Christine, don't go," he tried. "Please stay."

"No," she immediately snapped. "You're just like all the rest, Raoul, and I can't help but be disappointed to have misjudged you." With a final shake of her head, she lifted her eyes to mine. "May we leave, *ange*?"

"Anything you want, *petite*," I replied and did not hesitate to shoot a mocking glare at the brothers and a biting, "Thank you for your hospitality." With that, I led Christine out through a sea of odd, repulsed expressions, overcome with pride at the way she kept upright and unwavering in her defiance. Was it any wonder that I loved this woman so much?

Once we were outside in the warm night, her shoulders slouched with the weight of her exhaustion, and she leaned against me as we walked, setting her cheek to my sleeve.

"Christine," I softly bid, delighting far more than she could have realized in her nearness. "I'm sorry."

"Oh, Erik, I am the sorry one. I made you take me." She shook her head, and a few of her curls tickled my jaw as they escaped their elegant arrangement. "You did not deserve to be treated that way... And when I consider that you've endured such things your entire life..."

"It doesn't matter," I replied with an apathetic shrug.

"Yes, it does!" she insisted vehemently. "The way they looked at you... It had to have hurt you." I could practically hear the pained furrow I knew existed in her smooth brow. "And...and I did the same, didn't I? When I first saw your face, I looked at you the way they did...with such disgust... Oh, Erik, I'm so sorry." It shocked me because I could hear the catch in her voice with her tears; I had made the angel cry. "I don't deserve you in my life. And to consider how good you are to me after how I treated you..."

"Christine," I breathed tenderly, "don't consider that now. It isn't important anymore." As we walked with slow steps, I told her, "What you just did... You...you touched my face."

"I couldn't bear to have them look upon you." Her head suddenly lifted, her eyes meeting mine in terror. "I didn't...hurt you, did I?" She was absolutely frantic. "I didn't consider... I mean, does your face hurt to be touched?"

Oh, *that* was her worry! I nearly smiled. "No, not at all... No one has ever touched my face. You can't imagine how it felt."

"Pleasant?" she inquired hopefully.

"Very pleasant." I was unsure how to interpret the smile she gave to know such a thing. It was beyond my consideration, and with a wave of discomfort, I changed the subject, telling her, "It doesn't bother me that I don't belong to that world."

"Well, I don't belong either," she declared yet smiled still. "And I'd rather be here with you anyway."

I knew I was beaming; my smile was unfaltering all the way back to the opera house's doors. When we arrived, she lifted anticipating eyes to mine.

"May we go up to the roof?" she asked, and I nodded, loath to leave her presence. She didn't say a word until we emerged back into the night, the stars positively within her grasp, and I pondered that she had something on her mind that I was unaware of, something that intrigued me with the way it left her anxious and giddy.

I didn't have to wait long. Facing me with her sweet smile, she said, "Since we left the party, we didn't get to dance as I was hoping. So...will you dance with me now?"

There was not a word in existence to describe the emotions that washed through me. I almost couldn't even nod a reply, too stunned and petrified through every limb. Had any request ever been so exciting, so full of unuttered promise?

She was the one to guide me to stand in the center of the roof and to initiate our pose, bringing my shaking hand to the curve of her waist and setting her own on my shoulder. "Have you ever danced, Erik?" she asked, perhaps assuming her answer with my trepidation.

"No, ...not with a partner anyway." To admit it to anyone else might have been embarrassing, but Christine never made me feel awkward as we tentatively began to move.

Stars were dancing with us above our heads, moonlight streaming down and creating silver strands in her dark curls. I was sure this was heaven. To hold her when I had only ever imagined it, to feel her so close of her own free will and desire, to see her look at me with so many unnamable emotions in her eyes... I was overcome and never wanted it to end.

We didn't speak; what could be said when emotion alone was so blissful? After awhile, she laid her head against my shoulder, her body nearly flush to mine as we slowly moved, and I felt tears fill my eyes of their own accord. She was warm and soft and everything I had ever dreamed of.

And as we danced, I knew hope; it rose on its own and filled every space in my heart, making my entire body tingle with the desire for more, ...for forever. Maybe hope wasn't such a bad thing after all...

"The Anatomy of a Kiss"
Told from Christine's POV, she laments the final night at the opera and the importance of a kiss.

A kiss... A touching of mouth and mouth, lips to lips, breath given and breath taken. Who in the history of mankind decided that such a mundane contact should mean so much? It didn't fully make sense. Lips kissed, but lips also lied. Why were they given the important task of making a heartbeat hold significance? The rewarding act of a kiss, and it said more than the same words that past lips' threshold.

A kiss... It shouldn't possess the determining factor to change the world, not something so simple and so often indulged in frivolity. How many kisses were given in a day, and how many were genuine? Not every kiss shifted the earth's axis, more games from betraying lips. Kisses given, kisses received. Kisses thrown away, kisses savored. A kiss didn't *have* to mean love, but...it was intimate. There was no denial in that. An intimacy *I* had given, and at the time, I hadn't realized how much it would change things.

With a heavy head, I gazed at my reflection in my vanity mirror at the de Chagny estate. The beautiful, virginal bride, gowned in white, ready to marry the perfect prince and flee to happily ever after. I looked the part but didn't *feel* it. A kiss was the culmination of every fairytale. Why was I so sure I'd already given mine to someone else? I'd kissed the monster, transforming his soul, transforming *my* soul, and yet here I was about to wed the forgotten hero. And it was a sad reality that *Raoul* had kissed me numerous times since the fated night I'd chosen another man, and not a single one felt tied to my heart. Not a single one *moved* me or touched my innermost core the way Erik's had. What was wrong with me?

A kiss... I'd given one to the wrong man, the one who wasn't meant to be mine, and I was half-convinced I'd lost a piece of my soul in the act, granted it through touching mouths and committed it to Erik's possession. What had I done? That night was yet a blur. Weeks later, and I still could not fully recall the details, nothing beyond fear, terror, desperation, and then that kiss. It seemed to be the clarity in the fog.

I had kissed Erik... It was a truth I often had to repeat to myself to be sure it hadn't been a dream. And why? ...I had no answer, and the question tortured my brain at every second. I'd once denounced that face, cursed him for what he was, for the sins he carried and committed, and *I had kissed him*. It had been an odd impulse. Giving my word to stay with him and save Raoul hadn't felt like enough. It needed punctuation, and I had given it and made a vow into a surprising devotion. Had I wanted to shock everyone including myself? No one could have expected it, not Raoul dangling from a noose and perhaps calling it a betrayal, and certainly not Erik. I vividly recalled the way he'd tensed against me, *terrified of a kiss.*

A kiss had broken the almighty Opera Ghost, shattered his persona, and made him nothing but a man again. A kiss had indeed been a transformation, and it was bitter that it included a return of reality. He'd let me go because a kiss brought guilt with its awakening. It was...*magic.* I had no doubt that *it* had sparked his heart to truly beat for the first time. ...And it had inspired my heartbeat for the first time, too.

I hated myself as I stared blamefully at my reflection. Here I was, about to wed Raoul and only thinking of Erik and a kiss. I was *obsessed* with that one intimate act to the point that I did not care about anything else, not Raoul's good heart, not the future I was about to commit myself to live at his side. A kiss consumed me until I could no longer reason.

My mind turned its details over and over again. Erik, his misshapen lips, swollen and bloated on one side, as distorted as every other feature of that corpse's face. Disgust had been irrelevant; it had faded to something akin to wanting. I *wanted* to kiss him. The truth stung me and erupted more guilt and shame. It had been more than just the impulse I preferred to dub it; it had been an unconscious longing since the days he'd been my deceiving angel. A kiss, an intimacy, I'd given it to my angel and somehow turned him into a man. Opera Ghosts and angels couldn't love, couldn't exist on the ordinary plane of mankind, but...a kiss made me believe in his love and want it with a craving I could not quench.

Mewing in disgust at my betraying thoughts, I fought for focus and fingered my curls, drawing half back with hands I pretended weren't trembling. No, I was about to be *Raoul's* bride and give *him* my vow and my every kiss. He trusted me and hadn't pushed for more since the night at the opera. He'd been tender and gentle, over-attentive, and yet never forcing me to make promises in return. He said he loved me at every chance, and when I couldn't say it back, he acted like it was all part of the *trauma*, as he called it. He didn't put words in my mouth and took only sweet kisses. ...And those kisses were lies. *Lips kissed, but lips also lied.* My lips were lying to Raoul.

Secrets I'd carry to my grave. I refused to tell him any truth that would hurt him. He'd stood at my side through every horror of the past year; he'd given his heart without reservation. ...How I wished I could give him the same gift! He deserved it; he deserved to be loved.

But so did Erik.

"No," I muttered, rubbing my temples in a futile hope to wipe the thought from my mind. Erik... But Erik had given me away, hadn't he? He'd made my choice inconsequential and decided that my kiss wasn't important. In some way, I hated him. How dare he trivialize the bravest moment in my life? It made it easy to be the coward again and marry Raoul without protest. Bravery had won me *nothing* the first time; why try it a second time?

Desperate for distraction, I sought my veil, white lace and delicate, and lifting it atop my curls, I completed the portrait. The Vicomte's bride...

"Christine..."

My heart halted its constant pattern before speeding like a drumbeat against my ribcage. At first, I told myself it was imagined, the voice that played in my dreams, but...hope made me turn upon my vanity bench.

He looked out of place, standing within my open balcony doors, illuminated in the peeking sun's beams when I was so accustomed to seeing him by shadows. It felt like the fairytale had clawed its way into the real world and dropped my dark prince upon my doorstep. But...he wasn't the man I'd left that final night; no, he was the Opera Ghost again, masked and powerful, untouchable by any detail in the ordinary, mortal world, a god back upon his pedestal. I detested this image and had the urge to rip the mask away and hopefully, the persona with it.

"Why...are you here?" I fought to make words when my eyes longed only to stare. All I could glimpse was a lower lip exposed from the mask's protection, and it wasn't enough. I wanted to see the full mouth and learn if *my* mark was still imprinted upon its malformed shape.

No explanations, no excuses. He extended one gloved hand, his eyes alone insisting his fear that I would refuse him. He was far too good at putting on the show; if not for the revelations in blues and greens, I truly would have believed that this was all about control and regaining a lost possession. No, his eyes spoke his heart, and losing my held breath in a sigh, I obeyed like the dutiful student I had once been.

Rising on shaky knees, I crossed the meager gap and took that offered hand, weaving my fingers between his when I had once only set a palm. I wanted it clear this time that this was my decision to go with him without a single coercion on his part. No, I was too curious to know his intention, and...how could I refuse the rapid anticipation beating with my heart?

His fear calmed with my acquiescence, and drawing me near by joined hands, he lifted me off my feet and cradled me in his arms. I could feel his own unsteady heartbeat insisting more uncertainty, more anxiousness. He wasn't the confident Opera Ghost, and I felt an urge to cry in relief.

As if it were only so easy, he carried me. I pressed my faced against his jacket, unwilling to look and observe a single detail of the betrayal I wittingly committed, but I felt the hasty motion and his every flustered breath and knew he was being extra careful with daylight to reveal his crime. Purloining a bride from her wedding. No one would believe I'd gone willingly.

My gown was like a beacon, but I did not feel the heat of the sun's rays penetrating, only a chill of shadows as he rushed our pace and kept me firm to his heart. But I could not help my nervousness. My white gown, his white mask, each their own revelation for what needed to be hidden. We were practically a walking sin.

The journey felt short when I longed to remain in the protection of his embrace forever. There, nothing could touch me; there, I didn't have to be brave and change the world. I could just *feel*, and it was enough. But as he halted our escape, I dared to lift my head from his erratic heart and meet his mismatched eyes far closer than usual to my own. That masked face so near my touch... There was a certain appeal that guilt dubbed unacceptable. It wasn't right, and here I was encouraging it. I was another man's bride!

Purposely dragging my gaze away, I tried to concentrate on our surroundings, but one view brought new confusion. "Erik, ...why did you bring me here?"

He lowered me to my feet, and the stage stretched out before my white slippers, its surface caressed by my thick, bridal skirts. The stage of the opera house... I had not been back upon its platform since that last night when I had surrendered and sang an impassioned duet, knowing full well from the first note who my masked partner was. Yes, I had known *Erik* had slipped into Don Juan's role, but I had claimed ignorance afterward to my flustered fiancé. Better Raoul think me a fool than know I sang desirous lyrics and made provocative gestures to his enemy.

"It's the perfect setting, Christine," Erik quickly replied, pacing an unsteady path before me, and I watched him with growing worry. "The stage, of course! Are not the best performances acted out in exactly this place? Another show for an eager audience. And your goal is to make them believe you, to *feel* with your character. Yes, yes, this is ideal!"

"Ideal for what?" I tentatively asked, noting that he could not seem to keep still and jittered on his feet. Was it inspired only by anxiousness, or...was there something off-kilter with him? He had been on the verge of madness the last night I had seen him, ready to kill or die to be with me... "Erik, ...this is no opera show, and I am not here to perform another role. I...am to marry Raoul today."

"Well, of course I know that!" he suddenly snapped, rounding on me with fire in his eyes. I preferred his rage to considering him crazy and was grateful to see it. "The Vicomte's virginal bride...unless he already soiled the illusion, but...that's not my concern at present. No, ...no, he's entitled to you, isn't he? I sent you off with him for that very thing. That...isn't my concern today," he repeated, and I didn't believe him, not when I saw that the idea alone made him quake with a possessiveness he obviously did not think he had a right to feel.

"Then...why are we here?" I pushed and inched closer to force his focus. "You snuck into the de Chagny mansion to get me; certainly, it is for something important."

"Yes, important, an issue in need of a resolution. You are about to become another man's wife, and if I waited any longer for an answer, I would have been prompting adultery. You don't deserve sins on your soul because I hesitated."

Crazy... I began to call it a valid theory again. He wasn't making sense, those mismatched eyes darting the open space and never remaining on me. This was the one Erik that truly scared me; broken, and I wasn't sure I could fix him this time.

"Erik, ...you said you needed an answer. Well, I do not know the question. Won't you tell me?"

"That kiss, Christine!" he exclaimed, and I jumped from more than his abruptness. So I wasn't the only one fixated on meeting mouths. "I can't get it out of my mind! I was so sure in my assessment that it was done purely as a ploy to save your lover. A lie! I called it a lie! But I've spun the details over and over in my head, and then it dawned. I know *nothing*! How could I? I have no basis for comparison. I called it a lie and let you go, but how did I *know* there was not truth lingering somewhere? How can I know I made the right choice if I can't decipher that kiss? I need *you* to help me; you're the only one who can. I will go *mad* without an answer, Christine!"

I believed him...if he weren't mad already, but shaking my head somberly, I asked, "How? What can I possibly do to help you?"

"Kiss me again, and make it a *lie*. I want to know for certain what it feels like to receive lies from your lips, and then I will know the truth. And what better place for a show than the stage? You are a superb actress when in the spotlight. Here is your spotlight, and here is your role. You may close your eyes if you like. I don't care if you can't hide your disgust this time. Please, Christine, will you do this for me? Will you kiss me as a lie?"

I trembled, shivering from head to toe merely with the concept of kissing him again, never mind the rest of it. But as his words slowly registered and reminded me to stop staring at his exposed bottom lip, I stammered, "That...that's *absurd!*"

"No, it's not. I've analyzed it from every angle, and this is the most logical way to gain my answer. I need to know without a doubt what a *lie* feels like to determine the *truth*. There *must be* a difference. You wouldn't kiss the man you loved the same way you'd kiss a monster. So kiss the monster, make it a lie, and if you know disgust, all the better. *Act*, Christine. Make it believable. Kiss me with contempt in your heart, the hatred you must have felt that night. I just stole you from your life again; that should give plenty of inspiration. Take up the role. If it feels as it did the last time, I'll know I was right and sending you away was the correct solution."

"And if not?" I pushed, unable to stop trembling.

His breath left in a huff, heavy with his thoughts, and I wondered if he'd considered that side of it, perhaps only dwelling on being disappointed again. "You don't want such an answer, Christine, not standing before me in your bridal finery."

I felt my stomach knot, desperate to understand him. If he were wrong and saw reason to regret sending me with Raoul, ...would he recant? Keep me this time? Was that what *I* wanted? One kiss would give him the answer I was still reluctant to speak in my heart.

As he approached and began to lift a hand to his mask, I hastily insisted, "*No*, I won't kiss you."

"Why? I already told you that disgust is irrelevant. I won't hold you accountable for it. I *need* to understand a kiss. I need to feel you lie to me as you did that night and know that there was no hope. You didn't love me; there was no chance you could. I need to *know* these things and stop letting doubts waver in between. You *kissed me*; it *was* a lie, wasn't it? ...But *no*, I don't trust your words. I need proof when your lips have lied so often. *Showing me* a lie will be the only way I'll know without question left."

"Why do you think it was a lie?" I demanded, unable to fully denounce a rush of annoyance. "It was a *kiss*; not every kiss is a lie, but you are adamant mine was. I gave you no reason to think that."

"Your *fiancé* did! He was the one dangling from a noose a tug away from expiration. You *chose* me to save his life."

He said it was such conviction, a detail he obviously was certain to be truth, and yet...I was the one wavering. It seemed obvious: choose Erik and save Raoul. Those were the terms that had been laid out, and I had played right into Erik's hands with my so-called choice. Make the sacrifice of myself to preserve the man I supposedly loved, but that night, even as Raoul had struggled for breath and his existence had been *my* responsibility, *he* wasn't the impetus for my choice. He was the final push to a choice that had *always* existed and raged in debate in my secret heart. I wondered if Erik would believe me to say so. Perhaps it would only ignite more confusion from a man straddling the border of insanity.

"But...why did I *kiss* you?" I demanded instead and did not falter as his eyes flashed in flames.

"*Why? You* tell *me*, Christine. *Why?*"

"I...I don't know," I admitted honestly, and yet it only infuriated him further as he forced a grating laugh that made me tense.

I wasn't afraid; fear hadn't been relevant in longer than I cared to admit. Even that final night, fear for the unmasked villain ready to bring death and destruction hadn't been real. My fear was not rooted in Erik; it was rooted in my own shortcoming. Fear to be brave, fear to embrace a life that was unacceptable by society's terms, ...fear of a love that I knew would destroy everything I felt sure of in life. Loving Erik would change the world, and I wasn't sure I wanted such an epiphany.

Erik huffed his obvious disbelief and quickly decided, "All right, don't kiss me as a lie. Pretend instead that I am your darling Vicomte and kiss me as you kiss him. Kiss me with love, and I'll decipher the *differences* between this kiss and the last you gave me. I'll feel what was *lacking* from that kiss to make it true."

"What? *No*."

"You are an *actress*," he reminded as if that were the point that would change my mind. "You act all the time on the stage. My God, you produced a love scene with *me* in my opera, and it was prodigious! I almost believed you! You are quite accomplished when you apply your skills."

His words brought an impulse to cry. This was all my fault. I'd never given him anything to believe in, never a single concrete truth from the instant he'd stopped being an angel, and now the truth meant nothing to him. He saw lies; he saw *only* lies. For all my confusion and uncertainty, I found threads of truth that I was afraid to sew together; he was adamant that even truth was deceit.

"Do you require an audience?" he pushed on when I gave no answer. "Is that it? We had an audience to every detail that night. Perhaps having someone watching makes it easier for you to lift the façade into place. Can you imagine one, and will that be enough? An audience watching us act a farce on the stage. Just close your eyes and envision it, Christine. It will help if your eyes are closed, and you do not see my face. Then disgust won't come, and you can truly convince yourself that you are kissing your fiancé."

"*No*," I abruptly insisted. "No, Erik. I will not play these games with you."

"Then how am I to learn, Christine?" he asked a question that seemed so simple, and yet I stared at his hands and saw them fist to hide their shaking.

He was afraid. The Opera Ghost was the confident persona; the angel was strong. He was neither of those. *He* was *terrified* of learning the truth as much as I was terrified to give it. It wasn't just *my* world that would be altered.

Trembling as hard as he was to face my fear, I softly bid, "Let us be ourselves. No roles, no lies; let me kiss *you*, Erik, and we'll learn together."

"No, no," he whimpered. "*You* have knowledge of kisses and their nuances. You will be able to interpret, but I know *nothing*. I have never been taught what a kiss is and what it means. You could lie as you did that night, and I wouldn't know."

I shook my head and concluded, "You know better than I do. You felt the *truth*, and you came for me. You're teaching *me* more than I could ever teach you. So...kiss me now without the mask, without threats and ultimatums, without an audience, and we'll find the truth together."

Simply to speak the words made me shiver. How I ached for it! I'd never felt anything as I had that night, and despite every trepidation, I yearned only to feel it again. A kiss... Who decided it would change the world if it were true?

Erik made no motion, petrified in place and unsure whether to believe me. I couldn't blame him; bravery was new for both of us. So I edged the remaining distance to stand before him in my wedding gown, two words from belonging to Raoul and yet about to seal vows with Erik. And which would have been the real façade? I had no doubt when I let myself be vulnerable and did not bury my heart as it shown in my eyes and steadied the hand I lifted to his mask.

He shuddered, desperately trying to read me at every breath, but he did not stop me from removing that intrusive barrier and finding his damaged face.

"No roles," he whispered without sound, "and yet I find no disgust in your eyes. Are you acting, Christine?"

"No," I answered honestly and trailed my gaze over his scars, recreating them in my lackluster memory. How much better reality was! "I am only me, and you are only you."

"And without a ploy in place, do you wish to

kiss me, Christine?" His heavenly voice wavered with
the words, and I knew how desperately he fought to
trust what he saw as I nodded. To my surprise, he
inched a step back and ducked his mismatched eyes
from mine as he admitted with unhidden shame,
"I...don't know how, ...not as myself. Playing a part
was different. I could *be* the Opera Ghost and never
waver, but...I don't know what a kiss *is*, what it is
meant to be and feel like."

"Neither do I," I admitted, and he raised eyes to
me again. "Kiss me, and teach me what a real kiss
feels like."

He nervously licked his misshapen lips, and I
shivered with my desire to feel them upon me. Oh
God, I would have *begged* him for it had he not given
in. But to my delight, he slowly bent and barely
brushed his lips to mine. Tentative, hesitant, and he
met my constant gaze with an unspoken question,
making certain I did not regret before he took more.

As he sought another attempt, I met his mouth
with mine, raising myself on tiptoe and sliding
trembling arms about his shape to stop him from
disconnecting. *Not yet...* An urgent cry vibrated the
abnormal swell of his misshapen lips, and he suddenly
caught me with demanding arms, weaving them about
my waist and holding me to his body. I longed to sob
in relief and too much emotion for one person to hold.
This was truth and revelation; this was genuine and
seared my heart in one ordinary contact.

A kiss... A touching of lips to lips, and for the
first time, I understood why such a mundane
connection meant love. Love swelling my heart,
streaming the paths of my veins, love to every corner
of my soul and echoing in every heartbeat. Mouth to
mouth, lips to lips, and only one breath caught in
between. To breathe meant to live, to love meant to
live, and I was alive for the first time.

His kiss was gentle, unsure, and so very timid
that I *loved* him more for it. I followed his lead,
learning the same, and as my fingertips pressed

restlessly against the nape of his neck, a groan rumbled low in his chest and enchanted me. I wanted to make more sounds like that, to inspire such fitful responses that the word 'lie' would be forgotten in my boldness. And so I guided my hand along his neck and jaw and found his distorted face, cradling dead scars and bringing them to life.

He shuddered, and I felt him start to draw away. No, I refused to let go and took the reins, kissing his misshapen lips hard and intent, molding my mouth to his and stealing every gap that would ever exist between us. No more. This kiss meant love, and I wanted him to be as certain as I was. My hand was still upon his scars, gentle when my lips were anything but. I wasn't sure if I could cause him pain; every touch became a tender adoration, and as my fingertips grazed the open place where a nose should have been constructed, I felt his desperate exhalation tickle my skin.

"Christine," he finally dragged his lips away to gasp, "is this kiss a lie? Oh, you must tell me! I don't know what it means."

"It means love," I vowed and did not doubt it. "Love, Erik; it *always* meant love. The only lie will exist if you send me away again."

"No, no," he whimpered, and his arms clutched tight and hugged me to his heartbeat. "No, my love, never again. ...You love me, Christine? *I* am *your* choice?"

"Yes," I replied and pressed my cheek to damaged flesh to feel the wet of tears smear in between. "And I learned it through a kiss. Promise me that you'll never let me go."

"I promise. ...Oh, Christine."

He pressed kisses to my cheeks and brow, shivering when I did the same, and I felt *love* in every single delicate token. Love and a kiss and an answer in its intimacy.

The inventor of a kiss sought one perfect touch that spoke love more than words. I had never

understood it until that final night when I made a kiss
out of a vow and learned love in joined mouths. I
loved, and a kiss spoke the words before my lips ever
could. It was a revelation and set me on the path to a
happy ending. A kiss...and now I knew what it meant.

"Lie To Me"
A dark story told from Christine's POV.

I am an anomaly; I am a puzzle even to myself.
I am an actress; I am a liar. I am a hypocrite. At
times, I am selfish and vain, a materialistic idealist,
too concerned with my own appearance to notice the
rest of humanity and its struggles. Other times, I am
compassionate, sympathetic, empathic to suffering,
caring wholeheartedly and entirely generous.

With such a tremendous repertoire, is it any
wonder that I lack an understanding of myself? That I
am constantly searching for the true nature of my
character? Am I a heroine or a villain?

In the operas we perform, the categories are so
vividly black and white, pronounced and clearly
defined. Being a soprano, I am typically cast as
heroine: the beautiful, pure, the innocent. But, of
course, that is onstage. In real life, I fall into the void
of grey existing in between, ...maybe a dark grey,
...tinged with more black than white. I was white
once, pure white, virginal white, ...but once you add
even a hint of black, no matter how much white you
desperately stir back in, you will never have anything
other than a shade of grey for the rest of your life.
After my first taste of the darkness, I was overcome
with so much guilt that I tried to return to purity, but
temptation is black and temptation is strong. I was
unable to resist another taste and then another and
another until my soul was tarnished, and purity
became only a bittersweet memory.

I call myself a liar, a liar to everyone including
my own conscience. I pretend to be the same
Christine that I always have been. Sometimes I even
convince myself of it, that the blackness I can feel so
sharply beneath my skin isn't real; it couldn't possibly
be real... But it's undeniable in its potency, this ever-
present, ever-growing stain within me that I can't
control or refuse. Maybe it was always there, lurking
just beneath the surface, and I failed to acknowledge

it, ...didn't want to acknowledge it. Or maybe it was thrust upon me, the influence of a force I willingly allowed inside. Either way I came upon it, all that matters now is its presence, its constant, gnawing ache within my core, like a ravenous hunger that never seems to find satisfaction. I am beginning to wonder if I myself am blackened as well. ...More than that, if I am evil...

Staring at my reflection in the full-length mirror of my dressing room, I ponder the very term 'evil'. I don't look evil. The blue eyes staring at me are ones I recognize, ones that have looked back at me for a lifetime. The face, the contours and features, I know well; I watched them go from child to woman with a sense of fascination over the years, the changes so gradual and subtle that I only realized them after they occurred. I have always considered myself beautiful; that is the vanity within me. I attribute it to a father who lavished compliments and praises on his daughter with every breath. As I grew older with my father dead and gone, I learned that beauty is subjective and virtually indefinable, thriving in unexpected places and occasionally going against the norm. ...And yet even as I formulate my own definition for beauty and its perimeters, reshaping my core aesthetics, I still consider *myself* beautiful.

But... If I stare deep enough into the vision of my reflection, if I seek out the essence of soul lying within the pretty packaging, I can almost glimpse something unnatural, something strange and perverse, ...the darkness. Will it eventually become plain on my face? Readable in my eyes? Will the darkness steal every bit of what I believed myself to be until only a stranger remains behind? ...And will I care if it does?

An acute sense of loathing attacks me like a blunt blow to the gut, and I am forced to look away from my suddenly guilt-ridden eyes. The things I have done are like a nightmare that, try as I might, I cannot shake. And that nightmare is about to be relived once again; I am unable to stop it. I am weak.

Careful to avoid any accidental glimpse at the girl in the glass, the girl who has fallen under the dark influence and too eagerly shuns the light, I draw a thick, woolen cloak over my dark blue gown and reach for the hidden latch that unhinges my mirror and reveals the concealed passageway into the catacombs below.

A hundred times I have traveled this path, both in my waking and sleeping mind. I know every bend and curve, every step, every trick that brings me to him.

Him... My dark angel... In what bit of conscience I still possess and cling to with the tips of my fingers, he is Satan himself, the devil come to tempt me to sin and fall. And weak as I am to resist, I continuously return to him, continuously succumb and even beg for more. It has to be evil; the guilt that I always know afterward tells me that it *must be* evil, and yet I always go back. I always demand more.

Flying with black wings soaked in the blood of a moaning heart, I make my way through the cellars into hell's domain and to that fabled house on the lake. He is there within those fiery walls; I am aware of his essence before I even pass the doorway's threshold. I can feel him; I *always* feel him, ever since those deceptive days when he played heavenly angel to my vulnerable mind. His aura calls to me, always calls, always keeps a firm, unyielding hold on me. I no longer struggle against it. I need it too much now.

My shoes make soft whispers against the cold, hard stone of the catacomb floors as I reach for the doorknob and slip within that accursed, condemned sanctuary. In the back of my mind passes the fleeting thought that I am equally as condemned. I have willingly made this choice, and the eventual consequences are my own to bear, as I am sure they will come.

The house on the lake is lit with a warm glow,

inviting, welcoming my presence, and I feel it radiating into my bones, calming and stealing away my guilt. Guilt doesn't exist here; guilt only comes afterward. In its place, anticipation bubbles in my chest, and I can hardly wait until I am in his presence. Faster, quicker, my very soul is racing ahead of me to find him.

The moment I enter the living room, he meets my gaze, always with that initial disbelief that I have returned to him. He is sitting in his throne-like chair before a raging inferno of flames in the hearth, and even though he acts like I have come upon him unaware, I do not doubt that he knew of my presence long before, just as I knew of his.

He is...*majestic*. Erik, Angel. His pose is regal, his attire flawlessly formal, and that white mask glints unthreatening off the flames. This image of him is etched with intricate precision in my mind so that when we are parted, I can conjure it up in my most intimate of fantasies. His mismatched eyes, one sapphire blue and one deep emerald, never once need question my intentions; they immediately begin to smolder like hot coals gradually glinting and blazing with a fire more intense than that in the hearth. Fire... He is all fire, ...fire and heat.

My feet barely touch the floor as I float nearer to him. My skin is already tingling, though we have yet to touch, electrified like lightning is grazing the surface. I give him very little to decipher in my expression save a determination, a resolve that I *will* have what it is that I want so desperately.

Coming to stand before him while he patiently remains seated, studying me with great care and intent, I reach for the mask. I hate it right now; I hate its presence and the barrier it presents. I know that it is a necessity at all other times for both our pieces of mind, but at this moment before we are to make love, I want only to destroy it, to crush it and tear it until it is gone. My hand finds the coldness of its manmade material, and he doesn't stop my movements; he never stops me. My fingers fit around the edge, and I slowly draw it away a bit at a time, revealing that deformity to my eager eyes. It is ugly; it is ravaged and hideous, a twisted mockery of what a real face should be, and in spite of my eagerness, I feel the pull of aversion in my belly. I am disgusted by him, and strangely enough, it only makes me want him more. I need to see this repulsive face if only to assure myself that this is indeed Erik, *my* Erik, who I am taking into my arms and into my bed.

The mask slips out of my fingers and onto the carpet, and I immediately touch his face, cupping that ravaged side in my palm. It is instantaneous, the thrill that overcomes me, desire from head to toe, black and wrong and so unbelievably powerful. I can't deny it, even if I want to.

Erik knows the same fervent reaction to my touch; I can read it as he closes his eyes and gives a low growl in the depths of his chest. The skin of his disfigurement is so sensitive to any sort of caress, having been so long shunned and concealed, that simply the grazing of my fingertips along the thin layer of flesh that covers his sallow cheek makes him shudder violently from head to toe. I cry out, a nonsensical appreciation for that demon face, and bending down to him, I press my lips reverently to that cheek, lingering in a necessary kiss for a long, still moment.

This is not love. No, it can never be love. He has murdered mercilessly; how could I ever feel love for a murderer? This is desire, black desire; it is raw and savage and consuming. Not love... Never love...

Pulling my lips away, I stand before him, and with that same determined expression in my eyes, I push my cloak from my shoulders, hearing it fall with a hushed breath to the floor around me. As he stares transfixed, I gather my skirts in my hands and climb atop his lap, straddling him on his throne chair with a knee on either side of his body. I do not speak, do not make any false utterances of affection. He already knows what I want; why bother with words?

As I lower myself, fitting my body against his until I can feel the growing hardness of his manhood even through the layers in between, I tilt my face towards his, inviting his kiss. Without a dared complaint, he accepts the blatant enticement and captures my mouth with a hunger that makes me tremble. It is always like this; I can be brave, can take control, but in the end, I let him take the reins. I like being the subservient victim; ...perhaps it means I am less guilty.

Erik's mouth is hot and demanding, his kiss hard and bruising, and I match his fervency with my own. To glimpse such savagery between us, one would be shocked. Considering the other Christine, the light Christine I feign so well, this lewd behavior is unimaginable and aberrant; no one could possibly realize how deep this streak of darkness runs within me. Only with Erik do I know it. I felt it in dull tremors from the moment his angel's voice called out my name, and it has only grown since then into the inferno it is today. With Erik, I am not myself. I allow him to do things to me that I could never allow of anyone else. And I! I am unbridled, wild, passionate, craving in perverse ways for things that I could never fathom existed. The hunger is staggering, and whenever I try to refuse and stay away, it builds and assaults me until I can take no more and must yield to it with relieved abandon. I am addicted to this! To these incredible feelings! To the power he has over me! I love being his willing victim! And I cannot imagine a life without this and without him!

His hands tear at the clasps of my gown; they still tremble as we begin on this exhilarating carousel once again. I wonder if they will always tremble that way, as if he fears touching my body, a body that he already knows as intimately as his own. But as those infernal clasps open and my gown is stolen, I quickly forget the trembling of his hands; they have taken on a new sort of mystery, like an accomplished musician about to play his instrument.

With utter delicacy, he removes the pins holding back my dark curls and releases a thick cascade that is heavy on my shoulders and down my back. His fingers idly twist and entwine amidst the coils; he told me once that he would love to be lost in my curls and never come out. It is a memory that curves the corners of my lips even now as I watch him intently, a memory that I do not share with him.

Erik sits back in his chair and assists my eager hands as they discard his suit jacket, tie, and vest. But he lets me unbutton his shirt unaided, simply watching with that ravenous need glowing in his brilliantly bright eyes and scorching my flesh.

I am purposely slow in my endeavors; I want him to suffer, to be nearly bursting with desire, ...desire *for me*, and I play a part, feigning innocence and ignorance to what my torturous actions are doing to him. As he succumbs, only shifting uncomfortably and holding his breath to keep restraint, I thrill in the knowledge that I am in control now. I enjoy having such power just as he does, only I never let him know it. I keep my eyes wide, innocent, almost virginal, as if I am still hesitant and uncertain, and this makes his passion burn. Finishing with the last button, I am careful not to let my skin touch his as I push the material from his torso, noting with satisfaction how he arches toward me, expectant and desperate.

In a small voice, I innocently ask, "What would you have me do?"

"Touch me," he nearly growls. He could have grabbed my hands and forced them upon his skin, but that is not how he wants me.

Holding his passion-clouded eyes with my own, I very slowly extend my hand to his white chest until my fingertips lightly caress the cool flesh. I play the tease, the vixen, the virgin, and keep my touches light until I feel him writhing with need and only then do I press my palms flat against the smooth expanse of his chest and run them up and down as he arches into my touch.

Erik is in a frenzy of desire, and with a feral cry, he kisses me once more, demanding, fierce. Just one kiss, only one, and he pushes me off his lap back on my feet before him.

"Disrobe," he commands. His voice is so tainted with need by now that I hardly recognize it as his. When he is aggressive in this way, I do not dare argue; it isn't the time to pose a battle with him.

Moving with all the grace of my femininity, I obey, discarding petticoat, shoes, and stockings. Slower, I capture the hem of my chemise between my fingers and lift it over my head, exposing my breasts to his ravenous gaze, and then without pause, I lower my pantaloons, leaving myself bare. I am being ravished with his eyes alone as they trail up and down my every curve. I know that he adores my naked flesh; he has told me numerous times. It is his unending appreciation that makes me unashamed and confident before him, reveling in my own skin and my sexuality.

"I must have you *now*." It is a statement, not a question, and never daring to take his eyes from me, he hastily sheds the rest of his clothing and sinks back into his throne chair, beckoning me with a crooked finger.

Oh, he need not request. I am only too eager as I climb back atop him, this time sans the oppressive boundaries of our clothing. The very instant our flesh comes into contact with one another's, I feel my knees shake under my weight, anticipation dancing up the length of my spine. He is warm, a phenomenon that only occurs when we are making love. Usually, his skin is frigid to the touch, so like the very cellars he lives in. But not now. Now his flesh sears mine with each gentle brushing, the dead brought to life.

Quivering all over in spite of my prior bravado, I lower myself onto him, straddling his hips between my thighs. I am deliberately slow in my efforts, yearning to savor every second and every possible sensation. Even though Erik is in agony, his hardness straining between our bare bodies, he lets me play, but he is always ready to sway things in his direction. In that vein, he captures my breasts in his palms, cupping their generous weight before he lets his fingers pinch the hardened tips. I can't control the cry that I let loose; he knows exactly how to touch me to make me melt. Infuriating man!

With a grin of the seductress I truly am, I part my legs and lower my hips enough for the very tip of him to graze the length of my wetness. I am so ready now that my aching body is only liquid heat. One more long, insufferable moment, and I begin to take him inside. I am still playing, still toying with him as with each inch I take, I draw back a long second, making him wait.

But Erik is not a patient man, and with a roar of annoyance, he clamps my hips with his hands and forces me down until he is fully sheathed within my wetness. I cannot control the delirious cries escaping my lips. Sweet sin! This is exactly what I wanted. To feel him so deeply embedded within my body! To feel so stretched and full with him, *only him*! I throw back my head so that my curls fall across our joined bodies and tickle his thighs as he continues to hold my hips motionless in place. My every instinct begs for movement, for that primal rhythm to take over, and acquiescing, Erik begins to maneuver my hips in a torturously slow pattern, rocking us with contained passion. I know that he enjoys this and revels in making our union last as long as possible, and I concede, equally certain his control will not last long.

How right I am! For only a few blissful moments, he retains that savoring pattern, leaning close to find my mouth with a tender, exploring kiss. His tongue slips between my lips, and I can taste the dizzying deliciousness of him as I kiss him back, as gentle as he is. My tongue trails the length of his in my mouth, twirling and dancing around it. And that undoes him completely.

I feel his fingers digging into my hips with bruising force and marring my skin. They are not my first bruises from him in the unconsidered heat of passion and will certainly not be my last. Gripping my body viciously, he suddenly rises from the chair, and with a cry against his lips, I wrap my legs securely around his waist locking my ankles, curious to his intentions.

Erik wastes not time. He carries me to my bedroom and to the foot of this bed we've used so often. It is tall with a lush mattress, and he rests me upon its softness so that my backside just barely rests upon its edge. With a smirk at the end of our kiss, he lifts his hands to catch my forearms, disentangling them from his neck, and lowers me back onto the bed while he stands at the foot, our bodies still joined as one.

For one breath, he holds my eye as I stare up at him, mesmerized and overwhelmed with the unquenched passion in my veins. And then he creates a rhythm, thrusting into my aching body as I keep my legs wrapped around his waist. His torrid gaze wanders up and down from the column of my throat to the swells of my breasts and on to the apex of dark curls where our bodies are united. He often studies my body in this way while we are making love, looking more than touching; he likes to look at me. It is as if he is always trying to convince himself that I am truly here in his bed, sheathing his body within my own. Tonight, however, he doesn't just want to look. Never once disturbing the pattern of his thrusts, he presses his palms to the flat expanse of my stomach, curling his fingers around the sides of my small ribcage.

I shiver and tingle all over, staring up at him through cloudy eyes. Just as he usually likes to look upon me, I like to look upon him as we are lost in this most intimate act. I like to watch his tangled face, to see the desire and the passion build and twist those malformed features into something akin to what I consider beauty to be, my very own learned definition, uncommon and against standard conventionality. But how could it not be beautiful to watch this man give himself entirely to me?

Erik keeps his palms splayed across my belly for a long time before they slowly make a path to my breasts, cupping them and exploring as they have done dozens of times before. His fingers brush over each stiffened peak and then settle in a frenzy of tugs and pinches that drive me mad with the fervent need for release. I want to cry. I long to sob tears of my desperate yearning.

"Say my name," he hoarsely demands in that unarguable tone, and when I cannot find my voice to reply, he becomes harsher, repeating with the hint of anger, "Say my name."

"Erik," I whimper, clutching the blankets on either side of my head with handfuls of my thick curls tangled between fingers.

His eyes are glazed over with a flash of madness near insanity, as he continues sharply, "Tell me you're mine."

Erik's hand suddenly seeks the epicenter of my passion just above the place where our bodies are joined as I yell out, "I'm yours, Erik! *Yours!*"

"Mine forever," he growls, manipulating my flushed, craving body until I can feel release dangling so close to my grasping fingertips.

"Forever," I repeat of my own accord, hardly realizing that I spoke aloud. My heart is racing violently, my breathing in harsh gasps as I writhe on the bed, tossing my head from side to side amid my soft curls. So near, so close to what my body is burning for, and then in a great swell of passion, I find pleasure with a dizzying explosion so violent that I am left exhausted and weak in it wake.

Erik's bruising grip has returned to my hips, leaving new marks on my creamy flesh as with a guttural cry, he thrusts with savage intensity a moment more and then explodes deeply inside of me.

I study every expression, every sound he

makes, every detail of him during his climax. He has never looked as beautiful to me as he does right now, a revelation partly induced by my sated state of bliss. Dangling on that cloud, I allow myself to see him through the eyes of a lover, to regard him as if my heart is in my expression. As he fights to catch his breath, he leans down to me, pressing his sweat-coated flesh to my own and lays his flawless, unmarked cheek to my chest just above my beating heart, savoring its sound like a lilting symphony. I idly extend my hand to caress his deformity with unrestrained tenderness, as close to him in every way I possibly can be.

Long moments blend one into the next until I am unaware of the passage of time. This peace will be short-lived, but I refuse to remember that now. Let me live this illusion a little longer.

Erik is the first of us to stir and find reality. Raising himself, he gently disentangles our exhausted bodies, and even though I avoid his gaze, I feel the unspoken words there. Oh, not now. I cannot tolerate his words now.

The moment I am free of his hold, I scurry off the mattress and reach for the dressing gown I discarded across my chaise the day before. As I draw it on to conceal my nudity, I inadvertently glance down to the aching skin of my hips and notice the burgeoning purple bruises forming darker and darker.

"I have hurt you," he states matter-of-factly, and I jerk the robe closed, tying it tightly into place before lifting my eyes to his. Regret and compassion saturate his expression. How I cannot abide to see it!

Shaking my head, I reply in an emotionless tone, "No, I am fine."

"Don't," he bids as he reluctantly reaches for the extra blanket I keep beside the bed and wraps it around his waist. I know he is doing this for my sake without him ever having to say so.

"Don't what?"

"You always behave this way. You open

yourself so completely to me, and in the next moment, you become hardly more than a distant stranger. Is it really necessary to leap out of bed and cover yourself from my eyes? You come down here begging for my touch as if you will perish without it and now you shy away and avoid it like the plague."

"I...I'm cold," I lie. I am not a very good liar when I do not have an orchestra and an audience before me.

"No, you're ashamed of what we have done, of what you truly are, ...what lives and breathes within you."

It is as though he has somehow read my mind to know these things, and I cannot deny their validity.

Erik continues on sadly, "Why won't you let yourself love me?"

I cringe and lower my eyes to my idly twisting hands. "I can't love you, Erik," I softly reply. "You know I can't."

"No," he immediately retorts. "You *won't*. You will come down here and beg me to satiate your passions, but then not an hour later, you will go and lavish your affection on that damn Vicomte."

Raoul... It is a sore subject on both Erik's and my account that is better not broached and avoided altogether. "The Vicomte is a gentleman," I hear myself insist only half-considering what I'm saying.

Erik gives a bitter, grating laugh. "And I guess that makes you a common whore then. No lady would behave in such a shameless manner. Wouldn't you agree?"

A *whore*! My anger seethes like fire under my skin. How dare he! And yet a small voice in my head wonders at the possible truth in such a claim. I must bite my lip for a long second to calm my rage, and as a bitter retaliation, I reply, "Maybe I am not a lady, but Raoul is a gentleman, the sort worthy of my heart and my affections."

"Ah, but I am worthy of your body? Worthy enough to take your virginity and to use to squelch your unladylike urges?" The sharpness of his comments dwindles away, his expression becoming melancholy as he thinks on his words. He shakes his head, and I am doubtless that for the briefest moment, I glimpse the silhouette of a tear. Just as fleeting, it is gone again. "If your body is all I will have of you, then I will accept it. It may not be love, but it will do...for now."

"For now? My body is *all* that you will *ever* possess." Sometimes, I can be cruel; I'm not sure why I act in such a way. I just want to hurt him.

With a sudden abruptness, he darts to stand before me and catches my upper arms in a tight, viselike hold. "Naïve fool!" he roars. This is when I cannot endure looking at that face, when it is so twisted with rage that it can only be an ugly horror, and I vainly wish for the mask to hide it. "What will it take for you to admit that you love me?"

"I don't-"

"Oh, don't you? Then ask yourself why it is that you keep coming back to me? Why you keep begging me to take you? I am not blind, Christine. You do not desire that arrogant boy as you desire me. Your body is screaming at you that we are meant to be together. Why won't you listen to it?"

Before I realize his plan, he releases my arms only to grab both my small wrists in one of his quite larger palms, jerking them above my head to prevent me from struggling. With his free hand, he parts my tied robe at my thigh, groping my soft flesh as his fingers travel upward. I want to scream and rage at him for this violation, but I can only mutter a helpless, little cry as his fingers plunge into my womanhood, already throbbing and growing wet again from his attentions.

Erik moans between clenched teeth and expertly strokes my yearning body. "Listen, Christine, listen to what your body is screaming out. Your body knows whom it belongs to. Why do you refuse to acknowledge it? Do you truly believe the Vicomte could ever satisfy the darkness within you? It is for me alone."

"No," I weakly protest, squirming against fingers that will not cease.

"Yes, Christine, yes." Erik's voice has grown hoarse again, and I am enveloped in the heat radiating from his body. "Lie to me. Tell me that I am wrong while I have the essence of you dripping from my fingertips." His hand will not stop, and leaning in near to me, he huskily whispers against my ear, "Does your Vicomte make you burn this way? Does he make you yearn and ache and grow so wet?"

I want to lie. *Yes!* My mind is screaming. *Say yes!* But the heated warmth of his breath still brushing my ear is making me tremble all over and close my eyes, mewing my wanting. I don't want to be thinking of Raoul now! I only want Erik, only ever Erik.

"Christine, Christine," he chides in a singsong tone, taunting me with that angel's voice. His fingers are so deeply within my wetness while his thumb purposely flicks across the hard bead at the top, making my knees sway under my weight. "Such darkness thriving inside of you. It shames you when you succumb to it, yet it is far too powerful to resist."

Erik brushes his misshapen lips to the sensitive flesh below my ear and down the side of my throat, nuzzling his face into my loose curls as he goes, and I shudder violently from head to toe. If not for the tight grip of his hand holding my wrists captive above my head, I am sure that I would have fallen to the floor. My head is spinning in waves of dizzying euphoria, and my limbs are heavy and numbing. Oh, dear Lord! I can feel myself losing control, can feel my imminent release as his fingers move with purpose. Words no longer make sense, protests abandoned, and all that I can do is mutter nonsensical syllables of delirious desire.

Erik burrows his scarred face against the crook of my throat. "Say you love me." This command is firm. "Say it."

I meekly shake my head from side to side. "I...I can't... I don't..."

His fingers pause a moment as he brings his lips to my ear and desperately breathes, "Lie to me."

I arch my hips against his fingers as they stroke again and concede, whispering back that blasphemous lie, "I love you."

Erik growls his delight, and his caresses increase in intensity until I hear gasps and hoarse cries coming unknown from my lips. One more harsh pass of his fingers. My knees give out completely and only his hands hold me up as I climax with a jerk of my hips, my body spasming and clutching at emptiness as it seeks his to fill it and make it whole.

It takes me a long while to recover and Erik, ever patient when in the midst of our intimacies, continues to trail his fingertips delicately over my satiated womanhood. Such caresses always make me feel worshipped, as if he is in silent awe of my femininity. He lowers my wrists and releases them so that he can enfold me into him with his arm, and as my passion relaxes, he removes his hand from beneath my robe to make the embrace complete.

It is a lie; it is all a lie. I don't love him; I can't love him, but he will not accept that. He wants the lie, and he wants me to believe in it as well. ...And if I do, if I choose to believe, will the lie then quit *being* a lie and become a reality? ...Do I want it to be a reality?

Erik's embrace is tender and warm. I force the unending plethora of questions and the ever-torturous thoughts away if only for this moment. Let me forget them, forget the world outside and the guilt that will certainly come once I must leave him. The guilt always comes... But not now... Now I want to live that longed-for lie and pretend that it is indeed our future.

Closing my eyes, I breathe his scent in deeply and rest my cheek against his collarbone, weaving my own arms around him until we are sharing an embrace that is as necessary as it is passionate.

"I love you." Erik's voice is hardly more than an exhalation of a breath. He does not expect a response from me. I won't...

And yet I can't keep a passing thought from my mind: if this *is* love, why does it do nothing but cause us pain? It's not supposed to...

Much later, back under my guise as the prim and proper lady, I leave Erik's house on the lake. Just as I knew it would, the guilt attacks almost instantly with an intensity that steals my breath away. I can't continue this way; I know it is impossible to even consider. I feel as though I am living a double life. No matter what I do, I am lying to someone, whether it is to Raoul or to Erik or to myself. Someone is always victim to my deception.

Hanging my head low with the ferocity of my shame, I wander the cold, lonely paths back to the world. I cannot say how this must end or how it *will* end, but whatever happens, I fear the darkness that Erik uncovered will always be a part of me, something that I cannot deny or hope to lock away. And just as Erik claimed, I know that he is the only one who can make it burn. Whether I like it or not, I am intricately tied to him and will be for the rest of my life.

With the secret of my sins blackening my soul, I emerge into the sunlight above, knowing with absolute certainty that come sunset, I will once again lose myself to the darkness...

"A Revenant's Love Story"
The Vicomte makes a final attempt to keep Erik out of Christine's life.

Raoul de Chagny grimaced his absolute distaste to traverse the dank, dark pathway through the corridors beneath the opera house. Three weeks back and an ill-fated night with a threat of death at its culmination had left the Vicomte swearing that he would never set foot on this condemned bridge to hell again, and yet here he was, calling himself a fool at every turn and bend in the trail that would lead him to the doorstep of a murderer.

"Ludicrous," he muttered between curses under his breath, but as he insisted to his dwindling sense, he had no intention of repeating the last performance of these events. No, this time it would be he who had the upper hand, and noosed ropes would not matter. Let the monster attack; physical games to establish superiority were about to seem trite when the heart broke without a fist as its cause. A broken heart... Oh, more than that, a *destroyed* heart.

"Monsieur Vicomte."

A soft call shook Raoul from his reverie and reminded him that the projected outcome he'd been envisioning still needed its final bricks laid into place, hence a clandestine meeting in the recesses of the catacombs.

"Monsieur daroga," he greeted in return with more gentility than he typically would have granted a foreigner. A modicum of respect existed between them despite their vast, immeasurable differences; a commonly shared glimpse into the face of death certainly had a decided way of uniting its victims. "I'm pleased to see that you received my note. I had to take extra precautions to be certain no one else intercepted it by mistake."

The daroga was a small man in stature compared to the broad scope of the noble Vicomte, and he only appeared further a contrary as he nervously kept his dark face ducked and half-hidden in the shadows beyond his oil lantern. Frantic glances were cast into the depths of encompassing blackness at every angle under the unqualified fear that something would leap out at any moment as he could practically feel the choking sensation of invisible nooses about a bare throat, and he quietly muttered, "I had to be equally as careful; if he suspected anything at all, if he even had one iota of a consideration to your plan, ...Monsieur Vicomte, Erik is not a tolerant or a forgiving man. We were fortunate to be granted mercy once. He would never make such a mistake again. You believed torture chambers and nooses were horrors; you have no idea what he is truly capable of."

Raoul tried to appear unaffected by the warning, but his actions gave him away as he peeked into the far darkness before straightening defiantly. "I refuse to be at his whim; he will not be the ghost always in our shadows, monsieur. That is why we are doing this. I will not live the remainder of my life with his threat in the background."

The daroga shrugged his narrow shoulders uncertainly. "But he let you and the young mademoiselle go free. He bid you to leave and have your happy ending."

"Yes, and at quite the cost. I told you as much in my letter." The true extent of his recent suffering came to the forefront in one honest look, saturating to every creased corner of blue eyes. Suffering, ...more like agony.

"How is she?"

Heaving a desolate breath, the Vicomte admitted somberly, "As well as one could expect. After every trauma she's endured, it's a blessing that I've been able to reach her at all. That first week, I doubted I'd ever get her back. The doctor called it a breakdown. He blamed her anxiety and the horrors she was put through by that madman. That night was the last point she could handle; it was finally too much."

Not a single word spoken proved to be any surprise to the daroga. Nadir had seen Christine as they had fled the opera house that last night, and nothing of herself had remained in her eyes. Every glance had been empty and had shown only a hollowed void within her. The Vicomte insisted it was Erik's fault; Nadir wasn't as sure. "You said in your letter that she wasn't talking. Is she speaking again? Has she said anything about any of this?"

"She *is* speaking again," the Vicomte confirmed, "but she refuses to utter a single word about that monster. Can you begrudge her that seeing as how she was nearly forced to be his *wife*? She doesn't want to recall it, but I fear that it tortures her mind anyway. She nearly had to sacrifice everything to save my life; in all her silent days, I would wager that was all she could ruminate upon."

With the occasional glance yet about, the daroga abruptly asked, "And where is she now? Not at the de Chagny mansion surely if I am meant to play my part in this scheme of yours."

"Of course not. I sent her off to my aunt's country estate, and I will join her there once I see this task completed. I want to make certain that it is as authentic as possible so that he has no choice but to believe."

"Monsieur..." Nadir was shifting on his feet in the face of the Vicomte's determination, knowing his own lack of enthusiasm was vividly spread along his features. "Must we truly do this? It just seems so...malicious and indecently cruel."

"Indecently cruel?" the Vicomte retorted. "Do you not recall that he was just as prepared to kill you as he was me without a single qualm or consideration to friendship and loyalty? You were his friend, and yet in that situation, your life meant as little as mine. I cannot call this cruel so much as justice."

"But, monsieur-"

"No, this needs to be done, and *you* must be the one to do it. He will believe you in spite of everything; I've no doubt of that. *Please*." The Vicomte was not the sort of man to beg for anything, but this was the one time when no amount of money could buy what he wanted. Christine, her heart and soul, there was no price for such treasures. "This is the only way, Monsieur daroga," he added desperately. "He'll never leave her be; you know that as well as I do. He'll come after her and seek to steal her away again and again until he finally destroys her. No matter what you think of my reasoning, consider Christine. She cannot have any sort of decent life with him lurking in our periphery."

Christine... And arguments faded with the known fact that the Vicomte was right. Erik was not a man to lose or to surrender anything; it had been a surprise to Nadir that Erik had released them in the first place, ...released the only woman he'd ever loved to a future with another man. Nadir had to conclude that Erik's seeming good will was only a temporary respite. A man who loved that fiercely did not just give it up. But still one thought nagged at his brain, and he insisted with a rush of compassion and regret, "This will *kill him*, Monsieur Vicomte. I don't think you realize the full extent of what you intend. Amidst all the horror and sin of his life, Erik truly does *love* her."

The Vicomte's jaw tightened as his words struck a yet-gaping wound within and tore it open once again. Yes, the monster loved her, *his* fiancée, *his* love as well. Erik with his deformed face had dared to touch her and kiss her with his disfigured lips right in front of Raoul as he had had to helplessly watch, unsure where the line of pretending ended and reality began. For the Vicomte, that was the greatest trauma still clouding judgment with its sting, but he did not let on of it to the daroga, nothing beyond clenched teeth and a solemnity as he argued without waver, "Yes, and his love is as damning as his hate. You speak to me of *his* well-being; well, my only concern is *Christine's*. Hasn't she endured enough at his hands and all because he supposedly *loves her*?" The demand was spat with bitterness as thrusting a hand into his pocket, he withdrew a folded scrap of paper. "Give him this, Monsieur daroga. He will want some sort of proof; here it is, written in her own hand. She composed its secrets a few days after we left this place during her silent quarantine. Once I saw it, I knew that this would be my answer. He cannot argue or deny her own words. Give it to him, monsieur, when you tell him." That was it. Details laid in place, and the Vicomte cleared his throat, vying for detachment as he continued, "I must get back and make sure all the loose ends are tied. I cannot afford a single mistake, for both Christine and my own life."

"Mine as well it would seem," the daroga somberly added as he clutched the blasphemous parchment between trembling fingers.

"I will contact you once I have left the city and send word where I can be reached. I want ample notification if anything goes awry." He was about to leave, about to turn away and let the wheels spin in their motion, but he dared to assure with the conviction Nadir lacked, "We're doing the right thing, Monsieur daroga. He let her go to live her life with me; this is just insurance that he won't ever change his mind."

Even as he nodded, Nadir carried skepticism that knotted his stomach until he felt nauseous with every breath. The right thing... If this *was* the right thing, then why was he so loath to agree to its content? And why, when pain had been the prevalent emotion through this entire ordeal, was there only more at the crux of this plan? Pain, and he was about to be its primary cause with one uttered lie.

Nadir waited until the Vicomte disappeared from sight before daring to finish the trek into Erik's world. The paper in his hand was searing him with its letters even though he had yet to uncover its secret musings, so certain that he'd rather guess than know he was right. Every word was about to be its own little dagger, piercing hearts, causing damage, and creating gaps for the blood to leak out in rivulets. This small folded paper was the equivalent of a murder weapon, and even if it would be a lackluster attempt on his part, Nadir was to be its wielder.

With weighted footsteps, Nadir came upon the doorway to the house on the lake and hesitated, knowing that this was his final chance to change his mind before outcomes were set. ...No, this had to be done, and he had to be strong for Christine Daaé and her misfortune of becoming the sole focus of Erik's obsession. She did not deserve that.

Before he ever entered the concealed doorway, the ominous stillness of the dark corridors was pierced with frantic pitches from a bellowing piano's suffering strings and pounded hammers. Music was a loose definition for what poured out; this was the audible sound of a damaged soul, agony in pitches and melody interlaced with the dissonance of anger and temper. It stole Nadir's breath from his lungs with its potency. Erik's music often carried such an effect since his first introduction to its exquisiteness, but usually it was a direct result of a beauty not meant for the world to hear. His reaction now was caused by its blatant heartache, almost like the final fall of some majestic angel. ...God's angels would indeed fall to such a song.

Nadir was reminded of Erik's initial deception and the day he had gushed the details to the skeptical daroga of his plot to disguise himself as an angel for Christine, a plot already in motion before the daroga could have ever attempted to stop it. An angel, ...the Angel of Music. Typically, Erik did not share any facet of his life with anyone, but he had considered his approach with Christine brilliant and couldn't help but boast. It had been the only time in their lengthy acquaintanceship that Nadir had ever seen Erik happy in any sense of the term, and his happiness had nearly been as frightening to behold as his anger.

Loath to interrupt the serenade he was

eavesdropping upon, Nadir was as silent as he could be turning the knob and stealing into the warm glow of the house. Any other visit would have left him pondering how oddly cozy it was despite the depth below ground, how Erik had truly transformed a seeming cave into a home with every implied emotion that term brought to mind, but tonight's view was altered from usual.

A foreign sense of anguish was thick in the air, deceptively masked by the safety of firelight, and as Nadir glanced about, he took note of the mundane changes in his surroundings, things he would not have noticed unless he was looking. Objects were missing here and there, random knick knacks, precious treasures, and as he warily made his way down the narrow hallway to the occupied music room, following a piano's cries, his eyes were caught on wreckage and casualty, the remnants of those lost mementos, the shattered evidence of fits of temper and lonely rage. So many broken pieces in various colors and sizes, some glass, some resin, intermixed in places like a splattered mosaic of unique art. Yes, even Erik's destruction would seem to leave a thing of beauty in its wake.

The daroga barely arrived in the doorway when so suddenly that he jolted with surprise, the music halted mid-chord and hastily broke off. Well, he knew that Erik sensed *everything*. And as such, the unmasked virtuoso behind the piano abruptly leapt to his feet and spun about to face his intruder.

"Daroga," Erik greeted, glaring with cold, narrowed eyes as every unspoken insult attached was etched to precise telling along the nuances of displayed, malformed features.

"Erik," Nadir stammered back nervously, trying to deny his instinctual urge to shift and sway on his feet. No, he bid to himself, no giveaways to a man who would deduce and interpret every one. "How are you doing?"

A grating chuckle was his initial answer,

amused and utterly unnerving in its timbre as Erik rubbed distractedly at his scarred cheek before suddenly recalling its exposure. With a groan of annoyance, he rummaged about for his mask, never once considering that despite its absence, the daroga had given nothing that could be taken as an unpleasant reaction. Still, the mask was replaced and secured before Erik dared recall that propriety insisted he give some sort of answer. *Words*, he insisted of himself. And yet what words could possibly exist to sufficiently capture his current frame of mind? So instead, he chose to snap, "I haven't seen a single glimpse of your interfering presence since the night you betrayed our unusual companionship and aided that damn Vicomte and his gallant quest, and you dare to suddenly inquire about my well-being? Since when has such a detail mattered at all to you? Or is this guilt I am being faced with and a misguided attempt at penance?"

"You have every right to be upset with me," Nadir attempted as calm as he could manage. "To your consideration, it *would* seem a betrayal, but if you would care to look at it from my view, you'd see that-"

"I wouldn't care to look at it from your view," Erik interrupted sharply. "And you have no excuse that I will take. But don't worry. I've well learned my lesson. I ignorantly dubbed you as a friend; I will not be that naïve again. One would think that I'd have realized long ago to trust no one but myself, but...the mistake was made, and it cannot be undone."

"Erik, don't be ridiculous. You were beside yourself that night; I felt I had no choice-"

"You *always* had a choice; you just made the wrong one. And in my effort not to go through with killing you where you stand, I insist that you leave my house. I've spared you once already, and you well know that I've killed for far less than the injustice you have done me. Get out." Erik gestured to the door but had already made his dismissal as he stalked back

287

to the piano and its rested keys and threw himself upon the bench, pounding out one long, aggressive chord.

"Erik," Nadir interrupted, raising his voice to rival the instrument's volume, but he was blatantly ignored as more chords resounded. "*Erik!*" he practically shouted, and knowing exactly how to break into music's trance, he added loudly, "I have news about Christine."

All at once, the tone cut off again, even the leftover ring halted to silence as frantic eyes shot back up with impatience and fury intertwined. "What did you say?"

"Christine," he nervously muttered, feeling the assault through eyes alone. He wondered how anyone could possess the power to hurt a person in a look, but then again, Erik wasn't just anyone. Apprehensively stammering, he posed, "Well, ...it's been three weeks. Have you...heard anything of her? Seen her at all? ...Checked in on her?"

"Three weeks?" Erik repeated with a modicum of surprise. "Three weeks, truly? I...hadn't realized. I've been busy."

"Composing?"

Erik nodded frantically. "A new opera...for Christine, of course. I thought...I thought I'd surprise her with it when she returned."

A chill overtook Nadir from head to toe and left a shudder as its evidence. *When she returned...* He almost cowered; the hope in Erik's mismatched eyes was so toxic, so masochistic in its way because once it was gone, ...it would obliterate him to nothing. And Nadir hesitated. "A new opera? ...Well, then I suppose that means you haven't been eating or sleeping or doing anything else for that matter. You take to musical binges as normal people do to alcohol and forget every space between sober jaunts. I've always feared that one of these days, you'll neglect to come out of it at all."

Shrugging off words and open concern, Erik

rambled, "I'll eat when she returns, and as to sleeping, I know I shall only be able to do so again when she is at my side. So don't worry over me, daroga. She *will* return, and I'll live on."

"You're so certain of that."

"Well, of course," he snapped, slamming shut the open manuscript set before the piano's keys if only to have some task to busy his suddenly shaking hands. "You would not understand how I can say that and know it to be true. It is beyond your comprehension, but Christine and I have a bond that nothing could ever break or destroy. She'll always come back to me."

"But...you let her go," the daroga argued, noting how vividly the Vicomte's fears had merit.

"Well, yes, I had to. You don't know Christine as I do, daroga. She can get confused sometimes when she is being tugged too firmly in too many directions, and she can be weak. She let that Vicomte twist her up inside, but that last night...oh, that last night..." The light of a disconcerting bliss was bright upon his masked face as he insisted, "She knew she loved me. She *chose* me, and my God, she *kissed me.* You saw it happen. I did not force her or manipulate her; she did that of her own free will. She knew exactly what she wanted at that moment, but there were too many doubts yet in between, all inspired by her milksop Vicomte. I never wanted her to wonder if she made the choice because I coerced her. And I was confident that if she saw that I loved her, *truly* loved her enough to give her up, she would finally be strong in her own heart. You'll see what I mean, daroga, when she comes back to me. I expect her at any time now, especially if it's been three weeks already. She's likely seeking the easiest way to escape the Vicomte's watch as we speak." His elation was frozen in suspension with one recalled point, and he suddenly pushed, "You said that you had news of her? What news? ...Or is it exactly as I said? Has she left the Vicomte?"

Nadir faltered and dared to demand, "And if

she hasn't, what then, Erik? Will you go to her and carry her off again? Will you take the extent of the decision out of her hands as you've done before?"

"Oh, don't say it that way," Erik retorted back. "You speak as if I have forced emotions upon her, and I have done no such thing. As I said, she is confused, and if she has not yet left the Vicomte, it very well could be because he won't allow it. To admit that he has lost to a disfigured monster is quite beyond his capabilities. And therefore going and fetching her myself is justified and not the sin you're implying it would be. She *loves* me, Nadir; carrying her off would be a blessing to her."

"Would it really?" the daroga muttered. He repeated the Vicomte's assurance in his head once again; what he was about to do was for Christine. It was the only way Erik would ever let her go. Keeping a somber expression, he forced himself to speak, knowing that hesitance would seem valid and solemnity warranted, that sympathy would be genuine in spite of words that held no meaning in their context. "Erik, ...I have to tell you something, and I'm not quite sure how to say it, ...especially to you. It's...a tragedy, ...an awful tragedy. ...Christine...is dead."

The expression upon a masked face was blank and unreadable, the fixed stare searching for the crack that would mean a lie, but beneath the pretense, simply the utterance of such words made Erik's heart drop like a leaden weight within the cavity of his chest. And even as he remained unconvinced, he fisted his hands atop his lap so that Nadir would not notice the subtle shake that was quickly growing into a constant quiver.

"You're lying," he accused and commended his own control that not even a catch could be detected in his voice. "I truly cannot fathom the depth of your betrayal, daroga. You choose to side with the Vicomte and his arrogant ways, and now you dare come into my home and utter such slander. What are you hoping for? Tears? Pain? Some unimportant proof that I still have a heart after what I did to you?"

"No, no," Nadir muttered back with a firm shake of his head. "I'm not lying to you, Erik. I truly thought you already would have known; the news is all over the city, but you haven't left the house in three weeks so it is no wonder. ...She's dead, Erik; she...she took her own life."

"No," Erik stated firm and inarguable, eyes bearing into Nadir with an internal blaze of fire. "*No*, how dare you stand there, my so-called friend, and post such blasphemies to my ears? Get out of my house, and shall we meet again, your neck will be in my rope."

"It's the truth, and no threat you throw at me is going to change it. Here." His hand trembled, but he extended the crumpled note out before him as he took the few steps that put him almost gullibly within Erik's reach. He had faith that his offering would be the very key to saving his life. "In her own hand."

It took a concentrated effort to make fingers uncoil and snatch the paper, and Erik knew that his shaking was an undeniable reality that told his fears even as he kept up an indignant façade. Quickly unfolding the scrap, his unfocused eyes immediately recognized Christine's elegant penmanship with every loop and scrawl to her letters. Yes, this was in her own hand. In a soft voice, he spoke those cloistered words, unsure why he shared their burden with his unbidden audience but unable to stop himself.

" 'My dearest *ange*. You have broken my heart for the last time. Once again you have seen it fit to make my choice for me and decide how I will love. I chose you; I laid heart and soul vulnerably at your feet, but that wasn't enough. It couldn't be. You prefer to control the workings of my heart than trust their secrets. You wanted a prisoner to be chained to you and your love, not an equal to love you in return. And it didn't matter that I professed my devotion to you in one kiss. You never wanted devotion; you wanted power, the power to decide how and why I will love you. It was never considered that I already did. My heart is gone, ripped free of ribs and bone, and an open wound is in its place. You wanted a heart you could manipulate, and in your selfishness, you've taken mine. For what you've done, I'll hate you to my death; I only pray it comes quickly to take me away from the anguish of living. You have destroyed me, Erik, and made me as damaged as you yourself are. I loved you... I loved you, and you condemned me...' "

That was all; the rest of the page was severed and gone, and as the last of her accusations soaked into his skin and sought to poison the blood coursing within, a gasped sob was sucked sharply past parted lips. "No," Erik moaned miserably, cradling that scrap of a letter in suddenly desperate hands. "No, no, no, it can't be the truth. She wouldn't... Not if she loved me... She loved me, Nadir... This letter is proof, and she wouldn't..." He couldn't even utter the sin, his head shaking an urgent denial.

"As you said," Nadir stated, his voice choked with his own unshed tears, "she was confused. This entire situation was some sort of trauma for her; they say she wouldn't speak a word for days. And it was just too much, Erik, ...too much. All the horrors put upon her shoulders. ...She couldn't take any more; it finally broke her beyond repair. ...She...she's gone, Erik. I'm sorry, but...it's true."

Erik's head was reeling, fluctuating dizzily between fragments of Christine's own words and the daroga's fitted details. His Christine, alone and broken, believing he'd let her go because she had *freely* loved him. ...Oh God, what had he done? "No, no," he whimpered, clutching the note to one temple and grasping his masked face between violently shaking hands. "No, I won't believe it. She isn't...dead. She *can't be* dead! She's supposed to be mine! I love her!"

Every lie left a burning sensation upon Nadir's tongue, and as he watched the tears filling blue and green eyes and cascading over a masked face, he hated himself for every fabricated deception. But...it was too late to go back now.

"Erik..." Solace was uncommon for both of them, and unsure how to offer it, he patted an awkward hand upon Erik's quivering shoulder. "God has a path for everyone and every creature upon the earth. Perhaps she was simply being set upon hers."

"Her path was with me!" Erik exclaimed vehemently. "Her path is inextricably entwined with mine! Don't you understand that? Why can no one see it? She is my *everything*! My very reason to exist! She is my verity and my life; she is the only one to show me that I am not a monster, that I can be more...*for her*. I can't *live* without her!"

"Erik, no!" It was his tone, his determination that finally made Erik lift his heavy head and meet his stare.

"What do you mean *no*?" Erik snapped, anger vibrant and peeking through the center of pain. "You came here today, and you *destroyed* every bit of me! What is left? This is no world that I live in, Nadir! This is no *life*! The rest of the human race despise me, spit upon me, have treated me as if I haven't even the right to exist and breathe, as if I am *nothing*! *She* was my salvation, and I...I... Oh God..." Bending suddenly in half, tensed down every muscle, he sobbed, his heart leaking out through every tear's essence. Words made no sense, comprehension gone; all he could do was gasp her name over and over again, clinging to a single word when it was all that was left.

"Erik, ...I'm so sorry." And Nadir meant it. Never before had he seen a man so feared and powerful, so unexplainably strong considering all he'd endured in his lifetime crumble to a fallible human being. This was not the mad Opera Ghost who had despaired Christine's loss that last night; no insanity to dim the blow, no hope to present an ever-flickering rescue, nothing but a man mourning the only fraction of happiness he'd ever been granted. And when music had given a beautiful anguish upon his arrival, sobs were an exquisite lament as final as a requiem, filling the small, lonely house and filtering out to echo emptily into the catacombs.

*****

'I loved you, and you condemned me...' Those final words and their bitter accusation were looped in a spiral that pirouetted mercilessly through Erik's brain. Condemned, ...*killed* her; killed replaced condemned, a more accurate conjecture. *Killed, dead, gone...*

Tears only ceased when they ran dry and none remained, when an agonized heart felt empty of all matter that symbolized life. *Dead...*

It was with an eruption of temper and threats too tempting to be indulged that Erik finally got Nadir to leave him be. Oh, how he longed for peace and solitude! And yet once he had it, it tormented him and made him regret the loss of a sordid friend.

Alone, ...and Christine would be alone... *Dead...*

It took only minutes for Erik to devise a plan beneath the persistent voice of denial that continued to speak hope, and within the moment that the idea was born, he concealed himself in a thick cloak and hat, hiding within his persona as he abandoned the catacombs for the first time in three weeks.

Three weeks... He still could not fathom time's passage. It was too easy to lose long minutes and hours within the music; Christine had once teased that if not for her lessons, he would willingly remain buried in notes and melodies and never come out to life and the world again. He had never told her that she had been right, that it was only the induction of emotions she inspired that brought reality back and an impatience to burst his musical bubble and go to her instead. Then music had no longer been a pleasure so much as a way to bide his time between her visits. Nothing else had needed to exist in between because nothing else could amount to her. Christine... *Dead...*

His heart ached painfully within his chest as if to remind him that even as bruised and battered as it was, it beat on. It had to, no matter if he only longed for it to stop and end in succession with hers. Why beat at all if it had lost its syncopation?

No...no, he would not think of it yet.

It wasn't difficult to steal into the de Chagny mansion, not for a mastermind ghost who haunted opera houses at every spare moment. Not a sound gave away his intrusion as he stalked the hallways, seeking out one particular presence, astounded by the unexpected stillness and quiet to the house and its corridors. Quiet...like a house in mourning.

"Don't bother to call for help." Erik prefaced his entrance into the study with a threat, already certain what he would find: the Vicomte de Chagny sitting solemn and somber with a liquor glass in hand before his lavish hearth. "You'll be dead before they get here to save you."

Raoul stared coldly at his masked intruder, stoic and condescending as ever, the very rival for the heart of the woman he loved, and that point made his pretense as real as any actor on the stage as he narrowed bitter eyes and demanded, "What do you want? Haven't you caused enough damage?"

"Murderer," Erik accused sharply, stalking to tower over the Vicomte's seat. Yes, the Vicomte triumphed in stature, but Erik was bearing enough pain and rage to kill him without a thought if he so chose.

"Murderer? You, monsieur, are the murderer between us. All the lives taken and now...now Christine..." It wasn't difficult for Raoul to call upon tears, not with one consideration of sitting at her bedside as she had stared out unseeing for days, not with the thought of the admissions in a letter, ones that still wounded his heart to know. She loved *him*, the madman and murderer, through it all, and Raoul could only wonder in every silent musing why then she had gone willingly with him that night, ...wonder but never dare question.

"It's a lie," Erik insisted without sway. "It *has to be*; she is alive and well; you're keeping her somewhere. You can't accept the truth: that she loves me."

"I wish to God it *was* a lie," Raoul fervently insisted. "I wish to God that she hadn't concluded her only option was to...take her life rather than deal with what you did to her. She was a *shell* after that night, monsieur, a *shell*, empty and hollowed out. She was *nothing*. And no matter what I did, I could not save her."

"No," Erik snapped back, a step away from lunging.

"You still don't believe it?" Raoul demanded, swiping away tears. "Check the obituaries in the paper, check the doctor's report, the death certificate. Will that be enough? Or will you have to dig up her beautiful, dead corpse to believe it as truth? Will you need to hold her, lifeless and gone as I did?" Tossing the liquor glass upon the coffee table, Raoul stood up at Erik's level and flatly stated, "I *found her*, monsieur, when she did it. I *found her* body, wrists slit, blood... Dear God, the blood... I have *that* image of her to take forever with me as mine, and to know that she did it because of *you*... I would argue that *I* have the right to kill *you* this time."

Behind Erik's murderous eyes flashed images, the very ones created by the Vicomte's words: Christine, laying deceivingly asleep, blood tangled in her curls, staining her gown... As vision built upon vision, he suddenly shoved the Vicomte back into his chair and fled the mansion amidst a pain so intense that it was unbearable to breathe through it.

Raoul stared after him, relieved that it hadn't come to blows or nooses. He had no doubt that he had taken care of their problem and had finally legitimately beaten the Opera Ghost.

*****

They used to call him a corpse; they saw his

face, and it was a mélange of insults, each and every one vividly recalled and endured again in nightmare's sphere. He had been forced to learn to detach himself from every unpleasant situation or else risk losing his soul in the chaos of cruelty. Corpse... A corpse who lived and breathed, who suffered emotion like every other man. For the first time in his life, he wished to indeed be a corpse but by its standard definition this time, entirely devoid of life, but he couldn't even seem to do that right. He survived when he yearned to be dead, as dead as she was.

Christine... Erik was being haunted by her ghost, her image moving as a revenant through his head, singing so sweetly in his ears. He couldn't seem to be rid of her. Not even losing himself in his music could steal the vision or the agony brought with every fantasy. She would materialize practically between molecules of air, but the instant he would reach out, desperate for one touch, one idle caress, she would be gone, an apparition vanished from sight. Never to touch, never to hold, ...never again.

Death would have been welcome, but despite his insistences against it, the daroga refused to abandon him, ignoring lapses of temper and fury, determined not to allow the reprieve of eternal rest. Nadir believed he was acting with mercy; Erik saw it as further torment. Longer to live, longer to be alone without her.

Days passed unnoticed; weeks moved slower yet. It was a common belief that time healed pain; perhaps that was the customary situation, but Erik was sure he was the exception to that rule. No, time made it worse and all the more real in its bitterness. Time was its own instigator of torture, snuffing out hope with every deafening tick of the clock. Hope, ...hope was in the grave with her.

"Erik," Nadir called as gently as he could and broke Erik free of a reverie that had only included staring into flames this time. This bout had been tolerable; Nadir recalled worse instances and stirring

Erik from his own mind as he stretched tensed fingertips to open air and whispered the name he would not allow either of them to speak in his right frame of coherency.

"Are you still here, daroga?" Erik snapped as his cold eyes averted to the intrusion. "I thought I insisted that you go home and end your nurse's watch for the night."

"You did that...*yesterday*, Erik; today you've yet to say a word to acknowledge that I am present." Studying him calmly and intently, Nadir inquired, "Do you know how many nights it has happened that we've acted out this scene practically in its line by line exactness?"

"Oh, you know I threw that infernal clock away days ago when the ticking finally frayed my nerves."

"No, you threw the clock against a wall and shattered it to pieces, and that wasn't *days* ago; it was *weeks* ago. It's been four months, Erik, four months of variations to the same conversation, four months of my endeavors at forced feeding to keep you from starving yourself to emaciation, four months since Christine-"

"Don't say her name!" It was immediate; Erik was out of the chair with Nadir hauled up by the shirtfront, flashing fire in a glare. "You know that I cannot tolerate the sound of it! I told you that if you were to be permitted in my home again, you must abide by my rules. You are *not* to speak that name to me, or I may feel inclined to break a rule of my own and strangle the sound from your lips. It's been ages since I killed something, you know; it would hardly be an inconvenience or undesired at this point. It would certainly break the monotony and alleviate my requirement to be hospitable and continue to exist in the semblance of a man. Without you about, I could truly *be* a monster, and if nothing else, killing something might shift a bit of the guilt that is running rampant in my brain."

"You aren't going to kill me," the daroga stated

without doubt. "Not for reminding you of her anyway. Now let go."

With a growl of displeasure, Erik complied to heave him aside and stalked in a fitful pacing before the hearth. "Go home, daroga. I'm not going to kill myself tonight if that is your concern. I haven't the strength for it."

"My concern exceeds suicide attempts or your lack thereof," Nadir solemnly bid. "Four months, and you've barely touched your music. *Music*, Erik! That was always your escape and your gift. It has always saved you, more than I ever have. You are giving it up so flippantly it seems, and I don't understand how it isn't torturing you. Through every trial in your life, there's been the music; now you are denouncing it."

"*It* had denounced *me* and forsaken me at every turn!" Erik exclaimed back. "*Her* voice in every melody, singing no matter the tune. Music... Every bit of me is hers, the music as well. Without her, ...there is no music."

"Erik-"

"No!" he roared back, abruptly approaching with fisted hands pronouncing their deadly potential in the air between. "I am quite through with your company, daroga. You betrayed me once, and now you betray me again with your misguided congeniality. My wish is to die, and you've denied me at every turn."

"Dying isn't the answer; you know that better than anyone."

"I'm *already* dead! Why will you not see that? I am dead and in the grave with her, and there is nothing left of Erik on this plane of existing. My heart has already been laid to rest." Each syllable lost anger and mutated into the true extent of piercing anguish until he was drained and softly bidding, "I am nothing now; she took my life with her. The sooner you can accept that, the greater mercy you'll be doing for me. ...Please just leave me be."

Nadir huffed a deep breath and somberly shook

his head as he consented, "All right, I'll go for now. But I will be back to check on you tomorrow. We've been in this place before, Erik, and just like then, I am not going to give up on you, even if you've already given up on yourself. I know that you can be saved, and I believe the answer is in the music; it's *always* been in the music for you. Just...try to play something, *anything*. It will do you good."

That was all he said. With one final stare into the endless depths of tortured eyes, Nadir hesitantly took his leave, scurrying soundlessly out of the underground house, carrying as much guilt as Erik and acting his own form of penance in a constant pattern that would repeat on the morrow. It seemed the least he could do.

Play something... Erik considered such an act a pointless waste of energy, but heaving a soul-laden sigh, he made a frazzled attempt, sitting before the untouched piano keys and striking random chords, nothing that could truly constitute a melody for fear of summoning spirits with legato lines. Mind and heart were disconnected and wandered aimlessly in and out of thoughts and feelings. But the longer he played, the more the music began to reflect his inner turmoil. Tears spilled unnoticed down his masked face with every single pitch until he could handle no more and broke off the created composition to the cadence of a choked sob. No more, no more music, no more Christine... No more living...

Eventually exhausted with an overbearing mind, he abandoned the house altogether, roaming the catacombs like the ghost he had once been, considering such a title to now be an aspiration rather than a role of pretend. It was a new fantasy, the only one he was certain he could have: to be a ghost and truly haunt the opera house with Christine for all of eternity. Maybe that could be their future...

His wayward musings brought him up that familiar pathway, one he had not traveled in months. Up... There was a world up here, a world he had never belonged to, only ever watching its pleasures from the shadows. Now he stalked its recesses again, taking to the rafters above their heads as it he could float in suspension.

Sounds welcomed him in a way people never could, that long unwanted music. Rehearsals were going on below him for a new production, and he lingered a moment and gazed upon the stage until the longing built to an ache in his heart.

On that stage, he had first seen Christine, so long ago that it now felt like just another stitch in the seam of his existence. Christine, singing in the chorus. Even with a dozen other girls, she'd shown to him like a beacon. He had learned what love truly was with his first glimpse of her beauty and desire to match. Her presence had brought to awareness emotions he had had no name for before her and no need to feel them. She had made their appearance essential and necessary. All of his memories coagulated into one particular image of her, that fated Gala night singing center-stage for him alone. He had known with her first pitch that she was his...

With a rush, he abruptly fled the theatre's view as every voice ringing forth sounded shrill and ugly compared to the one he carried in his inner ear. Down hallways, keeping above bustling heads and never suspected, until he found the one place he yearned to be like a tunnel back into time. Her dressing room... He loomed behind her mirror as he had all of those days before, gazing into a world he had only wanted to be a part of if it meant he could be with her. And he pondered a disparaging hypothesis: what if the last year was only some convoluted nightmare, and she was about to enter this room, fleeing rehearsal to be with his voice as an angel hidden from view? What if should he consider hard enough, time could circle back around and set him in the past? What if...

He was so consumed in the idea that he almost believed his wish had come into existence as the dressing room door burst open with a whining creak. *Christine...*

The disappointment struck him cold and harsh to find only the little Giry girl and the little Jammes, two of the ballet rats likely escaping Madame Giry's raging wrath and endless, repetitive rehearsals. Annoyed as he was, his interest rose to consider that this dressing room was currently unused, abandoned since it had been Christine's, and yet the girls were closing themselves within as if it were theirs.

"How long do you think we've got until your mother realizes we're gone?" Jammes asked Meg Giry as both girls warily eyed the closed door as if expecting the ballet mistress to burst in at any given moment.

"Not nearly long enough," Meg quickly answered, shaking her golden head. "She's been on a rampage since we began rehearsal today, and I daresay that it will be worse once she notices that we've slipped away when we're supposed to have been rehearsing on our own."

"All right, then tell me right away. You've been teasing about your big secret all afternoon."

Erik deafened his ears to their chirpy, little voices, yearning only for them to go away and leave him to his memories, and he was starting to consider calling upon one of his Opera Ghost antics to frighten them off when he was suddenly drawn to attention by the little Giry's very next utterance.

"It's about Christine."

That name, its letters spoken aloud and echoing through the empty room that had once been hers, and Erik was dragged heart-first into the present and their conversation. *Christine...*

"You're not supposed to say anything more about her," Jammes hastily insisted. "You're going to get into such trouble with your mother if you dare tell me another thing."

"Oh, what's the harm?" Meg frivolously decided. "The Opera Ghost is dead...or at least gone.

No one's heard a thing from him in months, and it's only you and I here. Mama doesn't need to know that I've told you, and I *must* tell you because I cannot keep it silent and within myself any longer! I shall burst if I don't share my news!" Giggling at her own melodrama, Meg withdrew a folded piece of paper from within the bodice of her rehearsal attire, and that alone convinced Jammes that it was quite a secret to have gone to such drastic measures to keep it hidden. "This is an invitation, requesting the presence of Mama and I for the wedding of the Vicomte de Chagny to Mademoiselle Christine Daaé."

Erik felt the world spin beyond control with brutal realization and its driving punch to the gut. Her wedding to the Vicomte... An invitation to a wedding, ...the wedding of a *dead* girl.

Laughing excitedly, Jammes snatched the paper and scanned its contents. "The wedding of the year to be sure!" she exclaimed, tracing her little fingers over the embossed printing. "I only wish I could be invited as well!"

"How?" Meg retorted, stealing the invitation away again. "You know that everyone believes Christine is dead, and that's supposed to include you. You only know the truth because I can't keep a secret."

"Oh, and what's the difference if I know? It isn't as if I would tell anyone! And who would believe me if I did? All the papers announced her suicide as if it was a national catastrophe! The death of the soprano diva! I guess with enough money, one can buy themselves all the publicity they want, and the Vicomte obviously spared no expense! Aside from you and your mother, everyone else in the city thinks she is truly dead!"

"Oh dear God," Erik muttered beneath his breath, his hand fisting over his rapidly racing heartbeat. *Alive... Alive* all this time! Alive and moving onward with her life while his had ceased and halted in its tracks!

"And how, may I ask," Jammes went on, "do

they expect to have a wedding if no one knows she's still alive?"

"Oh, the Vicomte is diligent. No one from Paris or the opera, but Mama and I. He sent a note attached to remind us to be extra careful." Meg shook her head with conviction. "And I think it's ridiculous! It's far too much when the Opera Ghost doesn't even care! He's gone, after all!"

Gone... And Erik would have remained the invisible specter, learning this transient news from the shadows if not for one detail that he suddenly realized he needed.

The girls were distracted, continuing on about what Meg would wear to the wedding and how they would travel as he unhinged the mirror in a trick he had not had use for in months. He had devised the mirror exactly for the purpose of treading between worlds, and now was no exception. Neither of his victims noticed, not until the doorway was wide and gaping and he was striding through its portal.

A gasp, and it was the little Jammes who spotted him first, her eyes growing to saucers with her rising panic.

"Jammes, what...?" Meg turned and matched her stare as she became the sole focus of the menacing Opera Ghost. White mask gleaming, Meg had a thought and memory of what lay beneath from that last night as Christine had exposed a distorted obscenity to a full opera house. A hideous monstrosity! A demon brought to life that had haunted her every nightmare since!

"Mademoiselle," Erik tightly greeted with as much gentility as he could muster for two petrified girls a wrong step away from screaming. "I have no intention of hurting you, Meg," he attempted, forcing anger at bay and away from his fierce stare. No, he couldn't take out his rage on the one person who had suddenly renewed his hope.

"I...I...I'm sorry," Meg stammered, unwanted tears in her large, green eyes. "I didn't... I mean it wasn't..."

Without another word of assurance, Erik's hand darted and grabbed the invitation from her, his wrist flipping about and turning abnormally to make it deceptively seem to disappear to their terrified stares when he truly had it contained safely within the boundary of his sleeve. Finally having what he wanted, he gave the girls one final look with the threat only laid in the air and vanished back behind the mirror, shutting them out of his world.

Erik hesitated only a moment to watch the frantic stumbling and gaping he had left behind as they cried out to one another in high pitches over what they'd seen before suddenly remembering to flee. A slammed door announced their departure, and only then did he stalk back to the catacombs with a new sense of purpose to every stride.

*****

Nadir knew something was off-kilter the next afternoon as he arrived at the underground house before he ever passed the threshold. It was permeating the catacomb air, a sense of unease and restlessness that put him on edge as he quietly entered the door and sought out Erik. He was not surprised that he did not find him in any of his usual places, not as bustling noises filtered about.

"Erik?" he called with an unqualified urgency of dread.

"Daroga, I was hoping that I would see you before I departed," Erik greeted with a feigned civility that made Nadir all the more anxious.

"Depart?" the daroga asked as he followed the voice to the music room and spied his friend on his feet, packing a box with random scores. "Are you...traveling somewhere? ...What is all of this?"

A trunk was in the center of the room, open and proclaiming its packed stature while boxes were scattered here and there, over-laden with music. One in particular caught his eye as on top sat a newly written piece, the ink still gleaming with its freshness and today's date scribbled on the top corner.

"Composing again?" Nadir inquired as he lifted the bound pages and scanned the notes, wishing that he bore a musician's mind to gain an idea of the piece from a glimpse alone. But alas, the notes and staves were a language all their own and completely foreign to his regard. "I did tell you that music would help."

"Oh, it wasn't the music; no, not at all." With only the occasional shrewd glance out of the corner of his eye, Erik continued, unwavering in his task and tossing another score onto the pile. "You know, it's almost a wonder what good the *truth* can do for a person. I daresay that it gave me an entirely new perspective on life."

"Truth?" Nadir demanded back, shifting on his feet and attempting to appear nonchalant as he leafed through the manuscript and let black markings blur to a mess for unfocused eyes. "And...what truth do you mean, pray tell?"

Erik halted his actions mid-motion and faced his once-friend coldly as he stated, "You watched me mourn her; you saw it tear me apart to consider that she was gone and that it was my own fault. You saw the agony overwhelm every bit of me, and you never dared to utter a word against it. You singlehandedly devastated me, and for what? What did the Vicomte offer you? Money? Some sort of noble title? What did it take to buy your deception?"

Denying his words was futile, but Nadir formulated a protest anyway. "It wasn't anything so frivolous. He was just...concerned about Christine's well-being."

"Her well-being?"

"She suffered what happened as a trauma; she was so distraught that he was surprised she was ever able to come out of it. You cannot condemn him for putting her welfare first. He knew you'd pursue her, and with your obstinacy on the issue, he was right."

"Damn you!" Erik roared, keeping a tight leash on a natural instinct to attack and strike back. He couldn't have said why. Perhaps it was an engrained loyalty to their odd relationship, as near to a friendship as he'd ever known; perhaps it was because in some vein, he feared that Nadir and his good intentions made some sort of point, however aggravating it was. "Of course he was right! Of course I would pursue her! To the ends of the earth if I must! But you saw that letter; you heard its words. *She loves me!*"

"And she also abhorred what you did to her," Nadir argued back. "You must see that this was done to protect Christine."

"No, it was done to keep me from her by an arrogant Vicomte who knew he never had her heart."

As he had posed once before on Erik's behalf, Nadir now replied for the Vicomte instead, "But he *does* love her. They are happy, Erik, at peace finally. Do you truly mean to destroy that by going after her and past follies? Why not just let her go?"

"Let her go?" Erik declared as if such an idea was ridiculous. "That hardly seems fair! And allow the Vicomte to build their life together on a blatant lie and mistrust?"

"And you're a hypocrite to say so. Did you not do the very same? You would have done anything to manipulate her into loving you."

"Yes, and I was wrong!" Erik shouted back at him as he yanked his music out of the daroga's hands and put it back into its designated box. "I came to learn it a dozen times over. Every manner in which I've wronged her has haunted me for months. ...It won't be the same this time."

"This time?" Nadir leaned across the full box with an urgent desperation. "Please, Erik, just leave them be. She's happy. Don't take that away from her again. You're going to end up dead trying."

"Death was a world without her in it," Erik insisted adamantly. "And don't presume to think that I will ever listen to you again. You chose your side, daroga. My loyalty to you ends with the plain fact that

I am not killing you right now, and if you bear any lingering guilt for the pain you've been the catalyst to instigate, then I ask one favor: that you do not send word to the Vicomte of my approach. If you value my life as much as you've always claimed to, then I believe that you can do that service for me."

It was a reluctant nod, but it was enough to act as a commitment as the daroga wearily bid, "I'm sorry, Erik."

His shaking hands were closing one of his boxes full of music, desperate for motion, and he refused to meet the daroga's eyes as he replied, "I doubt our paths will cross again, daroga, and I cannot say that I am regretful of that fact. I will merely call you fortunate to once again be saved from being my victim when for what you've done, you truly deserve a merciless death. Perhaps your Allah will find a fitting punishment where I am lacking."

And that was all he would say, shrugging his shoulders idly and returning to his packing. He had far more important things to worry about than his former foreign ally; he had a future to begin planning.

*****

It was nightfall when Erik left the city, traveling first in a shadowed train box and then an unlit carriage with yearning to guide every mile that put him closer to her. His heart was in turmoil, not sure what to feel, terrified to fully accept reality. Christine, alive, ...and with far too many hours wasted fantasizing a death scene that had not happened, he still clung to fragments of its visions and shifted them in and out of the forefront of his mind. Only when he saw her breathing and feeling would he be able to forget their colors.

An invitation to a wedding was his guide. It brought him through a vast countryside laden with sprouts of life that danced in the night breeze and reminded him that in his four months of confinement, the world had spun onward and spring had arrived. Green and an array of shades for batches of flowers waving from the roadside. He wondered how many similar seasons had come and passed their length without his notice in his secluded years. It had never been a concern, never a thought granted unless it was over the hardship of impending cold or the nuisance of a rainfall. Now such details held meaning because he knew that they were important points to Christine, that *she* would acknowledge the new warmth of spring and be *living* in this world with its trappings. Her views on such matters had somewhere along the way altered his until he had begun to appreciate the world that she loved so fiercely. She had some unconscious power to transform every detail of his existence if she so chose; he was determined that she would finally realize it.

Aboveground and interacting in situations he typically avoided added a cluster of new problems that seemed trite compared to the desperation to settle his heart. But he had taken care to send word ahead of his arrival to arrange some sort of temporary residence. Underground lairs were impossible to come by in the country, of course, but a salary as an Opera Ghost could buy him whatever he liked.

His contact was an acquaintance from days gone by when he had had a hand in constructing the opera house, truly his last legitimate communication with the world unless being a makeshift ghost to the opera's cast counted. Knowing someone to make arrangements kept his masked face out of the eye of the general population and assuaged the awkwardness that would have otherwise prevailed, and it acquired him a house not very far from the lands of the de Chagny estate. Convenient indeed, and when the previous owners who had occupied its quarters until just this evening had been offered an exorbitant sum to leave, more than what such a home could ever be worth, it reinforced Erik's knowledge that money could truly buy him anything he needed; *objects*, of course, because what he wanted, the only ending he could accept as the finale of these chained events, involved hearts and choices, and money held no sway in such unstable situations. He had to wonder if the Vicomte had taken note of that fact yet.

Erik barely observed a single facet of his new home, too distracted by a heavy head, but it was the hours before dawn, and that left him little choice but to impatiently wait. Sleep was unthinkable and hadn't been indulged since he'd begun this mission; unpacking a few of his boxes, mainly his music, had only served to make him yearn deeper. And so he willingly allowed himself to suffer and be overcome with visions of Christine, memory intermixed with avid fantasies of what was to come.

It was another sordid misfortune in a life over-filled with them that he had such a distinctive ability to recall details. It meant never being able to fully forget the hardships of humanity's cruelty and his own sins committed right back, but it also meant that his mind's eye could envision Christine practically to perfection at every urging. For months he had tried to stifle that desire, so sure it would only cause further agony, but now he called upon the image and dwelled on every sculpted detail, every smile she'd ever granted a man who was unaccustomed to receiving such tokens, every gentle look in her blue eyes, and incidentally, every tear he'd caused her, every pain he'd ignorantly incited. All he could conclude was that it would be different this time.

The sun was up and beaming before Erik left his new residence, surprised by the natural brightness that peered within every window and encircled him as he dared to enter its domain. Too many years in the dark made it a blinding glow that he squinted to endure as he instinctively ducked his masked face even when it was only nature that spied his presence. Was it any wonder why he preferred to shun such illumination when it was so much easier to hide in the dark?

It was the nearest to a challenge he'd had in years to avoid the telltale beams and sneak about, to

truly play a phantom who lurked about in the
daylight. He had to take extra care, lingering away
from the single road through the countryside as he
walked the meager distance to the de Chagny lands,
and it was from between tall, leafed trees that he first
glimpsed the large mansion house.

From what information he'd been able to
collect, this was the estate of the Vicomte's elderly
aunt, a Comtesse in her own right. Like most of the
aristocracy, this was only one of her homes, an escape
in the country while her city house awaited her return
during the bustle of society's busy season. Here,
guests would come and go, entertained and indulged
with plenty of extravagances, and certainly there was
space enough for a lavish wedding and the party to go
along with it. A wedding for the Vicomte de Chagny at
the Comtesse's country estate, and with its date only a
week away, Erik noticed the chaos already underway
as random workers rushed in and out of the open
front door, carrying packages and random items,
including pieces for a makeshift stage. Ah yes, this
wedding would be equally a production to an opera
show, especially if the bride was acting a role no
different than upon a stage.

The continuing melee forced Erik to avoid far
too many eyes as he crept into the large house with
anticipation lightening his heart. It was such a potent
intoxication that he had to hold it at bay to keep wits
and skill as stealthy as ever, refusing to chance one
misstep. Again, details blurred around him, and he
only half-comprehended the luxury surrounding at
every angle. No treasure meant as much as the one he
was searching for with every silent footfall. One
glimpse, only that would appease his twisting heart,
...but then again, how could *one* ever suffice?

Stalking the quieter corridors away from the
madness of preparations, Erik could feel presences
nearby, catching the softest, barely audible sounds of
shifting motion, and carefully, he approached, peering
into empty room after empty room. Before he even

finished scanning the hallway, a familiar voice called out of the last doorway.

"Andrew!"

The Vicomte de Chagny, and Erik felt an immediate rise of murderous rage with one recollection of their last meeting and the fictitious tale of a bloody suicide that had haunted Erik's waking and sleeping mind for months. He would have attacked without thought if he hadn't had to shrink into corners and allow the passage of a hurrying butler, who did not even pause and wonder at an oddly shaped shadow as he rushed to the Vicomte's command.

"Yes, Monsieur Vicomte?"

"Where is my fiancée? I'm expecting the arrival of some cousins at any moment, and I want her to be present to meet them."

Erik's ears perked at that, and even as he swallowed bitterly against the term 'fiancée', he kept to being the silent observer in the hallway if it meant he'd be set on a path to Christine.

"I haven't seen her this morning," the butler Andrew nervously explained. "Perhaps she took a walk out to the gardens; you know how she enjoys the flowers. I could go and check for you."

"No, no," Raoul quickly insisted, "I'll do it myself once I see that all the preparations are being tended to. Have they begun to set up that platform for the party?"

"Not yet, monsieur. They are just about to start."

"Well, I shall check on their progress first. I can't afford to have any mistakes. No, Christine deserves perfection, and that is what I shall give her."

Erik did not pause to listen to more of the Vicomte's seeming endearments, sure he would forget himself and snap out without consideration to what he truly wanted. Out in the garden... He had a peculiar thought over such a detail, but he did not yet indulge it as with the hinted curve of an uncommon smile upon his misshapen lips, he fled the house by the same path he'd taken to arrive, stealing back out without observance and searching now for flowers and nature instead. A garden... On an estate this large, it was no surprise to him that the garden was a fair distance from the main house, buried between tall, protective trees. But it was not the flower colors and scents that drew him to its confines; no, it was a voice...

His peculiar thought became a reality in that one sound, so desperately remembered and clutched for months. An angel on earth, the *true* angel between them, and it was that very sound that had convinced him in his first hearing of its gloriousness. Larger now, fuller, brimming over with the confidence it had once lacked, it lured Erik in with every brilliant note. Escaping to the garden, and he had guessed from the first moment that it wasn't for glimpses of flowers and velvet petals; it was to *sing*. A future Vicomtesse would not be permitted such a talent, but Christine wouldn't have been able to survive without it. She would have found a way to practice, to let the music pour forth once again even if it had to be done secretly, and if her darling fiancé knew her at all, he'd have realized that.

That voice! Erik shuddered down his spine as its beauty ensnared him. There were not many things in the world that he felt compelled to thank any sort of higher being for creating, but he would utter prayers to his eventual death for that voice. Most of mankind knew attraction by appearances, perhaps personalities, perhaps an encouraging smile; for Erik, love had come with one solitary pitch from those cords. One song, and he had known that she was meant to be his. How could any doubt be formulated against such an imperative feeling? He felt it just as strongly now as he had then, a recognition and familiarity, an insistence that that voice would be the impetus of his greatest blessings and equally his greatest downfalls. *Christine...* And how he had suffered to know its etherealness only in echoes for too long!

As mesmerized as she herself had once been once by an angel's voice, he unconsciously crept a soundless path after its timbre, half-afraid that it would vanish before he ever found it. Down a stone walkway with fresh, fragrant blooms on either side, extending their petals for any touch of his intruding presence, he was eager and hasty in every step. The vocalise she'd been singing higher and higher up the scale ended to silence, and he felt lost as if his constant had been snatched away and left him idly wandering. But no, God wouldn't be merciless enough to take her before Erik even glimpsed her silhouette, would He? And then...

A shiver raced his limbs. She was singing again, moving on to an aria, and her choice of song... He went numb and petrified in his place for a long, held breath. It was *his*, the very aria he'd written only for her in his ill-fated opera. Serenaded by his own music! Composed with heart and soul, with such love as he'd never felt before! It left him urgent for a look, and he rushed his last steps until the path before him ended at the foot of a white-wood gazebo, laden with flower vines up every rail and spindle.

And there she was... The world halted for him in its usual progression. A sob was captured and held between his lips, but the tears that came with its aftermath sparkled in his mismatched eyes until he had to blink them away with his frustration and let them fall if only to clear the blur and return her image. His Christine, his love...

Beneath the gabled roof of the gazebo, Christine spun and sang, moving in the exact motions she once had onstage and acting the scene far more realistically than ever before. She called her earlier portrayal innocent and naïve, the performance of a child without experience in such matters to make any emotion as believable as it should have been. This was the aria of a woman who had tasted love and longed for potent desire once again; she had not fully understood that at the time. But now...now she sang with full heart, closing her eyes to savor every lyric on her tongue as she had once been taught to do. Her voice rang and resounded off the ceiling, filling the small space with its vibrato and clear tone, and as she soared up and blossomed on a perfect high note, she felt a strange, undeniable sense of appreciation and pride, ...one she only ever recalled in memory. It shook her to her core, but it did not jar her from the music. No, what did that was the softest sigh, almost unheard as it teased her ear with its missed emotions.

Erik... She halted mid-aria, and slowly with an unqualified fear that she was encompassed in fantasy, she let her lids flutter open and stared out at the dark shape just beyond the gazebo's entrance that watched her back with every tear to proclaim his validity. Frozen in her place, she felt emotion, pure, raw, so long unfelt, swell and overwhelm her with an interlacing of fear she could not avoid. No, fear was as important as every other sensation, fear for the man who had changed her life so completely and irrevocably and had subsequently shattered its every facet in his murderous hands. Fear and anger on its heels, and such things left her to stare resentfully at that dark silhouette with its gleaming mask. Even when the presence of the man could have inspired variations and a sense of longing, the mask reminded her of coldness and damage, of an Opera Ghost and a persona that surpassed mortal man, one she hated as vehemently as she could have ever loved the man attached to its epithet.

It was almost impossible to move and create motion, and Erik stumbled in uncharacteristically abrupt steps into the gazebo's protection, holding her apprehensive blue eyes all the while. His mind taunted him with every detail of her life: breaths passing her parted lips in an erratic pattern, the quivering of her body, the gentle stirring of loose dark curls with wind that gusted through the open structure and claimed her as existing, as *real.* Words were incomprehensible and buried beneath too much emotion, and as he halted before her, running feverish eyes over every feature of her porcelain face, he dared to extend a hand that shook along every finger and joint, needing a touch with a necessity that frightened him.

Christine did not move, only watched the approach of that familiar hand, pondering that it had rarely ever touched her. Rarely a caress, rarely a contact. Usually, he would deny such impulses and recoil before skin ever met, as if always terrified to tarnish her, but this time, his intention was clear. And this time it was *she* who recoiled, shrinking back before he ever found her cheek with wide and horrified eyes that accused in their stare.

What features could be seen with the mask to conceal the brunt creased in a rush of pain, and instinct bid her to beg forgiveness, to catch that yet motionless and offered hand in hers and guide it to her skin, to kiss its every knuckle and its palm. But she did not dare. She only shook a solemn no against her internal pulling and kept beyond his grasp.

"Christine," Erik whispered sadly, unable to quit gazing and marveling over her reality even as she rejected him yet again. Perhaps that would always be the result to his every attempt, and yet his devotion and awe were undimmed in their constancy.

Tears filled her blue eyes, every feature crumbling with their power as her gaze shifted from his hand to his eyes and back again. And with fingers that tingled in their eagerness, she was about to succumb, to seize that hand, take it in her grasp, and make its weakness into strength when their moment was purloined and lost.

"Christine! Are you out here?"

The Vicomte! He had yet to appear and spy the scene happening in the gazebo, and without a word of explanation, Erik suddenly acted, letting an uncertain hand become determined as he grabbed hers, stealing it from her side and drawing her with him into the gardens without a single struggle. She was willing, and he savored that mediocre victory.

Reason shouted at her to demand to know where he was taking her, but like the gullible child she had once been, Christine permitted his intent tugs, staggering after him without the grace he unconsciously carried in his every footstep. No, she was practically tripping her way behind, hoping her inability to be as soundless as the notorious Opera Ghost wouldn't alert Raoul to their presence. Raoul, the fiancé she should have been running toward and shouting to save her. But Raoul became an unconsidered thought the further they went from the gardens, slipping seamlessly into the surrounding woods and never pursued.

Erik took no chances, bringing her to the far edge of the de Chagny lands where the ground was uneven and hills became irregular cliffs. At the base of one stone drop was a small alcove carved into the steep wall, and he drew her into its private shadows with only the residual evidence of sunglow outside to grant any sort of light.

All at once, he released her hand as if he had committed a vile transgression, curling his arms into his body as he once again studied her every nuance, seeking every alteration incited by four months of time's passage. Dear God, she was perfect! And he wanted her just as much. It hardly seemed ridiculous to consider that such desire could lead to the extreme measures he had once taken in his desperation. No, her exquisiteness was his justification.

"Why do you look at me that way?" she dared to ask in a soft breath, shifting uncomfortably beneath the power of his eyes.

"You were *dead*," he gasped back, unable to dull his intensity. "I thought I'd never see you again on this plane of life, ...never touch you." This time hesitation was an afterthought to an already reaching hand, and he shook violently to graze a bold caress along her cheek, watching her close her eyes not to see the sin as it was acted out.

"Stop," she commanded yet stayed rigid in her place.

"No, I can't," he insisted, cupping her face with fingertips that restlessly roamed soft features, yearning to know every one. "I can't possibly, not now that I've touched you...and learned that you're real. Christine, ...you were dead," he repeated the blasphemy, swallowing against more tears as they choked sound to a whisper.

Blue eyes fluttered open and watched him steadily with the undeniable weight of his hand against her skin and its every unuttered connotation suspended between them. "What do you mean? ...Dead? I don't understand."

That was no surprise, but the assurance was its own relief. His fingers were outlining her lips and being deliciously burned by her living heat as he told her, "Your ever-devoted fiancé convinced me as well as the majority of Paris that you had taken your own life. And you didn't know a single detail of it, did you? He brought you here likely under the pretext of peace and a recovery away from the eyes of society. He never told you that he arranged a fake death in your absence."

Even as her mind spun with his words, Christine flatly declared in automatic defense, "He did it for my protection, of course. Raoul only wants to keep me safe."

"And to secure his claim upon you," Erik added resolutely. "He knew that if I didn't believe such a lie, I would come after you."

"Come after me...?" Jolted back to reality, she suddenly jerked back out of his reach, creating a necessary distance and forcing herself to see the mask. Yes, the mask was there, and it was as unavoidable as it always had been. "Why are you here, Erik? Our goodbyes are over and past. I am marrying Raoul, this week in fact. If you are here to ruin that and play the phantom Opera Ghost all over again with murder and ultimatums as your game, then I tell you now that I want no part of it. I will have Raoul stop you any way I must. I don't want you here."

"And am I to believe that after you only just willingly denied your fiancé and came with me? After you allowed my accursed touch?" Cruelty was a strong point; it laced his beautiful voice and insisted hostility over the depth of his true pain. How often had he chosen to react with anger and malevolence over the breaking of a fragile heart? He fought to crumble the wall he himself was building, and softening the firm lines of his expression, he pushed honestly, "I mourned you, Christine. I mourned you so desperately that I died with you. I begged to be haunted by your ghost, *anything* to have you with me still, but ghosts disappear to the touch. I learned that bitter lesson over and over again. But...I was never allowed to touch you alive; why would death be any different? I should have endured eternity without a touch; I am undeserving. But if I beg you, if I offer any aspect of my worthless life for it, may I touch you again? May I convince myself that you are not the body in the grave that I have envisioned at every nightmare? One touch, Christine..."

His hand extended to her again, and though she never spoke a consent, her silence was acquiescence enough as she closed her eyes as she had before, terrified of their betrayal. Without a look, she simply waited until she felt the first tentative brushing of cold fingers. No, she should not recognize his touch with so little to recall in memory's chasm, and yet she still had no doubt that it was Erik's, that even without comparison, she would know it as his. His other hand found her skin as well, both holding her face between their curves and framing it delicately as if creating its shape. She never needed to look to know he was admiring her again and gazing at her with that wonder she'd been subject to since his appearance. And if he had truly believed her to be dead, then she understood why. *Dead...* He'd mourned her as if she'd been dead and buried. The realization made tears collect in the corners of her eyes and escape closed lids to deceive her with their presence as they trickled a path and struck his hands on their descent.

"But why do you cry?" he demanded in a whisper. "I am doing nothing to hurt you."

"But you are!" The admission poured forth and stung the air between them. "You *always* hurt me!"

"Do I? It is never my intent," he vowed in breaths, unable to force a cracking voice as his thumbs swiped tears from her cheeks. "It doesn't have to be so, Christine. I can be something more for you; I can show you that we don't need to spend forever hurting each other, that we can be happy together."

"You intended to come after me," she could not stop herself from accusing. "As always, you would have taken me away because it was what *you* wanted."

"And *you* wouldn't have wished such a thing?" Erik was half-afraid of her answer, half-afraid that the way she was leaning her face into his touch was unconscious and instinctual when tears and closed eyes could tell him no different. "You didn't wish that I would come for you? Did you truly want me to let you go, Christine? In all of these months, have you never longed for my presence?" No reply came as she bit her lip as if to clutch answers within and away from him, and running his fingers gently along her brow, he decided it for her, "You have. ...I came upon you singing *my* music in the way I always wanted you to; an open window to your soul, I once told you. That was what I expected, but you always kept up walls and divisions between your heart and...and the music. But not today. Today you were all I ever wanted you to be."

"Yes, the music," she suddenly insisted, forcing herself to open eyes and not be swayed by those mismatched ones from a long-forgotten dream. "It was the music. I've longed for the music."

"One more detail the Vicomte won't allow in

your life," he concluded, shaking his head with his disgust. "The wife of a Vicomte cannot sing opera on the stage. Is that what he's told you? That you must give up everything you love for him and the sacrifices he's made for you?"

It was a conversation she was unwilling to divulge, and furrowing her brow with her frown, she suddenly replied, "One touch; you said one touch. Now let go of me."

Every instinct within him begged not to listen, but with overt reluctance, he curled aching hands closed and away, missing the soft smoothness of her flesh in the first severing of contact. Unable to quell his sharpness, he pushed, "And will you now insist that you love the Vicomte and that I should go and leave you to marry him?"

"If I did, it wouldn't matter," she retorted. "You'll hear what you want to hear and never accept anything else."

Eyes bearing into hers, he stated with conviction, "You *don't* love him."

"But I don't love *you* either," she replied and wasn't surprised when his expression never changed. "You don't believe me."

"No, I don't." His hand dove into his pocket and withdrew a torn scrap of paper, tattered almost beyond recognition from so many empty hours spent with its words clutched beneath desperate fingers that needed to hold to something. "I have proof to convince me otherwise."

Christine's eyes widened as realization came to the surface, breaking into rationale and reminding her of the day she had written every word and the haze she'd been half-overcome with as she had acted. "Where did you get that?"

"It doesn't matter. Your words, love, in your hand. Will you call *yourself* a liar then?" With the tip of one finger, he underlined the evidence he was after. 'I loved you' in elegant scrawl.

"And were you told the state I was in when I

wrote that?" she demanded back, grasping her private thoughts free of his exposing hold. "I wasn't myself after what you did to me."

But Erik shook his head, unconvinced. "Your trauma was not the result of the events of that night and dearest Raoul's near demise; it was the result of a broken heart, one I myself foolishly caused when I sent you away."

"You didn't want me!" she practically shouted. "And it's far too late to change your mind now! You're right, Erik; you broke my heart. But now it's healed and well, and it is the Vicomte's. So leave me be. I am no longer yours."

Without a thought, his hands darted out and caught her shoulders, and he hugged her to him, refusing the whimper of protest she gave. "You are *always* mine," he fervently breathed, keeping her close with desperate arms. To feel her! To hold her! To know the soft gasp she gave meant breath and life! He had believed he'd never have this again... "Oh, Christine," he sighed as he pressed his masked face to the silk at the crown of her head.

For an instant, she allowed it; she even shuddered her consummation and almost, *very nearly* held him back. But in her next coherent realization, she struggled in a grasp that had little choice but to yield and abruptly broke free, shrinking away to create distance.

"No, don't," she insisted, wrapping her arms futilely about her own waist in an empty embrace. "I can't... Please, Erik, just go. *Please*...leave me alone."

She wished that her expression did not speak as many unuttered declamations as it did, revealing a longing she didn't want to feel. How much complication it brought! And she knew that he would glimpse it, and it would encourage what should have remained dead. But with a final adamant shake of her head, she turned and ran, abandoning him in that alcove of rock and rushing for the house as if the devil pursued her every movement.

But her devil stayed away and only watched her go with hurt eyes, still able to feel her in his arms as once again only a ghost remained behind.

*****

Christine stared up at the canopy of her bed with an empty gaze that did not reveal the inner chaos of her mind. White chiffon, and yet to unfocused eyes, it blended into a sheet of pure color and shifted like a kaleidoscope's ever-changing pattern until it reminded her of a mask, white and stark, hiding a face in its recesses, protecting its secrets and with it, a heart so passionate and yet always terrified to truly *feel*.

Months of contemplating it were nothing to prepare her for being in its presence again, for being the sole victim of those mismatched eyes and their power and a love so brilliant that it overwhelmed her. To be loved in such a way, it was as confining and restricting as it was wondrous. Love, but a love that was free to be felt on *his* side, free to grow and swell to extraordinary heights while her own return had always been chained in fear and the frivolity of youth. And then one time she had let it bloom and match his, escaping its barriers to its fullness of heart and soul. One moment of purely loving before the chains had been reattached, this time *by him*. He had made the choice for her when it was supposed to have been hers to make and had pushed her away, restricting a love that he was afraid to bear and believe was genuine.

Oh, Erik... How many long, horrible hours had she spent suffering his rejection? How broken had it left her to reveal the truths of her heart and feel him pull away, to find bravery for once in a weak life only to have it squandered and extinguished from existence by the very man who craved it most?

It had been a trauma; they had called it a trauma. Doctors parading in and out of the Vicomte's home, searching for physical ailments when she had purposely decided not to speak, when she had chosen to live in regret and memory instead. They hadn't realized that she'd heard their every ignorant word. A trauma, stealing basic abilities of speech and coherency with its weight. They never could have guessed that she had acted the entire episode to be left alone with her thoughts, to sort out their facets and seek some sort of conclusion. No one would have believed that, not when she was supposed to have been distressed for kissing a disfigured madman and practically signing her life over to him. She was supposed to carry the scar of it still in her soul, and that was why Raoul continued to treat her with intricate care, convinced she'd shatter if he pushed too hard. He had made a trip to his aunt's country estate seem like a token of affection, a gesture of his love; she now knew better, and the crumpled scrap of paper in her hand was her proof.

Christine was jostled back to a place where white chiffon was only white chiffon by the gentle knock at her bedroom door, and shoving the scrap of a letter into a pocket in her gown, she rushed on nervous knees to answer, knowing who it would be in spite of the unnecessary skip of her beating heart.

"Christine," Raoul called as soon as he glimpsed her, running frantic eyes over her features and looking for causes of alarm. "Andrew told me that you were ill. I would have been up to check on you sooner, but my cousins arrived and I had no choice but to be hospitable. You missed supper, darling. Are you all right?"

Leaning upon the open door for stability, she distantly replied, "Of course. I just...had a headache and wanted to lay down for awhile."

"Are you well enough to come down for dessert?" Raoul urged with that charming smile she read so well. He was looking to appease her and receive a smile in return, but she would not concede and kept a furrowed brow. "If not, I can make your excuses. Whatever you wish. I can't have you taking ill with the wedding so close, not when I'm so certain that it will be just the thing to finally settle every worry you still have."

She had to wonder if he genuinely believed that her frequent bouts of melancholy and supposed headaches were due to a continued fear of losing him or if that was just what he told himself to make it acceptable. Either way, a wedding would make things permanent and an inarguable ending for them. A wedding would make her *his*.

Shaking her head somberly, she replied, "I think it would be best if I continue to lay down. As you said, the wedding is too close for me to take the chance of becoming ill." Her mind persisted to say that he should have been disappointed or at least a bit irritated with her neglected sense of etiquette and congeniality to their guests, but it was no surprise that he chose to please her first and foremost.

"Of course," Raoul gushed, setting his palms gently atop her shoulders. "And ring Andrew for anything you wish. He can bring you supper and dessert, anything your heart desires."

Anything her heart desired... Those words bit at her with their uselessness, and the leftover wound was so undeniable that it built her courage and urged her to broach a cold subject. Adopting her actress' façade, she made an attempt for the truth. "I had a telegram from Meg today, and...she said something unsettling."

"Shall I guess?" Raoul teased, smile unfaltering. "Does she wish to stay with us when she arrives for the wedding? I'm sure that hotels are inconsiderable when my aunt's mansion house is a far cry above. Has she asked for her own room and a separate one for her mother, or did she at least offer to share?"

"No, no, not that," Christine emotionlessly replied, refusing to allow Raoul to gauge her reaction as she accused him in a quickly concocted lie. "Meg said she wasn't able to invite any of the other ballerinas as I asked because they don't know that I am not 'dead'. Dead, Raoul? What did she mean?"

The Vicomte's countenance cracked, and his flustered agitation left him shifting from side to side on his feet. "You...well, you weren't supposed to know, Christine. I thought I made it quite clear to Meg that it would upset you to be told. It...it isn't as horrendous as it seems."

Careful not to portray anger or blame, she flatly demanded, "Did you do this, Raoul? ...Does all of Paris believe I am dead?"

He huffed his discontent and was obviously seeking a suitable explanation for her sake, but all he could mutter was, "I did it for you; it was not some sort of deceitful crime as I'm sure it must seem. Your name was being spoken in conjunction with that monster's, as if the horror at the opera house was somehow your fault as well. I thought only to take you out of their vindictive gossip and give you some sort of new life detached from that one. It can hardly matter if Christine Daaé is considered dead; you are about to become the Vicomtesse de Chagny. Such a title suits you and puts you on a pedestal so high above those hellions and their conniving tongues."

"But you convinced everyone that I took my own life," she insisted with a fraction of her true perturbation filtering through. "How could you do that? And that is why you've argued every time I've proposed we return to the city, isn't it? I would be a walking ghost!"

"Don't be angry with me. It was a harmless lie meant to give us both some sort of peace. That other life would have always chased behind us if I had done nothing." Raoul knew she was unconvinced, and purposely softening his expression back to a grin, he ran appeasing caresses down her arms to capture her hands and clutch them between their bodies. "You suffered so much because of that terrible ordeal, Christine; you didn't deserve to carry its stigma and fallout for the rest of your life, not when it was no fault of your own. I wanted to free you from that bastard's mark."

Though she permitted his touch, she did not grant forgiveness so easily as she dared to pose, "And...then *he* believes I am dead as well." There it was, the harshest point of accusation, and she critically studied his response, looking for a reason for anger.

"Maybe... Would it be such a horrible thing if he did? If nothing else, it would guarantee that he'd leave us to live our life."

It was as telling as if he'd admitted it, but all she said amidst her disappointment was, "And then he'd never come after me again."

"Exactly!" Raoul exclaimed, nodding fervently. "He won't come after you! So you see, my reasoning was valid and for your protection. You're going to be safe, Christine, no more fears. I wanted to give that to you."

Never a smile, never a concession, she merely muttered, "I have a headache, Raoul. I would appreciate it if you told your guests as much and leave me to lay down."

"Of course!" he gushed. His overdone smile was still begging for acceptance, but he had no choice but to give up as she pulled her hands free and reached for the door. "Christine," he made one final plea, "I love you."

But she was silent and solemn, closing him out of her room and with him, his lies. *Protect her?* No, protect himself. And she had the proof in her pocket and withdrew it once again with shaking fingers. Raoul had clearly stolen her private musings and used them to his advantage, which also meant that he knew each and every one.

And what about the rest of this letter, torn with an uneven edge from the bottom of the page? It had obviously been discarded, but what had it said? She had a fleeting memory, and in imprecise terms remembered a pleading, a desperate begging to Erik to come for her and take her away, a recanting of every harsh word and a vow that she loved him in spite of it, that if he would only allow her to make her choice, she would choose him again and again. ...All of those internal musings seen by her fiancé, and *that* was why he had enacted a plan to feign her death. It would have been the only way to keep her and the most potent manner in which to tear Erik apart for *her* feelings.

Her heart urged her to hate Raoul, to pity what Erik had endured and love him all the more, but her eyes passed over her own scribbled words once again, the harsh parts of a broken heart's lament. Today had proven no different than four months before with Erik laying claim as if she were his to do with as he pleased and love only in the way *he* wanted. He wanted her, but only inasmuch as he could control her, and not even her supposed death had changed that. Love to him meant *his* love, and he had a terror of believing in hers that she wasn't sure she could stop. How could she possibly love a man who was determined to instruct her *how* to do it and why? Who could not let her love as she did because he was so certain that it was fabricated? Doubt would always be his folly, and in his need to keep control, he would devastate her a second time. ...And worst of all was the blatant truth that she would foolishly let him.

*****

"...And if you can believe it, she proceeded to throw herself at him like some sort of cheap hussy as if there weren't a ball going on with a hundred people all around them. Shameless!"

Christine fought to keep her attention on a conversation to which she was supposedly an integral participant. Raoul's aunt was going on about the behavior of another socialite in hurried excitement to the collected group of a dozen ladies having tea in the parlor of her country mansion. This was not the first tedious afternoon gathering Christine had been forced to join since her arrival, and as was typically the case, gossip of those not in attendance far outweighed any other more important topics of discussion. In the past few months, Christine had learned more scandalous details of strangers' lives than she ever had backstage in an opera house full of backstabbing performers and dancers with loose morals.

"Oh, Christine," Raoul's aunt Constance suddenly called over the crowd's muttered agreement with her previous story. "Here I am manipulating the conversation when this party is supposed to be about *you*."

Such a reminder only made Christine shrink back in her seat, wishing to disappear from all the eyes shifting to her. This was nothing like being the focus onstage, singing and performing to an audience of hundreds. This was a nightmare compared to that as she kept her posture poised and perfect, terrified to even shift one finger the wrong way. This audience was waiting for her to fail, to make one error in speech or attitude so that she could be the next victim of their gossiping tongues.

"Five days until you wed the dashing Vicomte de Chagny," one of the older ladies gushed with her seemingly polite smile. "You must be the envy of every unmarried girl in the country!"

"Wherever did the two of you meet?" another asked excitedly, and Christine felt her nerves teeter on their edge, knowing that she would have to be mindful of every word. Not even Raoul's dear aunt knew the truth.

"In Paris," Christine softly offered, hoping no one would take notice how tightly her fingers were curved and flexed into her palms. "But we had played together as children years ago. It was simply fortune that returned us to each other."

Aunt Constance shook her head with an intruding laugh. "My ignorant brother hired nanny after nanny to raise his boys, and oftentimes I would visit and find them off amongst paupers and lay people on the city streets! Thankfully, Raoul did not let his heart go to one of those dirty, peasant girls and saved it for you, darling Christine!"

Paupers and lay people, and Christine never let on that she had actually fit into those categories at the time. No, as far as Aunt Constance and proper society knew, she came from a family as well off as theirs, if not titled to prove it. Dear God, how ashamed her father would have been if he'd have ever known that his daughter was practically denying her own family name!

The lady beside Christine caught her arm with her wrinkled hand and bid, "I overheard you mention to one of the ladies at our last gathering that you spent some time while you were in Paris training in the arts. Perhaps you could share a song at our next soiree. The ladies often entertain with their talents, you know. My youngest daughter sang and played the piano so lovely at our last one; it would be refreshing to add another voice to our usual performances."

Ah yes, because singing to the upper class was a hobby, never a profession. Young girls, daughters of the elite who claimed their voices as beautiful as they themselves were, decided that warbling a few notes on pitch made them prima donnas in their own right. Well, prima donnas without a stage, unless one counted the parlor and impromptu renditions of popular songs. It was considered a point of good breeding to be educated and that included lessons in music, but only as a viable incentive in catching a husband. Christine had already been told quite clearly by Raoul's continued conditioning that the instant she was revealed as an opera singer, even if she chose never to set foot on the stage again, she would be cast out of society's bubble and vindictively slandered for the rest of her years. *Such a promising future indeed!*

"No, I couldn't," Christine gently insisted to the lady's open offer, "I don't sing anymore. I shall leave the performing to your daughter and her friends. I prefer simply to watch." The greatest point of annoyance was the plain fact that they anticipated she would be mediocre at best, and if she dared sing full voice with all her training and talent behind her, she would be condemning herself right in front of them. Perhaps that was what they wanted; with the vast majority of those she'd met exuding pettiness and jealousy, it seemed a plausible conclusion.

"Come now, Christine," Aunt Constance pushed. "You know, a lady needs something to keep herself inspired until the children start to arrive. You could learn new parlor songs for our soirees."

"Yes," the lady beside her agreed, "take advantage of such pleasantries now before the children come, unless, of course, you intend to keep a nanny. I tried to refrain from nannies with my first child, but the instant I realized I had no time of my own and could not even respond to telegrams or choose dress samples for an upcoming ball without my son squawking his unhappiness every two minutes, I hired one right away and intelligently, kept her on for the duration of my birthing years. She practically became part of the family! Do you think you'll hire a nanny, Christine, once you and Raoul are expecting?"

Eyes widening, Christine was desperately seeking some sort of unoffending answer when Aunt Constance interrupted before she could find one, "Oh, Agatha, don't push her so quickly. We haven't even had a wedding, and you're already talking about children!"

"Well, ...one never knows," Agatha replied with a secretive smile. "These days it seems quite a few babies are arriving nearly the instant the wedding is over." Her eyes scanned Christine's small figure intently, and Christine nervously scooted back into the cushions of her chair, unconsciously slouching away from observance.

"Oh, Agatha, don't be absurd!" another lady insisted with her own giggle. "Raoul is a gentleman! ...But even if there was a baby on the way, once they were married, such a detail as the conception date could be overlooked if it is the child of a Vicomte."

"Yes," another agreed. "As long as you were married, it wouldn't be any sort of disgrace, not for a Vicomte."

It was too much, too many prying eyes scrutinizing her and trying to catch a glimpse of what wasn't there, too many insinuations to nip at her skin with their sharpness. Shaking with her nerves, Christine suddenly leapt to her feet and hastily declared, "Will you please excuse me?" And without further explanation, she darted from the room to a few snickers of decided guilt chasing behind her.

She did not stop running until she arrived in her bedroom, slamming the door and leaning back against its sturdy construction as if it would ground her. This was like a nightmare she could not find her way out of, and worse yet, this was the rest of her life!

"What would be the more condemning offense in this society, I wonder?" a voice called from her open terrace, and her eyes shot to its curtains in time to see the dark silhouette appear against their material. "Wedding a Vicomte yet already carrying his child or being an opera singer? It truly is a perplexing riddle, isn't it?"

The sheer power of his aura made her waver on her feet and depend on that unaltered door in the moment he shoved the curtain aside and strode into her bedroom. It astounded her that any human being could have such an effect. "Spying on me yet again?" she posed, desperate to seem firm. "Seeking another window into my life? I asked you to leave me be."

"And you knew I wouldn't," Erik insisted with conviction as he strolled the corners of the room and appeared to inspect its details even if in actuality, his senses were too consumed being in tune with her to care about much else. "I can't... But it certainly is interesting to eavesdrop and watch you interact in that superficial world. They were practically baiting you to fall."

"Yes, I realize that," Christine snapped back. "I've been the unwilling recipient of quite a few guile and artificial grins in the past months. Most of them already hate me for no other reason save the fact that I'm marrying Raoul."

He made a face of his distaste, yet dared to push, "And what would they say to know you are an opera singer? Stage performers are frowned upon and abhorred as whores and conniving buffoons in that crowd, those to be pitied and shunned. I quite understand such reproach."

"They need never know about it," she answered, eyeing him as he randomly toyed with the jewelry box upon her vanity and surveyed its contents with another scowl of his annoyance. Gifts, all from the Vicomte, and Raoul never seemed to realize that she had yet to wear a single one.

"So you will deny what you truly are for dearest Raoul and his fake pretense to society," Erik stated matter-of-factly. "You will denounce everything I taught you and worked so adamantly to see you achieve, and you will kill that integral part of yourself to be accepted into their volatile circle. ...Given the option, I'd rather that they hated you because you were with child and cast you out already."

"I am *not* with child," Christine corrected, and as his eyes perused her in the same rude manner that a room full of ladies had, she did not shy away, willing him to see her honesty.

Erik ached to believe her so fervently that it constricted his heartbeat beneath a web of tension. Merely to overhear those women suggest such a thing and consider its ramifications had left him a step away from bursting into their party and demanding an answer, audience unperceived in his desperation to know. *His* Christine, and if she were carrying that damn Vicomte's child, he was sure the news would kill him. But...stare all he liked, the truth remained a mystery when physical proof wasn't present, so in determined strides, he faced her and leaned close enough that she could not flee between his shape and an unyielding door.

"Has he...?" The words for such an act would not come, choked back on his tongue with a mixture of shame and reluctance.

Blushing ever so slightly with her chagrin, she anxiously bit her lip as she shook her head in an inarguable denial.

"But...he's kissed you," Erik abruptly retorted, unable to tear his eyes from the unnatural arch of a bit lip, recalling with utter torture the one time he'd known its caress. "He...he's touched you."

The pain in his mismatched stare made her tremble down every limb with its potency, and unable to endure the guilt that came with it, she quickly revealed in a quivering voice, "Nothing more than chaste kisses. I...I couldn't let him touch me...not yet. It still felt too soon after...everything." A flimsy explanation at best when she had shunned Raoul's every advance, using her supposed trauma as reason to deter him. How could she have ever told Raoul that she didn't want him to touch her because his every attempt ignited only disappointment within her?

Shaking his head slowly, Erik wasn't calmed and muttered, "But he's held you, comforted you as you suffered memories and night terrors of a monster's attempted touches. He has stroked your cheeks and clasped your hands, brushed his fingers through your hair, all so much more than I've ever been allowed. I'm sure you've permitted him without a second thought while I...I had to endure your suspicion with every accidental contact."

She could not protest a blatant reality, recalling how often she had recoiled from Erik's hands, making murder and violence their only implication even when that had been the furthest truth possible. No, he had always sought to portray tenderness, and she had always forced herself not to look.

The blame fringing hurt eyes stung her so harshly that she suddenly acted without choice or contemplation, catching each of his hands with hers and thrilling immediately with the graze of skin to skin. He never questioned her intentions; he only accepted every touch as if they were all he'd have. Fingers wove with fingers, palms to palms, and she never gave herself the scolding that sense wanted her to, not when his masked face was so close, his eyes over-laden with a longing that was reflected in the empty ache in her chest.

"Christine," Erik slowly called the present to attention, "I never wanted my touch to be a punishment for you, not when I've forever been denied such pleasures. But you always recoiled from me as if I would taint you with the blackness of my soul."

She could not deny what was true, and how foolish she now felt to realize it! "I was an ignorant child. Such things are unimportant now."

"Are they?" he doubtfully questioned, lifting their joined hands. "And yet you tremble. This frightens you when we've barely shared a touch."

"It frightens me because it is a transgression," she reproved even though she never broke free and only clasped tighter, more unbreakable yet.

"And this? Is this a transgression?" As he asked, he drew her nearer by grasping hands until they were almost in a haphazard embrace, bodies so close that she felt burned and branded to her core. "Is it, Christine? Can it be a transgression if it is wanted?"

"It must be," she softly bid, and so overwhelmed, she bent her head and set her forehead to his shoulder, sucking in a breath that was too heavy with his scent to keep her from intoxication. "It must be because I can't rationalize through it."

"But it's always been this way," Erik protested and knew she heard the hoarseness creeping into his voice when a shudder racked her frame. "And it terrified you so much that you ran from me. You were so desperate to convince me that it didn't exist because if it did, then it was more of a sin to deny it." He could not help from resting his unmasked cheek against the crown of her head, nuzzling dark silk with his features and delighting in their unhindered tickle. "Will you deny it now? Will you force me away again and pretend this isn't real?"

"Even if it is... I can't have it." Swallowing a resolute breath, she drew away and left him no choice but to lift his head and meet her eye.

"Why, Christine?" he suddenly demanded. "Is it because this heart that adores you is so scarred with its sins and horrors? Is that why you push it away and pretend that you don't see its desires?"

Her hands were her own again, free and fisted at her sides with their loss, and she felt the misery creasing her brow to reply, "Mine bears its own scars, and it is *your* doing. And shall I allow the wounds to tear open again when it is *my* love that has never been enough for *you*. You gave it away; you handed me over to the Vicomte as if you had the right, and now you seek to inspire guilt for the relationship you condoned. *He* is allowed to touch me; he is my fiancé, and you turn even that into an atrocity. You are not allowed to feel envious of what you didn't want."

"Didn't want?" he spat skeptically. "*Always* wanted. It was a mistake; I never should have let you go-"

"But you did! Because you wanted more than I could ever give. You don't just want to be loved, Erik; you want to be idolized and revered. You want me to still see the angel you never were and not the man you are."

"Yes," he agreed, forcing his hands not to grab her again, "but could you have ever loved the man, Christine? You're so sure that your love wasn't enough for me, but I was always so certain that *I myself* wasn't enough for you. I'm not an angel; I've *never been* an angel, but you loved the angel and the man was a sorry replacement."

"And yet it was the man I chose," she insisted without sway. "Do you not recall it, Erik? There was no angel present that night; there was only *you*. And I gave him my life and love in one kiss and then was thrown away as if it meant nothing." Her hurt poured through, hurt she wanted to seem inconsequential. Tossed away...with her love seeming irrelevant, a heart that was called meaningless in the scheme of things.

"Christine-"

"No," she snapped, never acknowledging the tears in her eyes. "You want love only on your terms, and Raoul has never done that. He loves me without rules and restrictions in place, without pushing me to love him back in the way *he* wants. And I can't help but prefer that as my future when you so vividly destroyed everything else."

"You prefer this?" he shouted, unable to quiet his adamant doubts. "This music-less, emotionless, stale existence in a world of cruelty and bitterness? No music, Christine! No singing! No heart and soul and notes on a page! No stage and applause! No angel to adore your every breath! ...No belief in stories and happy endings, in magic and thrilling anticipation. You told an angel once that you knew what you wanted of your life. Do you recall it, Christine? You said your only dream was to sing. Will you give that up for this pathetic excuse of living?"

Every point hit her and made a definitive mark upon her soul, but he had avoided one detail, and she quickly brought it into the light for him. "I said that my dream was to sing *for you* or for your deceptive angel persona. And I was a naïve child who you preyed upon with your games and lies. Have I now proven why I can't love you?" The tears broke free of fluttering lashes and spilled down paled cheeks as she insisted, "You want to possess me, and I won't let you do that again."

Erik raced a furious gaze over her, accepting the weight of her tears as his burden and responsibility, and with a firm denial in place, he promised, "This isn't over, not yet. I've waited and ached for too long. You must see what I feel for you. Christine, I-"

His every attempt was severed in one knock to the door against her back, and as her eyes widened with anxious fear, Erik gave her one last look and disappeared behind her terrace curtains, lingering beyond sight to listen to the creak of whining hinges on an opening door.

"Mademoiselle," Andrew, the butler, greeted with a wary glance past her into the room. "The Comtesse was concerned about you after you left the party. She asked me to check on you. ...Are you all right?"

His intent expression did not accuse her of anything amiss, but she was sure that he must have caught the echoes of another voice as he once again peered into her room. A sweet smile was her pretense, assumed from her stage days and as believable as any other, and she quickly insisted, "Yes, you may tell her that I will be down in a moment."

Andrew hesitated. She knew he was after some sort of explanation, but she reminded herself that a future Vicomtesse had no obligation to explain anything to a butler and therefore was able to keep up her veneer without a single crack, leaving him to acquiesce to her commands. "Yes, mademoiselle," he replied and granted one more uncertain stare before leaving her room and treading softly down the hall.

As soon as he was gone, Christine rushed to her terrace and peeked out, searching desperately for a shadow amidst the sunlight, but she found nothing unordinary and no masked man begging to love her. It was almost a relief.

*****

Two matching squeals of excitement bounded off the foyer walls, one from the upstairs landing and one from the open front door's threshold but both combining to a deafening high pitch that made Andrew cringe and grimace his annoyance as Christine raced down the stairs with pink skirts trailing behind her and caught her golden-haired friend at the base of the banister in a flustered hug.

"Meg! You're here! It's been so long!" Christine was rambling and giggling her delight at the same time. It was the first genuinely blissful emotion she'd felt in longer than she could remember.

"I could hardly wait to get here! The carriage ride seemed an eternity! ...Look at this place!" Meg lifted her head to scan the overly large, elegant foyer and almost reluctantly recalled her mother standing stoic and with an unaltered expression in the doorway behind her.

Understanding all too well, Christine eagerly played hostess and hurried to greet her old ballet mistress with undimmed enthusiasm. "Madame, how wonderful that you were both able to come!"

"Well, you only get married once," Madame Giry stated firm and emotionless, as sober as Christine recalled in every detail unless scolding was involved. "And where is our room? I should like a rest after such brutal travel conditions; that carriage jostled so viciously that sleep was impossible to indulge."

"Andrew," Christine called, smile yet in place, "will you take Madame Giry to her room?"

The butler was still eyeing Meg and Madame Giry with sharp scrutiny, but he did as commanded without protest and carried their few bags up the stairs with the ballet mistress close behind.

Meg made a face after them and asked, "What was that all about?"

"Andrew doesn't know that you're from the opera, remember?" Christine reminded with a smirk. "He's convinced you and your mother are my wealthy cousins."

Giggling to herself, Meg decided, "And the societal elite wouldn't greet each other with shrieking and hugging. What shall it be then? A cold handshake and a 'how do you do'?" She demonstrated by offering a hand and kept a straight face long enough for Christine to oblige the game and take it in hers. "How do you do?"

Reserved right back, Christine flatly declared, "Very well. And you?"

"Boring, I'm sure." That was all it took to resume giggles and boisterous remarks without regret as Christine dragged Meg by the hand she still had into the study and watched her friend's eyes widen and sparkle at the scene.

"The Comtesse is known for her decorative styling," Christine insisted with a gesture to the imported furniture and thick, woven wallpaper. "The other ladies in her circle call upon her frequently for her designing opinion."

"And *this* is how you've been living for four months?" Meg inquired with a feigned haughty tilt to her head, teasing, "I don't like it, not rich *enough* for my distinguishing tastes!" Her eyes were still interpreting every detail when realization made them dart abruptly back to Christine. "And when you are a Vicomtesse, is this what you will have to look forward to? Is dear Aunt Comtesse de Chagny decorating your new home as well?"

"I truly don't know," Christine replied. "It hasn't been discussed, but I certainly hope not."

Laughing delight, Meg flounced down upon the couch, carefully spreading out her skirts and smoothing every wrinkle. "Oh, Christine, this is so wonderful, every overdone detail, and..." Almost abruptly, her smile faded at its corners, and her true somberness was hinted in green eyes. "I am loath to ruin it for you. You deserve all of these amazing things, but...I have to tell you something, ...something awful..."

An idea was already quite developed in Christine's head over what she would say, but she kept her features set and bid gently, "Tell me, Meg. What is it?"

"The...the Opera Ghost, Christine. He... Oh, I'm so sorry. I've ruined everything... Oh..." Tears were tumbling from her golden lashes en route down her pink-tinted cheeks, and she wrung little hands in her lap and mussed her once perfect skirts. "He thought you were *dead*; everyone does, and I was so careful to keep the secret. Only Mama and I knew the truth, but...well, he overheard me. Oh, my big mouth! I told Jammes! And he heard about the wedding and everything! Oh, I'm so sorry!"

But Christine's expression remained unchanged in its sculpt as she revealed, "He's been here, Meg, a couple of times. I...I've seen him, and...I'm as bewildered as I ever was. He has this indisputable way of tossing me off my stability. It takes little more than a look from his eyes or a single word, and I'm in the same place I was two years ago, his adoring pupil ready to give everything for his favor."

"What...what did he say to you?" Meg nervously stammered, clutching the material of her skirts. "Did he try to force you to go off with him?"

"No, no," Christine quickly answered. "He wouldn't force me."

"He did before and worse! All the horrors he's had a hand in committing! He's a monster, Christine! Have you told Raoul that he's here?"

"Of course not! Raoul would have the guards of France out in pursuit if he knew. No, I wouldn't dare speak a word of it. Erik...he doesn't deserve to be hunted and killed like an animal."

"Doesn't he? How can you say that after the things he's done to so many people? To Raoul? To *you*? He nearly forced you to marry him!" Meg's always-anxious nerves had her glancing about the sun-filled room as if looking for some hidden token in the shadows. "What are you going to do, Christine? If he's here, it can only mean tragedy."

"He isn't here to hurt me," Christine vowed resolutely, never a doubt on that subject. "He would never; he loves me, Meg. He's said as much, and...Raoul convinced him that I was dead." The mere statement of the fact shone with sadness in her eyes. Erik had mourned her as if she was forever gone from him. "I cannot even fathom that. And he looks at me now with such awe in his eyes, as if he's thanking God that I exist. It...it's overwhelming!"

Meg was shaking her head idly with her aversion. "I think you should tell Raoul."

"I can't, and you can't either. *Please*, Meg. You cannot tell anyone, not even your mother."

"As if I would! She'd have my head for ever betraying her and sharing the news with Jammes. We were sworn to secrecy, you know, but...well, secrets are not my strong point." Thin shoulders shrugged with an amount of blamelessness for a reality that just was, and she added, "But...you haven't answered my question. What are you going to do, Christine? Neither of your beaus is just going to let you go."

With a desolate sigh, she admitted, "I don't know. If I were only stronger! I'd force Erik away!"

"Maybe...maybe being strong is *not* forcing Erik away." The consideration wasn't one she could encourage, but it had a certain amount of legitimate honesty to it that Meg hated to ponder and yet could not denounce.

"You are far too intuitive," Christine commented with the hint of a grin to realize she was right. "Being strong is not running away and not taking the easier path. But...I don't know that being strong is loving him either. ...He makes it impossible to love him."

"And yet you do it anyway," Meg finished for her. "I can't give you an answer and tell you what to do, but I *can* tell you whatever you decide, be sure. Don't break hearts if you don't have to."

Christine nodded her agreement, but in her head, she knew broken hearts were inevitable. There was always bound to be damage.

*****

Later that evening, clouds were rolling in to shroud the pale colors of the sky and hint at rain as

Christine watched their ominous threat from the parlor windows. Madame Giry had dragged Meg up to bed after supper had ended with an insistence on a full night's sleep, and though Meg had promised to sneak back down at her first opportunity, she had yet to appear, leaving Christine with nothing but her own thoughts for company. How torturous a wandering mind could be! And perhaps a distraction would have been ideal, but the instant she caught the low rumbling sound of Raoul's voice in the hallway approaching, she leapt off the couch and scurried out the terrace doors into the embracing breeze of the impending storm. No, she couldn't take the guilt right now.

And she ran. She knew from the moment the house was beyond her sight that she was being followed and had no question to the identity of her pursuer. How often had they played this game? The Opera Ghost spying from the shadows, more phantom than angel, and though she did not let on, she purposely led him through the brush to a particular place as the scent of rain hung in the air and random droplets began to sputter out of the cloud's bed.

Her private escape. His had always been underground in the dark, his refuge from the world; hers was a vine-covered gazebo amidst the flowers of spring, equally as secluded from anyone's eyes, a sanctuary unto itself. How often did she resign herself to its protection to practice when she had no place else to go? It had been a sheer stroke of fortune that she had found it tucked away in the far reaches of the garden, and when being overheard mid-aria was inconsiderable and practically forbidden, it was a good enough distance away to keep her from worry.

Rain was pattering against the rooftop as she huddled inside, syncopated beats lacking any decided pattern, and as the growling of thunder called in the distance, she hugged her body tight and glanced about at the shadows peering in, seeking one specific and distinct amidst the shades of darkness. The mask came into view before his silhouette, its starkness too brilliant to remain hidden, and mismatched eyes danced with a mixture of amusement and longing that choked any greeting she might have formed.

Erik studied her intently, trailing a necessary stare along every limb, every feature, purposely savoring the manner in which her pale pink gown complimented her complexion and made her blue eyes look deeper and an entirely new shade than usual. How funny when a simple background color could alter the typical spectrum? Even her skin appeared more like cream, not as pale and white. Minor details, but he absorbed every one and was desperate for more.

Gathering as much of his typically-acted aloof demeanor as he could, he stated plainly, "For as adamant as you are about marrying your Vicomte and assuming the title of Vicomtesse, you certainly spend a good deal of time running from that life and its world. Is this your usual pattern of behavior? Or has my presence brought it out of you? Are you now seeing how empty such a life is? How unfulfilling? How not *you*?"

Avoiding an answer when it must be the one he was after or be a lie, she demanded back, "And do you spend every moment of the day watching me to know such things? Is that all *your* life holds?"

He shrugged idly and revealed, "Most of it. I am not ashamed to admit that you *are* my life. If only you had the courage to do the same, then perhaps I wouldn't have to linger in the shadows just to be near to you." As he spoke, he dared to approach in unwavering footsteps, joining her scene as thunder rumbled closer in its appearance and raindrops created a pulse to movement.

"The Vicomte would kill you if he knew you were here," she insisted, knowing he'd glimpse how she trembled with his nearness, anticipating a touch that had yet to come.

Another nonchalant shrug. "He'd try; I doubt

he'd succeed. Had he come after me, sword at the ready, any time in the past four months, he'd have easily bested me. I *craved* death when I thought that was where you would be. But now...with you here and before me, only a mere relinquishing of pride away from being mine, the Vicomte would lose. He wouldn't be able to defeat a man with a purpose for living."

"This isn't about pride," she protested, desperate to seem in control as her shaking fingers curved into her palms to make urgent fists. No, she would not touch him again. "Nor is it about courage. We are not meant for each other. Why do you not see that?"

Her statement was sharp in its attack, and his bravado shattered with one painful consideration that he uttered in soft, thick tones that revealed too much of his heart. "Is it my face, Christine? Is that the real reason then? Is it still so repellent to you that it keeps you denying me at every turn?"

"How can you even ask such a thing?" The guilt over past indiscretions was potent within her and had never fully been relieved. No, it still bore a blame that made her heart ache with *his* pain.

"It *is* a reality," he snapped with a flicker of that temper she so despised. "It can never be anything else; my face will always be the damaged palette it is. And it disgusted you so completely once. Beneath the mask, it is the same abhorrent disgrace as ever before. Perhaps its memory incites you to retain walls between us."

Bitterness creased her brow and kept her from being dismantled with his harsh blatancy. No, she would not falter, not on this issue, and she retorted in equaled flames of resentment, "I hate your mask! I loathe its very presence! It gives you a reason to hide and an excuse for your own immorality. *You* use it as the boundary that you accuse of me. You would never believe that it doesn't matter."

"You hate the mask?" he couldn't keep from

shouting back, matching and exceeding the volume of the tempest outside. "Then do away with it, Christine! Destroy it for all I care! Take that boundary and find the one that will *always* exist behind it! You forget that I have a necessary reason to hide."

"No! I *never* forget! You wear the mask so that *you* can forget!" she accused without sway, refusing the anxious reach of cowardice. She kept firm and insisted again, "I abhor the very image of your mask. It has been the travesty that haunts my dreams with its vision and every implication that it brings."

"Then take it away from me. If its presence is what makes you hate and shun me, then rid me of it. But will you then love the monster you uncover? Will that do it? Prove to me that you can!"

On the unshaken wings of impulse and fury, she obeyed and reached for that damning mask, tearing it free in one abrupt jerk and exposing the face it concealed and its every unavoidable flaw. The mask slipped unnoticed to the floor as her concentration was caught and held captive by abnormal shapes, by ugliness and deformity, by a monster or a devil or whatever other valid insult he had been called in his lifetime. It was veiled in the shadows of a hidden dusk, illuminated in flashing pulsations of lightning, or else it was little more than a nightmare of a subconscious mind. His mismatched eyes bore into her with more betrayal, *always* betrayal between them, and the emerald orb sunken so far into the circumference of a gaping socket pierced to her core, robbed as it had been of its manmade cavity and now heinously on display. A corpse, she remembered he had called himself upon her first stealing of his mask, and a corpse he was, so vividly dead in appearance like the decaying skeleton's revelation and yet equally as alive as the gasped breaths past his bloated lips pronounced. He was ugly to behold, and it hurt her to know that he believed it still mattered to her.

"Oh, Erik, " she could not keep from whispering, oddly grateful to glimpse that face in all its monstrous glory. That face made him suddenly real and suddenly hers. Edging closer with a silent question always in her eyes, she dared to extend trembling fingers to that horror, impatient to feel what she had so long avoided touching. Touch made things real as much as it had for him to believe that she was alive, and now to lay quivering fingertips against the malformed plane of his cheekbone, touch made him Erik.

His eyelids fluttered closed, brow furrowing with his unique urgency to savor every second of this indiscretion. Her trepid fingers against his disfigurement were almost too much to bear, the sensations acute and poignant as they raced little thrills along the surface of every inch of his body's flesh. One touch, and it extended everywhere at once.

Mesmerized by her own actions, Christine transformed a touch into a caress, brushing delicately along that irregular, sallow cheek down to his jawbone and up again to barely graze the blank canvas that should have been filled with the overlooked normalcy of a nose. And it amazed her as her mind pondered an odd thought: that the typical human face was something so common and almost boring while this face was something new, perhaps distorted but interesting in concept and design. She wondered what he would think of such a definition. Interesting was an improvement to ugly and could eventually lead to extraordinarily beautiful instead. It could if she let it and stopped holding such musings tight and refusing their acknowledgment. For too long under Raoul's encouragement, she had refused to consider this face as anything but unnaturally abhorrent and evil. But now if she looked upon its distinctions herself, she could not find evil; she only found Erik.

His eyes opened to watch her, to observe every expression to cross her features as she fixedly regarded her hand and its smoothness and ordinariness against his scars. "You are not disgusted," he stated confidently.

"I haven't been disgusted by this face in a long time," she replied, somber and focused on the motion of her thumb along the misshapen swell of his upper lip. "Disgust was a response of impulse, and it was ignorant and childish." Her gaze darted to quickly catch his as it was entranced always upon her. "Why are you so surprised? I chose this face that last night we were together in the catacombs; I *kissed* it. And yet you look at me now as if you cannot believe me."

"But you also once ran from this face and the man who bears it," he accused in soft tones. Anger lost to the rain outside and its incessant tapping.

"No, I ran from the man in the mask, and this man before me now was the one who broke my heart. And even though they are the same, and every version is you, I cannot love them all."

"No, you can't," he agreed, tilting his scars further into her touch and delighting in its wonderful sense of branding possession over him. "I've never loved you as I should have, Christine. I've never given you a man worthy of you. I instead manipulated a heart I longed to be mine and sought to control its every beat. You said as much yesterday. I never *let you* love me, not unless I was the one deciding how it was to be done."

Her own allegations and spoken with such genuine sincerity that it left her expression to soften and the corners of her lips to rise in the hint of a grin. "And what will that mean?"

The smile she was containing appeared on his lips instead and was strangely brilliant without a mask to stifle it. "I want to give you a love story rather than the tragedy we've suffered," he vowed gently. "I want to give you the love story you deserve."

It was so tempting to fall into the dream, to believe and cling to his every word as candid truth, but with her palm yet cupping his cheek in the most intimate caress she'd ever given him, she reluctantly replied, "Perhaps...until doubt returns and you remember that you must believe my heart solely on my promises and actions. You've always preferred to decide how it should feel and why. You once pushed me to Raoul because *you* believed I would grow fond of him."

"Christine..." Only then did he indulge his urge and touch her back, catching her face between his palms and cradling her delicate features. "I never knew how to love you until I lost you. And now...I'm learning, *ange*. Love has always been denied to me and held so far from my grasp. You must forgive me if it therefore terrifies me to truly feel it."

"You were once going to make me your prisoner if I didn't choose you, despite anything I felt in return," she pushed.

"And I don't want a prisoner...or a reverent worshiper at my feet. I want a love; I want *you*. But I equally want it to be your own choosing, your own love in return." His scars tingled with the imprint of her warm palm, their faces enshrouded in shadows of a dusk storm that consumed natural light, but his dark-accustomed eyes read her lingering apprehension. "Have I carried you off, Christine? I could have done so time and again these last days. I have a house just beyond the de Chagny lands; I could have abducted you as I've done before, brought you there, locked you inside with no hope of escape. I could have stolen your freedom and forced my love upon you whether you wanted it or not under the pretext of a choice you once made. But that isn't how I want you."

She was sadly shaking her head from side to side, and tears tainted her voice. "I am to marry Raoul in four days, Erik. He loves me, and even if he doubts my own love in return, my affection is enough for him. He's never asked for more."

"He told me that you were dead!" Erik exclaimed feverishly. "He stole your life in every sense of the word! And he won't ever ask you for more because he knows if he did, he'd lose you. The more you can't give is *mine*; it's the bond we share that he can only envy."

"No, Erik," she stated as she drew her hand away to his blatant disappointment. Her fingers clenched defenseless in the air, her body pulling away when he acted without thought to consequence.

Her face was still cradled in his firm hold, and Erik suddenly leaned close and pressed his misshapen lips to her perfect mouth, experiencing the shudder that racked her frame with her.

Kissing her this time was far more exquisite than the night in the catacombs because it was by *his* impetus. He was creating the caress, and without the surprise that had been prevalent then, he was able to revel in the sheer bliss of such a mediocre contact. Lips touching, his were deformed, and yet they were solely hers, claimed from their first attempt at this shared intimacy. They moved so timid and uncertain, awkward only until she succumbed and met the kiss and returned it, filling in his insecurities and making him brave. A kiss, and though its name dubbed it an established and common act, it was anything but. It was a revelation; it was vows of love and devotion spoken by the rain outside in linguistic patters. He held her in place, but she gave no struggle to leave. And in the midst of an incoherent fog of emotion, he had one clear thought: that this moment was a piece of heaven confined to earth. It must have been to be kissing an angel.

Tears, there were tears, rising to flood his eyes with their condemning presence, and with a rush of reluctance, he ducked his head away and severed their closeness, ashamed to allow her to see.

"*Ange...*," she whispered gently as her hazy eyes fluttered open and sought his dark shape in the gazebo, and he shivered simply to be called such an ethereal appellation again. "What...what is it? You're crying."

"No," he lied, still refusing to look at her, but all at once, before she could protest, he caught her and pulled her close to his body, pressing his bare face into her hair and thrilling when she tentatively embraced him back with willowy, trembling arms that weaved about his waist. "You were dead," he was muttering against her crown, and that was reason enough.

In that moment, Christine hated Raoul so fiercely that tears of her own stung her eyes. Dead and mourned. Lost to a grave. "No, Erik, no," she gently breathed, rubbing her cheek against his chest to revel in his beating heart. "I'm here and alive. You're holding me, and you're still terrified to believe that I am real."

"I blamed myself," he admitted in matching quiet. "It was my fault that you would take your life. I drove you to it. Loving me made you suffer."

"No," she insisted with sudden adamancy. "It was a lie; it never happened. My God, he made you believe it so certainly that you aren't even listening to my words. Erik, ...you're shaking so hard." Her hold on him instinctively tightened, granting him the strength he lacked and could not seem to find. "*Ange, please...*"

"I'm frightening you," he concluded, rubbing desperate hands along her spine to mold her closer. "But it was the guilt of it and the pain of losing you, ...to think I'd never have this when I'd been so sure that I would! I was broken, as damaged as you yourself were, and how the agony played upon my soul! ...Christine, don't let go."

"I won't," she promised, daring to press a random kiss to the place of his heart.

"I still have such fear every moment I'm not watching you from afar, that you'll be dead and beyond my reach once again and I will be alone."

His body still shook, and she clasped firmly with her sudden, unjustified terror of the same thing: separation and loneliness as if the past months weren't enough. And it shocked her to realize how intense the urging was to fall into this moment and never come out, to pretend that Raoul didn't exist and hadn't spent months loving her and taking care of her. Her heart was adamantly calling the Vicomte an enemy for the life he'd knowingly shattered, and yet... How could she condemn him for acting out of love? ...Especially when once before Erik had done the same? Taken to extremes for fear of a broken heart. It seemed impossible to hate one and not the other for the same sin.

With a spiraling head too full of confusion to find the path to decision, she reluctantly drew free of Erik's hold, surprised when he yielded and released her, applying his stoic pretense back into place.

"Four days," he repeated for her. "Four days until your wedding, and that gives me four days to prove my words and give you the love you want. Will you grant me such a chance, Christine? If I vow to you this instant not to be the madman I was that last night at the opera or the so-called phantom ready to murder at whim, if I vow to control my temper and my vices and show you a man and not a monster."

Sense argued that it must end badly, that his proposed idea was bordering on ridiculous, but her heart glimpsed such hope within them both. Four days, and she felt the thin cord existing between their souls, one tug away from snapping, and she nodded her consent with never a smile or a nuance of encouragement. It hardly felt something to be happy about when it was most decisively a betrayal.

That was obviously the answer he wanted, and with a trepid grin, he bent to retrieve his mask, replacing it and hiding the face she missed when regarding the Opera Ghost instead. And yet wasn't the man before her already so different and changed? She had grown accustomed to being steered in one direction or the next by his whims and temper, but this Erik didn't look as if he was about to rage and command her concession. He simply looked grateful for a chance at something else.

"Until tomorrow," he bid as a promise, and before she could argue or change her mind, he raced out into the rainstorm and disappeared in the shadows, leaving her to stare in addled uncertainty in his wake.

*****

From the moment they walked in the door of the next night's soiree, Christine felt all eyes upon her, crawling across her skin like leeches looking for a place to bite. These social engagements were growing more frequent, and though Raoul had previously allowed them to decline attendance, the approach of their wedding had him eager to follow protocol and make an appearance. This particular gathering was hosted at the country home of another wealthy comte, not very far from Raoul's aunt, and it seemed as if half the county were present.

"Have you ever seen anything like this?" Meg softly queried as she huddled closer to Christine and away from a furiously gossiping group of debutantes. "I'm not sure yet if I'm grateful that you asked for my company, not when I'm half-convinced that they're talking about me as well."

"Of course they are; it's what they do," Christine replied, clasping Meg's arm in support. "I am quite used to it by now. I spend most of these events as the outcast until Raoul's aunt takes pity and adds me to her group of older ladies. I fear the younger ones will always despise me for snatching up Raoul before they ever had a chance at him."

"What a revolting branch of society!" Meg decided. "I'd rather be destitute and polite than wealthy and conceited."

"I doubt a single person here would agree with you." A smile curved Christine's lips, and she knew that she had Meg to thank for its creation, for the first time not caring that the girls nearest to them were shooting whispered comments behind telltale hands held to their lips. "Oh, let them talk! Not a word they say would ever amount to one shrill insult from La Carlotta, and I endured dozens of her cold comments stated before cast and crew without a single tear or breakdown. These girls and their pettiness are trivial in comparison!"

"I wholeheartedly agree," Meg decided with a firm nod, "but will you be able to endure this kind of cruelty on a daily basis without me here to walk beside you? Vicomtesse may have to be your greatest performance to date."

Snapping her fingers with the thought, Christine replied, "Exactly! It shall be a performance, and I will portray it as flawlessly and realistic as possible."

"For the rest of your life?" Meg posed doubtfully. "That sounds utterly exhausting."

"Well, what shall you propose instead?"

Lowering her voice to a whisper with a raised hand to match the rest of the gossipers, Meg answered, "Forget all of it, and come back to the opera."

"The opera? Where I am a *dead* previous prima donna?" It was the first time she'd been able to add any sort of genuine laugh to the lie.

Shrugging idly, Meg nonchalantly offered, "Perhaps you'll fit right in. You can be the Opera Ghost's wife and sing concerts back from the dead while the Opera Ghost accompanies on the piano. Imagine it: a haunted performance!"

Opera Ghost's wife... Christine's smile faded with the realization of how near the truth Meg had jokingly come, but she was never given the chance to retort as Raoul's Aunt Constance caught her arm and drew her attention.

"Christine, the ladies have informed me that there is to be a little impromptu performance at the end of the evening. They would really adore a song." Lowering her voice behind a hand, Constance added, "It would be wonderful for your reputation and help you to make some new acquaintances. Society enjoys good talent."

As long as it was within society's guidelines, Christine silently mused. And she had the distinct feeling that if she sang, she'd acquire more enemies than friends. "I...I really don't think so."

"Christine, you should!" Meg quickly interjected, and despite Christine's frantically shaking head, she told Constance, "Christine is practically a diva. She amazes every person who hears her sing; they're always shocked that such a big and brilliant voice comes out of such a tiny girl!"

"Meg, you're not helping," Christine muttered, but Constance was already taking the choice out of her hands.

"Wonderful indeed!" the Comtesse declared. "I shall tell the ladies to add you to the program, last if possible. I should love to have a member of *my* family show up some of these little society daughters. New money can pose such arrogance; they believe they have a right to play equals with those of us whose bloodlines are rich! This will definitely put our name on their lips!"

As Constance rushed off, Christine averted horrified eyes to Meg. "I can't sing!" she breathlessly gasped. "Raoul doesn't want me singing, not in the public eye anyway! He doesn't want us to draw attention after what happened!"

"Oh, he won't care," Meg insisted, scanning the crowd only to find the Vicomte in a heated conversation with a group of gentlemen. "I doubt he'll even realize a performance is going on. It doesn't seem like the men pay much attention to what their ladies are off doing. Look. The majority of them have to be reminded that this soiree includes dancing. They're too engrossed discussing politics!"

It was true. Raoul and an entire throng were having a debate whose ruckus could be heard vibrantly over the orchestra's melody. A few perturbed wives had even gone over to swat their husband's arms and drag them out for a dance despite the breach of etiquette such behavior boasted. Perhaps Raoul wouldn't notice...

To Meg's delight as the evening wore on, a

young gentleman with kind eyes approached and asked for a dance, and though the little ballerina tried to play her part as a lady, she was a bit too elegant and graceful on her feet, leading their motion as her partner awkwardly followed and tripped clumsily at every beat. Christine took the opportunity to scoot away from too many observing eyes, and careful not to be noticed, she slipped out onto the back terrace and was captured by the eager arms of the twilight breeze. She felt utterly weightless and free after too long burdened by society's restrictions. What a preferred idea it was to linger outside and away, to allow the party to continue without her and go unmissed in the melee. *If only!*

Suddenly perking up in stature and poise, Christine called out to the emptiness, "A gentleman would ask for a dance instead of spying in shadows."

"I have never been accomplished at being a gentleman," Erik replied as he stepped into the revealing moonlight, trailing eager eyes over her exquisite appearance. She wore midnight blue, gathered into an elaborate bustle in the back and trimmed in silver lace. Never before had she looked more like a fine lady, and yet never before had she looked less like herself. As beautiful as she was, he silently missed unbound curls and comfortable gowns; this was too much like another costume of the stage. "Perhaps you should guide me in proper etiquette so that I may know what is expected in this world."

"And do you anticipate using such knowledge? I was under the impression that you do not favor social interactions if they can be avoided," Christine teased with a subject she knew to be bitter, but leaning idly on her toes with an almost playful tilt to her head, she made it seem trivial and unimportant. *Almost* playful, because she wouldn't consider being playful with Erik. No, not playful...

"Typically," he replied, mimicking her light tone; it was far too delightful to savor the brilliant twinkle in her blue eyes and know that it meant life and that it was his. "But I also typically do not seek to capture a lady's affections, and if in my endeavors, I must choose to dance rather than spy, I will do so wholeheartedly...for *you* at least."

Formality left with one hungry look that ran like wildfire over her skin and made her tremble through every inch of her body. Under that forcibly intent stare, he gave a slight bow and offered a hand that shook in its feigned bravado, explaining, "Unconventional propriety. I'll accept a dance under the moonlight and alone instead of in a room full of prying strangers who do not approve of a mask as an article of fashion. ...Will you permit me?"

Her grin still bore a tentative wariness at its corners, but she conceded and set her hand in his, weaving their fingers together as he gently tugged her into his arms. It was quiet, the night still with only the orchestra's strains to filter out through ajar terrace doors and accompany a private dance. With an unsure hand forming about the curve of her waist, he began to lead her in slow, languid footsteps, thrilling as she hesitantly inched nearer until she could lay her cheek to his shoulder.

His voice vibrated against her temple as he said, "I may be unaccustomed to propriety, but I've observed enough from the background to know that this is not the usual manner that dancing is indulged. Do you dance with every gentleman this close to you?"

"Do you hold every lady against your heart?" she posed in return. "You were, after all, the one to put me here."

"I've held no lady but you," he answered and turned to rest his unmasked cheek to her silken head, wishing to be bare-faced and free of obtrusions, to bury scars in the uplifted cloud of soft curls. "I am only fortunate that you allow my indiscretion and permit me to hold you as I will."

Closing her eyes and filling her senses with every detail that was him, she shattered the unbidden intimacy of the moment and revealed steadily, "I have to sing, Erik, in their impromptu concert at the end of the evening. They're expecting a pretty girl with a pleasant voice, perhaps a bit more refined and trained than other ladies but definitely not a diva of the stage."

"And yet that is what you are and what you shall be," Erik decided for her. "I did not spend countless months developing your technique and talent to have you purposely diminish it. I warn you now: if you dare shame yourself in front of this throng and depreciate the extent of what you can do, I will indulge my whims and let the Opera Ghost manifest in the midst of that ballroom to put an irremovable stain on your reputation."

She did not doubt that he meant it, and how could she hate him for it when he only sought to push her back to her potential? Brow furrowing against the rich material of his suit jacket, she continued with one solemn point, "Raoul doesn't want me to sing for anyone ever again."

"I assumed that," he replied tightly and huffed so harsh against her hair that fleeting tendrils stirred. "That Vicomte of yours could never understand how integral music is to your very existence. It lives and breathes in your soul, and without it, it leaves a gaping hole like a piece of your essence is missing and stolen away. He could never comprehend that without it, you are only half of yourself. He simply wants it gone and forgotten; the music was always mine, and that tortures him."

No valid argument against him could be assembled, and she simply stated, "Music always meant you; how could it be anything else when you have been the source of my inspiration, *ange*? When music was our only ally in a world all our own, I never had to question the toils of my heart; they were always vivid and did not condemn me."

"Music is pure," he explained, "and we both know its passion so intensely. We've always loved each other through its notes on staves; it could be the root to something epic if only we'd let it grow." It was as much of a hint to smoldering desires that he could give, and turning his cheek to graze a clumsy kiss that the mask prevented from speaking fire, he said, "You know what you have to do, Christine, and it isn't about *my* pride or ambition. You would choose to be true to the music with or without my encouragement. It's too deeply embedded within the marrow of your bones to deny it for the ugliness that world of society tries to place upon you. You are too good for that."

Christine did not deny his words, and yet she was still loath to leave the quiet comfort of his arms and the trepid dance they were still sharing at a haphazard beat. It was just too perfect with only star glow and moonlight to intrude, and when the urging to beg for more tickled her senses, she did not halt it upon her tongue. "Don't let this end yet. Please, Erik, ...I've waited all day just to *feel* you."

"I've waited four months," he countered. "And I'd choose to argue that I'm waiting still. I may hold you and have you here, but it is only a piece of you when I'm waiting for *everything* to be mine. I'm waiting until I can feel you and know without a doubt that you will not run from me or push me away ever again, that one moment in one dance is only the prelude to hundreds more. ...Do such admissions affect you, Christine? Do they make you long for the same? If I beg in return, can they be mine?"

An answer was yet beyond her with her fiancé in a party going on behind her, but by fortune's stroke, she did not have to give it with any sort of understatement or lie, not as they were interrupted in a flustered, quaking call.

"Christine...?" Meg was frozen in her place at the terrace doorway, staring at the dancing couple with wide, horror-stricken eyes that did not lessen their astonishment even as the pair parted and broke their embrace. "The...the performances are about to start, and...the Comtesse was looking for you. I...I told her that I'd find you."

Though Erik's stare was cold on the little Giry, he could not fully denounce her presence when it gave Christine a genuine companion in the vicious world of the elite. Yet still, ...he hated to be taken unaware and most especially when his time with Christine was so precious in its brevity. Ignoring the gaping ballerina, he dared to stroke his fingers down Christine's cheek with an acute swell of a possessiveness he knew she did not favor. He couldn't help it; she had always felt like solely his to keep. But his expression remained tender as he bid, "Show them what you can do, Christine, and how far above them you truly are."

But she read his yearning and stated with the hint of a grin, "I will never admit to being yours until you can say that you are equally mine."

"*Always* yours," he breathed with beaming hope and brought her hand to his face, brushing his lower lip along her knuckles reverently before he finally found the ability to release her.

Just as reluctant, Christine halted long enough to raise herself on tiptoe and form her own worshipping kiss set to his only bare cheek so that he would feel the depth of her caress. "Thank you, *ange*," she whispered sincerely, and that was all she could say in current company. Quickly turning about, she hurried to join a wary Meg, capturing her arm and guiding the little ballerina back inside and out of the moonlight.

"Christine...," Meg nervously stammered, but she could only shake her head. "Wooing the Opera Ghost with a fiancé a windowed wall away? I hope you know what you are doing."

"I don't," she confided back, but the smile on her lips said far more and shimmered in the confidence she had earlier been lacking. "When do I sing?"

Nearly the instant she asked, one of the younger girls lifted her voice to resound through the room, and both Meg and Christine cringed at her inability to remain on the pitch given by a piano's accompaniment. And much of the rest of their untitled concert was the same. Girls whose families boasted their supposed talent and training and not more than a few decent timbres in the bunch. At least for how conceited opera divas could be, they had the talent to back it up! This was rather pathetic in comparison.

When it came to be Christine's turn, she cast one idle glance over the group, but Raoul was in an adjoining study, chuckling and drinking with his comrades, not paying a bit of attention to the concert. She knew that was unavoidably about to change.

With a supportive pat upon her shoulder from Aunt Constance, Christine took her place in front of the crowd, noticing how many eyes were bitter upon her, ready to tear her apart with one single flaw. She was determined that they'd find none.

It was in the second she opened her mouth and released a voice that had felt trapped inside for too long that she suddenly felt like herself, like the soul she had been stifling and slowly suffocating was finally flowing unhindered and *living* again. How right Erik had been! Without singing, she was truly a step from death!

Her chosen piece was one of her harder arias, showcasing skill and musicianship, but she knew that she would have shined in anything she chose as the fullness of her timbre echoed to every corner of the room and stunned her audience to gaping expressions. And she was doubtless that watching just as intently from some undisclosed place was Erik; she could feel his pride radiating around her and encouraging more and higher, full sound, full voice, and every nuance as near to perfection as possible. Was it any wonder that she sang for him? She had never been a diva, so he had re-sculpted the title for her, pouring his own confidence into every space hers didn't exist. It definitely made her voice as much his as it was hers.

She was executing a flawless cadenza when a flicker of her attention averted to the other imperative member of her audience. The Vicomte de Chagny stood in the doorway, unable to fully conceal his shock beneath a proper veneer. Astonishment, annoyance that she would dare, and undeniably an inkling of his own extended pride. She sang, and he believed that she was *his* now that Erik should only be considered a shadow of the past. She would gain accolades, and the Vicomte would equally accept their glow; yes, he was the fortunate one to be marrying the little songbird. And even if he raged at her for singing behind closed doors, he would savor her praises from his precious society's mouths as if he'd approved all along.

Even as she thought such travesties, she did not falter in her last high note, making it come to life and bloom on its pitch into brilliance before a sweeping of applause carried it away. Envy all around from too many of the younger ladies whose parlor songs had been outshone, but many of the older socialites were genuinely in awe, reminding Christine of the patrons at the opera. People just like these, wealthy and supporting the arts, reacting similarly to the performance of the prima donna, and just as she had in that setting, she graciously accepted their acclaim, curtsying elegantly with her stage smile upon her lips. Only Erik would have known about her surge apprehension to be so appreciated, her modesty always a step away, and like a recollection of this scene acted out in days lost, she knew that only *his* voice and *his* praises would calm her.

But she never got a chance to search for him as she was accosted by a stunned Aunt Constance, who was unable to make words and only gave an uncommon hug, clasping Christine by her shoulders and squeezing her tight for a brief moment before she stared, wide-eyed.

"Comtesse," Christine attempted to be the intelligible one between them, "are you all right?"

"You...," she stammered, shaking her head to

break her flustered awe. "When you said you were trained in the arts, ...well, I never imagined *that* would come out of you. In one song, you've created a point of status; everyone will want to be associated with the new Vicomtesse de Chagny. I mean...I haven't heard singing like that outside of an opera production. No society girl has ever shown such talent..." It was half a conclusion, but Christine was unable to form a lie of explanation as Raoul joined them.

The Vicomte's adoration wasn't entirely real; Christine caught glimpses of his agitation beneath, but he put on a convincing show for his fellow comrades and captured her hand to set an acceptable kiss to her knuckles. "You were...wonderful, Christine," he tightly complimented. "Wonderful indeed. ...But I think it's time we take our leave."

"So soon?" his aunt inquired, disappointment pouting her lips. "But I would love to walk about the room with Christine and introduce her to some of her new admirers."

"We have to go," Raoul abruptly insisted. "With only three days to the wedding, Christine needs her rest; that is a valid excuse. But you stay, Auntie. I'll send the carriage back for you. I know you like to remain through the last bout of dancing. Don't feel obligated to leave with us."

"Well, ...all right then, I shall stay. Someone must be here to receive Christine's compliments. I cannot wait to gush over my new niece to the rest of them. It's good to be above the throng, Raoul, as I've always told you."

"Above the throng," Raoul muttered to himself with a dubious shake of his head, and squeezing Christine's elbow, he commanded curtly, "Get Meg, and we'll go. Quickly please. We need to be free of this group as soon as possible."

She didn't question him; she simply obeyed, skirting between bodies and grinning at the occasional kind sentiment until she practically dragged Meg away from her heart-struck gentleman. By the time they joined him in the foyer, Raoul was wearing a biting expression that even Meg cringed to endure. The argument was brewing, but silence was chosen for the carriage ride home, even if it did nothing to lessen the tension like a thick cloud in the air; it was hard to catch a breath when lost within its haze.

As they finally entered the mansion, Raoul abandoned the girls without even a word or pleasantry, stomping off to his study like a belligerent child.

"He's really *that* angry because you sang?" Meg asked nervously as both she and Christine stared after the Vicomte.

"He'll make it seem that way, but...it's more than that," Christine replied. "Go up to bed, Meg. I...I need to talk to him."

Hesitant yet, Meg hugged Christine tight and told her, "Whatever he says, you were amazing, Christine. You belong on the stage even if he argues otherwise. You come to life when you sing."

"Erik would say the same." Merely mentioning his name made Christine long for his presence, for his praises and pride, everything she had been denied in their hasty departure. He would have made her stand taller and more defiant than she felt as she wearily left Meg and approached the quiet study. Erik would have made her certain that she'd done the right thing in a way that she was unable to fully believe on her own; no, her bravery would crumble beneath the Vicomte.

Raoul was seated at his desk, staring blankly at fisted hands resting atop the wood, his expression matching in its tense glare, and he did not regard her until she broke his thoughts with a gentle call. "Raoul?"

"You weren't supposed to sing," he muttered, still staring at fists. "I told you months ago. I said that if you loved me, you wouldn't sing again. Do you remember, Christine? If you loved me..."

"Your aunt told those ladies that I would," she

weakly attempted, internally scolding the futility of such an argument.

"But in the end, it was *your* choice. *You* were the one to stand upon that platform, and *you* were the one to sing and be the opera star once again."

"They don't know that," she protested. "They don't know about the opera; they just know that I'm trained-"

"And how long until someone figures it out?" he abruptly shouted as he darted to his feet. "How long until even one of them recognizes you? I have had to create such detailed lies about who you are and how we met. *Acceptable* lies. But they are not fools! Most of them keep city houses; did you never consider that? Some of them may have even *seen you* perform on the opera's stage! For God's sake, Christine, you've put our entire future in jeopardy!"

Even as she winced beneath his fury, she did not allow herself to break. No, she had withstood the temper of the almighty Opera Ghost, and his wrath was deadly compared to this. "I think you're being ridiculous," she insisted as strongly as she could. "All I did was sing a song."

"No, you put your past on display before all of society, the past I have so desperately tried to disconnect you from. You practically shouted to an audience of the elite that you were once an opera singer and whore to the Opera Ghost!"

"What?" She did not refrain from shouts and temper of her own. Not when such a detail was hoisted at her. "How dare you?"

"But it's true!" he yelled back. "*Everyone* knew your story, and I have diligently worked to make it inconsequential and give them no reason to think you and the Christine from the opera of Paris are one and the same. No one would have dared question me; even if they suspected, they never would have said a word against a Vicomte. But now you've made me look like a liar and destroyed both our reputations. All it takes is one person to speak the thought, and everyone will know the truth."

"And that is such a shame to you, isn't it?" she accused coldly. "To be marrying the phantom's 'whore'? ...How could you ever imply such a thing? Especially considering that you know the real story; you know who Erik is. You saw it played out before you."

"And you would recall that now?" he sharply demanded. "I have never once uttered a word about that night for your sake and sanity. I have never blamed you for what you did."

"What I did?" Christine was shaking down every limb with her growing rage. "I saved your life!"

"You chose to give yourself to another man!" he corrected in matching tone. "I am no fool! I know *exactly* what you did that night! A single kiss said it all! It was never about my imminent death. That was just a convenience to choose *him*; have you any idea how such a truth tortures me, Christine? To know that no matter what I do to make you happy, I can never be the one you chose and the one you wanted." The anguish was vividly brought forth from its place of burial, and it stung Christine and made her anger fade to tears that pinched the corners of her eyes.

"And that is equally why you don't want me to sing," she added in a soft breath. "You don't want society to know who I was, but you also don't want *me* to recall it. When I sing, ...it will always mean *him*."

No protest came, swallowed back in a full throat; the Vicomte simply commanded, "Promise me that you won't sing ever again, Christine. If you love me, you won't sing again."

The same guilt-laced order, and it struck Christine as harshly as it had in its first appearance months before. With its statement, the Vicomte cast her one more look and abruptly stalked out of his study, leaving her there, alone with her tears.

Two minutes. Two minutes spent in such misery, and she refused any more. Wiping away tears with the backs of her hands, she ran for the door and silently stepped out into the night. Her one thought was to get to Erik, but although she knew his current home was nearby, she had no idea how to find it in the dark. Perhaps she would become a lost wanderer in the woods and never come out again. But would that be such an awful fate when she could cause pain so easily that it was almost another talent?

Sense was begging her to return inside when suddenly, a strong arm caught her about the waist and drew her close. Comfort and solace were in one embrace, and she eagerly grasped back with fisted hands clenching the material of his suit jacket.

"That damn Vicomte," Erik muttered against her temple, wishing he could give more than an awkward kiss. "How dare he defile what was one of your most amazing performances? He has no taste for music; no, he always went to the opera only to steal your thunder and glory. And how he's manipulating you never to sing again!" His jaw locked with his anger; she could feel the tension of it against her forehead. "I once tried to take your life away by carrying you off and denying you sunlight and the world, and he condemned it. Now he does the same and expects it to be acceptable? No! He is degrading your talent!"

Christine felt disinclined to discuss it any longer, and curling tighter against him, she softly begged instead, "Take me with you, Erik. Please... Take me home with you."

He was not about to argue what he wanted so much, and easy as could be, he swept her into his arms, cradling her close as though she was his. ...Why couldn't she be his? And like days never forgotten, he took her away from her life and her world and brought her into his.

The journey was savored as much as anything. He took his time walking between tree trunks and brush, already having traveled this path enough times not to have to grant it more than the occasional glance. No, his attention yearned to be consumed only with Christine, and yet she kept her cheek pressed to his chest, refusing to share a look or a peek into her heart as if it would have proven too dangerous.

It was only as they entered the house, and he brought her through the foyer and into his living room that Christine lifted her head to survey the scene. Boxes littered most of the gaps of empty space between furniture, most of them opened and rummaged through, and only the objects spilling from the cardboard edges reminded her of his home at the opera. The rest of the décor was so decidedly not Erik, screaming of too much uppity sophistication. The couch he delicately set her atop looked as if it had never been used, never sat upon until now, and her thought was proven by the firmness of un-dented cushions against her back.

Only one point in the room was reminiscent of the underground house: the grand piano poised near the terrace doors with random pieces of music strewn atop its smooth surface. The corners of her lips tugged upward into a hinted smile with the musings of her mind. For as meticulous and organized as Erik was, when it came to music in the fit of any sort of playing or composing spree, the vicinity of his instruments would be a disaster of manuscript pages and dozens of ink wells every few inches within reach wherever he was working. What a reassuring vision to see the same now! It felt so much like home to her.

"Rest now, Christine," he gently commanded, curious to her pensive contemplations but afraid to ask. "You're safe here...with me as always."

Always... Without question, she curled tighter onto the unyielding cushions, laying her cheek against one of the ornate pillows at the corner and watching her companion steadily all the while as fixedly as he stared back, observing every movement she made as if insisting to himself that she was real.

"Forgive me for not having a room ready for you," he suddenly stammered, unusually flustered.

Desperate for some task to busy himself, he rushed to the hearth and bent to light a fire, speaking more eloquently and fluidly with distance. "All of your things are yet in your room in Paris. I was hasty with my packing and considered little more than getting to you once I knew you were alive. I could fill an upstairs room for you if you'd like, decorate it to your tastes and not the stuffiness of the previous owners. Anything you want, Christine. Name it, and I shall do it for you."

Flames sparked to life, and their residual warmth radiated to her shape and brushed eager caresses along her skin that she closed her eyes to appreciate. "It's still odd to me to fathom you aboveground and in the sunlight. I had always been convinced that even had I not left that final night, our future would have remained under the opera house."

"No, no," he chided gently, turning to gaze upon her unnoticed and trail his own added caresses with fire's glow upon the smooth perfection of her skin. "I would have bought you a house, a real house in the world. I could not shackle you to shadows; I didn't want to."

"But...do you like being away from the protection of the catacombs?"

"It would have been easier with you beside me," he revealed and watched her eyes flutter open and regard him with apprehension at their corners. And yet he did not recoil from conversation. "I imagined it to exact precision in my mind. Every detail of our life together would have been simple in its complications if I had you to stand by my side and love me in spite of society's shunning."

"Society's shunning?"

"Well, of course. It could be no other way. You would sing at the opera with your adoring, masked husband in the audience every night and never caring that they stared; they'd always stare, but my eyes would only be yours. And I would arrange for us to own the largest, most elegant house in the city, practically toss our existence into society's face. We'd force them down together with no one to ever defeat us."

Another tentative smile was her response, far more than words could speak. "You'd have me sing, and Raoul...well, you heard him tonight. He would murder that piece of my life without a thought; he already did! All of Paris thinks I am in the grave... Some of his intentions are genuine, but some are purely selfish. He wanted to disassociate me from my life, but I think he's simply ashamed of it, ...of me."

"Ashamed of perfection? My God, what more could he want? You are worth so much more than a single person in that room tonight. You shined like a beacon was upon you, a light beaming across your skin, and when you sang, ...Christine, I don't think I've ever been prouder of you. I've seen you be the diva of the opera stage and occasionally stand up to La Carlotta and her ego, but this! You faced all of society and put your real self on display, not the persona the Vicomte has created and tried to mold you to be. You were glorious, and a part of that was a result of your bravery. I've never seen you so strong."

His praises made a red blush tint her cheeks, and she purposely kept her head low to the pillow in hopes he would not notice. But every word permeated into her heart and thrilled her as poignantly as days past when she had strived to please an angel.

Anxiousness was in the air between them, and almost suddenly, Erik got to his feet and hurried to his piano. "I have something for you."

"Music?" she eagerly asked, unwilling to share how desperately she'd missed exactly that: waking in his home to the sound of a melody echoing into her room, begging him to play for her so often that she adored every time he touched a piano. Now was no different as she lifted herself onto her elbows and watched him with expectant eyes. "Did you...write me something?"

His very inspiration in one beautiful body.

How often had he composed simply to impress her? "Music was playing to deaf ears when you were gone. I had no taste for it. It was as if it didn't make sense to me when you weren't in the world to hear it. ...When I learned that you were alive, I wrote this."

He was the portrait of a virtuoso as he sat high and poised atop the piano bench, quickly finding the piece he was after amidst the mess and spreading it out for observance. Truly, he did not need it, not when every note and chord was emblazoned in his soul. His only concern was faltering now that he was finally playing it for its muse when he'd fantasized this scene so perfectly for days. So he did not glance at her, but he did not regard written notes either. He stared fixedly ahead, seeing colors in melodies and emotions in every line as he began to play, feelings made tangible across ivory keys.

Tingling down her spine with the first few pitches, Christine listened and felt every emotion as acutely as she was sure he had when he had written it, seeping through skin and into bone with their power. *This* was music. How had she lived months without it? When every legato line made her aware that she was alive and breathing with its motion? Unconscious tears slipped free to tumble down her cheeks as his hope carried through a piano's timbre and insisted everything he'd experienced in one revelation.

As he struck the last chords and let them ring out to nothing, he insisted before even a look at her, "It isn't long. I composed it quickly between packing, and it was encumbered by my own impatience. By you..." He stole a glance at her and sighed softly. "You're crying, and I see everything I intended in your eyes. And why would I have ever wanted to compose again if I couldn't have this expression as mine?"

Brushing her tears away, she rested her head back onto her pillow and shared an unending stare with a genius. "Will you play more for me, *ange*? I...I long to hear your music."

He never hesitated, not when music always

spoke volumes compared to the limitations of words. Gentle, lilting melodies sang forth from the piano's hammers and crept through Christine's body, lulling her to sleep with every beautiful line. It was just too blissful to be like this, in the place she'd missed for so long, being serenaded by music that was as ethereal as heaven and certainly not meant for the scope of the living world. All she could think as her mind drifted to dreamscape was that this was what her future was meant to be.

Erik played on even after he knew she was asleep, hoping that his music would accompany the journey of her unconscious and sing to her soul. But even when he drew the mélange of melodies to a close, he did not quit her presence. With the fire in the hearth as his ally, dancing beams across her features, he sat in a nearby chair and watched her sleep, reading his forever in the nuances of peaceful breaths and closed, crescent-shaped lashes.

*****

Sunlight was a stark contrast to the warm implications of flames in the hearth, and the brightness of its natural glow peering in from parted curtains returned awareness to Christine as her eyes fluttered open and surveyed her surroundings. She was alone, and it seemed unusual when she could practically feel Erik's aura lingering in the room from the chair where she had no doubt he'd spent the night gazing at her.

It was hardly odd or disconcerting, not when she knew he had done so before, watching her sleep and marveling over her existence in his life. She had caught him once ages ago when she had spent the night in his house. She had been looming in that place between dream and reality when she had heard the click of her bedroom door and so careful, so as not to be noticed, she had peeked out of one closed lid and had witnessed the approach of a dark silhouette to her bedside. It should have frightened her then, should have made her loath ever to return to him, but he had done nothing that meant harm, not even a touch. And she had spent the night half-awake listening to his even breaths so near and feeling strangely safe in his company. Angel to no end, even when disfigured murderer had been the more fitting appellation.

Within moments of sitting up on the cushions and smoothing back her falling hair with anxious hands, he appeared, striding gracefully into the room with an uncommon smile that made masked features seem pleasant. "Good morning," he greeted en route to draw back the curtains and let creeping sunlight fully stream inside.

One unwanted thought came with the sun's glow, and reluctant to speak it aloud, she whispered, "I should get back."

All at once, his smile fell and faded as if its presence had been imagined. "Should you? A return to the world that is swallowing you in its recesses."

"Erik," she called gently, her expression equally as somber, "of course I'd rather stay here with you, but...I can't."

"You can," he corrected, approaching her abruptly and leaning near. "You belong here with me; you know that, no matter what you think that you owe the Vicomte."

"And how long until you doubt me again?" she suddenly demanded, attempting to match his aggression even if she failed in its inception. "How long before every dream you planned for us becomes only the nightmare again where you lock me up in your cage to keep me as yours alone, until fear makes you question every word of my affection and reverts us back to the place we were months ago?"

Fire blazed in his eyes, ignited and inspired with one vibrant conclusion. "You'd like that, wouldn't you? That's what you're doing with all of this! With your avoidance to rid yourself of the Vicomte! You want me to be the monster again and force you, to carry you off and lock you up and make the choice *you want* for you! Because if I do, then it lessens your guilt; then you can blame me for the fact that you love me and left dear Raoul at the altar. You want the monster to take the choice out of your hands!" He bent near to her as she recoiled in reply, shrinking back into the couch's cushions and refusing to admit a single word.

"You foolish child!" Erik snapped, fisting urgent hands to refrain from giving into his rage and clasping her, terrified he would shake sense into her before he could stop himself. "I've offered you more than that this time, and I won't be the strong one between us any longer. You showed me last night that you can be as convicted as I can and brave enough to accept your own choices. I won't beg for your love and let my desire steal it from you on my whims again. If you want me, if you *love me*, *you* will make the choice." His addled mind recalled the Vicomte's use of the same coercion, and he quickly corrected, "This is not a manipulation, Christine, and not some cruel game to be played. This is a liberation. You need to live *your* life as *you* want. The Vicomte has you twisted to his wants, and I have done little better, always pushing you down my own path. No more!" Impulse restrained, he jerked away and stalked a fitful path to the piano, leaning his fisted hands upon its wood. "Go back to your Vicomte and decide what you want. Decide if *I* am enough for *you*. You know what I offer; I've sought to show you as much. But I will not be tempted to fall to your ruses of avoidance. No, I'm determined *never* to be that monster again. Go on. Quit teasing me with your presence; I don't want to see you unless you are mine."

Christine hesitated, swallowing back tears, but he was refusing even one shared look, his stance rigid with his pent-up aggression. *To be his...* Could she ever be his? Stumbling to her feet, she gave him one last glance, shaking violently all over, before she fled the house, darting out of its protective door and into sunlit woods. All she could think about was the blatant reality that whatever she chose, lives were about to be ruined, and it would only be her fault.

*****

Daylight passed in an unending stagnation that Christine felt sickened to endure. The same routine over again, wedding plans interspersed, every detail achieved with a dull luster to her usual shine. And this was to be her life? Millions of moments just like these, survived half-alive and yearning, *always* yearning? Erik wanted her to make the choice when it was already made; the difficult part was following through on its details. But she put on a role for the Vicomte's sake and was the Christine he wanted, quiet and submissive and listening to his every word as if it meant something important all day long. If nothing else, it left her undoubting. A choice... And she knew that it had been made long ago.

Twilight meant supper with the Comtesse as per their usual pattern, but Christine was disinclined to wait any longer. Careful not to be observed, she slid out one of the mansion's backdoors, often used for her escapes to the garden. This time a garden was not suitable enough, and she went further, following the path she'd traveled only that morning with nervous anticipation lightening every step. A choice, ...and this was hers.

*****

It had been some form of unnamed torture to keep from her all day, but Erik had been adamant and unwavering, pacing the floor when music was an unkind traitor and produced too many thoughts of her. He couldn't even look at the couch as his subconscious returned memories of her asleep atop its cushions, peaceful and so unwittingly his at the time.

His, he was fantasizing its implications so intently that at first a knock at the door seemed a hallucination. It took a second utterance of its impeding sound for him to accept it as reality, and he was anxious as he rushed to reply, afraid disappointment would sever hope at its source.

"Christine..."

375

She barely passed the threshold before she was in his arms, darting into his embrace as if it meant salvation, and he did not put distance between, clutching her back and clinging to her as he had only imagined.

"I'm yours; I'm yours," she was muttering against the crease of his neck. "I'm *always* yours."

"And that is *your* choice then?" he pushed yet never dared to release her. His entire body shivered to feel her breath tickle the flesh just within his collar. "Yours, made freely and without manipulation; yours, that you will stand and defend even as the world aligns against us?"

"Yes, yes," she fervently declared. "But tell me that you believe me, *ange*. Promise that you won't doubt my heart."

"And what does your heart say, Christine?" His desperation was unavoidable and thickened his tone, the need to know, to hear words he had dreamt upon her lips.

"That I love you," she confided without pause, "and if you will doubt and distrust spoken oaths, then I have proof."

Erik was still reeling from the sound of one sentence, but his curiosity piqued as she drew away and slipped her hand into the pocket of her gown. Held up to his inspection was the letter she'd written four months before, the one he had brought with his appearance, and with it was another scrap, the missing piece that had been torn free, set in place now to weave its severed, jagged edge.

"My words in my own hand," she told him. "I found the rest of it in Raoul's desk. He couldn't get rid of it; maybe it reminded him why he did what he felt he must. Read the rest of the letter, Erik. It was meant to be yours."

Brow lined beneath the mask's concealment, he took the letter into his shaking hands and read her words aloud. " 'I loved you and you condemned me... Condemned to be alone with a bleeding heart. I beg you to make this torment stop. Hatred is my enemy, for it is as demanding and possessive as love. I cannot separate one from the other, and I cannot truly hate what I love so much. I want you still; I will always want you. Come back for me, *ange*. Repair the heart you destroyed. I will be dead inside until you do. What heart can live without its beat? I love you, Erik. I should have said so and gave my choice meaning. I'll say it now. I love you... Come for me.'"

Every sentence pierced his heart with its sincerity, and as he stared at it and let her elegant cursive become a blended mass of revelations, she filled in what wasn't there. "I waited for you. I was so sure that you'd eventually come, but you never did."

"I thought you were dead," he distantly declared.

"Yes, but I didn't know that. I felt sure it meant that you didn't want me." She was desperate to capture his attention when secrets on a page were all he'd see, and with little pause to consider, she brought her hand to his mask and lifted its interfering presence away. "I love you, Erik," she repeated to astounded scars and their variations.

"And do you realize what you say?" The edge of urgency in his voice inspired her trepidation as he dangled a letter between them. "You begged me to come for you, to take you away, the same things I condemned myself for. I wanted to be more than that for you, to give you more, and you would have taken me as I was: monster, murderer, every sin upon my soul. You wanted me... Christine, this is a monster before you, but he loves you more than any ordinary man ever could and needs you so intensely that he will die again without you. ...And does that please you?"

She nodded with resolution, and his stare was riveted to the motion of dark curls, only able to consider their graceful sway and the fact that if he wanted to, he could reach out and touch them as if he had the right to do so. Her eyes were practically goading him to it, and with a new sense of hesitation, he indulged himself and gently touched the silk of those spun curls, weaving his fingers into their soft mass.

"Tell me what you want, Christine," he encouraged, desperate not to let her see how deeply affected he was by such an innocent touch. For the first time, it was truly *his*; he didn't have to ask permission or consider the guilt and fiancé waiting in the wings. This wouldn't be taken away from him again.

"What I want...," she repeated skeptically, too focused on the fervency of his stare to conceive much else.

"I laid a future at your feet last night," he continued, thrilling to know that he wore no mask and it didn't matter to either of them. "I gave you my intended concept of our life together, and you were so careful not to say a word about its details. So I pose it to you. Tell me what you envision our future to be. Anything you want I will give you."

"I want you," she stated, simple as that.

"And to sing?"

"To sing," she breathed amidst an undeniable smile. "Yes, to sing...and the music, but you would have given me such things without a request."

"And," he hesitated a breath, tentative yet in his proposal, "...marriage, Christine?" As quickly as he suggested it, he hastily added, "I haven't hauled a wedding gown up from the catacombs with the intention of forcing it upon you again. It will not be the same. You thought I wanted you as a prisoner, to love me as I saw fit, and maybe at that time, you were right. I couldn't have just loved you and let you love me back. But now...you are the other half of myself. I've no doubt that such sentiments exist as truth. I want to love you as such. ...I won't force it upon you." It felt essential to repeat such an imperative point, and the hand still twined in her hair trembled with his wariness as he scanned the play of emotions upon her face for an answer.

"I was to marry the Vicomte in two days," she softly replied, "and it never felt right. He tried to please me, but it could only be empty when affection was one-sided. You tried the same once. You were so desperate to keep me that you wanted to love for both of us."

"This isn't the same."

"No, it's not. You've put it before me and *asked* for my love instead of taking it. And if it is my choice now with an answer to be freely declared, then I *choose* to marry you."

That damaged face with its resilient scars looked the closest to beautiful that she'd ever seen it as he smiled with adoration, trailing mismatched eyes over her features, still seeming afraid to touch more than her hair and have it be acceptable. "A marriage and a future freely chosen, ...and I leave the rest up to you as well."

"The rest..." She already had an idea what he referred to. *The rest...* And as his hand tightened its grip in her hair, she had no doubt that she was right.

"I would never force that upon you either, not even the first time marriage was our option. Back under the opera house, marriage meant companionship. I just wanted you to stay. Anything else, ...well, it wasn't intended. You were still so unsure and afraid of me that I couldn't rationalize expecting more than idle caresses that hopefully one day would bear no suspicion in their background or worry of disgust. But you are no longer that girl, Christine. You've allowed my kiss and touch and shown no disgust in return. And...marriage can just mean companionship if you want; it need not be anything else if desire will frighten you away."

She was thoughtful over his words, keeping her trepidation in the forefront and never denied, and still carrying her uncertainty in her hands, she said, "You've always treated me like porcelain a step away from breaking in your hands. Whenever desire would appear between us, you were as timid and apprehensive as I was, and you let me run rather than assuage my fears with answers. I was always terrified that it would consume me completely and I'd never be myself again, and I think you were equally as afraid but unwilling to tell me."

"I've never felt anything as I feel for you," he admitted plainly, toying with her curls. "I can barely control it; how could I keep from frightening you if I gave in?"

"I'm not going to be afraid anymore," she decided even if the tremor in her voice spoke otherwise. "I won't run, and I won't break. But you cannot run from it either. I want to feel desire, yours and mine, and know that it won't steal my soul with it. Show me, Erik. ...Will you?" Under her persuasive cajoling, she leaned close, always victim of his apprehensive stare, and dared to press two delicate kisses to the misshapen arch of his upper lip, whispering again in the fraction of air between, "...Will you?"

He couldn't refuse her, not as every bit of him gave a reaction in violent shivers and shudders of need. Everything he'd ever tried to keep contained within his grasp, only peeking out in fragments when it burned him inside, was now all he could consider. A letter of admission joined a mask on the floor, unneeded and discarded as he collected her into eager arms, dragging her willingly to his chest and pressing her close. "I would give you everything," he gasped, setting timid kisses to her temple and brow. "Everything, Christine. Everything I am and everything I'll be."

"Everything I am," she agreed and encircled him in her arms, molding her body close and fitting it to his shapes. "Everything is yours, *ange*."

As he found her lips with his, she anticipated the contact, tilting her face upward and meeting his motion as his mouth inspired sensation that traveled through her and settled with an empty ache at her center. It was as terrifying as it was wanted, and when she once would have broken away and fled, she forced herself to remain and respond, to allow the waves of need to overcome her.

Gentle was no longer a consideration as evaporated as constraint, and Erik did not avoid impulse's pull, parting her lips with his anticipating tongue to taste her. He shuddered at her sweetness and burned to feel an equaled reaction travel her limbs, her body arching closer, firmer to his, wanting to be an inseparable whole and not an incomplete half.

Christine felt comprehension fade in and out of her grasp, lost for a moment of pure passion and return to encourage more and urge her to touch him. It took a couple of attempts beneath such sense-stealing power to convince her hand to loosen its stable grip upon his shoulder and seek his scars, its compass briefly spinning without direction until she could cup his cheek. These scars were hers, and they grounded her in reality and whispered without voice that this was *her* Erik and beneath every confidence, he was as untouched as she was and as unavoidably timorous.

One kiss, and he drew back to search her eyes and their hazy languidness, but blue depths showed no rising terror, no regrets, nothing to unravel the web of need encompassing eager hearts. How he savored that sight! Engraining it into the eye of memory, it would be his for all eternity, the woman he'd loved forever loving and wanting him in return, holding his disfigured cheek in her palm as if it meant only skin and bones. He wanted to cry as intensely as he wanted to kiss her again!

"Come on," he bid, voice thick with wanting and emotion, and capturing her hand in his, he led her up the staircase at the front of the foyer, watching her at every moment.

"Why are you so surprised?" she inquired, reading it vividly across his unconcealed features.

"You are not the same girl I once knew," Erik

told her as he guided her through the doorway of what he loosely-termed his bedroom. "You were such an innocent child always on the verge of doubting every proof of your own soul. Now...you're so strong, Christine. It amazes me."

She did not deny his words; she only said, "Wisdom comes from having your heart broken and believing you'd never breathe again. The pain of loss... I had to be strong to endure believing I'd never have this again and see you look at me with such love in your eyes. I had to be strong to marry someone else and only have the love in *his* eyes as meager compensation."

"His eyes," Erik restated it solemnly, unwilling to show her the true bitterness such a bleak reality brought to life. *Almost...* Drawing her into the center of the room, he suddenly pulled her close again, rubbing claiming hands up and down her back to be seared with the natural heat of her flesh.

Even as Christine conceded, her curious gaze peered over his shoulder and wandered the corners of the room. More boxes and little of Erik. The only detail she could discern as his was the suit laid across a chair, dark as he liked when the color palette of this master bedroom was disturbingly bright. She was sure that come daylight when the sun would filter in, it would be positively blinding in its every hue.

"What are you thinking?" he asked with an undeniable rush of amusement to witness her revealing smile.

"Just that after we're married, I must insist upon a new residency."

"As if I'd want to live an estate away from your jilted fiancé's aunt!" he teased back, oddly comfortable in her presence. For the first time, teasing felt natural and *normal*, and when her smile only beamed, he savored its every nuance.

"Not just that, but...well, the underground house was more ours than this place ever could be."

"Ours," he breathed in awe before he could nod

agreement. "Yes, it was *ours*, and I promise to give you a home in the sunlight that is equally so. Every aspect will be fitting to *our* tastes. Does that please you?"

"Very much. But you forget that Paris thinks I'm dead," Christine reminded, lifting an impatient hand to outline the features of his face.

Eyes closing to savor every innocent caress, he concluded, "There are other opera houses in the world. Paris isn't the only capitol for the arts. We'll find someplace better." Her fingertips were grazing the space left vacant for a nose, and he abruptly arched his face upward to lay kisses to her gentle hand. "You're trembling, Christine," he revealed what she did not say. "Are you afraid to touch me?"

"I don't want to hurt you," she insisted, yet tentative as her fingers resumed their path and brushed stark formations of exposed bone. "Does my touch cause you pain, Erik?"

"No, no, not pain," he muttered, closing his lids again to concentrate on soft fingertips against dead flesh. "I've never been touched this way before. Not even my own hands have touched my face if it could be avoided, never gentle, never with such caring and longing attached. You touch me as if you are aching to do so."

"But I am," she said without hesitation, and leaning closer, she dared to transform a touch of fingers into a touch of lips, kissing a path along those tattered features and feeling his flesh quiver beneath her ministrations and a muffled cry of disbelief as it vibrated in his lungs. She was watching him carefully as she continued, noting that his eyelids were yet screwed shut and refusing to regard the scene, and as her lips gently grazed the space above his ear, she bid, "Open your eyes, my Erik. Don't be lost in a dream; this is real."

It was as if she had read his fear, and he was reluctant to comply, knowing how quickly dreams flitted away from those who yearned the most. But she was adamant to tempt him, fitting her mouth against his, a hinted kiss first before she grew bold and gave it meaning.

No doubts, Christine had not a single one, and she was determined that he wouldn't either as she molded her lips to his. No, this was hers, and she was marking it as such as she dared to taste him this time with the tingling tip of her tongue, thrilling to be abruptly collected in firm arms and held closer and flush to the length of his body, to feel the true extent of his desire, unhindered and never dimmed back to a smolder.

"You mean to outdo every dream I've ever had, don't you?" he teased in the merest gap between longing mouths as he leaned close enough to press his forehead to hers. His eyes fluttered open, passion displayed in his mismatched depths. "To prove your existence and that no dream could ever be so feverishly constructed? You know that I've dreamt of this so often that it feels like fantasy is now bleeding into my reality. Isn't that right, Christine? But tell me, *ange*, have *you* ever dreamt the same? In all this time, was I the dream you harbored and yet suffered as a nightmare to believe it would never come true?"

"It's coming true now," she insisted back, her hand tracing scars again. "And I refuse to recall the emptiness in between and doubt reality now that I am touching it with my fingertips."

"But I was *haunted*." Erik's soft admission caused a shiver down her spine; haunted by ghosts, ...*her* ghost. It was as disconcerting as being told that she was believed dead. "It was truly the nearest to insanity that I've ever been, and I would have embraced it fully if it meant I wouldn't be alone and without you. A ghost is a disappointment, worse than a dead body even, because it calls to mind what one can't have with such vivid realism that it is only intangibility that gives its true definition away. I would touch you, and you wouldn't be there, unsubstantial, cold, not this warm, breathing, *living* body I now hold. ...I was so certain that I'd only ever have ghosts as mine."

His pain created the tears in her eyes, and she suddenly wrapped both arms about him and burrowed her head against his neck, clutching tight enough to feel his heartbeat as an echo of her own. "I'm yours," she breathed as she had earlier. "And I will be yours in life and death and on every plane of existence. I love you too much to ever leave you alone."

His hands brushed idly through her curls, sliding in and out of their mass to tease the line of her back, and he was pleased with himself to feel her shiver and arch closer into him. His, yes, she was his...*finally.* "Christine," he whispered as he set random kisses to her brow, "do you desire me?"

She was sure that he already knew his own answer as she quivered eagerly against him, but she indulged his request and replied, "I desire you, Erik."

His roaming hands were within the curtain of her locks again, and his quaking fingers found the clasps of her gown. Diligently from the nape of her neck to her waist, he unhooked every one, impatient for material to part and give way to the gloriousness beneath.

Christine remained frozen in her place, feeling the tug and release of every clasp, and trepidation only rose as the last one succumbed and the gown was drawn free of her body. Their embrace was broken for his intentions, and she stared with eyes that could not halt their widening, for the first time feeling utterly vulnerable in only her underclothes. A ravenous gaze swept the length of her, and she was the victim to the sheer intensity he could exude in a look alone, the power of it practically sewn into his aura, a threat but also an omnipotence. It was his Opera Ghost persona, the phantom they called him, and it often surpassed the real surreptitious uncertainty of the man behind it. He wanted to seem in control. But she knew better, and it made her calm and smile.

"What is that look?" he demanded, trying to be coherent when his eyes were feasting on the vision of her in white silk with much more pale skin exposed than he had ever seen before.

But she did not dare tell him that she knew of his apprehension. She just held his eye resolutely and reached for the ties of her corset, unraveling its binding with suddenly steady fingers. It fell away with a soft plop against the carpet, and without hesitation, she began to discard the rest a piece at a time, refusing modesty to stifle her or appear as more than a faint pink blush upon the vast expanse of flesh coming into view. She halted when all that remained was a thin chemise that barely grazed the top of her thigh and trembled in spite of her bravado to watch him burn as his fiery eyes traced the lengths of her legs and lingered at every curve and joint.

"Why did you stop?" His voice was thick and hoarse, giving away his need so poignantly as it skittered across her skin, and words evaded her, nothing but a blush to be her answer. With a fond smile that upturned the corners of misshapen lips, he posed, "Are you shy?"

"As shy as you are nervous," she insisted back with the slightest waver as her betrayer. "Argue it if you'd like, but I know you well, *ange*."

Any banter grew tainted with an odd severity she had not expected, and as he solemnly drew off his jacket and reached for the buttons of his shirt cuffs, he softly said, "I have ample reason for hesitations. ...There's something I've never told you, Christine. I... Well, I never thought it would need to be considered when this situation seemed a far-fetched fantasy. And now...perhaps showing you would be best."

Buttons undone, he jerked his sleeves up and revealed the white skin of his arms, studying her carefully all the while. Scars, faded but obvious along each inner wrist. It was unneeded to say what they meant.

"Why...why did you do that to yourself?" she

demanded, overcome in an air of horror that she had not known since the days she'd learned his last secret built in scars.

Exhaling a harsh breath that deflated his usual poised posture, he was uncertain of the answer himself at first, pondering memories before forming an intelligible conclusion. "I've been treated viciously and violently all of my life; pain was never the issue or the sense of being unwanted and undeserving to live. I was accustomed to degradation and shame. No, I did this...out of guilt."

Christine edged close to him again, and catching his extended arms in her hands, she studied the damage. It would have been done brutally, deep cuts to leave this sort of lingering evidence. "Guilt..."

"I am not emotionless for the lives I've taken," he told her, watching her with never a glimpse at his own marks. "It may seem simple for someone like me to end a life. I have justification for the pain I've endured as humanity's monster. But...I remember each and every person that I've sinned against; most were victims of my rash need to play a god on this level of existence, to have power to make up for the injustices done to me and make them suffer instead. I actually convinced myself that it was my right to decide life and death because of my face. Ridiculous, isn't it? No human being should have the privilege of omnipotence at his fingertips. Guilt for my inflicted horrors made me long for death, but suicide is a damning offense, more so than murder. It takes away God's right to condemn to the hellfire by already condemning oneself. It is choosing eternal agony before it is chosen for you." Studying the rise and fall of stirring curls, he told her, "It was agony when I believed the lie and considered you had done the same. You never deserved condemnation, especially for loving me. My saving grace was the conviction that I would meet you there someday, somewhere in the hellfire. Eternal suffering seemed the only way I'd ever be able to have you."

Her fingertip traced the lines, unable to fully comprehend reality when the skin before her was Erik's, and with a furrow that marred her brow and tattled the depth of her thoughts, she asked, "How were you saved?"

"Nadir, my Persian friend, ...friend loosely-defined at present. He foolishly believed it best to help the Vicomte trick me, and that is only his most recent offense on our supposed friendship. Knowing my past... He was afraid I would return to such masochistic behavior when I was told that you were gone and barely left me alone. He never saw that I had learned my lesson and wouldn't follow that route again."

"But...did you never consider it?" Gentle as could be, Christine lifted one wrist to her lips and claimed its condemning scar with a kiss.

Half-distracted by her motions, he almost could not find the ability to speak, shivering at the contact of soft, warm lips making something beautiful out of a tragedy. "I...I won't lie to you. Yes, I considered it against better judgment. To find you sooner on that plane of damnation... But I had a ghost to keep me company and sing in my ear, and I couldn't abandon her yet. It's positively absurd, but my own hallucinating mind was my salvation. ...Oh God, Christine what are you doing to me?"

Her lips curved into a tempting grin even as her tongue delicately trailed the sensitive flesh of his inner wrist, innocence falling to the backdrop when his eyes showed such fire in return. "I'm making you grateful that suicide was the one thing you ever failed at in your lifetime. Just the idea... The concept of never having known you... Erik, you changed my life. I would have always felt your loss without ever knowing why, half a person wandering the world alone."

"That was my existence before you." His hand caught her wrist this time, clutching it captive, and he guided it to his misshapen lips, brushing thankful kisses to perfection instead of damage. As she held her breath within her lungs, he imitated her teasing game and let his tongue trail the undisturbed threads of her veins, life beating in a flustered pulse against him. "Christine," he breathed against her skin, "I want you so much that it is consuming me, *ange*."

Her lids were heavy with his promises and their husky letters, and he watched her succumb as he lay idle kisses along her inner arm to the soft crook of her elbow, knowing she was as overcome as he was with the power of need.

Eager hands were reaching for the hem of her chemise, and Christine was surprised at how stable his grip was, confident and determined when she still quivered all over. Quiver became a shake as the silk was guided up and over her head, each inch tickling her skin on its ascent and inevitable disappearance; it abandoned her and left her entirely exposed to feverish eyes that raked intangible caresses up and down along every nuance and pale, flawless flesh meant for only him to know.

Before intelligible speech could return to his lips, Erik guided an impatient hand from the rounded shape of one shoulder across the blank expanse of her chest and lower until he could barely graze one breast with his fingertips. A whimper slid free from her lips with the jolt that raced down limbs inspired by that one solitary caress. Such overwhelming sensation! And from only a single touch! It almost frightened her to consider the intensity that more would incite, and yet she equally had no desire to ask him to cease, not when his adoration seared to her inner bones with its flames.

"Why do I deserve the right to touch you with these blood-stained hands?" he was muttering more to himself, but even with such a musing, he did not possess the ability to sever contact. His fingers dared to trail the hardened peak of her breast, and as her contained whimpers swelled to a definite cry, he felt possessed by the responding throb his body gave, like an answer to an echo. Tentative was lost as his hand cupped the full weight with her eager nipple making its presence distinct and urgent against his palm.

Touch wasn't enough; for the first time, he was desperate to have more than that, and watching her at every motion so that her responses could become his own, he bent and laid gentle kisses along the side of her throat, burrowing wanting, misshapen lips against skin so soft and sensitive that she went rigid and nervously fisted a terrified hand in his hair.

Hovering an inch from yearning skin, he whispered with a breath that tickled its path along her goose bump covered flesh, "And if my hands have no right to a touch, then my lips are far more undeserving yet. They're ugly and malformed, and yet they are kissing perfection as if they could be worthy."

Arguments to be posed in return were flitting on her tongue, but she could barely sift through their phrases and make sense of them. Words, but words were lackluster when his body was so near to her own that it was tempting her to forget everything but this moment in the long stitches of time. Forget words, or so she decided, and the hand she tangled in his hair answered for her, guiding those malformed lips back to the expectant crease of her throat as an urgent necessity.

Complying with a groan, he ravished that spot with kiss after kiss, never enough, never another doubt. Doubt was inconsequential when she was arching so fitfully into him and losing sounds of her delight that were memorized by his musician's ear like an audible memory to be replayed at will.

Patience had never been his strong point, and it was minimally intact when she was bare and pressed to him as if searching for skin with his clothing as an obstacle in between. In mere minutes, patience dwindled, and with an abruptness that made her sway and start, he swept her body into demanding arms and carried her to the awaiting bed.

"Still shy?" he teased even if the hoarseness in

his voice etched it out provocatively instead.

"No, ...no," she muttered and missed his nearness as he delicately rested her upon the mattress, laying her amidst bright dyes. Her mind formed its own teasing replies about the very idea of Erik sleeping in such a bed, but a tongue-tied mouth never spoke them. How could speech matter when her eyes were riveted to his elegant, long fingers and their motion with each button of his shirt that they freed? One, another, another, and her eager gaze fixed on the white skin revealed, paler than hers in its tones, almost flawless, ...*almost*.

"More scars," she managed to state, soft and yet so very heavy in its insinuation, and scooting on her knees to the edge of the bed, she let her fingertips find each and every one as he worked to remove his shirt. She did not need to ask for an explanation to know the source of such brutality; mankind was just that cruel. And she was sure that even though these were the wounds to eventually scar, there had been others, too, less severe, and bruises that had faded as if they had never existed. Such injustice in a world over-laden with bitter reality, and it certainly made an old illusion of an angel with white wings seem preferred, a dream of perfection when so many flaws were the actuality.

Erik watched her in awed adoration, touching him without hesitation and fingers that were adamant in every trek across random scars. He had to wonder if she had any idea how honest his earlier statements had been and how unworthy of her love he truly felt. Perfection kneeling before him, *touching him*, loving him as if he mattered in the world he'd always abhorred. He could want her to the depths of his being, and yet he knew he'd always feel undeserving.

"Christine..." His hands were unable to keep still and weaved in and out of her hair, and the only thought making sense in his desire-filled mind was that he loved her. Dear God, how he loved her!

Patience was sought again and yet unfound,

and Erik finally gave up trying as his hands coiling in her hair emerged to catch her shoulders and guide her back, his flashing eyes insisting what he wanted.

And Christine did not recall to be shy or trepid, not as she watched him finish disrobing with hazy eyes, curling back onto the mattress and awaiting as if he brought her destiny with him. Her innocent eyes studied his body as intently as he still regarded hers at every opportunity, and as she observed every sculpted detail and every inch of white skin, she grew as impatient as he was, yearning only to know his flesh against hers.

With a silent question always in the background, Erik laid beside her on the bed, and he could not contain a sincere smile as she immediately wrapped longing arms around him and pulled him close, content to feel the blissful contact of skin.

His hands made idle paths over any inch, up and down the shapes of her arms, along the features of her face, tracing her spine, and as he thrilled himself with her warmth and tangibility, he dared to press his hardness more firmly against the soft skin of her abdomen, surprised that even though she felt its need, she did not draw away. No, he glimpsed not even an inkling of fear when he had been so certain that would be all she would know.

Christine was too intrigued to be afraid, the breath catching in her throat at skin, so much skin against her own. One touch was always overwhelming when it was granted by Erik's hands, a million at once were an exquisite sort of torture. It was touching the ethereal existence of a star and learning the exhilaration of its beams through every facet, deep enough to brand bones with its engraving to insist possession.

Focus shifted in and out, and as it was snared by the soft moan of delight that escaped him, she arched her hips closer, tempting and bold when his manhood gave a desperate pulsation in reply. And why then would she succumb to the pull of modesty when this felt so necessary? In another life and another time, she had run head-first, and this time she was choosing to fall heart-first. Running had lost her precious moments of truly *living*; she would never follow that mistake again.

"Please, Erik," she whispered when the only hesitation was yet his. Arching against him again to illicit another uninhibited moan, she insisted adamantly, "Don't stop."

Sense was already far too overcome as he felt himself burning along every contact with a searing flame, and never separating an inch, he shifted atop her, careful, so careful with her. The backs of his fingers grazed idle caresses along her cheek, keeping her yearning stare captive in his so he could marvel over everything she felt.

His heart begged him to be gentle, but as he felt her wetness, felt how much she desired *him*, he couldn't deny impulse as it ached to be buried within her. In a swift and determined thrust, he entered her, but the thrill was torn in two with her sharp cry as her muscles tensed and fingertips flexed rigid against his shoulder blades.

"Forgive me," he immediately begged in a hoarse whisper, setting consoling kisses to the crown of her ducked head. "Please, dear God, Christine, forgive me for hurting you, but...*ange*, you are so wet... I had to be inside of you." More kisses were pressed along her hairline and into a mass of disheveled curls, and delirious with the need to continue, he restrained movement and desperately sought to keep attention anywhere but on the consuming sensation of her wetness surrounding him. "Christine," he breathed her name like a reverent adoration, "I never knew it would feel this way..." He was teasing her with the words, tempting her with each utterance. "I'm *yours*, yours forever now. Won't you look at me? ...I may not be the most handsome prize, but..."

That did it, and he nearly smiled even in the

midst of twisting need when she immediately lifted her head, twining her arms tighter about him, and pressed kiss after kiss to his lips and scars as if to prove him wrong with every sweet token.

"You are mine," she insisted as she nuzzled her cheek against his damaged one, "and to me, you are beautiful." As she spoke, she was the one to shift her hips closer to him, gasping a breath with the surprising swell of sensation that overcame lingering pain; pain was an afterthought and only faded further from consideration as he gave in and slowly began to move.

"Christine," he bid in a moan, "I don't want to hurt you."

"You're not," she assured back, rising and sinking to meet his every thrust as shivers raced her skin with the power of her wanting. She pressed her lips in an infinite kiss against his cheek, and it muffled soft cries that tried to break loose and words that made no sense to her clouded mind, pleadings never to stop, never to let go, ...requests for more.

It was all too fleeting, something she was desperate to clasp forever in her hands, and yet it evaded her as suddenly as it started. Her body was as much her enemy as her ecstasy, letting passion build when she would rather have hovered in the state in between and savored it longer. But as he kept her firmly clutched to his body, touching at every inch possible, she felt the overwhelming crescendo take her away and lost fervent cries of his name against the side of his throat with a pleasure so intense that she shuddered and shivered even after its surging.

Erik wanted to speak endearments and praises, to dote on the beauty of her surrender and the intoxication of knowing he'd pleased her, but he was becoming a victim himself, driven so close by her climax that he could not suppress the ache any longer. Finding her willing lips with an urgent kiss, he succumbed and allowed the explosion of ecstasy to steal him in its delirium.

"Oh, Christine," he whispered, sharing her breath between lips as comprehension crept in and out of notice, "can this be ours forever? No more doubts or hearts struggling to deny their rightful place. This is where we belong...together as *one* heart."

She nodded and closed that mediocre gap to kiss him again, tasting him upon an eager tongue that begged for more for her. She never wanted this to end. No, never to end, never to consider the world outside again. She ignored the sounds of night that filtered in through the ajar windows, the chirping crickets and deceptive calm to unfolding darkness. She would have sealed it out if she could, buried them in this room as they had once been buried beneath the opera house so far away from life as if their world was impenetrable.

And she was determined not to remember or let him recall as she stole words in kisses and urged him to start again. But the world waited just beyond their haven in an awkward suspension, waited to creep in and return to its spinning. It was inevitable, and yet she was determined to stave it off as long as possible and live in a dream that was a step away from being hers.

*****

A step away... A step Christine knew she had to take. As the first rays of sunlight were dancing over the horizon, she carefully disentangled entwined limbs from Erik's sleeping form, unable to keep herself from staring at that mangled face and marvel how the warm welcome of daylight played along its malformations and illuminated the odd beauty of its abnormalities. A corpse at rest, and all she could consider was breathing life back into him. The tinged smile upon her lips reminisced the wonder of watching an ecstasy that could only mean *life* overcome those skeleton features over and over again with night to knit dreamscapes about them. One night when she was in pursuit of a million more. That

very thought renewed her adamancy as she quickly
drew on her clothes.

Silent as could be, she leaned over his sleeping
face and breathed without sound, "I love you." It was
her vow, and hidden in its simplicity was a promise of
the forever she was determined to gain them.

It was a task, weighing heavily upon shoulders
that only longed to be light and weightless with every
dreaded step back to the de Chagny mansion. The
unease was thick as it hung about her, and as she
entered the terrace doors that led into the study, it
dropped upon her and suffocated every illusion with
cruel reality.

"Where were you?"

Raoul's voice shook her off her base for a long,
guilt-ridden breath that saw visions flash in her
memory of Erik and the love in his eyes, of his body
over hers, claiming hers, every sin she now carried in
her hands. That crack in her veneer was so hastily
patched that she prayed the Vicomte never saw it from
his arresting placement, sitting arrogant and
convicted on the edge of the couch as if he'd been
waiting simply to catch her entrance. No. Guilt would
not be hers.

"Out for a walk in the garden," she lied with
skill, the actress at her best, so accomplished that her
mind designed that very scenario and made it half-
real.

"All night?" He posed the question she knew
would carry no valid explanation, and though she was
silent, she wasn't breaking as he obviously expected.
She was uncommonly defiant, and it prompted him to
toss forward the one point that rattled her. "He's
here, isn't he?"

Christine remained stoic even as the breath
collapsed her lungs and escaped as a sigh. Lying
would prove pointless as she well knew, and so
without a single waver, she replied, somber, "Yes, he
is."

"And...you were with him..."

The conclusion had likely already been assumed, probably dwelled upon through every dark hour, but Christine refused to consider the depth of betrayal and again let truth speak clear. "Yes, I was with him."

It was the vastness of Raoul's pain that surprised her. She hadn't expected it, half-sure that in a way he had anticipated this very outcome in the parts of his mind that knew she didn't love him. But what faced her was an undeniable anguish, as he demanded with defeat, "How could you? ...And how long has he been lolling about, spying on us and seeking the exact manner in which to go about usurping my life?"

"You convinced him that I was dead." She wasn't above accusing him; he could hurt for losing her, but when she thought of why and Erik suffering the same, it kept her unmoved. "You arranged all of that specifically for *him*, to destroy him and make sure he never came after me. Your admission of what you did has always been shrouded in your argument that it was done for my protection. But this wasn't for me at all. This was to *keep me* and was just as horrific as Erik carrying me off like a rag doll."

"And yet you've forgiven him for that," Raoul spat as he rose and dared to close the distance between them, running his gaze across her every detail as if she had been changed and transformed, contaminated somewhere deep inside. "Why are my own efforts to hold your love condemned? Is it because I am not a deformed murderer playing on your sympathy?"

"Sympathy is not what I feel for him," she stated firmly, never cowering under the burden of the Vicomte's anger. "I love him; I've *always* loved him. You know that. You knew it before I did or could ever admit it to myself, so you sought to depict him as a monster and build me something to be terrified of and hate. ...You loved me, genuinely so, and I'm sorry for that. ...I'm sorry that I could never love you back."

That was it, vindication for a choice made four months before, and as she accepted the pull of conviction and strode past his slouched shape, she expected it to be over and felt a swell of anticipation, considering that she would collect her things and be gone within the hour, back to Erik, maybe even before he awoke.

"You may not love me," Raoul called after her, "but you're going to marry me anyway."

Halting numb in her steps, she reluctantly turned back, only inches from the study doorway and freedom. "No, Raoul, I'm not. ...I'm going to marry him."

"He'll be dead before he ever makes it to the altar."

Christine huffed her annoyance, staring fixedly at his back as he slowly regained his full posture. "And shall we return to the last denouement with both of you ready to duel to the death over me? I chose him then, and I choose him now which leaves you no reason to wage war."

"Reason? I have quite the reason," he coldly retorted, still avoiding a look at her. "You will *not* make me a fool before the entire country. We are getting married tomorrow as planned; I will *not* carry the ridicule of being left at the altar for a disfigured freak and murderer."

"Forge a death," she suggested bitterly. "You are quite versed in such affairs. A demise for yourself...or me. I don't much care. Tell them that your darling fiancée took her life...*again*."

"Oh, no, no, as if I would make it so easy for you to run off with your deformed lover!"

"What do you mean?" This was not a new idea or plot in formation; she had a definite feeling that he had had this conspired to precision all along, and as he finally met her eye and she glimpsed the opposition that had overtaken pain, she knew she was right.

"I mean," he replied sharply, "that I can make threats as well as he can, only I will be better at carrying them through. All of Paris believes you are dead. It wouldn't take much for me to go there and insist that *he* devised the entire scheme and made *me* believe that you were dead so that he could once again kidnap you. He is a wanted man, you realize; the *gendarme* would be quite grateful to have a direction and yet another purpose to pursue him. And with the funding and aid of the Vicomte de Chagny in hopes of finding his abducted fiancée, it wouldn't be an impossible feat this time."

"You can't," she argued without showing even a fraction of her rising trepidation. "And if you tried, I would simply insist that I want to be with Erik. They cannot force a willing woman from what she freely chooses."

"The *gendarme* would never believe that a beautiful woman would *freely* choose a disfigured murderer. They'll believe he's tricked you, and they'll *kill him* without question." Raoul was as undeterred as she was, glimpsing the slight shake of her hands before she fisted them and tightened the joints of betraying fingers. "You know that there is no exaggeration in my words, Christine. If I send the *gendarme* after him, they will shoot before they'll ever let him get away again. Go on then. Run off and tell him of my threats, but I guarantee that I will see him dead before I am the one hurt by his ropes and tricks."

She swayed on her feet with the violent quivering her body suffered. And all she could think in a horror-stricken mind was that it had been warm in Erik's bed. ...Why had she ever left? "No," she said even if the tremble in her voice revealed her doubt. "No, I will *not* marry you, and Erik will kill you before you ever try to force me."

"After all I've done for you, you would truly destroy your future for *him*? Inevitably, you're going to see that I'm offering you everything. Don't make our marriage be the forced manipulation he failed at conjuring the first time. It doesn't have to be a death sentence." And as his eyes softened their glare, he insisted sincerely, "...I love you, Christine."

It stung her so brutally because she knew it was true.

"Break his heart," the Vicomte ordered, regaining his cold control, "or watch it bleed itself dry. What happens is in your hands now, but are you truly so inclined to take chances with his life? I know the difficulty in that path; I *lived it* once before. Loving you and yet wittingly putting you in danger with the fear of losing you at the next shift of plot... It was a dreadful weight to bear, and then to consider the guilt I would have known if something had happened to you... Is that what you want, Christine? Because you will endure terror for your remaining days, the terror of losing him at any moment. I can guarantee that if you abandon our wedding, I will do everything I must to find you, even if that means scourging the entire face of the earth. There is nowhere you can go that you would be safe."

"Why?" she suddenly demanded, fighting back tears that threatened more and more with every sentence. "Why won't you just let me go?"

"Did *he* not play the same angle? And he won your heart in doing so." Raoul shook his head, and the sneer he gave made her consider him truly ugly. The most handsome, most coveted man in the country, and all she could see when she looked at him was an abhorrent villain. "I am no fool," he went on. "I don't anticipate gaining your love this way, but I will choose enemy before unrequited lover, especially when your ignorance is threatening my reputation. All this time in society, and have you not noticed how important such things are? I made a new, fictitious girl to love and wed because of it, killed the parts of you that would have proved shaming to my family name and gave you the prestige you needed to be accepted. I am not willing to lose that so completely. Even if the girl I created never truly existed, you gave her life and played the role to perfection. I expect nothing less at our wedding tomorrow."

"Stop saying that," she snapped at him, hating the very words.

"Christine, finally strong and convicted in what she wants," he taunted. "But you can't destroy lives built to selfishly satisfy your heart; I won't let you and especially not with *him*."

"But...I love him," she whispered, and despite resolve, the tears were pooling in the corners of her eyes.

"If that's true, then you'll choose to save him instead of being the sole cause and reason for his death. Love means sacrifice, Christine; Lord knows I've made enough for you." Pain flickered through anger, and he quickly forced cold apathy back into place and glared at her. "You can be quite convincing when you choose to be. Play the actress. Convince him that you're through with him, and do it well. Intelligently, I will not be without armed guards until our wedding, so if he dares try anything, he will be dead. Simple as that. Dead for your love. It is so very reminiscent, isn't it? Four months ago that would have been my part. It's amazing how time changes things and makes one the wiser. I will *not* be his victim again."

Raoul's attention was caught and riveted to the slow fall of her tears, and every crystal drop sliced deeply into him. Once he had held her and soothed such sorrow, but now... With his heart unavoidably in his eyes, he vowed, "When this is over, I will make you happy with your choice. I promise you, Christine. I can give you the life you deserve, and even if you'll never love me, eventually you may believe that what I'm doing right now is rooted in my love for you, above all else, even my reputation. Someday you'll be able to look and truly see all I've done for you, and you'll stop hating me for it." Abruptly straightening his posture and adopting formality, he flatly commanded, "Go and get changed. The seamstress will be here shortly for the final fitting for your wedding gown. I shall be so pleased to see you in it tomorrow."

Finality was one last shared look and a denial of compassion when hers was saturated in solemn tears, and the Vicomte stormed out of the study with heartache in every footfall.

Almost immediately, Meg came rushing in, green eyes wide with every sentence overheard, but she was too late to stop Christine from slipping into a heap of skirts and curls on the floor under the power of her sobs.

"Oh, Christine," the little ballerina emphatically cried, crouching beside her and wrapping little arms around her sagging shape. "I'm sorry! It's so horrible! I tried to deter Raoul. He came charging about last night looking for you, and I told him that you'd gone to bed with a headache. Evidently, I'm not as believable as you are; ballerinas don't have to be stellar actresses, you know. He didn't listen to a word I said; he was insisting something about a missing letter from his desk."

Realization beamed through the rainclouds in her head. A scrap of a letter in her own hand, and no, she had not been the most adept at hiding her indiscretion, leaving the Vicomte's desk in a rummaged state when he preferred pristine order. It was such a mundane offense, but of course, to him, it only spoke of guilt.

"What are you going to do, Christine?" Meg asked nervously after the brunt of another sob.

But Christine could not answer because the very uttering of such words was too much. It was about to be the greatest sin on her soul. A step away from what she had wanted was now a brick wall, unbreakable in its construction, a future lost as quickly as it had been dreamed.

*****

Heartache was disguised as apathy, and every tear and wound was concealed behind its curtain. Of course, this wasn't the first time Christine had had to put up a convincing front; opera roles required such deception and separation of heart. How had she survived *Don Juan Triumphant* with its underlying plot of catching a murderer, knowing the theatre had been filled to its corners with armed *gendarme* on a mission of shooting upon sight? She had established a veneer that night and had allowed emotion to twist behind its façade. But opera audiences were a gullible sort, impressed mainly by stratospheric pitches and cadenzas; such virtuosic feats could surpass poor acting skills and create a diva among the masses of sopranos with believability second in its importance, but this time... One flaw, and she would no longer be destroying Erik's heart; she'd be responsible for the loss of his life as well.

Meg went with her, keeping beside her even though no words were spoken as they each pondered the horror of their current trek. Breaking the heart of the Opera Ghost seemed an inevitable execution to the little ballerina, and considering the hours of tears she had seen Christine shed, she admired her friend's strength to go through with it so stoically. Anyone else might have shattered, but as Meg was seeing, Christine was far stronger than anyone had given her credit for.

The only falter in countenance came when the house appeared within view. For one second, a shiver overtook Christine's limbs, one second and in the next, the evidence was gone as if it had never occurred. *Erik...* A single waver would have him going after Raoul in a rage, and when she had watched firsthand as armed guards were put into place at the de Chagny mansion as a so-called formality, she did not want such a chance taken.

She knew Erik so well. She knew that if he were aware of what the Vicomte was doing, he would react rashly with his belief in his own indestructible invincibility as his guide. He never could accept that he was fallible. No, not the almighty Opera Ghost.

But Christine knew better. She had once believed her father was a permanent staple in her life, that he would eternally be fixed in the world, and when he had died, she had had to learn that nobody was immortal and people could be lost as quickly as seasons changed. Never again would she take a life for granted, especially Erik's. She would not punish him further for loving her by watching him die for it. If she followed her own internal monologue to perfection, she would have him hating her but at least he'd be alive.

Just before the trees parted at the door, Christine halted Meg with a steady hand upon her arm and asked, "Will you stay here and wait for me?"

"Are you sure you don't want me to come inside with you?"

Christine shook her head solemnly. "You carry too much heart in your eyes. If I look at you, I'll forget to harden mine and go through with this."

"This is wrong, Christine." Meg spoke the words playing incessantly in Christine's conscience, but even as she nodded, she could not change things.

"Wait for me," Christine repeated, and then she was quietly opening the door and slipping inside.

A certain agitation brought her to the living room and the sound of flustered motion, and peering inside, her heart gave a betraying skip to see his shape, his details, his very body, pacing between half-unpacked boxes so lost in thought that he didn't even notice her observation at first. It gave her long enough to make one more memory, to engrain in her mind this last moment that he loved her. That was about to seem his greatest misfortune.

Abruptly shaken back to reality, Erik averted anxious eyes to her silhouette in the doorframe, and the smile that lit his masked face tried to seep into her heart, but her will to deny it was stronger this time.

"Christine...," he breathed with an inflection of uncertainty laced through every step he took in tentative approach. Right in front of her, so near that her body's natural heat welcomed his as its perfect echo, he halted and studied her nuances, making answers for unasked questions before she ever said a word. "...Is it regret? Regret for signing over your life to my heart? ...Or...what did the Vicomte say to you when you told him that you won't marry him?"

"Nothing," she stated without sway when lies flowed so smoothly, "because I haven't told him, and I don't intend to."

Even with a mask to dull the sharpness of expressions, she could tell that he was still trying to decipher her as he tested with more inquiry. "And...do you prefer that? Stealing away without explanations and broken hearts? ...We could leave this very moment if that is the case."

"No," she declared before he could set out plans. "No, I'm not leaving, Erik. I'm marrying the Vicomte tomorrow, and...I came to say goodbye to you."

Suspicion was piquing, and yet he kept it reserved and silent. "Oh? And is it customary for you to so eagerly share the bed of the man who doesn't get to keep you in the end? ...Marrying the Vicomte, and yet last night you were planning a future with me."

"It was a lie," she decided, and her composure was sewn so intricately that the seam could not be seen or unraveled. "It was one night; I wanted to give you one night. After all I have put you through, I wanted you to have something beautiful... Something to remember instead of only pain."

Erik raced his eyes over every feature of her face with skepticism that faded in and out of focus and twined with the inevitable rising of his temper. "And what is this then? More pain. You would truly stand before me and call every exquisite detail of last night a *lie*? Truly, Christine? Are these your own words, and is mine the heart that is breaking from their bitterness? Tell me what *you* want, *ange*."

Hesitating should have created fine cracks in her veneer, but she was too strong this time. "I want to marry Raoul. It *was* the future *you* gave me, after all. You knew that he was the right choice even if I was confused. ...I've loved him all along. How could I not? He is perfection, and you...you're a murderer and a monster."

"Don't," he coldly spat, and the fire flaming in his eyes made violent threats out of what had once been fevered adorations. "Don't do this."

"Speak the truth?" she posed with a shake of her head, detaching her heart when anger had such an undercurrent of pain. "I don't love you. How could I possibly? And every act last night was done out of pity and a sense of compensation."

"You touched me," he reminded sharply. "You weren't disgusted. There was no lie there."

"But there was no love there either. You feared exactly that once before, that I would only ever know sympathy for you and your deformity, compassion maybe. I could never love it, Erik; ...it's a *horror*."

Every instinct begged him to lash out and force every ugly word off her beautiful lips, but he clutched rage in tight muscles and fixed limbs and simply stared. "A horror, Christine? Then it must have been torture for you to touch such a horror last night, to kiss it, to make it so convincingly seem that you wanted it."

Feigning apathy, she stated, "You trained me to be a believable actress, and you wanted to trust me so badly that you never considered that when I shivered, it wasn't out of desire. I can be quite persuasive with I'm playing a part. You should know that better than anyone."

Mismatched eyes glared, and when his hands darted out and caught her forearms, he had to control his fury not to leave bruises in his viselike grasp. "Is this what *you* want, Christine? To destroy us both for *him*?"

She remained undeterred, even when his hands were inspiring memories and threatening to shatter her. "It is only *you* who can argue destruction. I *love him*, Erik; he is everything I've ever dreamt of. For so long, you wanted me to be strong in my convictions;

well, that is what I am doing, claiming what *I* want. And you cannot begrudge me. I gave you something that shouldn't have been yours. One night... Someday you'll be able to understand my sacrifice." *Sacrifice...* And how it was breaking both their hearts! Desperate to be beyond the power of those eyes, she struggled in his hold and commanded, "Let me go. I don't love you; there is nothing more to say."

Every bit of him longed only to drag her closer, to tear away clothing and any dared barrier between skin and lose himself in her, so certain she wouldn't argue a single point if he was overwhelming her with his love again and proving it so undeniably. But he didn't follow whims this time. He forced his unwilling hands to part and release, to move away, open and tensed down every joint with the need to grasp. No. No, not if this was what *she* wanted.

Taking necessary steps back, Christine laid the final stone into a constructed wall. "If you ever felt for me as you claimed to, then I ask that you leave me be. I don't want to see you again, Erik. Last night was all I could give you. ...Maybe someday you'll be able to think about it and appreciate it for what it was."

"A lie?"

"A fantasy," she corrected, desperate not to let real emotion show through. "A fantasy of what can never be. I'm sorry. ...I can't love a monster."

He wanted to argue it further, to force sense back into her head if necessary, but he didn't. He restrained impulse's pull and held her eyes one last breath in his, searching blue depths for the fabrication in the background. What was the true lie? He wanted to insist it was her words. But he could find no proof to agree, and with anger mounting to the height of pain, he turned, stalking to the piano with his back to her regard. With a huff so violent that it buckled lungs, he threw himself onto the bench and began to viciously play, heartbreaking pitches that tore from the guts of the piano as its hammers beat savagely against its strings.

For one tear-filled moment when real emotion glistened through, she watched him and let the music pose its attack, accusing and tearing into the very heart of her before she coerced uncooperative legs to carry her out the door and away.

"Christine." Meg rushed to her side and slid an arm about her shoulders as the music rang out and threatened. "What...what is he doing?"

"Making certain that I know his heart is breaking," she softly bid with tears pooling her eyes and tumbling loose to fall. "I don't know if he'll listen and stay away, but I called him a horror. A *horror!*" The tears fell faster as she gasped, "I told the man I love that he could only be a monster to me!"

"And he did nothing in retaliation?" Meg asked in surprise with one recollection of the Opera Ghost's antics in an opera house, too many to recount.

"Nothing? ...But don't you hear it in the music?" Christine demanded, half-distracted by every pitch. "He's breaking apart, Meg, and he wants me to suffer for my weakness. It's in the music, ...in the music." Notes and pitches to anyone else would not rip into skin and bone as viciously as words and weapons, but she felt every sting, every vengeful outrage and cry and knew they were deserved.

"Come away from here, Christine," Meg begged desperately. "You don't need to torment yourself further."

"I don't want to leave him," Christine revealed in a sob, but she did not struggle free as Meg pulled her toward the woods. Leaving her heart upon a piano's suffering strings, she abandoned the only future she wanted, once again appearing as the weak child when in reality, she was anything but that. No, she was strong, and that strength was a curse as much as a blessing. It made her choose him and equally give him up.

*****

The piano had barely ceased its bellowing in long, unending hours. Its agony could barely be called music when it carried so much emotion, and as pitches and chords poured out of every crack and wall to resound into the woods, it announced Erik's presence in a far more distinctive way than he typically preferred, ...announced like an undeniable beacon light. It certainly made it easy for Nadir to locate the house when he had taken to wandering nearby estates warily and half-sure he'd get lost before he ever found Erik's residence. Before the daroga even crossed the threshold to enter uninvited, he knew such music was a bad sign. If things were settled, then Nadir knew he'd be audience to major key sonatas and adagio lullabies. This was dissonant madness in comparison.

Almost immediately upon his entrance, the ugly chords stopped mid-ring, and a frantic stirring of activity brought a hopeful, anticipating Erik into the living room doorway. Anticipating and then rapidly annoyed in the first glimpse of his guest.

"Daroga, ...did we not act this exact scene months ago? You arriving uninvited in my home and shattering my hopes with your very presence," Erik coldly reminded. "If you are here on another errand from your kindred spirit the Vicomte, don't waste your breath. He's already played his next hand without you, and now I just have to figure out how to go about killing him and ending this ridiculous game we've been indulging far too long."

"And so we've returned to revenge against the Vicomte," Nadir concluded with a sigh. "Well, I'm pleased that nothing new has developed in my absence. I would have hated to be uninformed upon my arrival."

"Nothing new," Erik muttered beneath his breath before suddenly allowing realization to dawn. "We're not underground at the opera. What are you doing here? I don't recall leaving a forwarding address for former friends."

"Since my 'kindred spirit' the Vicomte, as you call him, neglected to send me a formal invitation to the wedding, that must mean that I am here specifically to see *you*, former friend. Can we overcome the injustices we've done one another if I merely apologize, or do you intend to hold a grudge forever? Considering your shortage of pleasant acquaintances who from time to time save your life and occasionally look after it, I would argue that you could use a formidable relationship, especially if we have returned to musings of murder or suicide, whichever the case may be." Even as Nadir made it seem a gross exaggeration, Erik's unchanged expression put him on edge as he worriedly inquired, "Is that the true state of things, Erik? Murder or suicide?"

"Decidedly murder," Erik stated plainly. "You know my aversion to suicide. And besides, I have too much worth living for to opt for an easy way out. ...If we are so avidly friends again, then you might as well know that I intend to stop the Vicomte's sham of a wedding by whatever means necessary, and yes, murder is a viable option. And if you are going to be so inclined to tell him and warn him of impending danger, thereby betraying this sordid friendship and ending it once again in its tracks, know that I don't care. Do what you feel you must for your inconstant conscience."

"I am *not* loyal to the Vicomte," Nadir proclaimed adamantly. "I never told him that you were here, and I am not out to keep in his good graces. But please humor me enough to tell me why we have decided upon murder, or do I already know...?"

"Because Christine loves *me*."

"And we have returned to that as well," Nadir stated, half to himself. "So what has it been? Have you been stealing her away, insisting that you know she could only love you? Have you placed ultimatums before her again and sought to force the truth out of her?"

A biting glare was his reply, narrowed eyes and a sneer as Erik snapped, "You know I don't think I want your lackluster friendship anyway. Leave!"

But the daroga shook his head without even a bit of sway. "All right, I'm sorry for assumptions, but...well, that was how it was played the last time. You can't blame me for following history. So...what was it this time then?"

"Christine loves me," he attempted to reveal again. "She chose me, conceded to marry me instead, and now...well, he has said something to convince her that she so adamantly loves him and only him."

"And how do you know that? Perhaps it's the truth."

Huffing his disbelief, Erik explained, "I know she is lying because Christine may be a wonderful little actress, but *I* made her that way. At first, I nearly believed her, when my temper got the best of me, but...hours of playing cleared my head and reminded me of her every flaw when she is on the stage. Anyone else would have been convinced by her performance, but I inspired her every trick." *Every* trick, and as he had been engrossed in notes, he had spent the last sonata condemning himself for ever letting her pass the threshold of the door without the truth.

"Erik..." Pausing a breath, Nadir carefully considered what he could possibly say that would not result in vicious tirades and being tossed out of the house altogether. "...You already know why I must doubt you. After the last time-"

"This is *not* like the last time!" Erik shouted, making Nadir cringe and regret speaking. "Because I could have forced her, but I didn't. I let her come to me and love me, and I also let her make her own choices. But there is a vast difference between free will and exploitation, and the Vicomte de Chagny is not as innocent in the latter as he'd have anyone believe. Ask him, daroga! If you don't believe me, go to him and get the facts from his own mouth. Of course he'll tell you; he'd love to have someone to gloat his triumph to. He thinks he's won already, but the hell if I will lose everything I've ever dreamt of to *him*!"

Erik would have continued with frantic utterances of every threat he could devise, but a series of flustered knocks at the door broke into his rage and had him racing for the foyer with Nadir right behind.

"Christine," he was whispering as he jerked the knob, but as it clicked and turned, his awaiting visitor regarded him with wide, horrified eyes and a quick glance back over her shoulder to make certain no one had followed.

"M...Monsieur Fantôme."

"Mademoiselle Giry." Erik's greeting was laden in his disappointment before impatience swelled with one abrupt thought. "Christine? Is she all right?"

"May I come inside?" Meg nervously stammered with more peeks backward although she was suddenly uncertain if she had more to fear from a pursuer or from the desperate Opera Ghost and the terrifying Persian. Meg only recalled seeing the Persian man that last night in the catacombs as he had followed Christine and Raoul from the underground, looking just as tattered and weary as the Vicomte. Only later had Meg learned why with an explanation of torture chambers from her mother, another point that was sworn to secrecy...even if Jammes had inevitably been included in that promise's boundary as well.

Erik scrutinized the anxious little ballerina one more long moment before stepping aside and allowing her in, and as she scurried into the living room, he cast his own perusal over silent woods to know without a doubt that no one lurked behind before he closed out the world and impatiently joined Meg. She had taken a seat upon the couch without permission or request, but she had been careful to perch at the edge of the cushion as if ready to leap up and run if needed. Perhaps it seemed an intelligent option when both men in the room were staring at her with eyes that were more determined than words to have answers.

"I...I...I'm sorry to intrude." Meg stumbled over her own voice as she scanned the abundance of half-packed boxes with arching golden brows. "You weren't...leaving, were you?"

"Not without Christine," Erik said, ignoring Nadir's overt doubt and audible scoff.

"Oh, thank heavens! I thought she might have truly convinced you!" Meg exclaimed urgently. "But you know she was lying, don't you?"

"Lying?" Nadir questioned, fitting the facts into place despite the terror-stricken look Meg granted him. "Speak the truth, mademoiselle. Why was Mademoiselle Daaé lying?"

"Don't interrogate the girl," Erik ordered coldly. "Stay back and just listen. You're scaring the wits out of her, and I need a comprehensible explanation yet from her lips."

"*I* am scaring her?" Nadir questioned the Opera Ghost doubtfully with memories of shrieking ballerinas scattering about and shouting terror over their resident phantom. But with a huff, he conceded and lingered in the doorway, watching as Erik tentatively approached the wide-eyed girl and knelt unthreateningly on the carpet at her feet.

"What did he say to her, Meg?" Erik calmly posed, never daring a touch or any quick motions when faced with such fright.

Swallowing hard, she forced a tremulous breath and replied on its exhalation, "He said that you would be dead before he'd ever let you marry her. ...But you already concluded that, too, didn't you? Only your life would be worth such a sacrifice for her. She was determined to keep you safe. ...I wasn't supposed to tell you, but...I'm not very good at keeping secrets. And to see her that way and know why... I couldn't bear it. What he's doing is abhorrent! I can't believe he can manipulate her and yet still claim to love her!"

Cringing to himself with the recollection of his

own abhorrent manipulations justified by love, he refused to bring focus to past folly and instead asked, "Where is she now? Is she all right?"

"She would barely stop crying; I only left her side because she fell asleep. But...," Meg glanced worriedly between the men, "the Vicomte has armed guards posted everywhere. I barely got away without some sort of pursuit and questioning. I overheard him giving assignments, and they are to shoot if they even glimpse a mask. ...What do you intend to do? You can't let her marry the Vicomte no matter what horrible words she said to you. None of them were true."

"I know," Erik assured before shifting attention to the observing Nadir. "Well, daroga? Whose side are you taking this time? I'd appreciate not being stabbed in the back again at your first opportunity."

"Your side, of course, and I'm sorry it's ever been any different," he declared sincerely, and an unspoken oath passed in a gaze that Erik nodded to accept. "Now how do we get to her?"

"Well, ...you insinuated how much you wanted to attend the wedding," Erik replied with an idle shrug. "But tell me, daroga; who will draw more attention in that societal bubble: a Persian foreigner or a disfigured monster? It will certainly be interesting to find out."

*****

The tension in the room was palpable that evening, and Meg had to wonder as she observed the scene with a meek sort of fascination how the Comtesse did not notice it or the lack of joy on a bride-to-be's drawn face. No, Comtesse de Chagny carried on her boisterous, one-sided conversation as if anyone else's input was inconsequential anyway, filling in every inadequate personality with her own overbearing loudness. Meg had to wonder if that was how the Comtesse endured quiet evenings at home when she did not have houseguests: one-sided conversations with furniture, a sad reality and yet

414

completely fathomable.

Not for the first time since an awkward supper had ended, Meg cast an anxious glance to Raoul, surprised that he had chosen sullen as his demeanor even if his current company only consisted of Meg and her mother. Well, it certainly revealed how little the Vicomte actually thought of them; even the butler Andrew made them worthy of fake smiles and seeming propriety!

As Madame Giry made a great declaration over the Comtesse's unceasing prattling to insist that she was destined for her bed and a decent rest before the chaos of daybreak, Meg shifted wide eyes to Christine in time to see her dull nod of agreement.

"Bed?" The Comtesse made her displeasure known like a child to a strict parent despite the fact that she was nearly the same age as Madame Giry. "But...it's still early."

And yet as Meg well knew, *no one* posed arguments with her mother and won. Within minutes, the party was dispersing and heading upstairs, even the belligerent Vicomte, and it left Meg nervously hasty in her actions.

"I will be up in a moment, Mama," Meg insisted. "Christine and I were going to discuss proper etiquette for tomorrow so that I don't make a fool of myself before all of society."

Madame Giry eyed her daughter skeptically, seeking the real answer without a single word, and as Meg shifted nervously on her feet, sure she was giving herself away, her mother glanced to Christine's somber expression and distraught solemnity before nodding consent. *Well, of course*, Meg insisted to herself. Christine had once been like a second daughter when an orphan starting at the opera. Perhaps Meg hadn't needed to lie at all, or so said the compassion in the last gaze her mother granted Christine. Likely, the old ballet mistress already knew the truth. Little went on in an entire opera house without her knowledge; mansion houses of Comtesses would be no different.

And just like that, the girls were left alone in the parlor, and Meg's apprehension became a proud smile as she declared to her sad friend, "You have an engagement out in the gazebo to attend."

"The gazebo?" Christine questioned, and yet could she deny the immediate leaping of her heart? "There are Raoul's armed guards positioned outside the house."

"Not in the gardens. And you are not strolling the night as the fiancée of the Vicomte. You forget that the Vicomte's armed guards are not society patrons. They've never seen you; as far as they know, you are Meg Giry, a guest free to come and go as she pleases. As Christine, you may be on the verge of a prisoner, but *I* am not." A laugh of delight escaped her lips to regard Christine's astonished surprise. "You hardly believed I could be so conniving! And if you must know, this part of the plot was entirely *my* idea; I couldn't bear to see you suffer unknowing until the real drama starts tomorrow. So go on then, Christine. Out the terrace door, and if any of them stop you, you are not you; you are me. And the real Meg Giry is going up to *your* room. I am posing as you, asleep with the covers over my head in case dearest Raoul sends anyone to check. As long as I can carry off a decent snoring and the lights stay out, we are safe."

In spite of every fear and doubt, Christine couldn't keep from smiling, and with a quick hug to her giggling friend, she insisted, "You are quite good at conniving. I never would have thought!"

"Oh, I am an absolute surprise to be sure! Well, when I'm *keeping* secrets and not *telling* them. But go on. You'll see the best part of my scheme awaiting you in the gazebo."

One last hug, and Christine darted for the terrace door, slipping silently out into the night as Meg watched her go with only a flutter of anxiety in the background of bravery.

Guards were lolling about here and there, most incompetent and having conversations with each other rather than watching the house, so it was without effort that she passed their surveillance and found herself in the stillness of the gardens with moonlight's path to guide her between flowerbeds. Better judgment was the only one to push protests in her way, but it was overpowered by far too much desire for one body. She *needed* to see him with a necessity that made her footsteps light and barely graze the ground.

The instant she glimpsed a dark silhouette within the vine arches of the gazebo, her heart gave an eager thud of delight, racing against trepidation to meet his. Hearts could greet and embrace each other, but her approach was hesitant and wary, her eyes holding his apprehensive gaze and reading the walls lingering in between. He was waiting, and she knew she would have to be the one to collapse them again.

Sweeping a feverish stare over her, Erik watched as she timidly entered the gazebo, lingering feet away and afraid to cross the chasm between when all he wanted was to forge its distance heart-first and touch her.

In the softest whisper fringed with tears, she bid, "I called you a horror, ...a monster... I made the most wonderful blessing I've ever had seem like a curse. ...Oh, Erik, I'm so sorry." She was too exhausted to play pretenses and too heartsick to form more lies, and as she watched a masked face soften its hard edges into the man she loved, she did not scold herself for her resounding relief and burst of gratitude.

Hardly able to endure the weight of urgent fingers anymore, he encircled her forearm and drew her close, only able to take a full breath when she was pressed to his lungs and hugging him in return. "I love you," he gasped against her hair. "How I love you! Say what you will; that won't change."

"You are *not* a horror," she was desperate to

insist, "not to me, *never* to me."

"Words aren't important. How quickly you forget that I've been called nearly every insult in recorded language; words don't hurt me anymore. But if I had had to see you marry that bastard Vicomte, *that* would have damaged me beyond repair."

"He wants to kill you," she confided as her lips formed idle kisses within the collar of his shirt. "If I refuse to marry him, he will come after us and *kill you*." She repeated the words with emphasis when the only response he gave to such news was contingent on kisses.

"You give him far more credibility than he deserves," Erik insisted, tracing eager hands along her spine to mold her body more firmly to his. "Why are you so afraid that he will best us? You neglect to remember that the last time I wasn't confident that I had your love as my own. Now knowing what I have to lose, I am stronger than ever. He won't win, *and* he is about to have every advantage his reputation has ever earned him tarnished in the eyes of his precious society. I am going to make sure that he has nothing left for all he has tried to take from me."

"Then you have a plan," she concluded, shivering at his nearness and inching closer with every moment until she willingly arched against the hardness of his desire and felt every reaction of his body with him.

Losing a moan against her temple first, he then insisted, "Four months ago, I would have simply spirited you away and buried us safely underground for the rest of our lives, but now...well, I want to give you more than that. I want the future we discussed, and since that includes being a part of the world and the opera, then I won't have you constantly worrying in the back of your pretty head that the Vicomte will pursue us. This has to be ended."

"Without murder or death," she added adamantly.

"Without murder or death," he agreed. "But you are going to have to be strong, Christine, stronger than loving a disfigured monster has made you."

The distance she created in an embrace was necessary as her eager fingers reached for the obtrusion of a mask and rid him of it, finding her disfigured monster beneath. Desperate to alter perceptions, she began to cover damaged skin with healing kisses, making his denounced misfortune seem something exquisite.

"Oh, Christine," those misshapen lips breathed as a returned caress that she savored. "My first consideration when you insisted that you loved the Vicomte was that you regretted last night and its every provocative detail."

"No, no," she fervently bid with equaled kisses to the rough skin of an unmarred side. "I've barely thought about it for fear I'd never have it again. If that had been the only time... Erik, never again to feel you inside of me..." Her words were breathless, and memory made him burn and clutch her tighter to his aching need.

"And you were going to wed the Vicomte," he stated tightly, "and so callously give yourself to him. ...That was the sacrifice you spoke of, not sharing my bed but sharing his."

Cringing with the mere mention of such a fate, she covered his jaw with frantic, beseeching kisses and insisted, "I would do what I must to keep you safe and alive."

"Ah, but what if you are carrying my child?" He dared to pose the thought, even as he worried what her reaction to such news could be, and rightly so as he watched her tentatively meet his stare with wide eyes. "It's hardly improbable," he quickly continued. "And what if the child bore *my* face? I doubt that the Vicomte would accept such a tragedy. A child that not only isn't his, but also bears the ugly horror of its real father. ...No, the Vicomte would accept nothing less than perfection."

"Then if that is his idea of perfection, he shouldn't want me," Christine decided, "for I have been marked and tainted by the Opera Ghost himself and I can only be his. ...And I would be proud if our children looked like their father." The smile that appeared upon her content lips said that she spoke true and not just to appease him. "You forget that I think you are beautiful, my Erik."

"But a child, Christine?" he pushed. "A child bearing my face?"

"Would be more loved than any other child in existence and would be taught tolerance as well as humility. Our child would learn that it is not a face that defines a human being; it is a *soul*. And if the soul beams bright and brilliant, then it can make beauty even on a damaged canvas."

Erik could not help but be moved by her words, and as he caught her face between eager hands, he bid, "And this damaged canvas before you? Does a soul make it beautiful? Or is it only the sheer adoration I radiate for you and *only* you?"

"Oh, that is equally as appealing," she decided, thrilling to be victim to exactly that adoration scripted so vivid that it made her ache. But beneath a surface of pure white bliss, reality was a dark ocean of waves that occasionally poked through to insist its ominous dread and make shadows in her smile. "Erik, why can't this already be our forever? Without threat of death or separation hovering over it? ...I am supposed to marry the Vicomte tomorrow, and today I nearly broke your heart. Why must it be that between every moment of exquisiteness are gaps of anguish?"

"That is life," Erik answered as he ran tender hands through her hair. "And if we can bind together the best parts of it and make something strong and unbreakable, then the bad are never that damning. So we cling to the happy respites when we have them even if they are fleeting and use their radiance to dull the moments of pain. Life is a web of both with nuances in between, but I vow to you, Christine, to give you more happy than sad and make up for the darks we've endured well enough to still harbor their scars. And I'll make this dark one only a blur without distinctions in the timeline of memories. I intend to weave so many better moments atop that it will be buried from existence."

Vows for a future she was yet terrified to accept, fearful that the instant her fingers closed about its corners, it would be ripped from her, and though she did not speak her trepidation, she knew that he felt it and wondered if beneath every assurance, he carried it the same. Her hand caught his at her cheek and held it still as she turned to press her lips to his concealed wrist where other scars lived, another bad moment that he'd buried in his spun web and chosen to forget. Such a fact gave her hope.

"I love you," she promised, rubbing her cheek to the spot. "And I will give you a similar anticipation: an abundance of wonderful times to shroud the bad. You've suffered too many tragedies, some that I myself have been responsible for creating. I intend to make you forget any time when I wasn't loving you as I am now."

Chuckling lightly, he inquired, "And was there ever such a time? Beneath everything else, you've *always* loved me, haven't you?"

She mimicked his uncontained grin and eagerly said, "Yes, even when I sought to push you away and ran from your love, I loved you. You *are* my heart."

"Oh, Christine," he breathed, leaning near to brush idle kisses along her brow. "How I wish this were over, and I could take you home with me!" Grazing another kiss down her temple, he spoke his desire against her ear as she shivered in his embrace, "I want you so much that I can hardly bear it."

Her eyes felt heavy with the thickness of passion, and as he dared to cover the crease of her neck with sudden kisses, she lost an eager cry and clutched his shoulders with desperate fingers. He seemed determined to make his desire known and shared, and kisses grew in heat and fervency as his tongue tasted her skin so delicately that her hand caught in his hair and encouraged more with a fisted grasp.

One more yearning lick from a tingling tongue, and he whispered, "I wish to lay kisses like that over every inch of your body, every detail and glorious feature tasted and cherished even if it is from lips that are misshapen and will never be entirely worthy. I almost cannot resist and keep control merely with the thought of it: these lips that I've always been ashamed were mine and abhorred at every chance buried within every heated place of your body. It is arousing in its blatant transgression."

Shuddering from head to toe, she had to collect enough wits together to form a reply. "No, not a transgression if I long for your lips upon me and would beg for it, and if my wanting comes solely from the fact that they would be *your* lips and it would be *your* tongue tasting me."

To hear such provocative ideas spoken in her sweet voice made him gasp and moan against her throat and whisper in husky tones, "Yes, Christine, *my* lips and *my* tongue, and I ache to devour every bit of you! Think about that tonight when you're lying in your bed worrying over tomorrow's dire events; imagine every second of it and how desperately I'll be burning for you. It will give you something to anticipate instead of only instances to dread."

"And will you be doing the same?" she asked with the hint of a still-shy blush upon her cheeks.

"Of course! I spend every breath not in your presence fantasizing you into existence. Know that it is always a disappointment when I long to touch you so much and for exactly this: you in my arms, safe and loving me in return." His dream brought to life, and it was a form of torture to reluctantly release her with only one more gentle kiss as compensation. "I won't jeopardize my plan and have the Vicomte realizing that you aren't in your room. The little Giry might be decent at concocting clandestine meetings in the moonlight, but she is an awful liar. I don't doubt that one question from the Vicomte will have the truth spilling out of her."

Even though Christine knew he was right, it was a sharp disappointment to watch him replace his mask. "And now you're a stranger to me," she said with a shake of her head. "The man in a mask might have been the one to pursue my heart, but the man with the scars is the one I gave it to."

Erik grinned at her analysis and decided, "Then I shall have to denounce the mask entirely and choose to only be the man you love all the time."

"And then I'll be able to kiss you whenever I like," she agreed with a flash of excitement and proved her point by setting a kiss against the mask's material. "I could be kissing your cheek right now instead. Imagine *that* tonight when we're apart as well."

"I love you," he stated with a reverent caress along her cheek. "Please stay safe."

Nodding, she slowly broke away, sharing a final adoring look before she abandoned the gazebo and let moonlight lead her back to the confinement of another life. And yet there was a new determination in every step. No matter what had to be done, with Erik's heart tied so intricately to her own, she would be as strong as she had to and win their future. She would *not* destroy them both again. And if that meant facing armed guards and a raging Vicomte, so be it. She would *not* lose her love.

*****

Nadir was the most nervous of them all as he paced the carpet of Erik's living room, glancing time and again at a pocket watch and then, as if its ticked time was a lie, out the terrace windows, considering judging the hour by the beaming sun's position instead. It was only a miniscule relief when Erik strolled idly into the room and joined him, his confidence exuding the aura of his past persona.

"Have you any idea what time it is?" Nadir

snapped before he could think better of it. "The wedding is set to begin in only a couple of hours. You can be sure that the guests have already begun to arrive, and where are we? Still confined to this house a mile away when we should be there organizing the perfect plot and its every detail to precision."

"Oh, calm yourself, Nadir," Erik replied with mock severity. "Everything will work out to my exact calculations. You anxious, little man! If it eases your pretension, I will tell you that as you slept the night away, I made the arrangements I need, thus why I am not rushing about with the same sort of insanity that has gripped you in its clutches."

"And so we are going to do what then?" Nadir demanded without ease. "Loll about here until the ceremony starts?"

"Of course not! But I cannot chance lurking about the less concealing corridors of a church and being seen by some of the Vicomte's stuffy comrades. I don't want to give my presence away before the overture."

"Overture? Wedding march, you mean," Nadir corrected sharply. "And watching your beloved walk down the aisle to another man."

Erik's glare was fringed in his temper as he insisted back, "If you do not intend to cease your agitation and the insults that are coming from it, then why not make yourself useful? Go on ahead and check on Christine if it settles *your* mind, daroga. Just avoid being caught by the Vicomte's inept guards. I need you in that church after the curtain is up."

"Curtain? Erik, you do recall that this is reality and not another opera show, don't you? And that those pistols the guards are carrying aren't props and contain very tangible bullets that rip through flesh when shot?" Shaking his head, he continued, "And that the girl in a wedding dress is your *Christine*, not one of her soprano roles brought to life?"

With a huff, he decided, "I don't see the difference, daroga. Another opera show." He shrugged. "If all goes to plan, this will be my best work yet. When this is over, perhaps I will compose a real score for its every ugly nuance and truly place it on the stage where it belongs."

"Oh, you do that," Nadir sarcastically bid, "if we live through this."

It would have astounded Nadir that Erik could be so careless with too many lives in his hands, but he knew the man seeming apathetic before him, certain they had had something that was the equivalent of this same conversation a dozen times over the past years. This was the Opera Ghost before him now, in all his glory: conniving, manipulating, scheming to every facet of a plot, and accustomed to achieving a desired result in the end. Yes, this was the Erik that never lost...except for one point. As he lingered near his piano, paging through the piece that was set out, he idly reached for his mask and lifted it off and away as if it meant nothing at all, resting that imperative article of clothing lightly upon the piano's keys and actually releasing it from his grasp.

That face gave Nadir a moment of unease with its visual oddities and their prominence; it was just too easy to forget the extent of its abnormal characteristics when it lay hidden beneath a mask. Unsure of the proper inquiry to make for this unusual and bizarre behavior, Nadir simply questioned, "Erik?"

Never looking up from his music, Erik flatly stated, "Get all your gawking over with and completed now, daroga. I won't have you faltering when I need you because you've momentarily been stunned to idiocy by my face again."

"But...you're not going to wear your mask?"

Shrugging as if such news were insignificant, he replied, "The guards are looking for a man in a mask, are they not? It seems counterproductive to appear in the very object of their obsession. I'll have better luck with the shock value of being without it as you just proved so well." To the absolute surprise of

Nadir, the misshapen lips on that face curved into a wry smile. "And besides, my lady favors the man without the mask. She loves the damaged shell more than the pretense that it is perfect. You'll see what I mean, daroga. Christine gives not even a start to glimpse my face anymore; she loves me not in spite of its ugliness but *because* of it."

"Well, Christine not included in this tally, but you are about to incur the horror and fear of hundreds of society's best. Are you so sure you wish to do that?"

"Not a doubt," he sincerely answered, smile unfading. "Now go on. I did mean it when I suggested that you go and check on Christine. ...Tell her that I love her and not to forget to perform to her audience. They deserve a glorious show."

Rolling his eyes, Nadir chose not to remind yet again that there was no fiction in today's production and simply left things at that. With a nod of assurance that spoke far more than the menial task he was about to undertake, he turned and abandoned the disfigured man knowing that a corpse stared after him until he was gone and undisturbed by that fact. Erik was supposed to be the odd and unusual one in a throng, but perhaps it was everyone else that was abnormal and a loving, feeling corpse was a step closer to what they should all hope to be.

True to prediction, it wasn't a difficult feat to sneak into the church, not amongst dozens of finely-dressed ladies and gentlemen. In a similar suit, Nadir was practically one of them as long as he kept his face from a direct view, knowing in that regard, he was as out of place as Erik would be. But lackluster guards never even cast a suspicious glimpse as he followed the fluid movement of the crowd and slipped unnoticed into a narrow corridor, not unlike the hallway of dressing rooms behind the opera's stage. Perhaps Erik wasn't entirely erroneous in comparing this to a production.

As he approached the furthest closed door, he noticed Meg Giry lingering outside and watched the young ballerina's eyes widen the instant she saw him despite the acquaintanceship they had achieved at their last encounter. It reminded him that though neither of them belonged in this world of high society, she had the better chance of pretending.

"Mademoiselle," he greeted tensely. "Is Mademoiselle Daaé inside?"

Observing him nervously, she gave a small nod. "And the Vicomte told me not to leave her. I guess it would have been too suspicious to post guards outside her room, so he hoisted me into the place instead. He thinks I am in some sort of alliance with him; he even tried to convince me that Christine is falling under a spell concocted by the Opera Ghost." A flicker of guilt tainted her expression as she admitted, "A year ago, I would have believed him."

Nadir nodded his understanding and asked, "Will she see anyone, or is she insisting to be left alone?"

"She's apprehensive, but go inside. I bet your presence will assure her in a way my words can't possibly." Without pause, Meg opened the door for him, giving Nadir no other option as the beautiful bride-to-be turned expectant blue eyes from their musings, and though he was a far cry from her disfigured prince, her expression still glowed with a certain contentment to see him.

"Don't worry," Meg promised them both. "I'll warn you if the Vicomte makes an appearance." And with that, she returned to her place in the hall, closing them safely inside.

Nadir was half-enchanted by the scene before him. Unlike the opera house, this was no dark, contained dressing room. Sunlight poured in from tall windows and created fleeting halos around a vision in white. She was the exact opposite of the damaged monster Nadir had left back at the house, the other half of a love story, but the glow in her eyes was identical in its radiance.

"Mademoiselle." He stammered a flustered

formality and was thrown even further into agitation as she approached with a rustle of full white skirts and caught one of his hands in both of hers.

"Have you seen Erik?" she immediately asked with such blatant anticipation that it made her eyes sparkle with life. "Please tell me that he is all right."

"Yes, yes, he's fine." All Nadir could consider was the last night he'd seen her at the opera, withdrawn and empty, numb as the Vicomte had taken her away with him. Nadir had assumed it had been the final repercussions of Erik's madness, never that it had been caused by heartache. But the girl before him now was healed and saved even though she was clothed in the Vicomte's wedding dress this time. "He was worried about *you* actually and wanted me to look in on you, unnecessarily so. You look...wonderful, mademoiselle, certainly more confident than I am currently feeling or at least better at hiding it."

"Ah, but I am playing my part," she insisted beneath her smile. "The defeated heroine, ready to sacrifice herself for her love. If I am not at my most believable, the Vicomte may start to wonder over the details."

"And how like Erik you sound!" Nadir exclaimed with a bit of a chuckle. "Roles and opera productions! The two of you are being rather flippant with the dire consequences should anything go awry."

"I prefer to think of it not as flippancy but as intelligence in this instance. We're playing the parts we are accomplished at portraying: he makes a flawless Opera Ghost and I've defined the role of weak victim. The fictitious aspect makes it easier to accept when good must triumph and love cannot be eternally lost."

"I'm too much a realist for your world of make believe," he decided, "and I've seen more tragic operas than comedies. It leaves me less optimistic." In the recesses of a kind smile was the undeniable pull of regret, and staring into Christine's seeming happiness, he felt compelled to admit in a tumble of words, "I'm sorry."

"Sorry?"

"I am partially the cause of all this. I helped the Vicomte and was the one to tell Erik that you were dead. So many lies, and I watched him fall to pieces because of them. Neither of you deserved such a fate, but I was so sure that the Vicomte's motives were just."

Christine listened intently and slowly shook her head. "And should I curse you for that or offer gratitude? The Erik I left four months ago loved me but would never let me love him in return, not unless he was controlling the very inspiration of it. The Erik that came here adores me *because* I freely love him. For the first time, he isn't trying to force the beating of my heart and tug its strings anyway he deems correct, and he isn't doubting every word I say and everything I feel. He believes me when I say that I love him."

Even though it didn't take the sense of blame he readily applied and carried as penance away, he replied, "It was a horrible situation, but at least something decently good came out of it."

"I know what you did for him," Christine revealed, lifting her wrists to insinuate a sin she did not wish to speak and give full credence to. "You saved his life once before."

"Yes, well, at the time, he was being impulsively foolish. For as immoral as his life has been, he can get overwhelmed by that heart of his, and he can take emotions to such a blatant extreme. I guess it proves he is *not* a monster, but... That was the implied merit in the Vicomte's lie and how I knew it would work. Erik would understand how you could have been driven to...to that. It was the ideal pretense, and I told it because I was convinced that it would indeed become your very real future if Erik continued to go after you. The idea that he'd push you to such a sin seemed logical. How could I know that you *wanted* him to pursue you?"

"Yes, Erik could understand the impetus for suicide, and he'd hate himself for not being there to save me as you saved him. You could have let him die; you knew what he was and the sorts of things he'd done. You saved him, and you thought you were saving me as well. I can't hate you for that."

"But in truth, I didn't save him at all," Nadir told her with an awed smile. "*You* did. If you only knew the atrocities of his past and what he endured, then you'd understand why it affects me so much to consider what I saw today: a man who was completely unafraid for the first time in his life." Plain as could be, he revealed to her inquisitive stare, "He isn't wearing a mask, mademoiselle."

"He isn't?" All Christine could think was that she yearned to see him right then, to glimpse him striding about with his true face on display, as normal as he could be. She held such pride just to hear it mentioned, but to *see* it, she knew she'd be overcome.

"It astounds me," Nadir continued, "to realize how you have changed him."

"*Love* has changed him," she humbly stated.

"Yes, but it takes a very special woman to love a man like Erik. Not everyone could. You are an amazement, and I will do everything I must to set things right and make certain that you end together, as it always should have been."

"Thank you," Christine breathed, patting his hand. "And, monsieur, don't worry so much about your sins against Erik. I've hurt him more than anyone and broken his heart over and over again, but he has a penchant for forgiveness that one might find unusual. You are the closest to a friend he's ever had; he will forgive you."

Nadir ruminated on the wisdom of her words before he could give a tentative nod at their validity, and with them as a sort of hope, he said, "Take care, mademoiselle. I am going to 'take my place' as you stage people say. Erik wanted it said that he loves you and to 'perform to your audience'; I'd wager that goes for me as well."

Eagerly nodding, she urged, "Good luck. Perhaps this will condition you to a life in the theatre."

"I...truly don't think so," he said to her teasing, and with one final smile, he slipped out into the hall as Meg rushed in.

"Well?" the little ballerina asked Christine. "Will this be another of the Opera Ghost's devices meant to wreck havoc and chaos?"

"To tell you the truth, I'm not sure what Erik is intending," Christine replied as she slowly smiled. "But whatever it is, it will be memorable. Everyone in society will be talking about the bizarre wedding of the Vicomte de Chagny for generations to come. This may be as close to immortal legend that we ever get, Meg."

"Yes," Meg agreed with a giggle. "Remembered forever for being a part of the story of the Opera Ghost. Too bad I can't be infamous for my dancing, but talent is subordinate to tales of disfigured phantoms and true love. Oh well!"

*****

Although in a typical opera role, Christine easily and methodically disconnected her heart and became someone else, this one proved a particular challenge. As she lingered in the church's empty foyer, she idly cast a glance down the long aisle lined by aristocrats in the pews while an equally pristine Vicomte awaited her beside a priest at the end. It was that scene that reminded her blatantly that this wasn't a performance, but it was *her life*, no matter how desperately she promised her heart otherwise.

Her life, yes, but her life equally included Opera Ghosts and music, the other details in an open-ended story looking for its finale. And despite a façade of weakness and slouched shoulders, seemingly odd for a bride or so her audience would think, strength was at her core. She would never be weak again.

That strength became a fire at the introduction pitches from a pipe organ announcing her entrance. A wedding march, and yet peculiar in its accurate and ornamented execution. As every ignorant head turned to watch her and gaze in adoration at a bride, she longed to look up to the organ loft and gaze in adoration at a ghost brought to life, playing his beloved down the aisle to wed another man. But as always, music from those fingers was cathartic to her soul and stole any lingering apprehension as she obeyed its call and followed a path lined in rose petals toward her deceptively pleased groom.

It was a miracle that Christine was able to keep her eyes forward and deny the urgent pulling upon the strings of her heart to turn around, but she consigned herself to the empty smiles on the lips of strangers and let only her ears delight in Erik's existence, ears that would give no detail away to betray. No, it was only as she joined Raoul at the altar that she dared a peek at their audience and nonchalantly the stain-glass, window-lined organ loft, and what she saw left her heart skipping in its usually constant pulsation. His silhouette glowing in a myriad of colors from the sun streaming through stained glass, only his back but so poised and stoic, the virtuosic musician playing for his love. She had to bury the true smile she yearned to give and force uncooperative eyes to the Vicomte.

As the march ceased, Raoul caught her hands in his, keeping her focus as he gently murmured, "Christine."

It was immediate in the echoing silence of the church from rafters to altar, a responding singsong call. *"Christine, Christine..."*

Half a performance, Christine's eyes widened, and she frantically glanced about, but there was no longer a shadow left in the loft, as Erik was unseen and taunting.

"Christine, ...*my* Christine..." His resonating voice came from every direction, never his true location, eerie and haunting, and everyone in their audience looked for the source with growing agitation.

"What is this madness?" the Vicomte hissed as

Christine shook a blameless head, appearing just as baffled and surprised.

In her seat amongst nervous aristocrats, Meg Giry cast a quick look at her equally confused mother, knowing that what she was about to do would result in a scolding later but unable to change her mind when this was her one important task in Erik's plans. As his wailing call for his bride resounded from left and right, Meg let out a shriek that drew attention solely to her and shouted, "The Opera Ghost! It's the Opera Ghost! He'll kill everyone for her! Oh God! Have mercy on us all!"

A sinister chuckle overcame the lilting music in an invisible voice, and as Madame Giry glared in horror at her daughter, Meg kept up a terrified expression, never once breaking to the giggle of pride that was going on in her mind. *Ha!* They would never doubt her ability to act again!

Christine contained the same giggles to observe the growing pandemonium in the church from priest to attendants to the enraged Vicomte clutching her hands in a viselike grip.

"Christine," Raoul snapped in growing annoyance.

"But Christine is dead," the voice replied from every direction at once, and then from the corners at random intervals came a delayed echo. *"Dead, ...dead, ...dead..."*

Abruptly releasing his bride, the Vicomte stood at the foot of the altar and shouted over his appalled crowd, "Come out and face me, you freak!" Even as he waved warning to the armed guards in the back, Christine noted that they were not paying attention, too engrossed in looking about for a bodiless voice.

"*My* Christine," Erik called again, and she shivered unconscious delight down her spine.

"*Always* yours," she dared to whisper back and knew he heard.

"Sing with me, *ange*," he suddenly commanded, and his beautiful golden voice lifted in melody; appropriately chosen for a church setting, it was part of the requiem mass, a ceremony for the dead.

Christine was momentarily as agape as her audience. She had known of Erik's ventriloquist skills as he had once described them from his tortured days in a Gypsy carnival as a boy, but never had she been witness to them beyond a voice appearing anywhere he chose. His current point of sound was the mouth of a glorious statue of the angel Gabriel on one side of the altar. She, like every person in attendance, was half-certain that the statue itself was singing the minor tune. It was just that flawless of a trick, so much so that even as her mind wondered where he was, her body unconsciously crept toward the statue and chose to willingly play along with angels.

As every set of eyes in the room was riveted to a marble statue, Christine savored the beauty of Erik's voice and sought to match its ethereal exquisiteness as she joined her own with its legato line. Even though she could not see him, she could hear his elation, a smile that slightly brightened the color of his tone, a shiver that jarred the stability of his vibrato; all clues so subtle to anyone else, and yet she knew to hunt them out and cling to them as proof of his corporeal existence, as not for the first time in their sordid relationship, she had to make herself believe in his tangibility. An angel brought into existence just for her, that was how she had once considered it and thrilled to be able to recall it again. *Her* angel.

As she sang and felt the power of her voice reverberating off the stained glass windows and filling space, Erik shifted to a counterpoint, harmonizing so precisely and inextricably that surely anyone listening could decipher how perfectly their timbres complimented and completed one another, how integral they seemed to each other. A perfect match and solitary fit. And heightening her performance, Christine lifted eager arms toward a singing statue, practically begging him to come for her and carry her away with him to heaven or wherever marble statues were apt to exist as reality, ...the world of fairytales perhaps.

Suddenly remembering that this was not a scene out of an opera, Raoul was shaken back into himself, and catching one of Christine's lace-clad arms to yank it down, he shouted over the melody, shattering pitch with dissonance, "Stop this!"

"Why?" Christine dared to demand as she defiantly faced him. *Strong.* Strong was remaining unwavering in a room full of people who thrived at the top of a mortal chain of hierarchy and admitting that one existed at the base of life below their rich-soled shoes. "Every word is true. I belong to the Opera Ghost and rightly so. You can't marry a dead woman, Raoul."

"Not dead, love," came the eerie reply, no longer out of the mouth of a statue but echoing in every direction again. "A ghost, but a bride befitting an Opera Ghost to be sure."

"What do they mean by dead?" The only one to dare speak up in an audience full of aghast but riveted spectators was the Comtesse de Chagny from her place in the front pew. "Every bit of this must be a jest; I cannot rationalize a plausible explanation for such a display. The wedding of a Vicomte treated like some sort of circus act! And now to claim that Christine is *dead*? It is unseemly and indecent to speak such blasphemy in a church!"

"And what do you call singing statues, I wonder," Nadir countered as he protectively came alongside Christine in the focus of far too many dagger-laced stares. "Marble that speaks and is mystically called to life, and the Comtesse is concerned over the most mundane and yet honest point of all." Sharing a look with Christine, he proclaimed over the throng, "Christine Daaé, opera diva of the stage, is by all legal accounts *dead*, and therefore, Monsieur Vicomte, you cannot marry her."

The enraged Vicomte was a breath away from

lunging at the daroga, and if not for the outraged stare on his aunt's face and the low humming drone of frantic whispers, he would have acted. It was the thought of fully destroying an already tattered reputation that kept him in place, but he still spat, "And so you've returned to abetting a murderer, monsieur, despite his actions against your life."

"What you've done is *far* worse in this instance," Nadir stated flatly before amplifying a call over the hum of the crowd. "Let it be vividly known that the Vicomte de Chagny wanted to wed an opera diva, and to hide such a seemingly disgraceful fact, he chose to lie and fake her death and disguise her as an aristocrat instead. A Vicomte and an opera singer is an unacceptable match, but worse than that is the revelation that the Vicomte is a coward who was once at the mercy of the great Opera Ghost, weeping for his life and actually cursing and denouncing his love for Christine while we sweltered in a torture chamber. Perhaps it was the heat that inspired your words, monsieur, but did you not say that the life of a Vicomte is worth far more than that of an opera singer?"

Growling rage, Raoul shouted, "I will *not* justify myself to *you*! I *love* Christine."

"Maybe so, but you love yourself more," Nadir replied with a nonchalant shrug. "You would have given her up for your freedom that night, and had Erik not let her go, you wouldn't have had a difficult time moving onward, not when Christine is a prize more than a woman to you. A trophy, and by your own ignorant doing, you can't even marry her."

Christine posed no protest to the daroga's claims, even if a part of her still wanted to believe in the love behind Raoul's every concocted manipulation. It was the lingering tie to the friend of her youth that did not want to see the truth and preferred to keep innocent eyes, but more and more, blatant reality peeked in and with it, the stark brightness that stole the fuzzy edges away.

"Christine," Raoul attempted with an appeasing expression, but she could not tell if it was for her or their observing audience. "Don't listen to this nonsense. I don't want to lose you."

"No," she argued back, "you don't want to *lose*, and most especially not to Erik. You threatened his life, not to keep me but to hurt him because he couldn't have me."

"Christine-"

"Well, I choose *him*; again and again, I would choose him whole heart and soul."

"Would you indeed?"

She knew that voice, and this time it was without the theatrics attached; it had one definite direction. As she lifted eager eyes that longed for his image to the rose-petal enclosed aisle, she saw him, her angel, her love, the very face of death staring at her with such adoration in his mismatched stare that it made her heart sing in her chest.

The gasps and horror that permeated the church should have been deafening, but Erik heard such telltale sounds as nothing more than a foreign sort of introduction to the final duet between the hero and heroine of their opera story. It could only exist in the background when the smile that lit Christine's lips outshone every unpleasant detail as glorious as salvation. But to a God-fearing people, the presence of a veritable walking corpse was not well-accepted, and as Erik stalked the aisle holding Christine's beaming gaze, many of the finely-composed aristocrats let out screams and cries as they fled from the church in terror with shouts that the devil had risen pouring backwards.

One such yell was caught by Christine, and even though it dimmed her glow with its sting, she sought to contradict every word and scurried past the equally stunned Vicomte to meet Erik in the aisle, hugging herself to him with no care for the vile remarks circling their embrace; they never found a single gap to sneak inside. No, hearts were protected even in a room full of thrown spears and launched arrows.

Erik stared at the top of that veiled, dark head, savoring her nearness and marveling over her very existence for the millionth time. So long watching a world go by from shadows, and now made fearless by a love he felt he did not deserve. Here he was, shunned and reviled but not caring for the first time. His true face exposed and abhorred, but the woman in his arms was lifting an urgent hand to trail his scars, and nothing spoke more to his soul than that sweetest gesture and the unconditional love in risen blue eyes that proclaimed he was beautiful and adored.

"Damn you both!" It was only the biting curse from the Vicomte that intruded, and as they turned to face a viable fury, Christine weaved her arm securely with Erik's, clenching fingers tightly into the material of his jacket sleeve. She was adamant that this would be her ending, and nothing would be taken away.

"Words are all you have, Monsieur Vicomte," Erik taunted without sway and gestured to the emptying church behind them. "Not even your paid guards have remained to pose your threat for you."

This was not the first viewing Raoul had had of Erik's unmasked face, but he still blanched when its horror consumed his line of vision and grimaced his disgust as he sneered back, "I don't need a threat, not when it stands willingly before me. There is your threat, Christine," he pointed with a hand that shook in its course to Erik and his face. "I wanted to protect you from every danger, but especially this one. How easily you forget all he's done, his past sins and every transgression he put upon your shoulders! You came to me out of fear for him; do you not recall it anymore? A fear for your own life because of what he is and a temper that is unpredictable and terrifying. You're so certain such realities don't matter, but what happens if you anger him, Christine? What happens if you digress from being his perfect, little porcelain doll?"

A sardonic laugh fell from Erik's lips as he added, "Well, she's already learned what happens when she refuses *your* chosen depiction of who she should be: you lock her in with armed guards and insistences of sacrifice."

"Not much different from what you yourself did, or has that been forgotten as well?" The Vicomte only granted him one last glare before focusing solely on his lost bride. "Christine, we've played something like this scene before. You made the same choice then that you do now, but you left with *me* that night. And I gave you a future worthy of you. That must mean something."

"You gave me a future that I never asked for," Christine stated, her grip never loosening on Erik, "and one you carried out for me with never a consideration to what I wanted. You took away music and the opera; you took away my very *life*, and in doing so, you hoped to kill my memories of Erik. Erik's sin was in wanting to control a heart that was already his; yours was in wanting to steal it." Shaking her head somberly, she whispered, "I never loved you, Raoul; you know that, and it could never have been enough. So to punish me, you tried to break my heart."

"Christine," Raoul warned one last time, and suddenly conscious of his aunt's observance as she watched in horror from her pew, he muttered lowly, "He's a murdering monster."

"No," Christine posed back. "Monsters don't have hearts, and Erik does. I'm loved by it every moment of every day to know it is true. ...I'm sorry, Raoul. Leave us be."

The Vicomte was searching for another protest when the Comtesse left her spot and rushed to grab hold of her nephew. In a sharp tone, Constance insisted the same, "Let them go, Raoul. You would have truly dared to disgrace the de Chagny name by marrying an *opera singer*? You are fortunate that your father isn't alive to see this day; all he did to establish our family, and you've practically ruined it with this stain! We'll be lucky if we can ever hold our heads up high again! What were you thinking to dabble with this tart?"

"I love her," Raoul attempted, but Constance was resolved.

"You should know better!" the Comtesse snapped, and it surprised Christine that to Constance, it really was that simple. "Come on, Raoul. Let's take our leave of this nightmare and never speak of it again!"

Any more protests were futile. With one last abhorred stare at Erik's face, the Comtesse fled down the aisle, careful as she passed him to not even allow the hem of her skirt to touch his shape.

"Now aren't you thrilled that you're not a part of *that* family?" Meg quietly bid as she came alongside Christine and contained an unavoidable giggle behind a raised hand.

Christine wanted to answer with her own sense of lightness, but all thoughts of smiles abandoned her as Raoul halted his exit before her. She noticed instantly how Erik tensed, fisting the hand at the end of the arm she still clutched, ready for an attack if necessary.

"I advise you to listen to your aunt," Erik tightly commanded.

Glaring back at the disfigured man, Raoul arrogantly decided, "Christine isn't worth my death. I won't be fool enough to play her hero again. God help you, Christine, if you come to regret your choices and their consequences because I won't be there to save you."

And that was all. The Vicomte de Chagny stalked past them without a look back, choosing a haughty air over the true defeat of a deserted groom, but Christine did not feel Erik's posture calm and relax even after Raoul was gone from sight. He was taking no chances.

"Well, I hope that means this is over," Meg said

before a shrill shout made her wince.

"Meg Giry!", and her mother came charging down the vacant aisle, casting only one glance at Erik before fixing her attention on her daughter. "Haven't I raised you better than that? Yelling out such obscenities at a wedding that we were privileged to be allowed to attend? Where is your propriety?"

Meg lowered her golden head dutifully, already having anticipated exactly the chosen literature of this particular scolding and what her response would be. "I'm sorry to shame our existence, Mama," she dramatically stated, "but I was only trying to help Christine win her true love. If you want to punish me, then I will not pose an argument, but I do encourage you to look at how happy Christine is and then consider what her fate would have been had I not interfered. Tragic, Mama, to be sure."

Her humility had the desired effect as Madame Giry looked at a diligently nodding Christine and a half-annoyed Erik as he made a face of disgust by the depth of such overdone melodrama. Not even the stage was that exaggerated!

Huffing a slight concession, the ballet mistress decided, "Let's go and see if the Comtesse will allow us back in her house to collect our things, and then I think it best that we start for home. Games of pretend are enjoyable only so long. Wouldn't you agree, Christine?"

"Yes, Madame." And Christine meant it wholeheartedly to consider four months lost to her own game as she inched closer to Erik and felt him finally start to calm beside her.

"Are you coming back to the opera, Christine?" Meg excitedly asked as she watched her mother impatiently gesture for their leave. "I say, blame the Opera Ghost for your disappearance and supposed death and then make a grand return." The little ballerina cast a wary look at Erik, and as the sight of his scarred face made her anxiety rise, she quickly insisted, "Or maybe not...not blame the Opera Ghost, not if that means that the Opera Ghost will return as well with a vengeance... You make the choice, but...it would be so wonderful to have you home."

Christine could not deny that as with a frantic hug, Meg scurried out of the church after her mother, giving a quick wave behind her.

"It *is* your choice," Erik reminded, finally able to face his beloved now that their uneasy audience had dissipated. "Say the word, and I'll have us back in Paris with you as the featured soprano. The little Giry inspired me with her incessant rambling. A torrid tale of the manner in which you cheated death would draw an even greater audience. Everyone in the world would want to see the ghost soprano."

"No more ghosts," Nadir piqued up, reminding them of his presence. "Or notes or opera house accidents or singing statues or potentially life-threatening situations, at least for a little while. Let me recover my wits from this one first please. Give us all a chance to get settled back in Paris before we begin this insanity all over again."

"Then you are returning to Paris as well," Erik concluded matter-of-factly.

"Well, of course. I have nothing better to do with my life than keep an eye out for yours, *and* I expect a wedding invitation as well as an official request for a friendly supper once we are back."

"And you're really so certain that you'd rather not return to Persia instead?" Erik offered with annoyance that only grew as Christine released his arm to hug the daroga. He realized at that moment that he'd always be a little disappointed every second of his life that she was not right at his side.

"Take care," Christine told Nadir, "and thank you."

"I should say the same, only I will add to take care of *him*."

"Of course."

With a wry smile upon his lips, Nadir exchanged a parting nod with Erik and insisted, "I will see you when you get back."

In lieu of a sarcastic reply, all Erik said with sincerity was, "Thank you." And that was enough. Every bit of gratitude was poured into two words and felt as if they had been a hundred instead.

Nadir accepted it with a full heart and left the couple with a new peace that his conscience had not been privileged enough to know in months. Finally, things were in their rightful place.

Eagerly hugging herself to his side again, Christine proudly stated, "You had quite a bit of help today, didn't you? You, the almighty Opera Ghost, who tends to weave his schemes unaided." But all teasing faded as she felt him sag against her with arms that only then shook as they encircled her. "That was all a façade. You were not nearly as confident as you were letting on. Erik, ...you were afraid."

"My fear, as you are apt to call it, was justifiable," he replied, brushing a kiss to her brow. "I had something so dear that I could have lost."

"Erik," she breathed adoringly as her fingers traced the features of his face.

"Devil."

The term alone caused Erik's body to go rigid down the lengths of every muscle, and he lifted a cold glare to the priest who had silently observed the entire scene crouched beside the altar. "Devil, monsieur?" he coldly demanded, lifting his face to make every distorted feature vividly apparent. "Is that what I am to a man of God?"

"Yes, of course, the devil incarnate," the priest nervously stammered with horror staring back.

But it was Christine who retorted before Erik could. "How do you know that?" she snapped defiantly. "How can you look at him and call him the devil?"

"He is ugly-"

"No," she interrupted, "he is *different*, different than every other human being, and who is to say that makes him evil? How can you be certain that his face doesn't make him an angel of God instead? Your ideals of beauty are composed in the principle normality of the human race, but God may consider him as beautiful as I do. You judge what you know nothing of, monsieur."

Erik watched her in awe of her every word and the strength she had grown into carrying. To a man who had spent his lifetime defending himself, facing a cruel assessment at every turn and bend in the road of existence alone, he adored her in that moment more than he ever had and formed a silent prayer to be able to live up to her version of his spirit.

"But his face makes him condemned," the priest dared to protest.

"No," Christine insisted, "*you* make him condemned, you and the rest of the world who deem his face as a curse when I who love him deem it as a blessing." As she vowed, she gazed at that face and its vibrant scars and read a story of ethereal brilliance in its oddities. "I love you, Erik. Let the world say what it will; it can't change my heart."

Mismatched eyes ran over every detail of her in her bridal finery as his mind recalled another paralleled time as she had vowed her love in a kiss and he had ignorantly given it away. He never would again and bent to graze his misshapen lips against hers, breathing in the merest gap between, "*You* are the angel, and I am only your adoring worshiper kneeling at your feet, unworthy of your love. I will always be undeserving, but I will cherish every detail of you until my dying breath. You are my *life*, Christine."

"And you are mine," she whispered back, cupping his face in her palm.

With one more delicate kiss, Erik kept her curved to his side and led her toward the door with never a look back at the appalled priest. It didn't matter, nothing did but the woman beside him gazing at him as if she truly was her everything. He felt as blessed as she had called him.

He had promised a love story to the girl who had broken his heart, but love stories did not always have happy endings. The ending had been a question mark that he had been afraid to fully consider until that moment when threats were gone and hope took their place. Now every glimpse down that road was sunlit and beaming, spread out before them like a tapestry of dreams for the choosing. And he had no doubt that love would make every one into a sort of heaven and chase away every shadow of darkness. Love was always the light...

"A Passionate Interlude"
This is just a bit of fluff and provocative fun.

The streets of Paris were dark and quiet. An early fall chill loomed on each gentle breeze, hinting at colder days, creating goose bumps on exposed skin and refreshing the senses. To Erik, who had never before given much regard to the change and modulation of seasons, it brought a new appreciation and delight. Didn't every aspect of the world amuse him lately? Every one previously overlooked and tossed aside without a care was suddenly being savored. And why such a blatant transformation? ...Well, love could do that, and for a man who was as ignorant to pleasant emotions as the details of the world, it had changed every facet of his life and created a happiness he was sure no other human being could know to such an extent.

Love... What a wondrous consummation of the soul! It could bring pleasure and pain to equaled insurmountable heights. Hadn't he been victim to its every shade of color? It had beaten and nearly destroyed him, and then in the next instant, lifted him on high golden clouds to taste heaven. He could not regret a single tear, not anymore, not when bliss had taken the place of hopelessness and fought to dull every sharp edge he had once suffered. Bliss and only one word defined it: *Christine.* Just pondering her name and its sounds made a smile curve lips that were misshapen beneath his mask. She did not mind their bloated, odd shape or any other deformity of his malformed face. She had even once called it a work of art; ...art was, after all, a subjective thing, wasn't it?

Christine... He was longing for her already, yearning for her presence and nearness, but alas, he was entering the damp catacombs beneath the opera alone tonight, destined only to miss her. If she had been with him on his stroll through the city, she likely would have insisted they remain outside longer and relish the fall air, would have found the delight that

Erik was only just learning and would have taught him why he should adore it even more. She would have cuddled close to his side, her arm looped through his, and would not have hesitated to smile up at him no matter the interfering looks strangers would have given them. She wouldn't have cared. With a sigh, he resigned himself to accept an arm that felt far too bare and strode the passageways toward his empty home. Christine was all he wanted, but he would have to put up with the reality that she wasn't there.

Light filtered out from cracks in the stone façade that served as his house front. He was glad he had left a fire burning in the hearth during his impromptu outing, keeping the inner rooms in possession of their heat and not yet taking up the chill of the catacombs beyond. It also provided a flash of comfort and eased his subconscious with the lie that someone was there awaiting him. Only when he went within those quiet walls would illusion shatter again.

Abandoning the heavy dampness for the rush of warmth that met him the instant he opened the door, he wearily entered the foyer, tossing off his cloak and hat with the intention of seeking a glass of brandy and then retiring early for the night. Nothing else seemed more appealing. Not even music held the usual charms that drew him in during his every free moment. No, tonight loneliness hung too low to be overcome. Sleep would give necessary escape, and then with any luck when he awoke, loneliness could be forgotten all over again.

A few minutes later, brandy glass in hand, Erik sat in his throne-like chair before the crackling fire in the hearth. He idly set to staring at the orange flames in an unfocused manner that made the subtlety blend into one kaleidoscope of motion and brightness. Thought was torture when it could only be of her; he preferred the trance that the flickering flames offered. As their victim, it was no wonder that when desire transformed into reality, he almost did not believe its tangibility.

As he sipped his drink and rested his glass and elbow on the plush armrest, a small hand suddenly reached from behind to caress a feather-light path down the side of his throat. A smile erupted across his face as his free hand caught that roaming one and drew it close for a kiss that could only be awkward with his mask still in place.

"You were gone," he gently accused, keeping that hand as his proof clutched at the hollow of his throat. "Or am I just imagining you again?"

A soft giggle fluttered near his ear. "Again?" she posed sweetly. "Do you imagine me often?"

"Only when you are not close enough for me to indulge my desires." Closing his eyes, he savored the tickle of her curls against his one bare cheek as she leaned from behind and rested her chin on his shoulder. "I was under the impression that you were spending the night at Meg's."

"I missed you too much," she sweetly replied, and as she stood upright and walked around his chair to his observant and intent stare, she reached for the brandy glass in his hand.

Erik felt all speech flee him as he feasted his gaze upon her, watching her gracefully lift the glass to her lips and take a small sip before setting it aside on an end table. Had he ever seen anything more openly provocative? She wore only her underclothes, a flimsy chemise with lace trim and her ruffled pantaloons with her curls loose and cascading over her shoulders. One look into her seemingly innocent eyes, and he knew her appearance was very deliberate.

"Christine," he breathed, the husky edge of desire already on his golden tone. Even as she kept a blameless expression, he knew she was already getting exactly what she was after. "Traipsing about the house in your under-things, sipping alcohol so teasingly from my glass in the same spot my own lips have been, ...it would almost appear that you were intending to seduce me."

Shrugging her shoulders with enacted naïveté,

she continued her timid façade even as she climbed atop his lap, her knees bent on either side of his thighs. "Seducing you? ...Do I really seem as brazen as that?"

His body responded violently. The warm softness of her weight upon him was undoing his mediocre control as his ravenous eyes ran along the smooth, creamy skin of her neck to the exposed swells of the top of each breast. Even as he ached to bury his lips in their lushness, he restrained himself to play her little game.

"Straddling me half-clothed *is* brazen," Erik insisted hoarsely, gripping his fisted hands to the armrests of his chair to keep from touching her. "It's shameless, absolutely whore-like. You want me to desire you, don't you? Is that why you ended your evening early? To tempt me so mercilessly?"

Her blue eyes sparkled in the fire's glow as her full, pink lips curved into a smile. "Oh, much more than that. I don't just want to tempt you."

"Then what exactly *do* you want?" he pushed, his attention caught by her lips with the urge to capture them in his. How soft and sweet they were to the taste!

Sensing his train of thought, she bit her bottom lip teasingly before she plainly admitted, "I want to fuck the Opera Ghost."

His desire surged, his hardened body throbbing as intensely as if she had touched him. "Such vulgarity! Where did you learn such things?"

A flutter of a giggle escaped her as she settled her hips lower to his so that his manhood pressed flush to her, clothing suddenly a frustrating barrier. Just as expected, he was burning for her and unable to hide it. "I seem to recall that you used exactly that word last night as you were performing the very act."

Even though he still would not reach for her, his hips involuntarily arched toward her softness, his erection straining to be lost within her. "I have no excuse, save that you and your enticing body arouse me to heights beyond comprehension. How could I not use such provocative words when I was buried so deeply inside of you? You tempt me to it." Waves of passion were ebbing and cresting within him as he demanded with desperation to hear her. "And...is that your intention then? To seduce me and fuck me?"

"Oh yes," she breathed, lifting her hips and then temptingly lowering them to him again. "I intend to have the almighty Opera Ghost begging for release."

"Indeed?"

Christine's smile answered for her as, to his disappointment, she scampered off his lap, and with his constant stare following, went to retrieve something hidden behind the chair. Coming around to face him again, she displayed a rope to his inquisitively arched brows. "Your arms?" she posed as if her demand was sweetly innocent.

No protest crossed his lips as he willingly complied with eager interest in her plans. Leaning teasingly across his body, she lifted his hands above his head and went about tying his wrists to the wooden trim along the top of the chair.

Erik watched her work, taking note of the way she knotted the rope with a flicker of amusement. It was going to be far too simple to flip this game around to his advantage.

Restrained so that touch was impossible, he waited as she lowered herself back onto his lap and met his eye. "You are a vixen," he accused with a grin. "It amazes me how passionate you are when you used to run from these emotions. Perhaps my own desire has corrupted your innocence and made you as tainted as I am."

"Or," she protested as her hands made a path up his clothed chest, "perhaps I've always been equally as passionate as you are, and you've just brought it out of me."

"It's beyond passionate; it's often quite naughty." Abruptly shaking his head, he added, "Do not take that as a complaint from me. I like you naughty."

"Oh, I know that," she replied with a giggle. Her hand finished its upward path until she could lift the mask from his face and toss it away, exposing his deformity to the glow of the firelight. "If I am naughty, then you are downright wicked. The things you've done to me... I can hardly believe I've allowed you."

"As if you ever had a choice," he teased. "And I would argue that I've made certain you've enjoyed each and every one...quite thoroughly."

"*Quite*," she agreed. Christine's eyes roamed his scars first, making a wayward path that she then took with the tips of her fingers. How many times had she touched him this way? And yet she never seemed to grow tired of it. Part of that was attributed to the sheer wonder always creasing those features to know her touch, as if even after everything she and Erik had endured and finally conquered to be together, he was still amazed and overcome that she would touch his face and not know disgust. Though she savored his expression, she was sure she would like it even more the day that such a thing no longer brought a single notice at all.

Setting aside serious thoughts, she gave him a devilish grin that hinted her devious plans before she slowly slid to her knees on the soft carpet between his legs, leaning forward so that her fingers could unbutton his shirt. From her crouched position, she gazed back up at his captive form with amusement.

"I find I like having you tied up as a slave to my whims," she revealed, spreading the material of his shirt wide and exposing the smooth, white skin of his chest.

"Don't grow to favor it too much," he warned. "I am the sort of man who likes to be in control of situations."

"And this is not pleasant to you?" she asked as she bent to press kisses down his chest and stomach, enjoying his squirm. "Ah, just as I thought. You don't hate it as much as you'd like me to believe. In fact, I think it intrigues you to be utterly helpless to me and so contradictory to your usual self." Splaying her palms flat against his stomach, she slowly brought them to the buckle of his pants, casting looks back and forth between her task and his expectant stare.

"Well, I *am* permitting you, aren't I?" Erik hoped she did not know just how eager he was for her to touch his aching body, but in the instant his pants were opened and his desire sprung forth, it could no longer be underestimated. "More than intrigued by your game; I am exceedingly aroused by it," he admitted before she could say it herself. "I am burning for your touch."

Christine seemed satisfied with his honesty, running her hand up the full length of his hardened shaft before her fingers closed around his vast width. Though he could guess at her lustful intent, moaning his yearning, the instant she let her lips touch the tip of him in a feather-light kiss, he felt the thrill race through his entire frame in a violent shudder.

"Tell me what you want me to do," she commanded even as she grazed another kiss.

"I thought *you* were the one in control of this game," he hoarsely gasped, arching his hips toward her mouth and groaning his disappointment when his eagerness made her draw back and create a torturous distance.

"Oh, I am," Christine insisted. "And by my own order, I want you to say the words aloud." How she adored the amused glint in his mismatched eyes as they hungrily raked over her!

With a salacious grin on his misshapen lips, he complied. "I want you to take me into your mouth."

The tip of one finger trailed up him as she asked so innocently that it drove him mad, "Shall I be gentle with you?"

"God, no!" he exclaimed, desperately trying to arch into her hand again. "You know I like it rough."

Frowning, she drew away and replied, "Yes, but as you said yourself, it is *my* game."

"Cruel, Christine," he growled. "I am aching with your teasing!"

His hips lifted off the chair with an arch toward her, and she was only too pleased to keep beyond his reach, shaking her head with her taunting denial. Only when he eased back into the cushions did she approach again, beaming her triumph.

"Gentle first," she insisted, and leaning over his throbbing manhood, she lightly circled the tip with her tongue, glancing at him to see his fevered regard of her every motion. Continuing in that manner, she licked and kissed, teasing mercilessly and yet admiring his control as he remained still and let her do as she pleased. Gentle only lasted until she could tell his patience was dwindling to nothing. Then leaning back again, she breathed, "And now rough."

A cry escaped Erik with his delight in the instant she took all of him into her mouth, the warm wetness encircling and overwhelming him. Every instinct within screamed to grab her loose curls and hold her to him, to take control from her and establish his own rhythm, but his captive hands prevented him from being more than the willing slave she had called him. All he could do was lean back in his chair and watch her build his desire to dizzying heights, moaning with unbridled need at her eager aggression.

Christine continued to devour him only long enough to bring him to the brink, not over it. *Oh no, her game would not be over yet!* And the smile that curved her lips said as much as she pulled away and met his desperate stare.

"And you mean to leave me like this?" he breathlessly demanded, his manhood and its dull and constant ache the sole focus of his desire-clouded mind. "If I swallow my pride and beg you as you want, will you continue?"

Slowly shaking her head, she rose, letting her eyes travel over her captive in his state of disheveled and askew clothing. Her fingers sought the ribbon at the neckline of her chemise, untying and holding his lustful gaze as she lifted it gracefully over her head. The discarding of her pantaloons followed, leaving her bare in the delicious warmth of the firelight, though the penetrating heat from his eyes was far greater to endure.

"You are so very beautiful," Erik marveled, adoring every womanly curve, every provocative detail. It was a constant impetus for amazement whenever he would consider that she was all his, that she had freely given herself to him that first night and again and again since without lingering regret or fear.

She beamed even as she feigned nonchalance. "You always say that when you have me naked in front of you. I feel you think you must compliment in order to have me."

"I do not need to give compliments to have you," he insisted back. "I am merely stating a truth as I think it in my mind."

She wasn't entirely convinced, and the furrow that suddenly creased her brow brought concern through desire as she asked, "You don't still doubt that I desire you, do you, Erik?"

Doubt had been a prevalent interference in the beginning. How could it not be when he still vividly recalled days of her running from him in horror? ...And yet how often since then had she proven herself?

Erik shook his head, keeping passion intact. "To so enthusiastically do what you do to my body, how can I question if you want me? Shy and modest left you in that very first night, and since then, I'd argue that your desire rivals my own."

"It does," she agreed, climbing atop his lap again as his eyes continued to worship her. Pressing her palms to the bare skin of his chest and with her lips hovering near his ear, she temptingly whispered, "I am so wet for you, *ange*, ...but alas, you cannot touch me and confirm my words with your hands tied."

"Untie the rope, and I'll touch every inch of you," he offered, writhing with her silken body atop him and so close to exactly what he yearned for.

"Not yet." As she raised herself up with knees pressed alongside his thighs, she commanded, innocence still in every provocative order, "Kiss my breasts."

Erik did not hesitate as their fullness lingered before him, eagerly catching one pink tip between his lips and teasing with his tongue before imitating with the other.

Christine mewed her delight, arching nearer to his tempting mouth and only aroused further to watch those lips, misshapen as they were, at her breast. What had once so long ago disgusted her at first sight turned out to light her own desire to even greater heights, convincing her a hundred times over that they were meant to be together. No one else could crave such disfigured features in the way she constantly did.

Purposely tilting his head back to end his caresses, he huskily inquired, "You love when I kiss your breasts, don't you?"

"Erik," she whined, desperate for him to continue, "you know I do!"

"Yes, but I want to hear you say it."

She knew it was her right to refuse and reestablish her control of this game, but the teasing fire in his eyes encouraged her compliance. "Yes," she answered, lowering her face to press idle kisses to his disfigured cheek in her need for more, "I love it when you kiss my breasts. It makes me burn."

"Even though my lips are misshapen?" he pushed, still refraining from continuing.

"I was just thinking that very thought: that I love it *because* your lips are misshapen. They are yours, Erik, and therefore the only ones I want on my body."

Growling his delight, Erik abruptly caught one

nipple between his lips and suckled it ravenously, driven near insanity when she cried out and dug her fingers into his thin hair to clutch him closer yet.

Christine only allowed his fervent assault a moment more before she positioned herself over him, holding his expectant stare all the while. Instead of taking his hardness inside as he wanted, she grinned wantonly and simply grazed the tip with her wetness.

Groaning his impatience, Erik hoarsely ordered, "Now, Christine! I can take this no more!"

But she shook her head and kept her hips lifted to continue to play, moving so that his manhood stroked the length of her, and never taking more than the tip within.

That was all Erik could handle. Wrenching his wrists free of ropes he had systematically untied from the very beginning, he roughly caught her hips between his hands and dragged her down, plunging deep inside of her.

"Cheater!" she accused despite the gasp that caught the edge of her voice with desire's surge.

"Well, you are merciless!" He held her motionless, content for the moment with the fact that he was within her. And then he decided to make his own game.

Easily lifting her meager weight, he brought both their bodies down to the plush carpeted floor, never allowing her to notice that he had the rope twisted around one wrist. As she immediately conceded to the urging of his motions and laid back, he quickly captured her arms and raised them above her head.

"What are you doing!" she exclaimed, trying to yank free, but he had already tied her securely in place, her wrists bound to the carved leg of his throne-like chair.

"Taking control," Erik matter-of-factly replied, giving one last tug to the rope. "You really should know better than to think ropes would hold me prisoner. But, you see, the knots I've just tied are impenetrable. You, *mon ange*, are captured and at *my* mercy."

Narrowing her eyes, she could not completely dim her mischievous grin. "And what will you do with me? Will you torture me as I tortured you?"

His eyes perused her naked form with his blatant desire on display as he stood and began to rid himself of his remaining clothing. "I am not so cruel," he replied lightly. "Or so patient. After your games, how can I stand to wait much longer?"

A delighted laugh escaped her, and with a desirous grin, she eagerly parted her legs, expecting his invasion and tempting him to it as he lingered to admire her.

Naked and aching, Erik knelt beside her, unable to tear his eyes from her flawless, creamy flesh. With growing amusement across his disfigured face, he suddenly moved between her legs, but instead of entering her, he bent and covered her with his eager lips.

"Erik!" she exclaimed even as her body arched toward that tempting mouth. His tongue teased her with gentle strokes before it slid deep inside, making her writhe with surrender. She could already feel her desire mounting with a need for release that stole her breath away, but to her moan of disappointment, he pulled back before she could have it.

"I thought you weren't going to torture me!" she whined, watching him sit up with his hands still caressing her inner thighs.

"It wasn't my initial plan," he admitted, licking her wetness from his lips. "But seeing you so erotically spread before me... That convinced me otherwise." He let one hand glide up her thigh and very gently tease her womanhood, making her entire body shiver. "Tell me what you want, Christine. What do you want me to do to you?"

She gasped in a harsh breath as his fingertip encircled her most sensitive place, and in a breathless whisper, she replied, "Fuck me."

Grinning salaciously, he dared to continue, "And do you want me to be gentle or rough?"

"Rough, Erik. Please, rough!"

He needed no more urging. Lowering his body to hers, he abruptly thrust inside of her, savoring her cry of elation and swallowing it in a desperate kiss. She met his devouring lips with equaled fervor, entwining her tongue with his as it delved to taste her.

By her urging, he was not gentle, thrusting harsh and feverish, and within minutes, she tore her lips from his to scream his name as ecstasy overwhelmed and stole reality away. As she recovered her senses, she took note of the way Erik's arms felt wrapped so tightly and securely around her body, clutching her as close as he could as he moved in and out. And then as passion suffocated reason and took thought away in its fog, a guttural shout fled those lips as he exploded deeply within her, riding out every last wave of sensation until it diminished.

A few minutes later, when words began to make sense again, he gasped out, "My God, Christine, you amaze me!" Though he remained joined with her, he lifted his hands to untie the rope from her wrists, shuddering again the instant her freed hands stroked his shoulders and along his back.

"You have a problem with patience, *mon amour*," she chided back. "I would have amazed you further if you hadn't ended my fun."

"Oh, I have no doubt of that! But I might have lost all control before you managed. You had me on the very brink of exploding, and not even *I* am strong enough to deny it that long." Bending his head, he laid teasing kisses along the side of her throat in penance. "And besides," he breathed against her skin, "that's more for next time...which, considering my current state of satisfied exhaustion, may not be until tomorrow at the earliest."

Laughing with amusement, she teased, "You're showing your age, *ange*. You cannot tire so easily; we are still newlyweds after all."

"Well, perhaps if my wife didn't please me so completely or so well, I wouldn't be as entirely spent as I currently am. That is not an issue of age; it is simply that you are far too provocative."

Erik placed a sweet kiss to her nose, and she giggled and turned her face to lay her cheek to his scarred one, delighting in its textures and oddities and knowing every detail was hers.

"So then," she said with a gentle nuzzle, "I guess you are not angry that I stole your evening alone and returned early from my outing."

"I suffered a lifetime of evenings alone, plenty to last me to eternity and back. In fact, I was *dreading* it. When we haven't spent a night away from each other in the last six months, I was afraid I'd forgotten *how* to be alone and how to endure it."

"And now you need not worry to remember how," she replied, weaving her arms more securely around him. "Never again, *ange*."

"I love you," he breathed near her ear, savoring still being one with her as he gently moved his hips. "...And I adore your naughty side."

She laughed again. "Well, that's good because it is all for you after all. My desire is only yours, as is my love."

"Forever, Christine."

"Forever," she agreed and cuddled deeper into his embrace. How blissful it was to be in love!

"Cadence"
A finale story told from Christine's POV.

And with a kiss, I sealed my fate. A kiss... It shouldn't have been a monumental event; it's such a mundane contact. How many kisses are given away so frivolously on a daily basis? How many hold no true meaning beyond the physical? I myself have been one to indulge in the triviality, granting kisses to Raoul for no more than his own desirous urging. How often had I used the act of a kiss as collateral? Giving them to reassure his doubting mind of devotions that were actually dwindling on my part? A kiss, a lie, a deceptive device...

That should have held true for my current situation. This kiss should have been only to procure Raoul's freedom, *should have been...*

As we parted, and Erik looked at me with those eyes, those damning, soul-consuming eyes, I saw a mirror image of my own astounded expression. We were both equally innocent to the emotions that had been stirred and ignited to life, both equally at a loss for logical comprehension. All we could do was stare at one another.

Before either of us could sort out reality and reason, we were rudely interrupted by another of what had been a stream of shouted curses from the unnerved Vicomte in the torture chamber. That was it; spell broken to fragmented shards of soul-piercing glass.

Without a word, Erik strode away from me with a very determined course and within moments, returned, dragging the enraged Vicomte, who was obviously annoyed to be manhandled but only made feeble struggles to get free.

"Christine," Raoul called, and as his eyes sought mine and ran frantically over me from head to toe, he did not attempt to hide his surprise to find me clothed in the elegant wedding gown Erik had insisted upon.

460

What could I say to him? What explanation could be given to what I myself was so uncertain of? Of their own accord, my eyes traveled from the handsome, flawlessly sculpted face of the Vicomte to the malformed, pathetic one of my once angel teacher, taking in every scar, every deformity in contrast. He was a hideous sight; he had never claimed to be anything else. And to my own surprise, he was all I wanted to behold.

Erik unceremoniously tossed Raoul to the floor, a flash of satisfaction passing his gaze to watch the Vicomte stagger back to his feet, but as that same stare met mine again, any pleasant emotion faded and was swallowed in despair. "Go," he suddenly insisted, that beautiful voice I so adored twisted in agony.

"What?" I was sure I had misheard him, sure he meant Raoul...alone.

"Go, Christine," he repeated, more firmly and resolved. "Take your Vicomte, and leave this place. Now."

"Erik..." Words floated in meaningless phrases and incomplete clauses through my addled mind. I wanted to go to him, to touch him, anything to reinforce the choice I myself had been the one to make, the choice I was determined to follow through to its completion.

Raoul, however, needed no further urging and was grasping at my hand and pulling me to the door without my acquiescence, even as my desperate eyes were fixed in a gaze over my shoulder with Erik's.

"No." I found only a meek squeaking of my voice and suddenly began to struggle against Raoul's viselike hold. "No."

But Raoul was undeterred and easily pulled me along with him; it wasn't a difficult task, most especially considering the traumas of late. They had left me quite a bit frailer than the girl I had been months before.

We were outside the small, hidden house, and he was leading me to the boat at the shore of the underground lake. In the distance of the nearby catacombs, I could hear the rumble of the impending mob. *My God, the mob!* I knew they would not be happy unless Erik was dead. Erik, ...my angel...

"Erik! Erik!" I suddenly shouted, nearly hysterical, fighting with renewed vigor against the flashed image of his lifeless corpse in my mind: never again to sing, never again to hold me in his arms, never again to chuckle with amusement at something I said to him. He had once told me that I was the only one to ever make him laugh, that I was his only happiness...

"Erik!" I shrieked again, and then he was there, coming from the doorway of the house, seeking me with urgent eyes.

"Christine." Raoul was the one to speak my name first with anger as he glanced between Erik and me. "Come on."

"The...the mob," I heard myself insisting, something, *anything* to be my seeming excuse.

As if on cue, loud explosions of gunfire resounded through the cave-like catacombs, reverberating all around us at such a deafening volume that I screamed in terror. They were *shooting*! Still merely an approaching glow of torchlight in a nearby tunnel, but already their vengeance had begun.

"Get her out of here!" Erik suddenly roared at Raoul.

And then it happened...

I saw it as if in a dream: a burst of gunfire and Erik suddenly falling to the ground.

"No!" I shouted and jerked out of Raoul's hold, running toward my fallen angel without a thought.

Raoul tried to stop me, terrified for my safety, but I was a step ahead and at Erik's side, catching his shoulders in my shaking hands.

"Erik," I whispered, tears filling my eyes.

"Sshh," he crooned and tried to lift himself to a seated position as I automatically helped him, too dazed to argue. "It's just a scratch."

Scratch! All I saw was the blood, wetting the leg of his pants just below his knee, soiling through the material to stain the ground in red, ...smeared streaks of red.

"Christine, let's go," Raoul insisted, trying to pull me away again.

"No!" I shouted at him with a sudden ferocity that shocked all three of us. "I won't leave him! The mob will kill him, Raoul!"

"So, what does it matter?" I had never seen the Vicomte so arrogant, so uncaring, and at that moment, I hated him.

"Christine," Erik called gently, and I eagerly turned my gaze to him, breaking away from Raoul to once again crouch beside my angel, even as he shook his head in an adamant denial. "Go, *petite*, please. I can't bear to consider anything happening to you."

"Not without you," I insisted vehemently, and lifting my eyes back to Raoul, I set my own terms this time. "I won't leave with you unless we take Erik with us."

"Christine-"

"You say you love me." I was once again using something that should have been significant to my advantage. "Prove it. I *won't* leave him here, Raoul."

The Vicomte was openly enraged, but I was confident that I had won, waiting patiently as his resolve crumbled to consent.

"Monsieur," the Vicomte hissed without cordiality to Erik and gestured to the boat. "If you will."

Erik looked dubiously between the two of us, but I didn't give him the chance to refuse as I whispered, "Erik, *please*."

He held my eye for a long moment, and I pondered how behind those orbs, one so blue and one so green, I could not decipher the inner workings of his brain. He was so accustomed to concealing emotion even from me, and despite the fact that I knew him better than anyone did or would care to, when he gave me that guarded expression, I was at a loss for what he felt he must first decide alone.

"Erik," I begged again, gesturing a hand to the mob's approach, and with a hint of reluctance, he nodded and started to rise. His injury, however superficial he had attempted to justify it, hindered even that simplest of tasks. It was I with my meager stature that caught him before he fell back again, helping him steady on his feet.

Only the most fleeting of thoughts touched my mind that it was a rarity for us to be so physically near one another and certainly something never considered for Erik, my own guardian angel, to be the weaker of the two of us and in need of *my* help, feeble as it was. But with Raoul obviously unwilling to offer any sort of aid, I did not hesitate to slip my arms around Erik's torso and allow him to lean on me. There was shame mingled with gratitude in his gaze as it met mine, but he set his arm upon my shoulders without argument.

"Well?" the Vicomte demanded coldly from where he had untied the boat, and we slowly made a haphazard trek to join him. If Raoul was jealous by my concern and eagerness to help Erik, he never said so, acting as much a surly child as he had all along, and I certainly did not have the time or impetus to care. Let him be jealous if it got me what I wanted, namely Erik alive and not the casualty of the bloodthirsty mob.

With only a modicum of my support, Erik climbed into the boat, grunting and cringing to himself, disinclined to share his pain with me and the overt concern I could not hide. As we launched off in the opposite direction as the shouts and occasional gunshot, my natural impulse bade me to bury my trembling body in Erik's embrace, guardian to all ends, but, of course, I had to deny anything of the sort, sustaining myself with solely an unbreakable stare on him. I wanted to curse Raoul's interfering presence, but my better sense reminded me that we likely wouldn't have gotten far without it. Raoul was the only one capable of rowing us to safety.

"Monsieur," Raoul sharply bid as he threw his weight into his task. "Some direction would be appreciated. I am at a loss for escape now that I must busy myself with concealing a fugitive as well."

"Straight, Monsieur Vicomte." Despite his pain, Erik matched his tone and even served in more spite. "To the end of the tunnel... Then we will have to hide."

Neither Raoul nor I asked what he meant. I was confident without a single doubt that Erik would keep us safe, that he would know exactly what to do. He had never failed me before, unlike every other person in my life. He was my constant.

My eyes idly ran over his face as he seemed to meticulously avoid looking at anything but the water around us. Had I really kissed those misshapen, bloated lips? ...And dear God, why did the memory of it alone make my body tingle and the desire to do it again twist urgently in my belly? It was one kiss, my sense argued. Some of the ballerinas gossiped about dozens of men they shared kisses with, dozens of kisses even. It shouldn't hold such sway, should it?

...And yet when I had kissed Erik, it had felt like the earth had moved, like ground, stable and dependable as it always was, had suddenly shifted beneath our feet, leaving every principle one clings to as logic flipped onto its head, upside down *and* inside out.

It would have been a lie to say that I had never considered the feelings I possessed deep in my heart of hearts for Erik in a romantic vein. For some time, emotion had been thriving within me, and I had no knowledge of where or when its origin lay, as if it had always been there waiting to be acknowledged, ...waiting for permission to exist. My loyalty to Raoul continuously stifled its possession, the immature vows we had once made to one another that should have meant forever. ...But an even greater obstacle than witting betrayal was my lingering apprehension to Erik, that vain voice in my mind that constantly reminded what lay just out of sight beneath the mask, hidden but omnipotent in its power to keep us apart. Denial became necessary for my very sanity. I was terrified to realize my own thoughts! And how long would I have continued down that path? Virtually half-alive because how can one truly live while holding at bay the very right and privilege to *feel*?

Was what I felt for Raoul even a fraction of what I did for Erik? If Raoul had been the injured one tonight, would I have been only *too* willing to leave him to the mob and run off with Erik instead? It shamed me to consider how appealing an option that was; ...if I would have known regret for such an act was the real unanswerable question.

Glancing to Raoul as he rowed furiously, I noticed the repulsed glares he cast to my unrecognizing angel, and I momentarily wished I had thought to grab his mask, not for me but for Erik. He did not deserve such stares, especially from Raoul with his mockingly perfect features. If I could have, I would have covered that tattered cheek, that absent nose, that sunken eye, with my own hands to keep it protected from unwanted observance. Raoul did not deserve the *right* to see Erik's true face. I wanted to jealously claim so aloud, to scream at his lack of compassion, that the face he seemed so disgusted to even share the air with was only mine, that Erik's dearly distorted features were *made to be* mine.

Raoul caught my glowering gaze and attempted a smile, and I had to look away. It had been an exhausting night; I no longer had the strength to play along.

My gaze drifted to my wringing hands, idly twisting in the crinoline skirt of the wedding gown. I still lacked the answer to whether or not Erik had intended for us to wed this night before all his plans had gone awry. He had only demanded that I stay with him in his hasty threat; the term 'marriage' had not come up in any vein, but an implication. For all his sins and the dark gaps within him, he had only ever remained honorable and respectable toward me, the perfect gentleman. Such a concept made me sure marriage was the only considerable route to his intentions. He wouldn't want to tarnish me and the perfection he saw me to be, ...despite how undeserving I always felt of such a title.

The tunnel ended in another shore up ahead and past that all I saw was a dark passageway. Dark had always been a fear of mine, and even now caused reminiscent goose bumps to rise upon my skin. Only with Erik had that fear been assuaged, as he had always insisted that he himself was the most terrifying thing that lurked in the shadows and I faced him on a daily basis. "Unfounded," he had called my fear, and I remembered vividly how he had gestured to his mask and even asked if I had seen anything else more worthy of screams and genuine horror. I hadn't, but I hadn't told him that.

Raoul did not help Erik as we arrived onshore; not that I thought he would have been considerate enough to "lower" himself to such a thing, but he retained his disgusted look with every glance in Erik's direction as if he considered that by merely touching Erik, his austere appearance would become disfigured as well. I, on the other hand, gave not even a hesitation, eager to touch him in any way that he would allow me, ...even in a way that went beyond aid. No, it was he who was the reluctant one, and yet, thankfully, he saw the necessity enough to permit me.

As he hobbled out of the boat, his malformed features contorted into a pained expression, his jaw clenching in a tight line, and overcome with the urge to soothe that intrusive tension, I brushed a caress to his unmarked cheek and drew his eye to mine. I would have touched his scars without a second thought; I wanted to far more than I even admitted to myself. But I was terrified of upsetting Erik, and in our current situation under an already annoyed audience of the Vicomte, I knew I would have to wait.

"Erik," I bid gently, "are you all right, *ange*?"

He forced a less severe expression; I knew it was a lie. "Fine, *petite*, fine. We have to keep moving."

I nodded and willingly slid my arms around his waist, grateful I could use his injury as an excuse to cling to him and draw strength from his guardian spirit.

To me, this part of our journey seemed never-ending. I wasn't burdened by Erik, who was obviously determined to do most of the work himself, pain be damned. But echoing around us, I could still hear the mob, albeit fainter with our distance. I wasn't sure that they wouldn't pursue, and neither was Erik; I could tell by the determined pace he tried desperately to keep.

As we walked the darkened tunnel, at some point that I considered random since there was no sort of landmark to decipher location, Erik ordered, "Here. Wait. Stop here."

He knew exactly what he was doing, releasing the meager hold he had on me to stagger the rest of the way to what appeared to be only a stone wall. I did not see how he did it, but the next thing I knew, there was a small click and the wall opened up to us. I should have known by now that he had a great many passages through the opera, but as always, I held an absolute amazement to consider his genius.

We found ourselves in a small room, stone walls on all sides, trapped once they door was closed.

Raoul rounded on Erik furiously. "And what do you intend, Monsieur le Fantôme? To lock us in?"

"For now," Erik replied. "If I were you, Monsieur Vicomte, I would be most concerned with keeping Christine safe."

"Of course that is always my main concern!" Raoul snapped back. "She is *my* fiancée. *I* will be the one responsible for her well-being."

Erik did not reply, but I recognized a brief flash

of jealous pain in his eyes, so subtle that anyone else would have missed it. I knew the emotion must have been striking with brutal fierceness for him to let it through his impenetrable guard.

Eager to do something to break the tension, I asked him, "What is this place, Erik? Did you build it in the walls?"

He shrugged with a modesty I was used to seeing. "I have a few similar rooms throughout the catacombs. I planned for hasty escapes, you see. There are provisions along the wall: blankets, towels, fresh water, lanterns." With a grimace of the pain he fought to endure, he slowly took a much-needed seat on the stone ground.

How my heart ached with him! "You need to let me tend to your leg," I told him matter-of-factly, seeking the towels he had mentioned. It felt absolutely wonderful to have some task to set my mind to.

"Christine," he attempted the argument I was expecting, "that is unnecessary." It was feeble; he knew I was right. His paler than usual complexion was enough to justify the necessity to both of us, his argument based more on a loathing to seem weak in any sense of the word.

"Tend to?" Raoul inquired with a cringe. "Must you, Christine?"

"Yes, it could get infected." There was more to it than a desire to keep me from helping his enemy, and I nearly smiled with amusement. "Do you not tolerate the sight of blood well, Raoul?"

"I..." The Vicomte, one of the richest and most respected men in Paris, was at a loss for words over what I saw to be a ridiculously mundane issue.

"Perhaps you should wait outside the room," I offered.

"And leave you here with *him*?" Raoul shook his head adamantly and watched me with a hawk's eye as I collected a few towels and some water and returned to kneel before an equally attentive Erik.

I met Erik's gaze for a brief instant and softly said, "This will hurt. ...I'll do my best to be gentle."

"I've endured far worse," he replied, and I knew he was not exaggerating, that if anything, he was yet underestimating what he had suffered in a past I knew only scant bits about, only what he would willingly admit. It was violent, the sort of nightmare one cannot even fathom enough to have. It was truly a miracle he had survived it.

My fingers found the leg of his pants, curving around the cuff at his ankle, and as carefully as I could, I lifted it to reveal a bloody mess over every inch of white skin and an injury that was more than the scratch he had called it.

"Oh..." Raoul moaned behind me, and I turned to see him run out the open doorway without pause.

To my surprise, Erik actually smirked; injured, bloody, in more pain than he was willing to reveal, and he still found humor enough to mock the Vicomte. I could not help but share his grin, meeting his gaze in a conversation that needed no words to qualify its existence.

In the next instant, I was back to my task and proceeded to clean the wound that thankfully still bled only a little. The bullet was not there; I could tell that much. It had been a graze, but it had certainly done its damage. As promised, I enacted gentleness with every stroke of the wet towel across the injury, and for the most part, Erik gave nothing away, only a couple of grunts and one hiss when I crossed the gaping center.

"You're a good patient," I softly said, glancing up at him as I diligently worked. "You've endured such things often, haven't you?"

"Often? ...Enough," he answered with an apathetic shrug. "I've never had anyone tend to my wounds before, though. Usually, I have that task to myself. I can assure you that you cause far less pain than my own hands and mediocre attempts have."

As the dried blood was gone from skin so white

that my own pale complexion looked creamy against it, I added a hesitant caress of my bare fingertips across the brunt of the injury and heard him give a slight hiss.

"Oh! I didn't mean to hurt you!" Guilt assaulted me for indulging my foolish whim. I had only thought to give a pleasant touch to skin that had been so violated, but as I met his stare apologetically, those mismatched orbs bore into me.

"You didn't hurt me, Christine," he softly revealed, eyes holding mine intently.

I wanted to push the subject, but was shaken under such a gaze, and blushing pink, so bright I felt my cheeks burn, I returned to my task of bandaging the injury, ripping a towel into long strips and forming a makeshift wrapping. Every time I attempted a casual glance at my patient, I found those eyes on me, and even when I didn't, their stare pierced my flesh, straight through to my soul. There were questions there, questions that hung unuttered between us, but left a visible mark in the air. Had they always existed? I couldn't remember a time without them and the pressure they brought, pressure to define what had so long remained indefinable. He had always wanted answers, and I had always avoided the questions.

With my chosen task complete, before I dared look at him and lose my courage, I followed a whim, something that was uncharacteristic for me but in this particular situation, necessary. Leaning near, I pressed a kiss just above the bandage's edge, against the smooth, white flesh alongside his knee, undeterred from prolonging it even as I felt him go rigid and heard his harshly gasped breath.

When I slowly drew away again, I lifted my eyes to his and saw his terrified expression as if my kiss was anything but the tender caress it had been. Tears were rapidly filling those mismatched depths, glistening and twinkling as he shook his head adamantly back and forth, denying something. *What?*

my mind demanded, but my tongue could not find a
voice to ask it aloud. He did not speak either; he was
too aghast for words. But he trembled; I could feel it
as every bit of his flesh seemed to share its possession
until a slight shiver became a violent shaking that I
knew I could never understand. Only a lifetime of
cruelty devoid of any form of kindness or love could
have given me insight into the depth of what he
suffered.

Staring at him all the while, I tentatively placed
my palm in complete delicacy against his ankle, and
almost immediately, a soft sob escaped his misshapen
lips, his flesh quivering beneath my touch. I
wondered if he would protest, if he would be angered,
wondered how far I was breeching the propriety of
our undefined relationship, but I couldn't seem to find
the will to stop. As he shook and cried silent tears, I
looked between that intense gaze and the touch of my
hand as it made a languid path up his white calf,
delicately across the boundary of the bandage, and
over his knee to the spot my lips had known, tracing
my fingertips over the invisible mark I had left in my
unthreatening wake.

"Christine," he whispered breathless, a million
utterances in his eyes. Perhaps he would have spoken
them, perhaps he would have explained why he still
bore such a look of fear in the background.

But a soft shuffle of footsteps made me
suddenly yank my hand away in the instant Raoul
called into the cave, "Christine, have you finished?"

"Y...yes," I stammered, casting a guilt-filled
glance to Erik, but he would not look at me as he
suddenly jerked his cuffed pant leg back into place
and scooted away from my nearness.

If Raoul could feel the tension boiling rapidly
in the room, he didn't mention a word of it. But
perhaps that explained his overcompensation, as he
came to my side and placed an unwanted kiss atop my
head, that I noticed Erik witness solemnly.

"My compassionate darling," Raoul gushed,

472

and I fought not to cringe and even shudder.

My eyes were again drawn to Erik as if through stare alone, I could explain that I wasn't at fault, that Raoul acted on his own without my encouragement or desire. But Erik stumbled to his feet, and under a limp from his sore leg, he went to secure the hidden door to prevent intruders.

"No one was following," Raoul insisted condescendingly. "I was standing by the lake this entire time and saw no boats or lights, heard no shouts. They are not in pursuit."

Erik did not reply as he came back to join us, and understanding even his unspoken comments all too well, I hurried to my feet and went to collect blankets for the night. I would never argue against Erik and his intuition.

As I handed a blanket to the sneering Vicomte, he demanded, "And you intend for us to sleep *here*, Monsieur? In a dank cave? On a hard stone floor? Isn't it a bit overdone to camp out from a nonexistent threat?"

"Raoul," I snapped, already beyond my levels of aggravation with his intruding presence. "Trust him. He's just trying to keep us safe."

"Is he, Christine? Or is all of this only another ridiculous game? How could I possibly trust that murdering freak won't kill me in my sleep?"

"Enough!" I nearly shouted, noticing Erik cast me a sideways glance tinged in pleased surprise.

"I can't be blamed for it," Raoul continued. "The bastard already attempted to kill me once tonight, you do realize. And now he wants us all to vulnerably sleep in the same room together? It seems a bit too convenient."

At that point, I could not say that I didn't wish that to *be* Erik's intended plan. Raoul had pushed me far too much tonight, reminding me in the process how many thoughts he himself had put into my head, how many times he had twisted things about to make me see Erik as the villain. Had I ever truly feared Erik before Raoul's ridiculous assumptions?

"You forget," I was arguing equally as vehement. "Erik was the one to release you once already this evening. If he wanted to kill you, he would have done it then."

"You are naïve, Christine, entirely a willing subject to his spells and far too trusting in an inherently good soul that does not exist."

I was on the verge of screaming a retort with blatant impetus for attack. I might have actually done it and even lunged at him had Erik not broken into our argument.

"Monsieur Vicomte," Erik snapped, "Christine is right, and you are no gentleman to dare question her character. If I had intentions of killing you, you would be dead already without regret on my part, I assure you." The rage in his eyes was one I had seen before, but I also saw his determination to keep it within his control. "And as to the nature of my soul, that is for God to judge, *not you*, Monsieur."

With that, he grabbed a blanket and went to the farthest wall of the cave from the two of us. Then with only one look in my direction, he turned his back and lay on the hard, cold stone floor, dragging the blanket over himself without pause. He shut us out, ...well, shut *Raoul* out; I was only included by default. It made my blood boil with a fierceness that left me shaking all over, for Raoul had not only enraged Erik but had caused him to shun me as well when all I wanted was to be in his comforting company. Damn him!

Shooting Raoul a cold glare that sang with the curses in my head, I went to the side wall away from both men and imitated Erik's motions, laying down facing stone. My hands curled tightly in the coarse material of the blanket, drawing it close not only to block out the dank chill looming in the catacomb air but to conceal from my eyes the wedding gown, smeared in blood, smudged with dirt, further attestation to the trauma this night had been.

Manifestations of a Phantom's Soul

I couldn't have slept if I tried. At some point, I heard Raoul lay down, thankfully making no move to approach me. I would have been happy never to speak to him again after this night, never to have to answer the questions I knew had been brought to life in his mind, never to have to justify myself, my feelings, my very soul. How blissful would it have been to close my eyes, drift off, and find upon opening them again that this had all been a nightmare, that the last *six months* had never happened.

I imagined it in my head as my eyes stared unseeing at the stone grey before them. I didn't want the days of an angel's presence in my life; no, I wanted the ones between, the ones when though I had known exactly who and what Erik was, I had gone to him anyway. Oh, how I would love to live those days again! Only I would do it so differently now. I wouldn't let myself be the meek, scared mouse. No, I was determined that if I could go back, I would be stronger and follow my heart's bidding, the exact longing I had shunned and run from right into Raoul's eagerly awaiting arms.

It stunned me to realize that *I* had been the cause of all of this and the pain attached. Never before had I considered myself worthy of any kind of dramatics, good or bad. Erik had always tried to prove otherwise to my unconfident self. Every negative comment that had ever passed my lips in his presence, he had always countered with double as many compliments. He saw me as special and so entirely different than I had ever seen myself.

One time, as I recalled with a tinge of a smile, I had been crying in my dressing room after some seemingly evil words from La Carlotta. She had called me plain and dull with the voice of a mewing cat, her jealous rants tearing me to pieces. And as I had sobbed to myself, Erik had breathed in such warm and endearing tones that I was so beautiful that when with me, he could not take his eyes away because every other object in the world paled in comparison.

It was always that way with him; he not only said beautiful things, but he genuinely thought them as well, which was why I was always so humbled when he would bestow such compliments on me. Of course, most had been spoken from behind my mirror, not in an angel's guise but with his own lacking confidence as his hindrance.

We were two of a kind and always had been, scared in our own ways of each other and the very tangible connection existing between us, unsure and ever so timid with how to act on feelings we were terrified to admit we possessed. At least Erik had not run from them. No, that was only *my* folly and burden to bear regret for...

Daring to peek over my shoulder under the command of an overwrought heart and a tormented head, I saw Raoul lying in the center of the cave, his back to me, but his breathing calm and deep. I was reasonably sure that he wouldn't be lying awake unless he had an eye on Erik at all times, suspicious of attack. And so to my impatient mind, I concluded that he had to be asleep.

Taking a deep breath, I dared to abandon my blanket and made a half-crawled, half-scooted approach to Erik's stiff back, sure before I even arrived behind him that he was awake. I didn't have to speak a word, for he was already turning to lay on his side facing me, those mismatched eyes hitting me with all the intensity of a punch to the gut and yet all the gentleness of a soft caress. Only briefly did he glance beyond me to the Vicomte, but assuming sleep as I had or perhaps not caring either way, he returned that stare to me, waiting, expecting, but what, I didn't know.

"You weren't asleep," I accused softly, lying on my side and curling up at the knees as I faced him.

"Neither were you."

It continued to astound me how he could have known such a thing, and how with equaled certainty, I could know the same.

Erik's gaze quickly traversed my small shape before with the hesitancy of a terrified child, he lifted his blanket and brought it close enough to encompass me in its cocoon with him. A small gesture that spoke the volumes that neither of us had the ability to say.

"What were you thinking," he asked in a hushed whisper, "to keep you from being able to rest?"

So many things! Too many to go into with the lingering walls between us. As I stared at that face so near my own, scars so blatantly on display, I pondered a long, still moment before giving him an answer.

"My mind was in a turmoil...of thoughts, memories, images, ...questions..." Bravery threatened to abandon me; I couldn't let it. I had to be the Christine I had intended to be if all of this could have been relived, the one who wouldn't cower away so easily. On the wings of my resolve, I dared to demand my most agonized of thoughts. "Tell me why you tried to make me leave you tonight, Erik."

He sucked in a harsh breath, his eyes drifting up to the ceiling, away, ...away from me. I wanted an answer; I was determined to have one. But after a long pause, he instead turned everything about. "What sort of things were you remembering, Christine? Are only the bad times haunting your mind tonight, or do you recall that there were good ones as well?" Before I could give him a reply, as if he was terrified to let me for fear what would be said, he insisted, still avoiding my gaze, "For me, even the most terrible of times and situations, ...like tonight, could never be considered bad if it included your presence. ...How could it be bad when it seems the only times I have ever known what it's like to feel, to truly *feel*, have been with you? ...Human beings, in general, give too much credit to the more pleasant of emotions: love, happiness, joy... They discredit the fact that they can only know the true extent of such things when they have also known what it means to feel their less than appreciated counterparts: anger,

And when you learn and know one, all
d and bad alike, are intensified to
_ights... I don't think I knew what
_u, pure and true, untainted in its most
concentrated and consuming sense could feel like
until I loved you..."

I couldn't form a coherent reply to such
revelations. Did any exist? To love and to hate; I was
entirely sure Erik had known both in equally
passionate quantities for me, and if anything, he had
just confirmed my thoughts.

"It's amazing, really," he continued with a
slight shake of his head. "I have been beaten, abused,
assaulted, called every possible insult known to man
or God; I have known torture, been both its victim and
its inflictor; I have committed sins too great to
imagine and have eternal damnation awaiting me in
the next life... And yet from the moment I began to
love you, I have learned what real pain is...and equally
well, what pleasure can truly be. You cannot possibly
know what it is to endure a lifetime without such
things, without happiness, excitement, ...the pleasure
of a simple touch..." His voice drifted off as if he could
not bear to continue on that current trek of thought.
"I...I just want you to remember the good as well for
when the time comes that we part. I don't want my
very existence to be nothing but a painful recollection
that you wish to repress. Perhaps it is selfish of me,
but I would like to know that I at least made some sort
of impact on your life that won't get washed away with
the fancy gowns and luxury of a Vicomtesse's life... It
wasn't always painful, Christine, ...to love you..."

"Painful," I whispered more to myself, and
before he could continue, I insisted, "Painful is baring
heart and soul so vulnerably to another only to be
dismissed from sight like a disobedient child."

My hand left its blanket security to gently force
him to meet my eye, turning his face with subtle
pressure to the unmarked line of his jaw. I couldn't
understand why he wouldn't look at me. Was I too

close to him? Did it unnerve him to share the air with me so much that he had to pretend I wasn't even there? I was certain it wasn't a residual shame for his face; after the extensive amount of time it had lain exposed tonight, surely he could tell that the shock of it had long worn off. But with the walls up to insurmountable heights within him again, I could not read his emotions and could not decipher what I yearned to, and it frustrated me to no end.

"Erik." I said his name with all the tenderness in my soul. "Are you afraid of me?"

A breath I had not realized he had been holding left his lungs in a sigh, and I could see him debating his natural instinct to look away from me again. My fingers remained beneath his jaw, a tangible reminder not to give in, and he complied and remained a willingly captive prisoner to my blue gaze.

"It's more than that," I concluded for both of us. "You say that you love me when really you are *afraid* to love me... That's why you wanted to send me away with Raoul, isn't it? Because you couldn't bear to give yourself completely, heart and soul, to me without trying to control what I felt in return."

"I am no fool," he retorted in as much of a raised tone as he could without waking the Vicomte. "It would have been a lie, every sentiment, every forced emotion. You kissed me to save your beloved, and for a moment, I wanted to believe you so badly that I almost held you to it. I had to ponder if it really would have been such a terrible thing to keep you, to make you live with the choice you had made. The voice in my head kept insisting that given enough time, I could make you love me back, that until then I could love you enough for both of us, and that eventually when the Vicomte became the distant memory and the recollection that instead I myself will someday be, that then you might love me and not him." He paused, the thinnest veil of tears in his eyes. "Yes, Christine, I am *terrified* to love you, but I do it anyway, against better judgment and rationale, against everything the world insists and punishes me for, I love you. I always have with whole heart and soul. Pain wasn't pushing you away tonight; it was the aftermath. And loving you wasn't keeping you; it was letting you go."

For the first time, I understood him, and I saw the heart he spoke of in his eyes: unconcealed, open, vulnerable to being broken. Its center bore small cracks on the verge of a surmised shattering in the *aftermath*. It was only held together now by my lingering presence in our current situation, and the hope I knew I had caused with my enacted courage. It terrified me to consider that when I left, it would be nothing more than jagged pieces and a black cavernous hole, and the man I now held eyes with would be as broken as that heart. Was I really so important? Did I myself matter that much to hold together this always strong, always powerful man? He made me feel like I was his salvation.

With the turbulent thoughts playing through my head, I hesitantly brought my hand up from where it still rested at his jaw, and dragged delicate fingertips to the disfigured side of his poor face. I could never have imagined the violent reaction my seemingly unthreatening touch would bring. An earlier touch to his leg had made him tremble; this touch, so much more intimate in comparison to him, made him shudder uncontrollably down and up his spine and give a muffled yet strangled sob, tears flowing down his face to strike my fingers. I was unwilling to be deterred.

With the curiosity of a child and not the woman I was, I explored those misshapen features, knowing the mistreatment this flesh had endured, knowing that *never* had it known a gentle touch. It wasn't grotesque; it was skin and bone, sinew and muscle, twisted unnaturally, ...differently, but it was just a face. How foolish it now seemed to be afraid of *this*, to shun the man and run from him because of something so trivial and meaningless. He had not closed his eyes although I knew he wanted to, and in those mismatched depths, the soul of this man, the heart, the hope, shone through with such blinding intensity. *That* was Erik. Not this accursed trick of Fate that he had been unfortunate to be afflicted with.

I stared into those brilliant eyes and into that passionate soul, and I whispered adamantly, "You are so beautiful, Erik; it astounds me that one as amazing as you could love me. I feel unworthy of your heart, ...and yet I want it so much."

His hand left our sheltered cocoon, and he mimicked my motion, cupping my cheek, exploring my features with fingertips that shook as if mine were as foreign to him as his were to me. It reminded me how rare a caress from him was, and my body responded in kind, tingling every place his skin brushed, flushing with a fire beneath the skin in my very blood.

"What if I changed my mind?" he softly whispered amidst tears. "What if I held you to your vow? Would you stay out of loyalty? Pity maybe? ...Compassion? Would it truly be a torturous obligation and punishment to be with me? ...I could make you happy, Christine. I did once before. Do you remember? Back before all of the pain..."

I gave a slight nod. "I remember... I remember everything."

We were laying, curled on our sides, facing each other, cupping each other's cheeks, mine smooth, his flawed, and both of us were crying silent tears beneath the weights of hearts that were too heavy to hold.

I scooted ever nearer until our knees touched and softly told him, "If I stayed, it wouldn't be out of loyalty or pity or compassion, Erik. It would be out of love." The word itself was a breathless whisper, and I watched it strike the air and attack him so hard that he shook from head to toe. It was a bewildering concept that one word, one combination of letters really, could encompass so much feeling.

"Love, Christine? ...Please promise me that you speak true. I will shatter to pieces if you are lying." The hope in his eyes was raw and unguarded by his usual walls, so intense that it made me cry fresh, unending tears.

Momentarily choked for words, I leaned close enough to press my lips to his scars, tasting his tears, kissing them away as he sobbed silently, his arms suddenly coming around my waist to clasp me, fingers curving so firmly and permanent. I knew he wouldn't let me go, and I didn't want him to.

Tilting my head, I dared to press my unmarked cheek to his scarred one, and as our tears mingled together, I whispered near his ear, "I love you, Erik."

That was all I needed to say to possess a heart that was already mine. And we just held each other that way, healing wounds, mending the gap that had been torn between us for so long, seeking solace for the assumed unforgivable.

At some point, I fell asleep, so warm and loved that my entire being was content. As I slept, I knew only the most delicious of dreams, not the nightmares that had plagued my every attempt at rest in my long months away from Erik's necessary presence. I was whole and complete, and my soul knew it.

When I awoke, I felt Erik's arms around me before my eyes even opened, and a smile came to my lips, lips that almost ached to form such an uncommon expression as of late. My stirring woke him with a similar smile. Had I ever seen him smile that way? So confident, so loved. It humbled me.

Suffice to say, that was the beginning of our happy ending. The Vicomte was gone from the cave without a trace, leaving me to conclude that he had indeed overheard every bit of our private exchange. I had been reluctant to admit it, but I think a part of me had known that he would hear, that he would know, ...that he likely *already* knew. Either way, he did not linger, and I was truly convinced that it was only because he had felt something for me that he left without consequence and did not send the mob after us or wage war with Erik. It was one of the only respectful things he had ever done.

      We left the catacombs that morning and Paris by nightfall, seeking a new life. And we were happy, happier even because we had known the pain separation could bring. We weren't afraid to love each other, full hearts, souls, bodies, more passionately than I had ever thought love could be. I marveled over such a thing constantly and was grateful beyond reason that I had found courage enough not to give up my darling angel. He was my life; he always had been and always would be for all eternity...

ABOUT THE AUTHOR

Michelle Gliottoni-Rodriguez earned a Bachelor of
Music in Vocal Performance from Saint Xavier
University in 2002. She has been studying voice
privately for sixteen years and is a student of Dr. Jan
Bickel. Michelle has won various musical awards,
including Semi-Finalist at the National Association of
Teachers of Singing competition, and Third Place in
the Josephine Lipuma Vocal Scholarship Competition,
and in 2002, she was the recipient of the Nicholas
Raimondi Scholarship. Her musical theatre
performance experience includes the roles of Nettie
Fowler in *Carousel* and Agnes Gooch in *Mame*.
Through St. Xavier University, she has portrayed
Sister Genevieve in *Suor Angelica*, Rosalinde in *Die
Fledermaus*, the Countess in *The Marriage of Figaro*,
and Yum-Yum in *The Mikado* and sang roles in scenes
from *The Marriage of Figaro*, *Fidelio*, *The Old Maid
and the Thief*, *The Impresario*, and *Suor Angelica*.
This spring, she will be playing the Queen of the Night
in *The Magic Flute*.
Also an avid writer since her youth, she published her
first novel in August of 2011, a Gothic romance titled
Opera Macabre. She is following that with the
publication of the first of her angel series *The Devil's
Galley*. She has written over 25 novels and hopes to
keep publishing and sharing her stories with the
world. She has also been posting stories based on *The
Phantom of the Opera* for the past 2 years and has a
worldwide following, including having stories
translated to German and Russian for other fan bases.
But despite keeping busy as a singer and an author,
her most important job of all is being a mom to her
two beautiful children, Noah and Cordelia.